THE DREAD SKINHEAD

THE DREAD SKINHEAD

JABARI ADISA

Published by:
Hardstyle Fiction and Boxcutter Books

The lyrics from "Street 66" by Linton Kwesi Johnson appear in this book with permission of LKJ Music Publishers, London, England. Originally released on the Bass Culture album (1980). Jamaican dialect assistance graciously provided by Mr. Andre Cuffe of Chat Patwah (@chatpatwah on Instagram & YouTube) and Mr. Roan Biggs.

Published by Hardstyle Fiction | Atlanta, Georgia | www.hardstylefiction.com

First Edition (Third Printing)
10 9 8 7 6 5 4 3 2 1

NOTE: This edition includes a newly added map of the novel's setting and an optional companion music playlist that follows the music as it appears in the novel. A full color version of the map is available for free download from HardstyleFiction.com.

Cover art by Rob Schwager, Tiny Bird Press (tinybirdpress.com)

Interior design and typesetting by Jabari Adisa

Typefaces: Hit Me Punk! (junkohanhero.com), Goudy Old Style, Westsac (Adobe.com)

Genres:
Hardstyle Fiction / Cult Horror / Urban Speculative Fiction

BISAC Categories:
FIC056000 FICTION / African American / Urban
FIC028090 FICTION / Horror / Occult & Supernatural
FIC038000 FICTION / Visionary & Metaphysical

Inquiries or bulk orders:
Hardstyle Fiction, PO Box 20064, Atlanta, GA 30325 | info@hardstylefiction.com

Dedicated to the originals.
The tips of every spear.
The ones who make history doing what only they would dare.

Thanks to Delma, Ix'Chel and Stokely.

Baby Lion

CHAPTER ONE

It was just supposed to be a bus ride. Ten years old. First time riding solo. I needed a bike part from Major Motors.

I was geeked. Real big-boy activities.

At the bus stop — 63rd and Normal — bike wheel in one hand, token in the other. Craned my neck like the old folks, trying to see when the big green limousine — that's what we called it — would pull up. I was trying real hard to look like an old pro, not a first-timer.

A hand gripped my shoulder.

"Come on, young buck," he said, steering me toward the phone booth a few steps away.

One of the older boys. A Disciple. Somebody I felt like I knew, even if I didn't.

He stooped to look me in the eye. "I'ma dial a number. When they pick up, you say—"

Twelve words. Six seconds.

"Say it back to me just like I told you."

I did.

"Put a little more bass in your voice."

I tried.

"Better."

He dropped a coin in the slot. Dialed. Pressed the receiver to my ear. I heard the trill of the phone ringing. He watched my face. Taking my temperature the whole time.

"Hello?" A male voice. Older than mine. Not a grown man. Combatant age.

I spoke the words. Just like before.

"On Folks, Boogie, we ain't gon' play with y'all too much longer."

I hung up, like I was told.

The silence felt serious. Like something had been set in motion. Like Boogie was already up off the couch, deciding what to do next.

The older boy gripped my hand. Took me through a Disciples handshake. Not a compliment. A confirmation.

I wanted to ask a hundred questions about Boogie. But I didn't.

Instead, I just stood there, feeling important. Powerful. Big-boy activities.

Wait.

Did I just get walked in?

◎ ◎ ◎

I grew up in Englewood — the motherland of the Black Gangster Disciple Nation. But I spent most summers with my aunt on the West Side. Behind enemy lines. In the shadows of the Vice Lords. The Disciples' main enemy. Deep in the projects of Holy City.

You've seen the projects. Those bleak, inhumane slabs of brutalist austerity that dominated every vista and obscured every sightline. They left an impression on everyone who passed by or through. You had to wonder who designed them — and whether they were satisfied with the results.

8

They baited with safety. Stability. A shot at respectability.

But once the people packed in, the trap was sprung.

"Y'all can live here, y'all can die here, but y'all shouldn't be seen here."

A contraband runner's dream and greased rails for the downwardly mobile.

If the national parks were America's best idea, housing projects had to be the worst.

I liked visiting. There were lots of kids, and every other floor had an enterprising lady selling penny candy from her kitchen table. We raced Big Wheels on the landing and had fun upsetting the pretty girls jumping Double Dutch. We played Strike Out against the broken elevator doors. And ran high-stakes games of Hide and Go-Get-It in the stairwells. I noticed the poverty but, for me, it wasn't a deal-breaker. I never understood why my aunt stayed put.

The elevators reeked of urine and were always out of order. The stairwells were poorly lit and anything above, say, the sixth floor, required significant exertion. Especially if you were carrying groceries. I think the area between buildings was supposed to have some green space, but the narrow, shady corridors spawned more trash tornadoes than blades of grass.

The common sentiment in the projects was to stick to the building you lived in and keep security top of mind lest you become prey. My aunt was the overbearing type and never let me go down to the playground unattended. From her 12th floor apartment I could see and hear the kids on the merry-go-round but they might as well have been in Alaska.

Every Tuesday the Chicago Housing Authority (CHA) would set up shop in one of the buildings and dole out lunches and five-pound blocks of government cheese. We called the lunches "Chokes" so that should give you some indication of how appetizing they weren't.

Tough white bread, bologna, block cheese, a carton of milk, and a foil-covered Jello cup stuffed with mystery fruit.

Still, Chokes day was an event. A reason to come down out of the tower. A chance to see the residents of the other buildings. The older kids used it as an opportunity to find attractive mates. It was the anti-carnival. Instead of rides and games we had people-watching and gut-busters.

This was where I got my first education in gang dynamics. Some buildings were controlled by a particular group while others were contested. The building my aunt lived in was a Vice Lords stronghold. It was important to know, even for the kids, which colors were allowed in which buildings. And sometimes, while we were standing in line for Chokes, the people on the floors above would throw bottles down on the heads of anyone they thought might be enemies.

Sometimes sirens woke us up. On the ground below might be the crumpled body of someone who'd been thrown from one of the upper levels. I remember pressing my face to the six-foot-high fence, craning my neck to see what a dead body looked like. It happened frequently enough that the CHA took corrective measures.

That was the summer of '76. They brought in massive cranes to erect 130-foot-high gratings over the open terraces of the projects.

I was there that day.

I was fascinated by the larger-than-life Tonka trucks. It was exciting. Workers rappelling whiles fastening bolts. Felt like a movie set. I didn't realize it, not then, that the new grating wasn't for saving people. This was the ceremonial capping of an open-air prison.

The gratings made the projects feel smaller. More confining.

Even the weather behaved differently. The wind whistled now. Raindrops clung to the small gaps in the metal, so you could never tell if the rain had stopped or was still pouring.

The CHA didn't bother to remove the old six-foot-high fences. The result looked like a design error. On the upside, we no longer had to worry about our rubber balls falling twelve floors, and now we had new dares.

"Climb the terrace fence and stand in the gap."

"Okay, now walk the four-inch gap from one end to the other."

"Okay, now go two floors down and catch this Hot Wheels car. If you catch it, you can have it. If you drop it you owe me one. Yell when you're ready."

We could also now hang our laundry to dry without fear of it blowing away down to the street.

That was it for upsides.

I didn't know it at the time but sealing the terraces was one of the insults that led to the Collapse.

Chicago was still Chicago back then. It was a city like no other. More Muslims per capita than any city outside of Baghdad. More Poles than any city outside of Warsaw. Black people — like my parents — in self-exile from the Jim Crow South came chasing opportunity. Relief. It was a city of immigrants, climbers and competitors. And back then you could still find decent factory jobs and grocery stores in the neighborhoods. You could live a full-featured life — birth, school, church, love, marriage, family, hitting the numbers, getting caught cheating, addiction, recovery, death — all within walking distance.

And yet, Chicago was and is gangland and survival in the gang context required mobility and expansion.

The big families, the Black Gangster Disciple Nation (BGDN) and the Vice Lord Nation (VLN) ran operations from these monoliths and orchestrated movements well beyond the dirt-lot turf rumbles the media portrayed. These weren't just street cliques anymore. They were start-ups, plotting growth opportunities, becoming high-risk, high-reward capitalist enterprises with their own corporate cultures, boards of directors and CEOs. As with any corporate war, the goal wasn't just profit. It was market domination.

If you want to understand organized crime, start by looking at a Fortune 500 company. Apple doesn't want to coexist with Samsung; Apple wants to bury Samsung. How? Dominate the supply chain. Undercut profits. Siphon talent. Acquire smaller players. Convince the world the Apple brand is superior. Superior service. Superior support. Superior product. Choose Apple because you *think different*. And when you do, you are superior to the fools who chose Samsung.

The street families formed for the usual reasons: security and identity. This is just human culture, the world over. For a brief moment there was hope that Chairman Fred could unify the important sectors into a working class movement — undermining the corporate ideal — but the police killed him and that dream died. The leadership void was filled by other, less radical, players. The street families became crime families and the crime families merged to become corporations. People Nation and Folk Nation. Apple and Samsung.

I know, it's nothing like what they showed you on Frontline.

The late '60s and early '70s saw federal programs throwing money at the big organizations which funded some day care centers and other useful public works, but that money also bootstrapped weaponry, and inspired envy, suspicion and betrayal. By the '80s the big organizations were changing. The money had dried up, the leadership was in prison or in the cemetery and the survivors needed to make a way out of what was left. They needed to innovate.

The BGDN was splintering back into sects — Black Disciple (BD), Black Gangster (BG) and Gangster Disciple (GD) — who frequently went to war with each other. Meanwhile, the VLN was more structured and focused on building their business culture slowly, methodically. Expanding beyond the West Side to set up shop around town.

I started with Englewood and the West Side for a reason.

The cultural center of the West Side — we didn't call it "The Scratch" back then — is Holy City. That's the motherland of the Vice Lords Nation.

Englewood, where I rested my head and went to school, on the other hand, was the birthplace of the BGDN. Nearly all my male cousins rode Disciple.

As a youngster, I was always pulled in different directions. "What you ride?" I heard that shit every day, on every side of town, even as a boy. I didn't have an answer. I wasn't ready to choose a brand. I just wanted to be a student of the code.

I watched how the big boys in Englewood leaned right, while the big boys on the West Side leaned left. Not politically. I'm talking literally. Body language mattered. The way you "crossed up" your arms — right over left or left over right. Wearing your cap "broke off" (tilted) to the right meant one thing and to the left, something else. I was a smart kid. I wore my cap straight to the back or straight to the front. Better yet, no cap at all! Zero confusion. Good for walking through, bad for standing still. If I was passing through, I didn't look like an invader but if I was at a standstill, like at a bus stop, I would get approached and checked. "What you be about?" "Where you stay at?" "You know where you at, right?" "Bet." "When I'ma see you at Service, young-blood?"

Service was where the big messages from the Vice Lord CEO would be shared. Who was moving what. Who was in jail. How to respond to new developments. What the new brand mark was. Sometimes the brand mark needed to change. Had to keep ahead of the regulators: Law enforcement.

I consciously avoided clothing that suggested brand marks. Six-pointed Star of David = Disciple. Five-pointed star = Vice Lord. Pitchfork = Disciple. Playboy Bunny = Vice Lord. I can't remember if we had the word "neutron" back then, but that would have described my style. These were my very first intentional fashion choices, long before I got seduced by an entirely different code.

Being a schoolboy in Englewood made things a little bit clearer. My upstairs neighbor was one of the hardest soldiers in town and he was Disciple from dusk to dawn. If I ever got static I just dropped his name and the signal cleared right up. Like the time I was riding my Schwinn Stingray. I loved that bike. I parked it outside Mr. Brown's corner store at 61st Street and Normal. When I came out a much bigger kid had claimed it as his. I tried to take my bike back. He pushed me in my face and laughed.

"You ain't got no bike no more, little pussy."

"Okay, bet." I walked back towards home announcing: "I'ma go get Robbie D."

The thief did a quick calculation, gently leaned my bike against the brick wall and hustled away like his mama was calling him. I later told Robbie D about it. He asked for a few descriptors, decided who it was, then marched me over to the bike thief's house. Made him apologize to me. Then Robbie beat his ass while I watched. Told me to never let that boy, the thief, punk me again.

The local Disciples gathered on my front porch at 440 W. 61st Place nearly

13

every day. I heard whispers of "Larry Hoover" and "King David."

I heard "On Folks, them BDs killed Sly."

"I don't give a fuck about no reunification. I'm a BD killer."

They took an interest in me.

"Why wasn't you there last night when we hit the freights? You the right size. Next time we hit them freights, you best be at the vidock ready to work."

"Man, you know his mama ain't gon' let him out after the street lights come on."

I loved it. I soaked up game. I knew I was rubbing elbows with cutthroats and gunrunners but they treated me like a little brother and I got the sense that I was maybe two degrees at most from Hoover himself. On the flip side, when I was on the West Side I was rubbing elbows with "Hoover Removers." That was one of the Vice Lords' loudest provocations.

As I did with the Vice Lords, I learned the signs and symbols of the Englewood Disciples. The older boys thought it was funny that I knew all the hugs, handshakes, and catch phrases. "All is One," "Folks Run It," "Third World" — this was many years before "Growth & Development" became the movement. They'd teach me the latest handshakes. Test me. Make sure I got it right.

Style mattered to me and I should admit that stylistically-speaking, I felt closer to the Vice Lords. Their colors, red and white, banging left, the walking sticks, the playboy bunny graffiti. And the Vice Ladies looked so good. Tight red t-shirts. Their names and clubs in white, iron-on lettering — Marsha. CVL. K-Town — Bone-white Levi's Street Brights, ironed to a crease. Curves on display. Everything right where it was supposed to be. These people were sharp. Even their language had me hooked. "All Is Well," "Keep the love in the club," "Peace Almighty," "First World." I devoted a wirebound spiral notebook to their signs and symbols.

If I had stayed on that path, I probably would have chosen Vice Lord. But choice is a luxury that is granted to a precious few. Tremor knew I was drawn to Vice Lords and nurtured crushes on Vice Ladies. They seemed like my kinda people, as illogical — and possibly disloyal — as that may sound.

For the time, I stayed neutral but, at some point, neutral becomes political.

That point? It's different for everybody.

It might be the first time a boy starts sniffing around a real operator's sister. Or it might be when you get taught to shoplift. Or it might be the first time you get thrown onto the freight train and do a good job shifting merchandise. Or maybe the first time you get hemmed up by police and give up nothing even though you definitely saw everything. Or it might be the first time you get a can of the right color spray paint and put your name on a wall a little too close to the brand mark. Or the time you get pressed into making a threatening phone call for the Set.

It's different for everybody, but I think we all agreed that after ten years old you ain't a kid no more and you better start thinking about hopping off the porch and running with the big dogs.

The other option? Go Poindexter. Go in off the porch. Close the door on your heels. Play with your toys. Watch from the window. No knowledge of the game, but the game will know you.

CHAPTER TWO

Tremor wasn't having it.

"I'm getting you out of here."

"But my friends—"

"Ain't no friends in Englewood. Only purse snatchers."

The movers handled everything. Packed up the whole family — Tremor, mother, two big sisters, and me, the baby. 440 W. 61st Place, now something less than home, shrank behind us as Tremor pulled away from the curb.

We drove east on 63rd Street.

Crossed the Dan Ryan expressway. Turned south onto King Drive.

Stopped in at Parkway Gardens to say whattup to some cousins.

Drove east again on 67th Street.

Skirted Jackson Park.

Turned south again at South Shore Drive. Stopped in front of a yellow brick building.

We moved into the top floor of a six-flat apartment building at 7158 South Yates. South Shore. On the south side of what used to be called Chicago. In what we, the people, would come to know as Fourth World.

South Shore was different. And it had a secret. Terror Town.

Holy City and Englewood were landlocked concrete jungles cordoned off by El tracks and expressways. Terror Town was steps away from a beach at South Shore Country Club! Wasn't nobody golfing, but I could smell the lake from my front step. The sun rose and shone into my big window. Sun and beach meant girls and that meant everything to me. We didn't have El trains rattling by. We didn't have expressways and overpasses. We had birds and trees. Whereas it seemed to get dark and deadly when the street lights came on in Holy City or Englewood, Terror Town always felt like a party was about to pop off.

I loved these streets. Clocked countless miles that summer drifting around on my Huffy, taking it all in: The block parties. Roadblocks at both ends of the street. No cars. Kids everywhere. Families. Big-belly men tending to their grills. Sun visor, white towel slung over one shoulder, directing traffic, making sure everyone got a plate. Then there was the music. A mix of "dusties" — oldies — and new joints. I recognized the DJ as one of the on-air personalities from WJPC. I felt like I was looking at a celebrity.

Terror Town breathed culture. Curtis Mayfield's kids hung out there. Donny Hathaway's kids partied there. This is where Earth, Wind and Fire was from.

The afros, the braids, the handshakes, the Blues festival at the Country Club. The Hamilton movie theater. Run down, but walking distance. The Afro-Caribbean bookstore on 71st Street. The Fulani hats. The Garvey flags. The open air squares where people debated ideas. The closeness to black people with money — like the ones in Jackson Park Highlands. This shit was my oxygen. This felt like a place with a future.

And the hustles? Oh, the hustles!

Every corner in Terror Town had a lesson to teach. Like Rainbow Beach, just a mile or so south of the Country Club. This was where the raw talent congregated. This was known as one of the best places to take a date, but also a fine place to get your pockets turned inside out if you didn't know the code.

Basketball sharks. They controlled the courts. If they spotted an opportunity they'd switch to playing like amateurs, trading what we called "dummy money" back and forth, gassing gullible spectators into thinking they might be able to outplay the locals. With eyes on a potential mark, the charade would slowly evolve. Missed shots. Hands on head. Weak excuses. "Today ain't my day." A lot of cursing. "Aw shit! I can't believe I missed that one!" Sooner or later a tourist would get cocky enough to put real money in the game. Easy money, right? That's the hook. With the flip of a switch, that brick-tossing scrub transformed into a pill-dropping pro. Another sucker, yanked. Another slack-jawed tourist trying to figure out where they lost the thread. The shark would draw out the charade for maximum potential. Pretending to be surprised by his own skill. "You bringing out my best, playboy. I never hit like this." Feeding line to the fish. Punctuated by a couple of easy misses to make the mark believe they had a chance.

The psychology of the mark is that they never want to admit that they've been beaten and in the best cases — for the hustler — that mark could be convinced that he could have much better luck and maybe even build a legend for himself simply by putting a little more money in the game. "Double or nothing, Rockefeller. Get yo' money back. Don't let *me* break you." This went on until the mark's pockets were empty and turned "inside out." Once the shark was confident he'd squeezed all the work out of a mark he'd kick his game up to sniper-level accuracy and trash-talk the mark for thinking he was good enough to go up against Skyhook.

"Yeah, that's who took your lunch money. Sky Motherfucking Hook." Swoosh! "Go back to wherever the fuck yo' goofy ass came from and tell them that you a pussy ass bitch who pays Skyhook's rent." Swoosh! "All net, baby!"

And that? That was a typical day at Rainbow Beach.

I still missed the familiarity of Englewood but I understood why Tremor packed us up and out. And, shit, this place breathes!

Yeah, I'll have to deal with new school shit. New questions. New friends. New enemies. All that. And, just so you don't forget, Chicago is gangland, so I also discovered a new corporation.

The Black P Stone Nation (BPSN) had rituals that were heavily influenced by Noble Drew Ali's "Moorish Science Temple," a proud, mysterious fraternity that borrowed from the *Quran* and enhanced it with Black political thought. They broke with orthodox Islam by naming Noble Drew Ali their savior. In their world, men could be God.

Some people argued about what the P in BPSN stood for. Outsiders were told that it stood for "Peace, Prosperity, People and Power." Insiders knew better. The P was for Prince. Jeff Fort. The Black Prince. Eventually, the Stones leadership, under Fort, went full Muslim and dropped "BPSN." They renamed themselves the "El Rukn Tribe of the Moorish Science Temple of America." They declared themselves a religion — Sunni Muslim — and claimed they weren't "African," in the sub-Saharan diaspora sense, but instead were descendants of the Moors — the North African Muslims who ruled Spain and Portugal in the Middle Ages. Moorish was shortened to Moors, and thanks to the way we talked, Moors became Moes. That's how they greeted each other: "Peace, Moe." And that influenced how us kids in Terror Town greeted each other. Quietly.

The way they talked, "Stone to the bone," "Peace and Love." These phrases hit my ears like poetry. The way they moved, like they were tapped into music only they could hear. I wanted to hear it, too! I did what I always did. I tuned in and soaked up game.

Terror Town was more than a scary nickname for a neighborhood — it was the name of one of the original — "Main 21" — Sets in the BPSN. They were a no-nonsense People Set with their own mystique, culture and mythology. The kind of Set that other Sets wanted to be like.

The surprise here, though? Everyone on this side of town knew everything there was to know about Tremor. What the fuck?

The first time I heard myself called "Lil Tremor" it threw me off my game for a beat.

I didn't even like the goofy little nickname that I had as a kid so, yeah, "Lil' Tremor" was an upgrade. But still, what the fuck does that mean? I mean, yeah, even Ray Charles could see that I looked like Tremor, but I didn't hear other boys being called "Lil Ralph" or "Lil Leroy." No — this meant something. It was more about Tremor than it was about me, but it became about me too, because people started to treat me differently. And once I locked in and started to introduce myself that way, the whole calculus shifted. It was mostly little shit. Free haircuts, and food, and dry cleaning and shit. My friends noticed. They liked free shit, and it made me popular.

On the flipside, mothers would hang up the phone on me when I called their daughters. *"Ain't no 'Lil' Tremor' gon' be calling* my *house."* Or straight up lying when I came to the door. *"She ain't home."* Or telling their daughters to pretend they didn't know me if they saw me at the beach.

This shit was bad math.

CHAPTER THREE

After a fucking excellent summer, September rolled around and I walked into Myra Bradwell Elementary School. Bradwell — the kids called it "Bad Hell" — was a hard fork in the road. That's where I began to hate school. Where my trust for authority took a nosedive. And where I learned to hide my thoughts from my parents.

My old school, Lewis-Chaplin, was all asbestos and clanky boiler, but at least everyone agreed on a dominant culture. Disciple. Here, two cliques, The Kingston Raiders and the Colfax Killers, fought for the top spot. And not no "meet me at the flagpole at three" shit. I'm talking 30-on-30 game-of-death, heads-banged-into-lockers kinda brawls. Their goal was to eliminate the other team, impress the P Stones, and hopefully get absorbed into the Terror Town Set.

I read that as a cheap way to become Main 21.

The Raiders and the Killers clashed every day at Bad Hell and out on East 75th Street — from Essex to Exchange — right in my path to school.

Word got out that I was from Englewood. They tested. Tried to push my buttons. Called me Dirty Folks. If I really was Folks those would be fighting words. I had already decided they were beneath my ambitions. My stand-offishness meant suspicion — and fights. Toe to toe. Mainly with a Raider named GoGo.

I learned to take the long way around the Raiders-Killers war zone, so to get to school I'd walk the far side of South Exchange Avenue from 72nd to 77th. Turn west on 77th, then south on Burnham. Clear. Reverse order on the way home.

The school was always on lockdown. Closed campus. No playground time. Bars on the windows.

Class. Lunch. Class. Go home.

The lunchroom was the only place we really got to let loose and express some personality.

In my favor, I'd become a fiercely witty signifier — some people call it "playing the dozens," but not where I'm from — so while I had two flanks of enemies I also had some hangers-on who stuck close to hear my latest takedowns.

My greatest hit was "Yo' mama so fat even Jesus can't lift her soul." I had another. I told Peaches that her house was so dusty that the roaches needed dirt bikes to get around. She capped back with one that accused my mother of being so horny that her vibrator needed a kickstand. Murder!

It wasn't all fun and games, though. Your id, ego, and your superego all took turns in the ring. We might even hit you with some Oedipus. The knockout blow. That's how I got close to Viddy and Peaches. We tried to destroy each other, then decided we needed each other. They didn't have those names back then, of course. Back then, they were just two wild-ass kids like the rest of us.

Peaches's family was among the white stalwarts who never left. They were regular old South Side Democrats. The kind of people who looked out for their neighbors but also marked off their preferred parking spot with kitchen chairs and would fight anyone who moved them.

They worked the steel mill, post office, and printing press jobs alongside everybody else. They got laid off alongside everybody else. They never got the notice about "white flight" because they were too busy trying to keep ends met. And they didn't get the alarm bell about property values tanking because they rented — like the rest of us. There was a growing trend among white families to pack up and move to the suburbs, but this one stayed put. Peaches wasn't "the white girl" to us, she was just a cold-blooded cutie who knew how to slap-box and signify.

Besides Viddy and Peaches, fifth grade sucked. New kid shit. Sixth grade sucked harder. I had a teacher who hated me.

Kids always say that shit and the usual response from the listener is to wonder what the kid did to offend the selfless servant. You're probably doing it right now. No. This bitch hated me. She would have aborted me if she had the chance.

She knew I cared about my appearance, so she gave me all the shitty jobs like cleaning out erasers that left me covered, fro to toe, with chalk dust. I know, you're thinking "what's the big deal? Stop being so dramatic." Keep listening.

Fast forward to the class Christmas party. We were all having a good time. Butter cookies, Mr. Juicy juice, Vitner's potato chips. All the shit that Chicago kids love. Peaches decided to be sneaky. Stole an extra fistful of butter cookies. She slid up next to me to show off her loot. I wish I'd thought of it. I laughed. Too loud, I guess.

The teacher's troll face snapped around faster than her wig could follow.

"WHO IS LAUGHING LIKE A BARBARIAN!" It was only half question.

GoGo pointed at me.

It's a party. Big deal, right? Yeah. Apparently it was a very big deal.

She pulled her desk chair forward. Grabbed the pointing stick.

"GET UP HERE!"

I knew what was coming.

"Drop your pants."

"Lay across my lap."

"Grab the chair legs. Both hands."

"And you better not let go."

She brought that stick down on my ass like she was trying to exorcise demons.

You ever seen a kid get beaten so hard they start convulsing? That was me.

For laughing too loud. During a party. The class Christmas party.

Bitch hit harder than a tax bill.

Her out-sized reaction to regular kid shit seemed extra personal, like she was beating more than just me. Like she was beating every black boy that was less than perfect. As if she was beating every man that ever cheated on her. As if she was finally beating the life choices that landed her at Bad Hell. One lash would have been too much but once this bitch got started, she couldn't, or wouldn't stop.

She broke that pointing stick across my ass. The pointing half flew off and got stuck in the cork board.

Her burst of violence killed the party.

What did she expect? Applause?

She looked up. Didn't like what she saw in the kids' eyes. Shoved me off her lap like she'd just got caught with a dirty secret. Ordered me back to my desk. I walked slowly. Flesh aching. Eyes blurry. Hyperventilating.

I swear I saw GoGo laughing.

I put my head down in my arms.

A few classmates came by to slip me cookies or juice cups but nobody touched me. They knew not to put hands on a kid who was recovering from a whipping.

Nobody tried to console me. They knew this feeling. We all knew this feeling. "I hope she die." And then, the pivot. "I wish I was dead, then she'll be sorry." And the conviction. "When I get bigger ain't nobody never gon' hit me no mo'. I'ma be the one doin' the hittin'." That feeling.

But then...

Someone — I didn't know who — violated the code. Put a hand on my shoulder. I reacted. Terror? Anger? I don't know. I lashed out with ferocity, grabbed the wrist. I twisted. I wanted to snap it.

She screamed.

I quickly let go.

It was the teacher.

I saw her eyes do a quick calculation. She smirked.

She ran to her desk to call the principal.

Said I attacked her.

They called the police.

No one asked my classmates what they saw.

Then they called my parents.

My side was never considered.

Back then, people didn't question teachers.

Everyone believed her. Even Tremor. That hurt almost as much as the beating.

I got kicked out.

Do you know how bad you have to fuck up to get kicked out of a broke-ass public school?

Do you have any idea how fucked up it feels to not have fucked up at all but still get treated like the fuck up of all fuck ups?

I learned a big lesson that day.

You might be able to beat a case but you can't beat a set-up.

CHAPTER FOUR

For the next couple of years I was bussed across town. My life was limited to going to school, having my older sister micromanage my homework, and sitting in hair salons while my mother and my sisters titivated.

I lost touch with my Bad Hell associates. Yeah, we'd catch occasional glimpses of each other but, for the most part, I ceased to exist in Terror Town.

My main escape was through books. Pulp fiction, mainly. Donald Goines, A Clockwork Orange, Ray Bradbury, Octavia Butler, The Outsiders, A Wrinkle In Time and all that.

"The Twilight Zone," "Friday," the ABC comedy show, and "Saturday Night Live" were my windows to the broader world. It was there that I got my political education. Richard Pryor, Steve Martin, George Carlin. And I fell in love with British television shows like "All Creatures, Great and Small," "Benny Hill," "Prisoner: Cell Block H," and "Doctor Who."

Seventh and eighth grades zipped by and, other than summer trips to Memphis to attend Mid-Southern Wrestling matches religiously with my grandmother, Tremor's mother, there's not much to tell.

Along the way I got taller, sharper, cleaner. The way I presented myself really began to matter.

Weekend sleepovers with my cousin saved me from Poindexter status. We dressed the part, hit the parties and stayed in touch with the game.

It didn't always work out, though. My cousin and I went to a Set in Chatham. We were supposed to meet two girls there. His mother dropped us off at the party. Told us to call when we needed her to pick us up. The Set was in a half-finished basement and there were way more boys than girls. We had the prettiest girls and we kept them close — until it was time to make that call. We went upstairs to use the phone and came down to find our girls dancing with other boys. We rode in the back of her AMC Gremlin looking sadder than the last grape on a long stem. It's funny now, but it wasn't then.

For the first year of high school my mother sent me to Mendel, an all-boys Catholic school, but my grades hung near the bottom. The results were not worth the expense. For tenth grade I was launched back into public high school. Kenwood Academy. That's where I was reunited with Viddy and Peaches and where we all met a new kid, Nigel, from London.

Nigel's father had landed a job teaching Computer Science at the University of Chicago and moved the entire family from London. Instead of sending Nigel to the University's high school with the upper class kids, his parents threw him into the shark tank that is Chicago Public Schools, with nothing but his wits and his charms.

The first time I saw Nigel, he was wearing penny loafers with coins in the slots. When pressed, he said that it was emergency bus fare. We — Me, Viddy and Peaches — got a good laugh out of his innocence and his accent. We'd never met a Black Briton before.

"It's a good thing 911 is free," Peaches joked, "because you'll be needing help when you get hood checked for a shoe violation."

He didn't get it.

I explained to him that the coins were a clue that he was riding under People and that while that could fly here in this People-heavy school, out in the streets it was a reason to get checked for who you know and "what you ride," and in the wrong hood it was a green light to snuff a Preppy.

I gave him the nickname Brixton and a crash course in the signs and symbols. A Kangol cap and Clarks desert boots? Englewood, under GD and probably a hard six soldier. Stacy Adams shoes, a wide brimmed hat and a fashionable walking cane? Undoubtedly a Vice Lord. A pyramid necklace or ring, a Fulani hat and a dashiki? El Rukn. Blackstone elite.

His mind struggled to understand how he could possibly learn all this and stay alive. How could we? "Why ain't you lot dead already?" And thus began a long friendship of signifying and schooling each other in the cultures that raised us.

The first lesson he gave us was: "Reggae is poor people's music. Sufferah's music. Just like the Black American Blues. Once you understand that, the rest will begin to make sense."

"Britain is a mess hall of subcultures. From the Teddy Boys onward, every tribe has its rules and its rivals. Rockers hate Mods. Teds hate Punks. Skinheads hate New Romantics, Soulboys, and Hippies."

Something about that word "Skinhead" caught my attention. It wasn't completely new to me. There were mentions of them in The Stray Cats song "Rumble in Brighton" and before that, Generation X's "Running with the Boss Sound," and before that, "The Warriors." I also knew Chicago's history of Baldie gangs — they were adversaries to the Greasers — but these kids that he described sounded like my kind of people. Functional dressers. Rugged in the day, sharp at night. Clean cut. Serious attention to detail. Proud. "Hard and smart" is how he described them. "They ain't no angels and you might not want to meet them down a dark lane, but having one as a mate is as good as having ten of any other mate."

"Skinheads are the result of Mods mingling with Rude Boys. The Mods dressed super sharp but after some bad dust ups with Rockers on Brighton beach, some of the Mods decided they needed harder gear, and they borrowed from West Indian youth. Some people say the short hair comes from copying Black kids. Others say it was the Borstal crop. When kids went into Borstal — I think you lot call it juvenile detention — their hair got chopped off. It became a badge of honor through hardship. The whole style became extra hard, more territorial and gang-oriented. That's how the name "Gang Mods" came about. The old timers say that for a while, it seemed like every kid — Black and white — was sporting the Skinhead look."

"But Rude Boys, like me — we run tings, eh!"

"Rude Boy is a counterculture, not a subculture. Our clothes are like armor. The dark shades. You never know what Rudie is thinking or feeling or going to do next. A real rude youth will do whatever it takes to survive but, more than anything, Rude Boys are always on the cutting edge. You want to know what's new and what's next? Watch what we are wearing. Pay attention to where we shop and hang out. Tune into our pirate radio stations. We play what the people want, but what the BBC won't—"

"Tell us more about the Skinheads," Peaches interrupted. These kids caught our imagination. They dressed like we dressed, a sort of Ivy League lite, but they had an exotic twist on things. And Brixton spoke about them with a degree of seriousness that sent us on a deep dive into the microfiche archive at the big library downtown. Brixton accidentally indoctrinated several of us Fourth World youth into this Skinhead business. Viddy claimed "A Clockwork Orange" as his new personality. I got hooked on Prince Buster. Peaches was the first to get her hair cropped short.

During one of our lunchroom sessions, a sharp youth named Von slid by our table to drop off a plugger for the Set he was having at his house on Saturday night. Handwritten on an index card, the style of the time, was:

```
    Andre Hatchett + guests on the wheels.
        Pure Prep. Dress to Impress.
            Rep your school!
            6911 South Bennett

                9 until...

        $1 with plugger, $2 without
```

I decoded the plugger for Brixton. "'Pure Prep' means no gang markers allowed. Collared shirts. Only certain footwear — Stan Smith and K-Swiss, yeah, but no Pony turf shoes. 'Rep your school' means no old people. '9 until...' means it's gonna go late. No one knows how late."

Brixton noticed the address. "Cho! Mi flat is right by there. 67th & Constance."

"Bet, it's time for you to get your Fourth World cherry popped, playboy."

◎◎◎

BOMP! BOMP! BOMP! BOMP!

Von's house was set back from the street but that signature four-on-the floor bass thump could be felt at the curb. The big brick house with its Prairie School identifiers looked like a mansion to us Terror Town kids. Von had hit the lottery. He'd been adopted by a white family who had money. That's how he was able to pull and pay real DJs. His parents bought a house in Jackson Park Highlands and sent him to public school because they felt it was important that he stay connected to regular ol' black folks. The kid was a charismatic mover and an architect of what would later be called "House."

You see, the older folks... my sister's crowd... the "party people," would go to Ron Hardy's Muzik Box or The Warehouse in The Gold Coast. They called their thing "Rice & Beans music" — a clever twist on, but also away from R&B — and they called their clubs "Church." We were too young for Church. Some of us managed to sneak in and get proper educations but we knew that their thing was different from our thing. The closest thing to Church in Fourth World was The Jeffery Pub, at 71ˢᵗ Street. They played the music but they catered to gay men and party people, and carded heavily at the door.

House music, proper, got its name from the parties that took place in people's *houses*. Not just big houses like Von's. It was a regular thing to drop into a set in somebody's drafty, unfinished basement — like the one where me and my cousin got dumped. That's where the culture was incubated before it broke out into high school gyms and event spaces. Long before it got its name.

Hypnotic. Symphonic. Seductive. Tribal.

The expansive porch of Von's house was crowded with party goers who had spilled out to smoke or drink or flirt. We pushed through, into the spacious house. BOMP! BOMP! BOMP! BOMP!

Everyone styled to stand out. Hands in the air. Bodies moving. In unison. The walls sweating. Shadows and silhouettes. This was where we lived. This was where we learned to love. For many of us, our first intimate encounters happened in the dark corners.

Brixton was mesmerized.

Andre was on the wheels blending a very explicit spoken word poem with a four-on-the-floor bottom. BOMP! BOMP! BOMP! BOMP! The only light in the room came from the street through the band of windows to Andre's right and the small desk lamp illuminating his DJ coffin.

Brixton was drawn to the turntables like a moth to a flame. He craned his neck to see what Andre was spinning but like all the DJs of that time, the labels were obscured. A trick of the trade. The only identifiable marks were scribbled BPM notes and tiny hashes to tell the DJ where to drop the needle. Hieroglyphics. A secret code that Brixton felt compelled to crack. Andre, wanting to guard his intellectual property, elbowed Brixton away from the edge of his coffin.

I caught the vibe and pulled Brixton away to introduce him to a group of girls called, coincidentally, "The Rude Girls." They were one of the elite cliques and were closely watched for what they were wearing or how they were styling their hair. My middle sister was a Rude Girl, as was my down-stairs neighbor, Ajoa.

BOMP! BOMP! BOMP! BOMP!

Brixton was hooked.

◎◎◎

I mean... I loved that shit, too, but for Brixton it was a drug. While his crowd swam deep into the new wave, underground, and Hot Mix waters, I was seeking something different. I just didn't know what it was, yet.

Like many of the kids of that generation I stayed awake late at night won-dering if that would be the night that nuclear destruction would rain down on our heads. I feared the apocalypse was imminent but most of the dance music of that time was bald escapism. I craved something that touched the raw nerves of my worriment. I needed to hear from someone who felt what I was feeling. Something that shouted for attention and demanded change. I didn't know what it was until I saw The Plasmatics on "Friday," Fear on "Saturday Night Live," then The Clash at ChicagoFest. The urgency of The Specials and The Selecter began to make sense. They drew me in and made me a believer. My curiosity turned me on to The 4-Skins, The Last Resort, The Strike, and other deadly serious Skinhead bands of the time. Ironically, while Brixton was becoming a student of Fourth World culture, my imagina-tion was thousands of miles away — in London.

"Why don't I ever see you around Lion Order?" Brixton asked. "It's right by your flat, and they have a book on your beloved Skinheads"

"What's Lion Order?

"Mate. You're missing out on a goldmine. Fix that up, nuh?"

◎ ◉ ◎

Lion Order sat inside the 75th Street Raiders-Killers war zone that I actively avoided but, gang strife or not, I needed to check it out. I barreled into the shop, sending the overhead bell into a minor tizzy. I was immediately overpowered by a heavy cloud of sinsemilla smoke. Thundering through the sound system was the hypnotic opening bass line of "Street 66" by Linton Kwesi Johnson.

There was a serious-looking Rastaman behind the glass counter. I approached. His eyes were closed, lost in the music — but somehow, he knew where I stood. He lifted one finger: the universal sign of "cool your jets."

LKJ was just getting started:

> *The room was dark*
> *Dusk howling softly 6 o'clock*
> *Charcoal lite*
> *Defying sight*
> *Was moving black*
> *The sound was music mellow steady flow*
> *And man son mind just mystic red, green, red, green*
> *Your scene*

I stood transfixed as Ras Piankhi and LKJ communed within the dub poetry. It wasn't until LKJ uttered his closing lyric three and a half minutes later, *"Yes, this is Street 66, step right in and take some licks,"* that Ras Piankhi opened his eyes, looked toward me and, as if my presence was an intrusion, asked:

"Wah yuh waan?"

Ras Piankhi was a hard faced, gravel voiced, Old Testament-spewing, Jamaican Rasta who seemed to know everybody who was anybody in the world of Reggae music and, of course, the weed business. It was impossible to tell how old he was but the grey in his beard and locks suggested he was well past 50.

"Do you have the book *Skinhead* by Nick Knight? How about 'King Pharoah' by Delroy Wilson and Coxsone Dodd? And why did everyone make records going at Prince Buster?"

"And why Lion Order, Mr. Piankhi?"

He paused. Pulled on his pipe. Slowly placed his pen on the counter before him. Took a breath, and said, "I and I cuh sekkle di question, but reason it out for yuhself."

After a brief pause I jumped in, eager to impress. "Okay! The Lion is Selassie. The Lion of Judah. Christ in his kingly character. King of Kings, Lord of Lords, Conquering Lion of the Tribe of Judah. Elect of God, the Light of the World."

"Book learnings," grumbled Ras Piankhi.

"And 'order' could be like structure, rules or it could be like a command..."

"And."

"Sir?"

"Not 'or,' 'and.' Two ting can be true, mi yute. The command is the authoritative utterances of Rastafari Himself. Many ears may hear the command but only the righteous may receive."

"But who is righteous?" I asked, ready to spar.

Ras Piankhi laughed. "Waah real baby lion question, dat... In due time." He picked up his pen and went back to his ledger.

"Di book yuh look fah is deh pon di shelf." He gestured with a grizzled finger, never looking my way.

With that, I sensed the conversation was done. I bought the book I'd come for and rushed back home to read every word, twice.

Nick Knight's *Skinhead* became my bible.

◎◉◎

"If you want to grab an English thing, Dennis Bovell and Mad Professor have the game on lock. Cho! Saxon Sound System is mashing up the streets, mate!" Brixton said. "Papa Levi and a singer name of Maxi Priest—"

I registered every redirection but I stayed on course for Skinhead infamy, to his chagrin. "Make me a tape, man."

He tried. "Skinheads are stuck in time, mate. Tethered to tradition. Watch the Rudie dem. Once you start staying home listening to oldies or pulling out last year's clothes," he jabbed, "you're no longer a Rude Boy."

"It's a good thing I'm not a Rude Boy, then," I laughed.

"Mate! You ain't even got a football team! A Skinhead without football?" He was right, but he also had an agenda. I scanned the room, reached for the only name I knew, from a Cockney Rejects song. "West Ham! Now to find some claret and blue," I quipped, turning the screws back on him.

Vexed, he grabbed my copy of the Nick Knight book. "If you're gonna do this Skinhead thing look to the originals for your style. This right here. Page 45. Pure class."

"None of that tight pants, tall boots, shaved head business. Too scruffy."

I knew I'd won. I had successfully worn him down.

"You already have the hair," he continued, "the only thing missing is a part. We call that a trench back home."

"Nah man, that is leaning too hard into gang-banging. You know I like to keep it neutral."

"Let me guess. Right side is Folks and left side is People."

"Sho yuh right."

"And both sides would be..."

"Goofy," we said at the same time. Goofy was one of the worst insults you could use on a person in Fourth World.

"Ay mon. Now I get why you don't have pierced ears."
"Right. That would be a hard claim and I ride straight neutron. I mean, I'm associated just by being where I'm from and walking where I walk, but I don't fight no wars that I didn't start. Now, perpetrating, pretending to be something you ain't, that's something you just don't do." To his credit, he never turned my words back. Never questioned why I was so enthralled by a subculture from thousands of miles away.

Brixton took on more Fourth World styles. Started dressing like us. His old standbys like Fred Perry, Sta-Prest, and Ben Sherman lost relevance. Now he chose Polo, Izod, Pierre Cardin, and Sergio Valente.

He cleared his closet. Knocked me down some of his old gear. He laid them out with care.

"Most people think Skinhead is all about the boots. That's part of it, yeah, but the shirt — the shirt is the key. It's a holdover from when Skinheads were switching over from Mods to the new thing. But it can't be just any button-down shirt."

He pushed a shirt into my hands. "Put this on."

"See. It's got to have a roll collar. Here. Put your fingers in here. A three-finger collar is what you want. Some go for four, but you gotta have a long neck to pull that off. Turn around. And, here. The back collar button. It's meant to keep a necktie in place, but Skinheads don't wear those. Now it's just for style."

"Now, hear what — and this is crucial — this second button on the shirt. It's placed intentionally high. That button makes the collar roll pop. And never, ever button the top button. It flattens out the collar roll, and that's not Skinhead, at all. Skinheads are tightened up, but never uptight."

The details in the Nick Knight book came to life.

"The locker loop and the back pleat. Got to have those. But this. This!"

He pointed to where my arm pressed against the opening of the short sleeve. There was an inverted v-cut with a decorative button at the apex.

"The sleeve cuts. Skinheads like tight sleeves. The sleeve cut pulls your eye

38

in. Lets you know you're looking at the real deal."
"That's it. You look crisp, mate."

I felt like a giant. I wasn't just wanting a part. I was becoming the part.

I couldn't get him to give up his Crombie or his shearling coat, though. Those I'd have to find on my own.

And charity would only get me so far.

Viddy and Peaches saw me fully turned out and wanted to be in the club. Confided they were frustrated in their searches for the right gear.

Brixton gathered his accidental Skins — me, Viddy, Peaches and Herb — for a trip. We hopped the bus to downtown. Transferred west to Maxwell Street. The Scratch.

We found real Levi's Sta-Prest. Red Wing steel-toed postman shoes. Levi's Type 3 trucker jackets. We found Arnold Palmer and Towncraft short-sleeve button-down shirts—with most of the desired features. We were amazed to find London Fog Harrington jackets. Brixton cautioned us to avoid the suspiciously-priced Brooks Brothers shirts. "Most-likely counterfeit."

"You lot have got a goldmine here. Right under your bleeding nose. And it took an immigrant to show you," he grinned.

Looking the part was half the battle. An origin story was taking shape.

◎ ◎ ◎

Lion Order was a Mecca for Reggae and the shop became my home away from home. Ras Piankhi had almost all the records listed in the Nick Knight book. Buying them all was out of the question so I parked myself at one of the listening stations and gave myself a thorough education in Skinhead Reggae.

Lion Order's stock of 45s was a collector's dream arranged in massive hand-built floor-to-ceiling sliding stacks that were organized first by artist, the second stack by label and, for the real seekers, the third stack was arranged by producer. Ras Piankhi also stocked albums, hand drums, t-shirts, books, and a ever-changing array of Rasta and Ethiopian ephemera.

A table full of Elders quieted down to take a look at me. They seemed to size up my clothing and decided I wasn't worth much consideration.

Near the door was a cork board where artists, artisans, and handy people posted their availability for any jobs for cash or barter. Some of the more philosophical members of the community tacked their thoughts onto that board. I found a diatribe entitled "THINGS TAKEN: AN EPISTLE" that raked Christopher Columbus, the pope, and the whole concept of the Thanksgiving holiday over a bed of flaming hot coals. The polemic was handwritten on notebook paper, and I was captivated.

I wanted to understand everything the author professed. I pulled a pen and notebook out of my MA-1 jacket and began to transcribe it word for word. I planned to consume it in my own time alongside encyclopedias to chase down every thread. The Elders silently observed my diligence and decided that maybe I was a genuine seeker of knowledge and, despite any first impressions, I might possibly turn out to be worthy of their regard.

Ras Piankhi pulled on his pipe. "Jus tek di ting, mi yute."

"Excuse me?"

"Di paper. Have it."

"But if I take it then no one else will receive it."

"Respect. Respect, mi yute," he replied, drawing on his pipe.

Ras Piankhi gave me the nickname Jackpot before he ever asked my real name.

He said that I reminded him of George Dekker from The Pioneers. "Unno two studious." And since I was into "dat bal'head ting," whenever I came into the shop, he would put on The Pioneers' 1968 Skinhead Reggae classic "Jackpot."

The nickname stuck. It made me feel important. A unique alias with its own theme song? Yes, please. It also helped that it was loaded with suggestive potential that I exploited to flirt with girls, telling them in countless ways that spending time with me was as sweet as winning the lottery.

My mother hated the nickname, but even she was forced to acknowledge it when my friends called. I got the sense that Tremor was secretly glad that I could move around Fourth World and not be weighed down by his name. His past.

◎ ◎ ◎

Ras Piankhi had been in the sound system business in the early days of popular Jamaican music. His job was to mash up sounds and mash down soundmen. His boss man wanted to rule the dancehall, and to men like Ras Piankhi, the dancehall was the spark that lit all fires. "Ska," he said was first "dancehall music before the money man grab it." Rocksteady, again, was simply "dancehall music" before it got another name. Roots, again, was first known as "dancehall music." Only the groundation was "pure Rasta music," he explained. "Every yard man have one foot inna di dancehall and the nex' foot inna him gates." Only the harps, the holy trinity of the Nyahbinghi drums, the Bass (*"di eart-quake"*), the Funde (*"di tunda"*) and the Kette (*"di light-nin'"*), could evade the clutches of the money man. "Di whole ah dem ah mi heartbeat... but the people dem want Reggae so mi sell Reggae... And herb," he said with a gleam. "More herb than record, fi true."

"Now buy sint'ing. Dis a nuh charity."

This was much more than a record shop. This was Ras Piankhi's yard. His gates. His kingdom. He owned this corner, and above the storefront was his home which he kept with his wife Sista Evangeline, a beautiful black woman from Gales Point, Belize, and four children. An adjacent storefront housed a gaming arcade, and the next a laundromat, all connected by walkways, and all owned and managed by Ras Piankhi and Sista Evangeline.

Immediately behind the storefront was Sista Evangeline's Roots & Bittas Shop and kitchen. The racks were loaded with dry roots and tinctures. Mysterious names like Yohimbe, Abrus Precatorius, Ibogaine, and Guifiti. One wall was labeled "Fi Di Man." Another labeled "Fi Di 'oman."

Behind the building, hidden by a tall wooden gate, was a large garden sprinkled with chairs, tables, umbrellas and a small, wooden stage. To one side was a bottle tree, a prayer kettle and a large altar built around a tree stump that had been transplanted from Congo Square in New Orleans. The stump itself could have made a decent sized breakfast table for a family of four, but here it served as a place of remembrance — and maybe goat sacrifice.

The yard was capped on one end by an imposing stack of handmade sound system speakers. They were painted to read "ROOT TEMPLE VIBE-FI." Red, black, and green musical notes wrapped around the giant cabinets.

At the other end was a thatch covered drum circle.

This was where Ras Piankhi held his groundations. Where the elders elevated the Dancehall. This was where the materialists and the "heartical, rootical" people became one. An oasis in the middle of a concrete jungle. "Dis yard ya..." Ras Piankhi emphasized with a hard finger, "Dis a nuh Terror Town. Dis ya Root Temple."

Terror Town breathed. Fourth World was my oxygen. But Root Temple? Root Temple was the nerve center. It hummed. It moved. It sang. Literally and figuratively. I could imagine the Orishas themselves — all 400+1 — coming here to recharge.

Ras Piankhi watched me. He sensed what Root Temple was doing to me. "Yuh a good yute. Dat mi si. But yuh haffi leggo di bal'head ting. Bal'head nuh build great man, dem only kill great man." I joked, "I don't know... I can't see myself with dreads." Sista Evangeline's eyes widened. She moved quickly into the yard and put her hand over my heart as if to steady me. "That's a word that must not be used lightly, and an energy that has no place in Root Temple."

I rifled through my memory and landed on what I gathered was the troubling word. I didn't understand, but I accepted.

I took the word out of my vocabulary.

◎◎◎

Ras Piankhi was a teacher to his core, so he welcomed the youth who came there to shop and reason, and it was this atmosphere that inspired a generation of youth from the South Side to organize ourselves, unofficially, as "Lion Order."

There were some in Lion Order who clung to the Rude Boy aesthetic, others who were turning Rasta, a lot of Preppy types, and several revivalist stalwarts, like me, who loved the Skinhead thing. What united us was a love for Lion Order. We weren't a gang, and only rarely referred to ourselves as a crew. We weren't mature enough to be a family, and we shunned hierarchy, but we had each other's backs and tolerated each other's peculiarities. Each one of us came from our own "trouble block" — that's what people from The Gold Coast called it — but we loved Lion Order enough to cross any number of war zones to get here, and we needed Lion Order enough to leave any outside affiliations or rivalries at the door.

"How yuh get rope inna dat peelhead ting, mi yute?" Asked Ras Piankhi while I thumbed through the *Kebra Negast*. He was polishing the blade of the machete he kept behind the counter, and was in the mood to listen. I laid out my origin story.

Ras Piankhi drew on his pipe as I told him how I'd gone looking for anything and everything about these youth and how the more I learned the more it seemed to fit me. Their style. What I imagined to be their demeanors. The brands they clung to. Similar brand choices positioned me as an undeniable insider to Fourth World culture but also set me off as just enough of an outsider to be mysterious.

"Careful, mi yute. Only slave master love brand...Gwan."

I told him how Tremor thought my buttoned up look was out of place. Ras Piankhi's eyebrow raised at the mention of the name. "Tremor didn't hate it," I explained. "But he thought it was strange how me and my friends wore work clothing but never did any work in them. Like we were 'going to a fashion show at the steel mill.'" That amused Ras Piankhi.

"Yuh fadda call dat right, nuh rass," he laughed.

I told Ras Piankhi how Tremor was much more appreciative of the nighttime Skinhead gear and appreciated my attention to details. It was Tremor who took me to Kham & Nate's shoe store on 87th to buy my first pair of Florsheim's brogues. He even handed me down a shoe shine kit, complete with a horse hair brush and shoe spreaders. Once I saved enough money he took me to his tailor to get my first suit. I had to settle for sharkskin because tonic cloth was a rarity in the United States, but he surprised me by paying for the suit himself. He told me to keep saving until I could get myself a proper tonic suit.

Ras Piankhi looked at me with deep regard. "Yuh Tremor pickney fi true. Unno two do tings wid intention, mi yute. I and I does admire dat."

I felt like I'd passed a test and, from that day forward I was never "bal'head" or "peelhead." I was either Jackpot or "Soon Ras."

I had avoided this stretch for years. Now, it was my stopping place after school. I'd saunter in and annoy Ras Piankhi with my questions, but a key turning point was an old blade. Tremor had been holding onto a military-issue Ontario machete for years. The edge was dulled, the sheath tattered. It needed a better home. Tremor knew Ras Piankhi loved machetes and cutlasses and he also knew I was spending a lot of time at the shop. He sent the relic with me as a gift to Ras Piankhi. That was the moment that Ras Piankhi accepted me as more than just a wide-eyed upstart.

I clocked hundreds of hours at Lion Order and, under the wings of Brixton and Ras Piankhi, I became much more than an appreciator of Jamaican music. I became a genuine student of Reggae.

I did the sweeping and some of the organizing. I helped out at the arcade or the laundromat. I gained an understanding of his 45 filing system and helped collectors find hidden gems. I did all this just to be involved. Useful. Ras Piankhi couldn't pay me in cash, but he frequently sent me home with books or records that he thought a "Soon Ras" should have. The first of which was I-Roy's *Step Forward Youth* album. He topped that with a pristine copy — "straight from Jamdown" — of "Jackpot" by The Pioneers, on the Amalgamated label. The 45 was autographed by George Dekker, himself! This was worth so much more to me than cash and I still have it to this day. Still other times he'd send me home with a "care package" of collie weed for Tremor who, like Ras Piankhi, was a real herbalist.

With some coaxing Ras Piankhi allowed me to mark the sleeves of Skinhead Reggae 45s with yellow masking tape. I leaned heavily on his encyclopedic knowledge of the music. He wouldn't let me make one whole section, saying it was "lone Rocksteady" and "unno baldhead nuh run Reggae. Dis ah yard man ting."

Keeping the Skinhead Reggae tunes in the larger collections highlighted an important facet of his inventory. Customers wanted to know what the yellow tape signified. "Why does Slim Smith's "Rougher Yet" have the yellow tape while his "Born to Love" does not?" It sparked conversations about the subtle distinctions — subject matter, mood and instrumentation — between the sides and, once collectors caught wind, some would travel great distances specifically for those tunes, oftentimes buying big batches. Ras Piankhi would grumble about what he saw as their narrow interests but he couldn't deny that they were great for the culture, and for Lion Order.

The practice of marking the Skinhead Reggae tunes blossomed into a whole system of categorizing the sides with a distinct color each for Dub, Roots, Ragga and even the little known John Crow Skank offshoot. Simply by browsing the stacks, customers were taken on a journey through the intricacies of Jamaican music.

"You and Brixton… unno two special yute. Unno give I-man hope fi di future," Ras Piankhi confided.

◎ ◎ ◎

Brixton became a true Fourth World citizen. He rapidly fell in with our culture and fell in love with the Rude Girl, Ajoa, my downstairs neighbor, which meant he was around my home all the time. His new obsessions led him to try his hand at DeeJaying small parties which required equipment and transport so he was one of the first of our Set with wheels. His father's Volvo 240 DL station wagon. He convinced Ras Piankhi to let him throw an afternoon Set inside the shop. Brixton didn't have much of a name as a DJ but Fourth World loves a party so the local youth came by to check it out. This brought the shop and Ras Piankhi onto the radar of curious kids from around Terror Town. I can't say his first attempt was elegant — his blends were rough and his mic chat lacked finesse — but it was good enough to get him remembered. The gangsters didn't like the neutrons walking freely across their borders, but a wall had been quietly dismantled. In hindsight, Brixton could, by rights, be called the first face of the Lion Order movement.

I admired Brixton's outlook on life and the unstressed latitude that he enjoyed. As an immigrant, Brixton was aware of, but not weighed down by, all our claustrophobic customs of who could wear what and who could walk where. He enjoyed a degree of freedom that was unavailable to the rest of us. His accent gave him an extra layer of cover. He'd get a free pass out of trouble once the hearer determined he wasn't from around here, and that any offense had been unintentional. Brixton discovered that away from London he could let his guard down and just be human, and he showed me that the world was so much bigger than Fourth World. He became a best friend to me, maybe even a brother, though I never got a chance to tell him that.

◎ ◎ ◎

One afternoon while sweeping up at Lion Order I felt a tap on my shoulder. I turned to see two older, fully-formed Skinheads. One a light-skinned Black man in his early twenties. The other a serious looking carrot top. My eye quickly clocked that all details were exactly where they were supposed to be.

The Black Skinhead introduced himself as Moonstomp. I mentally connected the dots to the lore of "The Bronzeville Bully." He leaned in and whispered, "What size boots are those, freshcut?"

I stiffened.

"I'm just fucking with you. You look like the real deal, man. Props."

I exhaled.

The other Skin, Bubba, talked with Ras Piankhi about some 45s he had on special order. They tucked their new vinyl away then scooted off on their Lambrettas.

While I'd see Bubba again, that was the last time I ever laid eyes on Moonstomp. He got shipped out to Beirut with his Marines unit and was one of the unlucky two-hundred-twenty who took the long nap in that operation.

By then, the streets knew me as Jackpot. A name that would get heavier with time.

CHAPTER FIVE

The Walls
Joliet, Illinois

They call it the Slave State.

You see the wall of the old prison before you see anything else.

The gothic medieval facade — with its pointed arches, towers and battle-ments — evokes a very different era. And yet, despite its hints of antiquity, it is the most modern structure in this bombed-out burg.

And the walls... Those fucking walls.

Designed by humans to hide the inhumanity we inflict on other humans.

The roundhouse. The panopticon. The guards in their tower. Everything can be known. Nothing can move without being seen.

What did the architect want us beholders to think?

What did the architect want the beheld to feel?

◎ ◉ ◎

From the Book of Black Teeth: Immoral Tales
Joliet, Illinois

A dark room. Too modern to be a cavern. Too rough to be any home.

The shuttered movie theater. The abandoned firehouse. The music shop, which was where the only signs of life could be detected by outsiders.

Then you catch it. A stench so nameless. Age, earth, iron, body. Carrion. Corpse flower.

A rot so deep it no longer smells like death. It smells like the moment death itself dies — the slackening. The leak. The stink of an illicit tryst of vultures, hyenas, and jackals. Intertwining. The sensation threading its way into the soft meat behind your nose. Nesting in the sinuses. Coiling in the reptilian brain. Tickling that deep, dark remnant of primordial sludge.

Days later, it claws its way up from the ooze. Grows limbs. Spinal needles. Vocalizes. Knocks. Reintroduces itself.

You wonder if something's wrong with your hygiene. Or your mind. Does no one else notice? Or do they all?

No shower scalds enough to shed a stench so nameless.

A maze of corridors connect the structures. The corridors began as homage to classical ideals, but were constructed without the fascism of the ancients. As if the modern craftsman had read of them but never seen the actual arches and angles and vestments. As if the modern craftsman had to accept their limitations. That in this singular case, verisimilitude was just a hair's breadth beyond reach and would have to do, for now.

Heavy drapes hide secrets meant only for devotees and aspirants. The oblique passageways would only confuse and ensnare the uninitiated.

The theater's carpet had long been ripped away, leaving only acid-burned concrete.

Walls smudged floor to ceiling with ochre.

Along the wall, meticulously hung at precise intervals, an array of well cared for greatswords, broadswords, maces, and pikes. Sharpened. Honored.

An ornate bookshelf in the corner tells a story of its own. The Grand Grimoire, The History of Surgery, The Picatrix, From There to Here: Ancient Sex Worship, The Pale Fox, The Iceman Inheritance.

The books – not merely arranged, but divinely arrayed. Return as found. Flaying awaits the careless.

Tomes that live. Fecund tomes that claim a piece of the reader with each crack of the binding. A bloody thumbprint along this spine. Eye water on this page. Frustrated spittle flecking an obtuse passage in this one. Notes scribbled then furiously stricken.

Tomes that live.

Tomes that take.

Tomes as oblique as the corridors.

Tomes that feint and torment and occasionally answer.

Tomes that know when you've read too far.

The inhabitants, ten in number, silently watch the screen, rapt.

On this night, on the screen, an endless loop of "Immoral Tales."

◎ ◉ ◎

The Pen CNN: Grapevine, the Divine
Joliet, Illinois

Some men do bitter.

Some men do sweet.

Grapevine did hardstyle.

Not jokes. Not rumors. Truth.

He made words float. He made words land. He made sense out of no-sense.

And when Grapevine stood up to do his thing? The walls between Here and There disappeared.

They couldn't jail Grapevine.

49

The law? Just another knot for his words to untie.

The institutional lighting and high ceiling cast a cold, eerie glow over the space. These walls, chipped by time and projectiles. Years. Violence.

Same walls. Mocking the men. Psychologists and paint sellers tricked the State into believing Baker-Miller Pink would salve the trauma and solve the poverty.

Rows of long, metal tables with attached benches stretch across the room. Scratched. Dented. Years. Violence.

The air. Bleach. Sweat. Government cheese. At the far end, a serving line. Sneeze guards and prison guards. Inmates. The lucky ones. Dishing out kale and pepper steak to the slightly-less-lucky.

Normally, this place hummed. The din. The clatter of trays. The scraping of chairs. The low murmur of conversations. Occasionally punctuated by the sharp bark of a guard's command.

Now, though, all eyes were on Grapevine.

Prison-issue jumpsuit. Loose around his waist. A matching cap tilted defiantly to the left. His afro spilling out the sides.

I know y'all wanted me to tell y'all about "The Ball of the Freaks."

(They know this rap)

Let's leave that to a lesser poet, or a slow news week.

(He paused for a beat)

They call this the Slave State, but we freer than most.

(The men murmured in agreement)

This the Pen CNN. The squares call it a toast.

(He let that land for the fresh meat)

I don't sell no lies. No wolf tickets. No doubt.

(The men said it with him)

Grapevine, the Divine signing the fuck out.

He stepped down from the cafeteria table. A guard's finger found his trigger. Just in case.

His fellow inmates: Cards shuffled. Dominos slapped. The walls returned.

CHAPTER SIX

Some lives leave fingerprints. Brixton's cut grooves. Deep and loud.

Brixton worked to climb the ladder of the DJ set. Any date. Low pay or no pay. Anything to sharpen his skills.

He got booked to open for an up-and-coming Harlem rapper and his DJ at The Blue Gargoyle, a small gothic-themed theater on the campus of the University of Chicago.

Hip Hop culture walked tall, here. The big glasses. The fat gold chains. The shell-toe ADIDAS. The lyrical cyphers, beatboxing and breaking. It was all foreign to us locals. They liked bass drops while we liked bass lines. When our DJs played, the rap lovers couldn't connect with the 4/4 beats and held up the wall. When their DJs played we cleared the floor so they could do their breaking. They were brash. We saw ourselves as smooth.

This was hostile territory but Lion Order showed up to support Brixton.

Don't get me wrong, we liked Rap. We'd get geeked when Herb Kent played the latest releases on his "Punk Out" show, but we saw it as a New York thing. Fourth World liked what Fourth World made so it wasn't just Rap from New York that was on the sidelines. GoGo from DC, Detroit Techno and even Minneapolis Funk all had to fight each other for second class status. A culture clash was inevitable.

Brixton turned in a solid early set but it was clear that only Lion Order was entertained. At the end of his round another DJ, with a distinct New York accent, dragged the needle across one of the platters and shouted "NO

MORE WACKNESS!" The Hip Hop crowd was thrilled. We bristled.

An insult. From outsiders. Invaders.

We saw ourselves as war fighters in need of a war. We'd grown up on a diet that included "Tony Brown's Black Journal," "Pixote," "The Spook Who Sat By The Door," "Enter The Dragon," "Assault on Precinct 13" and "Cooley High." Those works of art radicalized us. Rendered us ready to answer every challenge, intellectual or physical.

The insult put us on edge.

I joined the breakers in the middle of the floor. They assumed I was serious and made space for me. Instead, I made a mockery of it. Disrespected their movement. My crowd roared in approval. The insult had been answered.

The Hip Hop DJ grabbed the mic. Screamed "GET THAT FAGGOT OFF THE FLOOR!" That was all the provocation Brixton needed to clock him in the jaw.

That was the blow that set off the melee.

The two cultures clashed.

Chairs thrown. Mobs going at each other. Months, if not years, of tension were spilling out and, to the Rap crowd's surprise, these Fourth World kids could fight. Viddy and Herb turned up the heat by toppling the Rap DJ's coffin and dumping out their record crates. The music stopped. Viddy grabbed the microphone. Yelled what would become a Lion Order battle cry, "give these generals some new stripes!"

It would be easy to say this was a noble battle during which rules of engagement were respected, but that would be a lie. We weren't angels, and no part of this was a fair fight. Our billy clubs and brass knuckles couldn't be answered. We wolf-packed — we called it "siafu," after the African ants who can collectively bring down an elephant. We destroyed their equipment. We humiliated them. We wrecked the opposition.

We wanted to send the New Yorkers home with stories to tell and scars to show. This is how Fourth World defends itself. We wanted to let any local Rap movement makers know that second class status was the best they could hope for.

Brixton was more bothered by the absence of music than by the melee. He pulled a couple of wires, plugged them into his 4-track and piped his experimental bass track through the speakers. A symphonic score for violent, youthful excess. Like A Clockwork Orange, but real.

Brixton was in a trance. His music sounded bigger than ever over the sound system. Bigger even than he'd experienced at Lion Order. He was hearing it as he intended it to be heard and we practically had to drag him out of there before he — and, by extension, his father the professor — got blamed for the ruckus.

News of this brawl reverberated around all sectors. It became nearly impossible for Hip Hop to find open doors in Fourth World. We'd walked into their home, pissed on the couch and gotten them evicted. We, on the other hand, were very happy with our results. Told them that Lion Order was responsible, and that we could be found at 75th and Kingston if they needed to file any complaints.

Lion Order had a newfound swagger after that performance.

We felt unstoppable.

◎◉◎

Brixton was inspired. He wanted his Lion Order Sets to deliver that same symphonic experience, but his Sears-Roebuck PA system was a limiting factor. His research for a replacement led him to the wasteland of Joliet, Illinois. A music shop called CACOPHONY.

He knocked on my door and dragged me out of bed. 50 miles. Neither of us had been that far beyond the Scratch so this was an adventure. A very flat adventure with a lot of dairy farms.

"Remind me why the fuck we have to go way the fuck out to klan-land for some speakers."

"They aren't just 'speakers.'" Brixton responded. "These subwoofers are gonna create a low-frequency bass that motherfuckers in Milwaukee will feel!"

"Why can't you just get Ras Piankhi's guys to make you some?"

"That's where I started but Ras Piankhi put brakes on it. Told his man not to do the job. Said I shouldn't be copying his sound. I should be trying to obliterate his sound. And he's right."

I went back to counting cows. Until... The walls of the prison rose up from the horizon. I'd heard of it but never seen it. It was somehow both bigger and smaller than I imagined. I wondered about the men locked inside. I thought about that "Scared Straight" bullshit and decided, ain't gon' be me.

We slowly wound our way around the prison and through town until we found what we were looking for. Right next to the rundown movie theater and the decommissioned firehouse. CACOPHONY. A homely windowless storefront. It smelled like what I imagined a slaughterhouse would smell like.

In the gravel yard behind the shop was a jumble of parked carnival equipment. Rising above the fence was a broken down dragon that laughed and sneered. Part house of fun, part house of horror. Across the street was a funeral home. Next door to that, a tattoo parlor. Parked out front were a couple of Harley FXR Shovelheads. Club-style bikes. Tanks decorated with "DEATH ROCKERS MC." A new patch to me.

We parked in the gravel lot and went inside. They froze at the sight of us. As if we'd interrupted a seance. Venom in their dead eyes suggested something deeper. I reminded myself of Tremor's words. "Go into every place as if you belong there." I squared up my shoulders and claimed my space.

The room smelled like a mixture of rotting flesh, urine, sweat, Marlboros, and desperation. The fake wood paneling was a throwback to prior decades. Tacked haphazardly on the walls were posters from obscure bands, and pages pulled from photocopied newsletters.

"WELCOME TO HELL"

"NO LIFE 'TIL LEATHER"

"BLACK METAL"

"TRIUMPH OF DEATH"

"MOTORHEAD"

That last one I recognized.

I sized up the shopkeepers. Two men, two women. Ragged. Long scraggly hair, ghostly pale skin. Late teens to early 20s. Distorted guitar sounds from the mid-sized boombox. A lot of treble. No bass. Fast drums. Not much of a groove. The instruments competed with each other to get out of the small speaker. I caught a brief glimpse of the teeth of a man. Saw that they had been filed into sharp points.

I was on guard but Brixton was oblivious. He found a used Alembic bass and, without asking, pulled it off the rack. He plugged it into a Gallien-Krueger GK 800RB bass amp.

He tuned the bass, plucked some strings, then turned a knob to knock out the bridge pickup. On the amp he cranked the bass knob up to ten and the treble down to about nine o'clock. He plucked some strings again and, satisfied he had a usable tone, he dropped right into the bass line from Derrick Morgan's "Teach My Daughter." This tune was one of my favorites. I jumped in and beat out the rhythm on a floor tom and sang along, off key but that didn't matter. He smiled at me with his eyes, getting lost in the groove.

The dirtheads shot glares our way but we carried on.

Brixton then blew my mind by playing a sublime bass line that oozed dubby sweetness. He shouted it was from "Dream a Lie" by UB40. I'd never been a fan but this bass line changed that.

The dirtheads behind the counter cranked up their tinny cassette player but it was no match for Brixton. Eyes closed, he segued into the "Good Times" bass line by Chic which naturally led him to "I Need a Freak" by Sexual Harassment and then into a thundering four-on-the-floor bass line that pushed the GK 800RB in directions the rock-tuned amp wasn't made for.

The strings of nearby acoustic guitars came to life with a buzz. Snare drums joined in. The whole shack bent to the will of Brixton's bass trance.

This was starting to feel like Church, but...

I tapped his shoulder. Showed him the price tag. He understood. He might be buying the amp if he pushed it too far. He shut down the concert. Straightened up. Put the bass on the rack and got back to looking for his subwoofers.

I drifted in the other direction, humming, trying to remember the "Dream a Lie" bass line.

Pinned to a cork-board near the door was a strange flyer. "Which third grader banged this shit out?" I asked no one in particular.

1560/1614

THE FEAST OF THE COVEN°ANT/

WE ARE THE EATERS OF THE PUREST UNCORRUPTED UNTAINTED/

TESTIMONY OF THE *9* DEVIL'S ADVOCATES/

BE NOT RULED/

CLAIM \ EXPLOIT \ SNUFF

EXSANGUATE/ EXCEREBRATE/ IMBIBE/ RECEREBRATE/

1560/1614

ON 4 AND 20 TERRE BLANCHE ULTIMA THULE IN THE SHADOWS OF THE SLAVE STATE

RAPE WITHOUT REMORSE
PLUNDER WITH PRIDE
KILL WITH PRECISION

I heard a whisper... more like a growl say, "That's not for you!" Before I could register the meaning, a pale hand ripped the flyer off the wall and took it behind the counter. I turned to face the fucker.

Brixton called out to me from the back corner of the shop. He'd found what he was looking for.

The wooden shipping crates were marked Cetec Gauss 5181. The cabinets that he swore would produce a bass that would push people off the walls of Lion Order and make lake trout tap their toes.

In his rush he brushed past one of the women, briefly resting his hand on her shoulder. "Pardon me, love," he said in his London brogue. She froze. The horror spread across her face like she'd tasted bile. Quick. Sharp. Unmistakable. A silence rippled. Not heard. Just felt. Brixton didn't clock it. He was fixed on his subwoofers.

Brixton didn't mince words. "$850 each? I'll take all four for $3,000 cash. And I'll need help loading."

They bristled but they took his money and followed his direction.

"Man, I don't know if you can trust these people," I said, loud enough for them to hear. Trying to get under their skin. "You better look inside every crate. Could be a bricks-in-the-box scam."

They moved slow. Sullen. Brooding hard on being bossed around.

One of the dirtheads slammed the hatch angrily, prompting Brixton to take an exaggerated look at the door, checking for damage. I think he finally got that we weren't welcome. Satisfied that no damage had been done, we climbed back into the fully loaded station wagon.

I caught something being muttered.

"Night Skins." Didn't bother me. I happen to like my dark skin.

Brixton fired up the chariot and pulled away, anxious to get back to Lion Order, rattling off all manner of horns and crossovers and preamps that he would use to string the cabinets together.

In the side view mirror I noticed a primer-grey Chester the Molester van pull out behind us. Were they tailing us?

I watched it for a while.

"Mate! You have a good voice! You owned that Morgan chune. We should start a band."

"Man, I can't even hold a note," I replied.

"That shit can be taught. Just like I taught you to be a Skinhead."

"I think you just needed a tough mate to get you out of scrapes and intro-duce you to girls," I said, laughing.

"Mate, you never even kissed a girl until I gave you some hand-me-downs."

"Bruh, your crusty shirts are a liability. How did you get pee stains in the armpits?"

We kept signifying until the road took over.

I dozed off thinking Night Skin would be a cold-blooded name for a band.

CHAPTER SEVEN

"We've got a lot in common with the blacks from the point of view that we both get police pressure, and we both get spat on..." the bass player said.

I was sitting with my crew — Viddy, Brixton, Tremor, Ajoa, and Peaches — in my living room watching a bootleg of the BBC "Arena" documentary about the London Skinhead band Combat 84.

Peaches sat on the floor watching the TV. Ajoa sat above her with barber shears, tending carefully to Peaches's fringe and feathers. Peaches had gone full crop once, but now her feathers added softness. Maturity, too. She was a Skinhead girl, but growing up into a Skinhead woman.

Brixton was giving his assessment of the speakers. "The singer is clearly not on our team but the bass player seems proper sussed. I remember that youth. He's from Tanners Hill in Deptford and has always been the best dressed of his kind." Tremor came in on the tail end of the conversation, joint balanced on his lip like it had been attached with Krazy Glue. "Brixton my boy! You startin' to look like a Fourth World original." I always joked that Tremor liked Brixton more than he liked me.

Viddy prodded, "Go ahead, Brix. Ask Tremor the question you asked us."

Brixton had been picking our brains but none of us had the whole answer. "I know that Chicago ain't Chicago no more. And I know that it's all chopped up into quadrants now. And it all seemed to happen overnight. But what caused it?"

I sighed with mock exasperation. "Man, please don't get Malcolm Y started.

He'll have you building bombs and shit."

Tremor bounced the joint on his lip. "First off, mister musical-chairs-of-names, be more like Brixton and less like you, and second, I'm already started. Buckle up."

"1983 was the year that Chicago collapsed."

This was secretly one of my favorite Tremor raps, but I couldn't let him know that.

"Da Mayor and The Fed are why the city imploded. Both men were dead by then but the wheels they'd set in motion reached peak velocity in 1981."

"It was a slow collapse but, in hindsight, all the markers were there. Da Mayor believed a segregated city was a well-functioning city and he used the Chicago Police Department to enforce that. He didn't come right out and say it but he never addressed de facto segregation and inequality. He actively opposed fair housing measures. And his urban renewal platform was, everybody knew, just 'Negro removal.'"

"The Fed's Counter Intelligence Program (COINTELPRO) was the weapon that blew it all up. He was afraid that Chairman Fred could be a 'black messiah,' so he and his Bureau did everything they could to undermine, weaken, and compromise."

"The Scratch, more or less what was the black part of the West Side, was the first to secede. Some people call it "The Morgue" but people from The Scratch take that as fighting words. Still, it was spoken of as a kind of purgatory of its own making. The Scratch had its own legends and lore, but they were closely guarded by the residents who felt disaffected by the political structure of the city. The people of The Scratch suspected they were being intentionally impoverished as a form of collective punishment by the rest of us. All of us."

"The Scratch is where The Chairman was from — it wasn't called that back then — and it never recovered after the police murdered The Chairman. Everybody says that happened under orders from The Fed and Da Mayor.

The Chairman's whole Rainbow Coalition? Shattered.

That felt like the last hope for a desperate people. After that came a couple of blizzards where they couldn't get plowed out. Then came the teacher strikes. Then came the 1981 mayoral race where every grimy trick was played to undermine our Harold Skytalker. And then the dumps. Businesses just dumped all their toxic trash in The Scratch, and the right grandmother got sick and tired of being sick and tired. She'd had enough and told the whole world. She struck a chord. For The Scratch, there was no coming back from these assaults and slights. I'm not sure how it got the name "The Scratch" — rumors say it started with that grandmother saying "scratch us off your list of dumping grounds" — but it fits. At first, The Gold Coast tried to wield it as an insult, a bludgeon, but then it became a badge of honor. And then, before anyone even realized, it was a battle flag."

"Now, when we talk about access to resources, The Jewel has that to a science. They got all the best parts of a suburb — good schools, police that actually live in the community, politicians that will go to the mat for their constituents — and all the best parts of a city. Nightlife. Jobs. Museums. Think of European cities like Paris and Milan. You have a wealthy center surrounded by poor areas, the service class. That's The Jewel. A shiny kingdom surrounded by a dirty moat. The wealth ain't as concentrated as it is in The Gold Coast, but it's there. What's strange, though, is that The Jewel never figured out how to take care of its children. As resource-rich as they were, they left the kids to fend for themselves for recreation, entertainment, whatever. That's why they never solved their gang problem. They never figured out how to treat the kids as something other than a parasitic drain."

Brixton jumped in. "I've seen it! Kids in The Jewel just waste whole summers away at these little concrete parks, wedged into congested intersections. They sit there with fuck all to do. Then the police come along and say, "Let's keep it moving people. No loitering." But it's a park, with benches, and chess boards. No loitering? Those places are made for loitering."

"Or the way they shut down the skating rink," interjected Peaches. "They said it was a magnet for gangbangers. Oh, really? How about this, then? The kids clearly love skating. Open more skating rinks. Put one in each area. That way you don't have kids feeling like their rink is a limited resource that's being invaded. If my public school ass can think of this shit, why can't they?"

Tremor picked it back up, "I'll tell you why. They hoard the resources until the right youth become the right adults who, if they made it that far, can be trusted to keep the wrong youth in check."

Brixton was hanging on every word.

"The Gold Coast is the bank. It looks down on the rest of us, literally and figuratively. The high-rises. It's like an all-seeing eye, but with cataracts. They can see The Scratch but they don't see the struggles, mainly because it wouldn't profit them to lean in. They don't see that their machinations, their waste, their pollution, their hoarding, have a direct effect on where we live, how we live or even *if* we live. The slums they lord over are just rows on a ledger. They don't even bother checking in on the ants to see if we are onto them because in their minds, they ain't up to nothing. The order of things is simply as it should be. They deserve their abundance as much as we deserve scarcity. But, the funny thing is that they are so sure that the asylum is airtight that they don't realize they are inmates, too. Any system that hasn't invested in solving poverty has not invested in protecting the wealthy."

"I heard that they can live whole lives in those buildings," said Viddy. "Like, they have grocery stores, schools, clothing shops, everything right in there."

Tremor picked up the thread. "I think they are secretly miserable. The women starve themselves for unattainable beauty goals. The men compete with each other in a vacant cycle of material one-upmanship, and their kids... They say the cobblers kids have no shoes well, these high society kids ain't got no home training. Let me tell you this — if you ever meet one of those kids who comes out of the towers to slum it on The Grid, run as fast as you can in the other direction. They are always the ones to set off some crazy shit and they are the only ones who don't get burned. They are the ones brandishing daddy's shiny new revolver and the ones with the chief of police on speed dial. Nah. Steer clear."

I could see questions in Brixton's eyes. Tremor kept sailing. He was in his zone.

"Fourth World, that's where we are now, is marked by a jagged border that loops in all the neighborhoods from Englewood to Lake Michigan, and Bronzeville to Roseland. The local legend says that it's called Fourth World because every religion in the world has a temple here. It's a patchwork of third world enclaves within a first world city — I always liked how they claimed 'first world' for themselves as if Africa wasn't the cradle of civilization. Anyway, Fourth World wasn't no planned utopia. Immigrants got dropped here because they were Black. Black Brazilians, Jamaicans, Bajan, Belizean, Nigerian, Haitian, Ethiopian, whatever. Take your black ass to Fourth World. But that coalition of faiths, languages, foods, people — including white families, like Peaches and Herb, who never left — became our secret weapon."

"In a segregated city this became an accidental oasis. We lived together and agreed to mind our own motherfucking business. Well, with the exceptions of the gangsters, but that's a different story. It's said that it's impossible to build culture during wartime. Fourth World proves that to be a lie. Like that Afro-Caribbean bookstore over by the movie theater. Burned down. Twice. Da Mayor, up to his shit again. Got rebuilt. Still open. Still spreading ideas that are stronger than their handcuffs. We used to work from 'can't see to can't see' — that's 'so dark you *can't see* in the morning' to 'so dark you *can't see*' at night' — now we can make a dollar out of fifteen cents."

"They hate our superpowers," Peaches said.

"But how did you *do* it?" Brixton was on the edge of his seat. He'd read theory but he realized that, at that moment, he was sitting in an actual rebel town.

"Conspiracy," replied Tremor. "The goal? Starve The Gold Coast. The strategy? Deny them revenue. The tactics? Those damn vehicle registration stickers. Police officers that came from Fourth World turned out to be a trojan horse. The people agreed that everyone would stop buying the registration stickers and that all drivers in Fourth World would scrape theirs off. Silent protest. They couldn't ticket us all."

"These kids right here, sitting next to you? Every single one of them went out with scrapers to do what had to be done."

"Police hate writing tickets, but as back-door tax collectors that's what they spent all their time doing. So, at first they went ticket crazy but quickly got burned out on the grind and just gave up. Then some of our more persuasive people met with some of their more flexible people and came to an agreement that when they did write tickets, because they had to look productive, they would get the state on the license plate wrong, or they'd write an F instead of an E. The courts got flooded with cases they couldn't close and one of their biggest revenue streams dried up. We made street-level law enforcement obsolete. The courthouses were empty. The only tickets being written were on cars in The Gold Coast but the courts didn't want to piss those people off. The city had to tighten its belt. Judges started staying in their chambers. Public Defenders suddenly had time to clear backlogs of cases. Prosecutors went into private practice."

"And the vidocks," I added. "Their city planning had huge blind spots. Those train lines that they ran through our neighborhoods could get choked off any time we needed to apply pressure and get some results."

"And The Scratch was where they parked all the trash trucks," threw in Viddy. "Nothing went in, nothing was coming out. The Gold Coast smelled like an outhouse."

"Put it all together," said Tremor. "Think of the beams they made at the steel mill. They served a purpose. Reinforcement. Structural support. Load balancing. Whatever. But sometimes metal flexes. If it flexes too much, it work-hardens, and if it work-hardens it eventually breaks. The system — the metal — we broke it, not because we were naive but because we wanted to see what would happen next. The people decided that Chicago, as a concept, had outlived its utility."

"Yeah, outsiders still called it Chicago but those of us on the inside, we led with where we were from. You could tell a lot about a person based on where they came from."

"After all those years of regular old segregation, the people decided that Da Mayor's approach was child's play. Let's dial it up a notch. This time, not based on race, but based on culture. On vision. On talent. On resources."

He paused. Locked eyes with Brixton.

"And by *choice*."

"It's said that the song 'Let No Man Put Asunder' by First Choice was the lightning bolt that lit the fuse that caused the cataclysm that created the implosion that crashed the wheels that The Fed and Da Mayor had put in motion. If true, it's the most Chicago thing in the world for a dance song to kick off a revolution."

"There I go calling it 'Chicago,' again."

"We gave 'Disco Demolition' a whole new meaning."

"No one can agree on the exact day and time, but sometime in 1983, "Chicago" was laid to rest. Youngbloods like your friends, here, started calling it 'The Grid.' Part map. Part cage."

Tremor paused. Point made.

Brixton sat back, speechless. We were all speechless.

Brixton exhaled, slow. He let the silence stretch. Let the words sit. His fingers tapped against the table — not to a beat, but to a thought forming somewhere deeper than language. He looked around. This wasn't just resistance, it was an art form.

No words. Just the weight of it all pressing onto him, reprogramming everything he previously thought was possible or probable. He looked at Tremor like he was seeing him for the first time. Or maybe not seeing him at all, but seeing dots, circles, and lines connecting.

I saw a change wash over Brixton. He looked at each one of us and saw an undercurrent of history and struggle and self-determination that he'd missed before. These people didn't want handouts. These people didn't even want revenge. The people simply wanted to choose their own way, even if it meant poverty, so long as it was a dignified poverty.

CHAPTER EIGHT

But dignity didn't guarantee safety, and the war for the soul of The Grid was pure pressure.

At the macro level, The Gold Coast still exerted control, doling out chastisement when and if it could. And, at the micro level, anyone regarded as combat age was prey for the local vultures. That's why Viddy walked a narrow line. He'd been my ace since fifth grade. Other than the years when I was at-risk of achieving Poindexter status, he and I were thick as thieves.

He lived a few blocks over from me at East 74th Place between Kingston and Phillips, ground zero of Terror Town.

Viddy lived in a rundown single family home with his adoptive parents. His mother was actually his aunt. She took over raising Viddy when her sister decided that a baby would just be a chain hanging off her.

Their house was three stories tall and had a scary ass basement. They also had what sounded like a big ass security dog that they put on the back patio whenever visitors came. I heard that dog thousands of times but never once laid eyes on it. The house, a drafty wood structure, was covered on all sides with cheap roofing shingles and seemed destined to catch fire. If you slammed a door too hard, the whole house wiggled. Scotch, Viddy's father, would cuss us out like we were seasoned sailors. *"Slam another motherfucking door one more time and I'ma knock somebody's dick in the dirt!"*

Out back there was a rickety wooden staircase that ran from the top floor to the ground but that shit didn't have any support pillars. I always wondered "who the fuck built this shit and, more importantly, how the fuck did they build this shit?" His house wasn't much to talk about, but it was one of my favorite places to hang out and argue about music and movies.

Viddy didn't just love *A Clockwork Orange*. Viddy lived inside *A Clockwork Orange*. He became Alex and was the first Clockwork Skinhead in The Grid. He peppered his speech with Nadsat. He played the film score for enjoyment. And he dressed the whole part: painters' whites, white Ben Sherman, black Dr. Martens, black braces, black bowler. Everything about him said cross the street instead of crossing his path.

The craziest part? He was funny. An effortless comedian with a gift for spotting and naming the absurd. Throw in his ability to imitate almost any accent and it was clear that this Fourth World youth should have been stealiing the spotlight in Hollywood. Instead, he was trying to be invisible to Terror Town.

His street was both the cleanest and most dangerous block in Terror Town.

While I lived in the nosebleeds, Viddy had front row seats. If you sat on his porch and looked to the right you had a clear view of the Terror Town Black P Stone headquarters. A dark brick six flat. Marking its entrance was a seven-foot-tall Egyptian pyramid expertly painted in the foreground of a foreboding red, black and green striped fence.

The twenty-one bricks of the pyramid represented the "Main 21" – The 21 individual Sets that made up the Black P Stone Nation. By this time the other 20 Sets collected under the new El Rukn flag, but the Terror Town Set clung to P Stone. Their "Little Prince" Adze carried outsized weight within the Main 21. Terror Town still had to pay tax to the El Rukn organization but they flew their own banner.

There were full time sentries posted at the entrance of P Stone HQ. If you didn't have a reason to cross their threshold it was best you didn't approach. Old ladies with their shopping baskets were quite safe, but the rules changed for potential soldiers like me and Viddy.

From Viddy's front porch, pivoting your head ninety degrees to the left gave you a clear look at a three flat apartment building. Married couples lived there. We later learned they were undercover Feds. They were posted there to keep an eye out for Jeff Fort or any other People Nation leadership. We didn't know that at that time. Shit went sideways for them the year before.

The local drug squad jacked me up in the street. Stupidly overplayed their hand. And blew up the Feds' operation.

I wasn't even trying.

Viddy had two cassettes of mine. Some live-in-the-park NYC rap and a Sound System clash. Kilimanjaro versus Volcano Hi Power. I needed them back. Viddy wasn't home but his mother let me in. I darted up the stairs, grabbed the tapes then quickly dashed back towards my house, the same way I came. On my way past the three-flat, two men, one black, one white, jumped out of a Chester the Molester van. Hemmed me up. Pulling on my clothes. Hands on my throat. Throwing me up against the van. Real extra shit.

I was stunned. Insulted. Pissed off. I wanted to grab the closest one by his throat, press into his jugular veins and send him to sleep, but I sucked up the abuse. Kept my mouth shut and my hands to myself.

I clenched my jaws while they stripped me down to my underwear right there in the street. They went all through my pockets, asking dumb questions about where I'd been, what drugs I bought, and from who. They looked real goofy when they found I was cleaner than a hound's tooth. Their rough handling of me caught the attention of the P Stone sentries.

The hard-up-for-a-bust drug squad quickly became the talk of the zone. Everyone's attention turned to that side of the square. The P Stones zeroed in on the three-flat. Ran multiple plays to bait and mislead the Feds. Eventually, the Feds accepted that their cover was blown and cleared out. The Stones bought the building outright. Moved some of their high rankers in.

Entirely by accident the legend of Jackpot began to take shape — accident and foolishness, I should say. I knew better than to go back the same way I came — the rookie route. I had an excuse though! I wasn't doing dirt, so it never crossed my mind to run the junkie route: in one door, out another. And remember what I said about Viddy's dog and the staircase? There was no other door for the kid.

After that, when they saw me on the block, the Stones would dap me up and give me credit for helping clear out the Fed roaches. And, as far as I can remember, that was the last time I ever saw a cop in Terror Town. One day, Prince Adze pulled me by my coat. "Peace and Love, Lil' Tremor. You did the Nation a big favor. You ready to hop off the porch?"

I responded respectfully, "Peace and Love, Prince, but with all due respect, I'm just a guard for my yard. War ain't in my blood."

Prince Adze laughed. "Ain't in your blood, huh? We'll see, Lil' Tremor. We gon' see." Something about the way he emphasized "Lil' Tremor" echoed in my head.

He signaled the end of the conversation in the way that was customary in the Nation for real insiders, not spectators like me. He clasped my hand and took me through a handshake that ended with our index fingers forming a pyramid. A handshake I knew, but shouldn't know. A handshake that I practiced with my cousins but would never show publicly.

"Stone Love," he called.

"Stone to the bone," I answered.

"Five Poppin'." He gripped my hand tightly.

He was testing me.

"Six droppin'." Any other response would have been a grave mistake.

"Sho yuh right. If Big Tremor wasn't yo daddy, you would already be over here banging Stone."

I kept my face still but my lungs threatened to collapse in on themselves.

"Tremor... Why the fuck motherfuckers always bringing him up?" I thought.

"Peace and Love, Prince."

I put some distance between us. I turned towards home.

Tremor. Always Tremor.

Prince Adze's words reminded me of some shit that had popped off in '83...

CHAPTER NINE

I called my father "Tremor."

Everybody did. For me, "Dad" or "Daddy" didn't fit.

At 6'1" he wasn't the tallest in town but he had the swagger of a dangerous man and the shoulders of a football player. He was effortlessly charming and had a reputation for being quick-witted, often giving people their forever nicknames, whether they wanted them or not.

He was a good father, but he was from a generation of men who didn't play with children, literally or figuratively. He'd teach — he loved to teach — he'd correct, and he'd discipline, but he was not the lovey-dovey sort. Every now and then he'd smack the back of my crop and tell me that I was "not as dumb as I look," which was high praise coming from him. Other times he'd look me up and down and say, "you look like a damn fool with that bald head and no facial hair." Balance.

He ran the household with a firm hand but he wasn't a tyrant. As long as we weren't bringing cops or new grandkids to his door, he was alright.

My mother was an accountant in The Gold Coast. She put herself through college and was the first from her family to do so. Her Master's Degree hung in our living room where most people would have Martin and Malcolm.

Tremor was street. My mother was all about the books. Balance.

◎◎◎

BAM! BAM! BAM!

It was Tremor.

"I need you up. We got a problem. Put on some street clothes. None of that Skinhead shit. Meet me at the car."

I knew better than to question. I got dressed as quickly as possible and hustled down the stairs. The engine was already running. He pulled off before I closed the door. He looked wound up. He drove north on South Shore Drive. "I just got a call from Jimmy Twist," my sister's friend. "Some gangsters got Callie and they want money."

I rode along silently, waiting for details that never came.

"I wouldn't pull you into this if I didn't have to."

He didn't have to tell me that. I knew. But he was explaining himself. Something he never did. That spoke volumes. So did the way he careened through traffic.

"Open up the glove compartment. Check out The Situation."

I squeezed the buttons, lowered the vinyl door. His chrome Smith & Wesson 1911. I knew that Tremor kept guns. He always had. In cold defiance of Chicago's strict prohibition against handguns, Tremor, like all the other adults in my family, kept firearms. They believed in self-preservation. They didn't trust that job to anything but their own instincts. Tremor once explained to me "Crooked cops, criminals, and klansmen all have guns. You don't want to be the only one that's empty-handed." Point made.

I knew that Tremor's 1911 had some history, and being entrusted with it gave me a small sense of pride, but I was also wondering what the fuck this Sunday morning would become.

He ran me through a quick admin check on the pistol. "Show me the safety." "Chamber a round." I hesitated. "Lil' boy, we been over this shit a million times. Get on the ball!" I chambered a round and flipped the safety off. "Good." Every now and then Tremor looked me over. I think he was taking my temperature. 47th and Greenwood — where the kidnappers were holed up — was coming up faster than I wanted. I secretly flipped the safety back on. I'm not sure why.

◎ ◎ ◎

My mind drifted...

I was caught up in the Skinhead thing with all the associated street drama. My middle sister was the fashion plate Rude Girl, and my older sister was party people. The kind of people who always knew where the best parties were happening and who knew where to score all the best party favors. Drugs, sex, whatever. Never broke. Always floating. And always steering a seeker to whatever it was they sought.

My oldest sister was tight with one of the big dope dealers. A man named Matt "Haint" Givens. She was part of his crew along with some other cold blooded players like Rodney and Rasta Fox. Those three all got lost to the game. Haint was smarter than most, but he was also vulnerable in special ways. He bought over a small diner called The Stop at East 66th & King Drive. A cash business. A solid choice for cleaning money. But also a location where he could be counted on to return to, again and again.

Haint also made the mistake of including his family members in the business, including an older aunt. She loved the money but wasn't cut out for the hard edges of the lifestyle. The Feds zeroed in on her. Sank their hooks in. She folded. Told them everything they needed to know, including Haint's biggest mistake. Haint wanted to distinguish himself from the other underworld CEOs. He loved luxury. Once he got some money, he moved to a condo in The Gold Coast. The Feds found him very easy to grab.

◎ ◎ ◎

Tremor's wheels crunched into a gravel lot. He never said anything about having ransom money, but he was so calm that I assumed he had all that figured out. He hopped out and left the car running. He came around to my side. He nodded subtly in the direction of a brown steel security door about sixty yards away. "You post up at the phone booth and be a hawk on that door. If anybody come out and it ain't me or your sister, pop 'em."

He crossed the lot and disappeared behind the door.

Game on.

The building, a plain brown two-story brick box had probably served as a livery or a coach house in the past. The only windows were along the top floor but they showed no signs of life.

Inside my jacket the big .45 felt heavy and cold. Would I be able to pull the trigger? What if I missed? What if I didn't? What if I shot the wrong person? I'm not a killer... But Tremor said...

It was a bright, clear morning and the weather was perfect. I was overtaken by a heightened sense of everything around me. Faces became clearer. Sounds became more distinct. It was as if I was experiencing all these sensations for the first time. I can still remember the big hats and faint perfume of the passing church ladies. They were devout, and dignified, and wholly oblivious to the bloodbath that threatened to ring out of that coach house.

I felt like I was floating outside and above my body. Watching myself like I was the main character in a video game. I felt exposed. Awkward. Obvious. I stepped into the phone booth. Pretended to search the white pages. All the while keeping my eyes on that door. I waited. I don't know how long, but I waited.

The door swung open. I snapped out of my dream state. I steeled myself. My hand inside my jacket.

I flipped off the safety. Ready.

◎ ◎ ◎

That motherfucking Haint... I remember hearing about that motherfucker getting pulled in off the streets. That was around the same time that Rodney started to talk about tails on him. Rodney got paranoid. Turned into bad cop with Haint's inner circle. He flipped over every rock. Connected dots that might not have been the right dots. Decided that it must have been Rasta Fox who dropped dime on the crew. Rodney made himself the chief. Took it on himself to plug the leak. Told Rasta Fox to meet him at 63rd Street Beach. They had some quiet words. Then Rodney, as he told Tremor, "gassed the dread."

Rodney disappeared after that. Some people said he went into witness relocation, others said he was at the bottom of the lake with a car battery as an anchor, next to

Rasta Fox. We don't know. He just vanished. Haint was hit with a heavy sentence. Federal penitentiary. There was a mad dash to fill the void – lock in his connections, lace up his customers. The rest of his associates were getting pressed for information and leverage. Like my sister, Callie. The same sister that was under heavy manners in that building.

◎ ◉ ◎

A figure emerged from the doorway.

I tensed up, gripping the .45 so tight that my knuckles blanched. What if I...

It was Callie.

I exhaled.

She looked tired but she looked like herself. She half-walked, half-ran to the car. Tremor came out a few seconds later. Pointed to the car. His focus was on his back, letting me know that the transaction had not gone in the kidnappers' favor. I hopped in the passenger seat, tense, alert, eyes scanning the door and the windows.

My sister puddled herself into the back seat, head down. Tremor grabbed the wheel, mashed the gas, lurched, punched a lane and pushed us out into traffic west along 47th.

The hum of the engine was the only sound. Once we turned south on Drexel it seemed okay to relax. I asked how it had gone down. Tremor ignored my question. Commanded: "Settle the Situation." I switched on the safety and put the 1911 back into the glove compartment.

Tremor replied coolly, "I explained to them that there would be no ransom paid, and that now that they see that they are dealing with Tremor, they must know that it would be easier for them to just let her go, and chalk this one up as a loss. That was pretty much the end of it."

That was also the end of any explanation.

When we got home my sister went quietly to her room. Tremor stood at my door as I laid out my Skinhead gear, eager to shed the civilian clothes, eager to return to my idea of normal.

I selected a Arnold Palmer blue-brown windowpane shirt that had a perfect roll collar. My white braces, my signature gray Sta-Prest and my Red Wing Postman shoes. He joked, "Now that the streets are safe again you can put on your Skinhead costume and go do whatever you crazy baldheads do." He chuckled at his quip. I countered: "Only crazy people laugh at their own jokes."

He parried, "You 17 and you dress like you 57. You textbook 'crazy.'" I didn't know it at the time but he kind of had a point.

"Now that the sun is up you can go get some sleep, Blacula," I shouted, getting the rare last word.

The kidnapping episode was never spoken of again. I never got the full story. No word on who the kidnappers were. No clues on how my sister had gotten hemmed up. I never thought to check in with her. We just moved on.

Still, whenever I got hints that Tremor was a name that had been earned the hard way, this episode came to mind.

CHAPTER TEN

"Mixin'" Brixton's stature as a DJ grew steadily.

He built a crate of tracks the average Fourth World DJ couldn't touch. And his blends made anyone who followed him work harder. They had to scramble to match his vibe or, if they dared, top it.

He wrapped himself in Fourth World. Talked like us. Dressed like a native. He cast himself as a Fourth World Patriot. He wandered every quadrant of The Grid that used to be Chicago, bright-eyed and curious, but it was Fourth World that felt like home and fed his fire. He wanted to give something back. Something born of how he saw us. He called his new sound "Fourth Wave."

That sound? Funk bass riding a deep, West African Dunun drum bottom. Reggae downbeats for the swing. And soulful vocal runs to take the people to church.

Whenever he hit the decks he dropped jaws. He was climbing the ladder. He could hold his own against Silk, Remix, Vince, or Jesse. He had his sights on Frankie and Ron, and with his built-in boosters, The Rude Girls, he was central to a grass-roots insurgency to challenge the reach of Farley. How? Post-Set party-line chatter and tape trading.

Fourth Wave was the newest home grown vibe. Brixton's name on a plugger drew party people like faithful parishioners. But it wasn't just the locals who knew his name. Music industry people were calling. Wanted to buy his creativity. They could get him heard by more ears. Get him on the radio. Get his work in stores. If only he'd sign on the dotted line.

◎◎◎

Even without amplification Ras Piankhi's gravelly voice slashed through the silence. In a lyrical DJ style he conjured the Groundation:

"Dis a new ting fi di King's offspring.
Jah Rastafari lead and guide us along the way.

Once was hard pon di boulevard.
Dis time bare livity from temple ta yard.

Dis sound ah di hola sound.
Dis sound ah di royal sound.

From Jah lips ta unno ears.
Days on days and years pon years.

No destruction. Lone Creation.
Civilization. Elevation. An' Livication.

"JAH!" He roared.

"RASTAFARI!" The people answered.

The Groundation drums rumbled in. DUN DUN dat DUN DUN DUN.

A different voice, female, equally strong — not Sista Evangeline, a different elder — sliced through. *"CREATION! CREATION!"*

The words hung in the sky like two new clouds.

"LIVICATION! IRATION!" The drummers answered.

The bass drum, the funde and the kette danced around each other. Sank into the hypnotic rhythm.

DUN DUN dat DUN DUN DUN

"CREATION! CREATION!"

We sat at a corner table in Root Temple sipping on Sista Evangeline's Hardstyle ginger beer. The Nyahbinghi session thundered from across the yard. The bare essence of the drums. The pervasive weed smoke. The clarity of the night. Only in Fourth World.

"Creation! That's what they don't understand," Brixton asserted.

Record industry people were calling him. Trying to get him to cut a single.

"Why don't you just sign, man? Go world wide. Take me on tour with you."

"Vultures, man. The music industry. Culture vultures. They don't care about the how and the why. They only care about the how much."

"Who cares, man?" I asked. "Just get out there and get heard."

"I'm still trying to hear it myself. All art starts with inspiration and incubation. That's where we are. Creation. It comes organically from 'the people.' Artists echo it back, artfully, beautifully — if that's a word — to the root culture."

He was talking about himself. His dream of mattering to Fourth World.

My eyes followed the shape of a beautiful Skingirl. She sat at a table across the yard. Peaches clocked my focus. "Yinka ain't thinking about you. She already got a boyfriend."

"Well, now she got two. I ain't the jealous type," I joked. Peaches laughed, rolled her eyes and turned her attention back to her boyfriend, Herb.

Brixton was in his zone.

"Fourth Wave ain't shit until the people grab it and see it as theirs. That's when it becomes native. What's in. What's out. Does it move us in the direction we want to go? That's Codification."

"An artist might want to experiment and stretch the boundaries but if they lose the audience — the root culture — then it's all for shit. Look at Soul and Reggae in the 70s. So much garbage. Violins and shit. They almost forgot about the grit. The streets. The people stopped listening. Couldn't relate. And if ain't nobody listening, maybe you ain't said shit worth hearing."

"*CREATION!*"

"*IDITATION*"

"The call and response!" He motioned to the Nyahbinghi session. "The call wants a response. The reaction — the attention of the audience is the feedback loop that tells the Creationists if they're truly in tune with the people."

"I love that some people like Fourth Wave. But right now? It's just my mistakes. I need to feel that it's more than that."

"I don't know, man. You don't make mistakes. You make connections. Maybe you are afraid of running out of ideas?" I framed it as a question but he barreled past.

DUN DUN dat DUN DUN DUN

"*CREATION*"

"*ITATIONS*"

"The danger," Brixton cautioned, "is in the next period. Commodification. That's when the art gets bar-coded. Boxed up. And licensed to the slickest liar. The liars put their own faces on the label. The root culture, the Creationists get forgotten while hired help, skillful imitators — The Poachers — get the fame. The vultures — The Fatbacks — get fatter."

"That's real," I agreed. "Look at R&B. Can't even recognize that shit no more."

"The sound becomes aesthetic. The culture becomes optional. The ritual becomes invisible. And the world starts mimicking the culture without honoring the violence, the vision or the vocabulary that birthed it. And the whole thing winds up being controlled by outsiders."

"And the Fatbacks don't even care what Creation truly cost" I said.

Brixton's eyes lit up.

"The Fatbacks don't call. Can't respond. They pretend to respond but it's a cheap trick. They get to keep the rights, the royalties, and the name. All we get is scraps and disease." He said it like it was two words. Dis: the opposite, and Ease: comfort, relief. Dis-ease.

DUN DUN dat DUN DUN DUN

"If Fourth Wave is going to be a thing then I want it to be owned by Lion Order. Can't nobody call their thing 'Fourth Wave' without us being involved. And we ain't got to stop at music. Clothes. Art. Everything."

"Make a way out of no way," I said, borrowing a phrase from my mother.

"Yes! Make our own art with our own talents." He pointed at the Nyahbinghi drum. "If we need a new sound we invent an instrument that makes that sound — I didn't buy those Cetec cabinets because I want to make Cetec or those dirtheads rich. I bought them because I want to learn what makes them good so we can build something better."

I was in. I believed. And when I say I believed, I'm talking like Disciples believed in King David, the way Rukns believed in Moorish Science. I wasn't just backing up Brix on general principle. This shit made sense.

"Let's get Fourth Wave poppin'," I said.

Brixton sat back. Finally able to relax.

He called. I responded. It gave him hope that he could speak to all of Fourth World, like a native.

"CREATION! CREATION!"

◎ ◎ ◎

We went to The Jewel.

We piled into two cars. Brixton's Volvo and Peaches' Falcon. Brixton, Viddy, Peaches, Herb, Ajoa, and me. Made our way north. South Shore Drive to Lake Shore Drive. Past The Gold Coast. Crossed into The Jewel. Exit. Catch Armitage. West for about a mile. Catch Racine. Head north.

"There it is. Find a parking spot."

Frankie Knuckles, an iconic DJ, was spinning at Beautyful Ones. He rarely played outside Church so this was a can't-miss opportunity for our young, Fourth World ears to hear what he could do.

The scale of the place was amazing.

It had been a glass factory. Now it was a Mecca for dance music. It was big. Stripped down. Cold and industrial. The whole place vibrated with bass.

Frankie was up in the rafters. High above the dance floor. Giving him an almost god-like stature.

The warehouse setting fascinated me. The storerooms. The loading docks. One room was built up to resemble an oversized playground. Another room had a wall of small TVs that showed random clips from obscure movies. I got lost in the spectacle and Frankie's soundtrack. I drifted from room to room.

I spotted an extremely pretty young lady. Dressed to kill. One exposed shoulder. A skirt that both amplified and hid secrets. Her hair channeled Supremes-era Diana Ross. Classy. Swept-forward sideburns that pulled the whole look together. I needed to know her.

She read my style — fully encoded as a Skinhead — and knew what it meant. Opinionated, drinks too much, allergic to longterm relationships, and likes to fight. What she didn't know was that I was a tragic virgin and terrified I'd die that way.

We went through the pleasantries. Names, ages, where we grew up — she was from The Gold Coast — our relationship status — she'd recently broken up with some nobody. All useful information. Her body language transmitted silent signals and I was catching every one. We exchanged phone numbers and promises to be in touch, then she dashed away to find her friends. This was an amazing feeling. So natural. So immediate.

The dating rules dictated that a young man should wait two days before calling a girl or risk looking desperate. I didn't care. I called her the next day.

"I'm glad you didn't do that whole waiting-two-days thing. That's so annoying."

"Why wait? We're already married," I joked. She laughed.

"What are you doing with your Saturday?" I asked.

"Nothing. Just homework. Laundry. You?"

"Just talking to you."

"You should come hang out."

I was out the door before the handset hit the cradle.

The bus and El couldn't move fast enough.

We were supposed to have dinner at Bacino's on Lincoln then go to see a movie, but instead we fell onto her bed and finished what we'd started at Beautyful Ones. She liked that she was my first.

Our bodies fit together perfectly. It was everything I ever imagined and more. She was firm and sweet and receptive to my touch. So brown and pretty. The sweetest voice and laugh. I was already in love and wanted her to know it. We moved inside and around each other. It felt like we'd known everything about each other for years.

I moved down her body. Kissing my way between her breasts. Lingering at her belly button. Then further down. She tensed up. Tried to close her legs. "You don't have to do that." This was a degree of intimacy, vulnerability that she wasn't used to. But I wanted this. I wanted to taste her. To thrill her. To show her that there was no part of her that I'd ever neglect.

She lay back. Threw her arm over her eyes. Her body did all the talking. Told me everything I needed to know. She pulled me up. Kissed my mouth. Swore undying love.

It was perfect.

From that point forward it was Siobhan and I. She became known around her university as the girl who ran with a Fourth World Skinhead gang.

She wanted to introduce me to her parents. When I stepped into her parents' Gold Coast high-rise I wondered if it was where Haint once called home. I searched the doorman's eyes for permission to ask questions. I looked at doorknobs for signs of forced entry. I listened out for police radios, as if they'd still be on the job.

Her parents, Mr. and Mrs. Soltare, were the first faces I was ever able to put to The Gold Coast. Her father, a Black man, was the president of Soultare, a Soul music label. He talked about his work in terms that made him seem very Fatback-ish. All polish, no roots. I wondered if he knew about the musical movement incubating just a few miles south. I kept that to myself. Her mother, a tall redhead, had been a high-flying fashion model until she married Black. That tanked her trajectory. The offers stopped. The invitations dried up. She retired early and focused on her family.

She was the one with the street smarts. She pulled me aside and asked, "What's your relationship like with your father? Does he live at home with you?" I gave her the broad strokes. "Good. Good. That's important. I like you. I don't mind you dating my daughter. But don't get her caught up in city life. And don't disrupt her studies."

The second part was easy.

The first part was... well... cooking up mayhem in The Grid was my team's specialty.

How could I possibly keep Siobhan sheltered from that? Tremor cautioned me about pulling her too close to my chaotic world but I didn't listen.

She lived near Wax Trax Records and that was how I met the Pama City Skins, the largest and toughest Skinhead crew in The Jewel. They held down fort at a little concrete strip called Aetna Park. The park sat at the intersection of Halsted and Lincoln. Just blocks away from the Fullerton El stop. Steps away from the record store.

I heard a shout of "Oi! Skinhead!" His name was Necro. He introduced me to Jake, Icepick, and Broomstick. They didn't go for the traditional Skinhead gear. They were all T-shirts and raggedy jeans. They liked their music fast and heavy.

Their graffiti told the story. The Effigies. Rights of the Accused. Bad Brains. Battalion of Saints. Articles of Faith. 4Skins. Iron Cross. 7 Seconds. The Last Resort. The Crucified Skinhead. Punk rock was their religion.

We talked a bit, sized each other up — music tastes, personal style, perceived mettle. Now I'd have names to put to the faces I saw at shows and they'd have a point of reference for how Lion Order Skinheads did things in Fourth World.

After a polite conversation I turned my attention back to Siobhan and continued our mission to Wax Trax. Pama City Skins was very different from Lion Order. They were the real deal, in their own way, and we'd surely cross paths again, but it remained to be seen how compatible the crews might or might not be.

Brixton would be wary.

◎◎◎

A few months later, Brixton needed to go back to CACOPHONY, this time for a Gauss meter, he was sure he'd seen one there last time, but this time he had to go alone.

"Wake up, mate. Mek another Joliet run with me, nuh?"

"I can't do it today, playboy. On my way to The Jewel to do you know what with you know who."

"Alright, then. I know I can't compete with that. Push once for me, nuh?"

"You're disgusting and disrespectful!" I laughed. "Just keep your hands to yourself this time, though. Don't be getting fresh with no dead gyal."

"No promises, mate. I might wanna try some vampire punani."

We laughed. Gripped hands.

"Hit me when you get back, playboy."

What I tell you next is what I've pieced together from my mother.

◎◎◎

Brixton made it to CACOPHONY.

He found his Gauss meter.

He was walking back to his car. Feeling great. Dreams of obliterating Ras Pianki's sound system.

An engine.

A gray van.

That gray van?

He didn't have time to react.

They ran Brixton down.

Threw it in reverse. Ran over him again.

Somebody got the plate. Called it in to the Illinois Division of Criminal Investigation.

Didn't matter.

They ain't give a fuck. Half-assed investigation.

They slapped cuffs on the driver and passenger but that was about it.

They got charged for murder.

They said they didn't know what they hit.

Backed up just to see if it was a rock. Or a deer. Honest.

Judge knocked the charges down to involuntary vehicular manslaughter or some shit. "*He was wearing dark clothes.*" "*He wasn't watching out for cars.*" "*He was distracted.*" "*The deceased, a foreign-born immigrant, may have misunderstood the direction of the flow of American traffic.*"

That was it. Brixton was gone and, to America, it was his fault he was dead.

His funeral was one of the saddest days in Fourth World. The church couldn't hold the crowd. The preacher talked about justice and struggle and urged everyone who loved Brixton to leave whatever happened next in the hands of God and the justice system. He assured us that the truth would be found out and that any wrong doing would meet the mighty hand of correction and consequence.

To this day I'm ashamed of myself for being afraid to take one last look at Brixton. There's not a day that goes by that I don't curse myself for letting him go out alone, for choosing my dick over my blood brother. My last words to him, "hit me when you get back," seem hopelessly callous. I never thought twice about letting him ride solo.

I chastised myself for never telling him he was my best friend or how he'd been one of my best teachers. Instead, I feared that his lasting memory of me was of a goofy Skinhead wannabe who was always cock-blocking him and Ajoa. I wanted to shout that I loved him and that we needed Fourth Wave to take over the world. That we couldn't do it without him.

Instead, I just sat frozen to the hard oak of the pew.

Regret is loudest in silence.

◎ ◉ ◎

That night, the sacred harps of Rastafari beat like heartbeats into the night. The drums — the Bass, the Funde, and the Kette — united us as one organism. A single spiritual, corporeal organism... the riddim serving as the connective tissue binding us to each other. Not as tethers, but as sinew.

Brixton danced one last earthly dance among us. Brixton sang one last terrestrial hymn through us. Brixton directed his last and greatest symphony... and then took flight.

DUN DUN dat DUN DUN DUN

"One bright morning when my work is over I will fly away home..."

DUN DUN dat DUN DUN DUN

CHAPTER ELEVEN
The Pen CNN
Mixin' Brixton

Grapevine, the Divine climbed up slow, like the band was about to drop *that* number. Tongues stopped wagging. Dice quit tumbling. Every ear in the house leaned close for the one drop.

You expecting to hear "Sweetback Slim" and "Sportin' Life,"
But this one right here cuts deep like a knife

This one is for Mixin' Brixton

Mixing Brixton, so young and so bold,
London can't fuck with Joliet, the land of the cold.

Every child enters the earth as an act of will,
The spirit of Jah no man can kill.

That young brother distracted by his bright-eyed gaze,
Unaware of the dangers in this motherfucking maze.

Youngblood ain't know he stirred the wrath of men,
Them pale motherfucking souls who strike again and again.

He ain't know nothing bout that hatred, burning fierce,
Them teeth, sharp as daggers, looking for something to pierce.

In this world of shadows, youngblood lost his way,
Them motherfuckers was hungry for scalp, that fate filled day.

Mixing Brixton paid the ultimate cost,
Under Joliet's wheels, his innocence lost.

Mixin' Brixton's queen, tears flowing with grief,
Her cries a haunting echo, no hope, no relief.

What touches the now the ancestors also feel,
What touches the now future offspring shall feel,

His street family stood silent, their hearts full of fire,
Vowing to honor him, lifting his name higher.

Lion Order stood close, their sorrow kept tight,
On the cold, hard Grid, where shadows meet light.

For every moment lost, a vow they would keep,
To carry his story, in waking and in sleep.

Fourth Wave died that day, when the devil played his hand,
Now Brixton lays down the bottom in Zion's livication band.

He ain't just in a better place, he is in a stronger form,
An ancestor for those left behind, and those yet unborn,

How will they go on without him, we'll have to watch and see,
They'll need strength and guidance, through trials yet to be.

(He let that hang for a beat)

They call this the Slave State, but we freer than most.

(The men cosigned.)

This the Pen CNN. The squares call it a toast.

(If you didn't know before. Now you knew.)

I don't sell no lies. No wolf tickets. No doubt.

(The men said it with him)

92

Grapevine, the Divine signing the fuck out.

He stepped down from the cafeteria table.

Conversation resumed. Hands fanned cards. Dominos hit like gunshots. And the sharp clack of backgammon dice filled the air.

Chapter Twelve

Ajoa and the Rude Girls fell apart.

Our parents didn't slow down to guide us through trauma.

They had an embarrassment of riches when it came to trauma. They had to wear a mask of outward resilience even when they were at their lowest. They hid their hurt because any expression of pain was an invitation for more of the same. Generations of sustained low-intensity conflict had work-hardened them, but they refused to break.

They thought Ajoa could be like them. They assumed she was strong enough to absorb the pain and get back to "normal" the way my sister had after the kidnapping.

She tried. We all tried. But Ajoa, she took it hardest of all.

She's only talked about in whispers now.

You can see her downtown, today, unwashed, incoherent, nearly unrecognizable. Always right by that State Street preacher who tells everyone that everything they do is doom-worthy.

I once tried to give her some money, to ask if she was alright. Her eyes took a moment to focus. When she finally recognized me she screamed at the top of her lungs, "You! You did it! You killed Brixton!"

She pointed a long, dirty fingernail at me.

The preacher's eyes bored into me. "The sixth commandment says 'Thou shall not kill!' Murder gon' send you straight to hell!"

"HE DID IT," Ajoa screamed.

"HE KILLED BRIXTON!"

"HE KILLED MY BABY!"

"HE KILLED MY BABY!"

I ran. I ran as far and as fast as I could but I could still... *can* still hear the accusation.

"HE KILLED BRIXTON!"

Did I?

Chapter Thirteen

Brixton's killers were sentenced to 30 days in jail, to be served over fifteen consecutive weekends. They were to check in to a local jail on Friday evening, serve their weekend, then get released at five am on Monday morning so they could make it to work.

Lather, rinse, repeat. Fifteen times.

Insult, meet injury.

We mourned with violence. We wanted everyone to feel how we felt. Whether they deserved it or not.

We lashed out.

We were fractured.

Rudderless.

We tried to numb it. We cried.

Then we made the streets cry.

We picked fights. Didn't care who won. Or who walked away.

[Knock]

I think we secretly wanted to self-destruct.

But not before we made the streets cry again.

And Siobhan? She became a liability.

She made shit more complicated than it needed to be.

◎ ◎ ◎

Siobhan and I were at Club Dreamerz with Viddy and a few other Lion Order players. We were trying to get back to normal after Brixton's death and this was something like that. As a team, we had one steadfast rule. We show up together and we leave together. Our lifestyle and appearance was a magnet for all kinds of attention — the good kind and the bad kind — and it was better to be mobbed up than solo.

Siobhan wasn't into it. Or maybe she had somewhere to be the next morning. Whatever it was, she wanted to leave. My squad, on the other hand, was having a great time. The ladies seemed to like my guys, which always helps, so when I said it was time to jet they gave me blank stares. Instead of closing up shop and rolling as a team they broke the rule. Sent me off with a fucked-up mood.

Siobhan and I made a brisk, silent walk to the Damen El platform and waited for the Blue Line train to take us east for our Red Line exchange. I quietly seethed. I planned to drop her at her dorm, then sprint back to Dreamerz to close down the bar with the crew. One hour at most. Maybe one and a half.

There weren't many people waiting for the train that night. Mostly late shift restaurant workers. A hard-looking man drifted over and told us we made a lovely couple.

"Yeah man, thanks."

He kept talking. "You guys got anything for the head?" Code for drugs.

"Nah man," I replied, flat.

"Y'all got any spare change?"

"Nope."

Then he flashed a knife. "One of y'all gon' give me SOMETHING I WANT!" He eye-fucked Siobhan. I understood.

I tuned myself for combat. I was carrying a clear, plexiglass cane which was my style of the time. It also served as a makeshift weapon. Cops in The Jewel rarely gave it a second glance.

I didn't wait for his next move. I jammed my cane straight into his jaw. He dropped his guard. I knocked the knife out of his hand. Swept it off the train platform. The knife clattered onto the tracks and fell through a gap. Tumbled in slow motion to the street below. His eyes followed the knife. He couldn't believe what he was seeing. He was distracted.

I raised the cane.

There was a pop. The platform went dark. I brought my cane down on the top of his head. I wish I'd had a hatchet. He staggered. Almost fell onto the tracks. His scream came out two octaves too high for his frame — exposing fault lines in his cold-blooded facade.

We both noticed it at the same time. The hook of my cane had snapped off. Now I held a plexiglass dagger.

"Oh yeah, motherfucker. You just hit the Jackpot."

The tables had well and truly turned. His eyes jumped from my eyes to the dagger, wondering if I'd really stab him. I was asking myself the same thing.

The train came squealing into the station. Doors slid open. He watched me. He dove on at the last second. The doors closed between us. He glared through the glass. A mix of shame, fear, anger, and awe. I memorized his face. Hoping I'd see him again.

Once the train pulled away, I turned to Siobhan. She was holding her eye. Crying. In the chaos, I'd shattered the lone bulb illuminating that end of the train platform. Fragments had flown into her face. I rushed her down to the well-lit lobby. Her eye was fine, but she'd walk away with some small scars that her mother would be extremely curious about.

I was furious.

I marched back to Dreamerz with Siobhan on my heels. Tore into my crew. Chastised them for letting me walk solo. Shouted that their fixation on getting their dicks wet had left me exposed. That I nearly had to kill a man. That if they'd followed protocol none of that shit would have happened. Viddy tried to explain. They weren't to blame for all that shit.

"Why didn't y'all just stay here?" Peaches asked. The obvious, unspoken, answer was Siobhan.

I snapped. "This is the kind of shit that left Brixton ass out."

Blaming them.

Blaming myself.

I was irrational.

My team closed out their tabs. We walked, silently, back to the Damen El.

We took Siobhan back to her dorm then they went off to finish out the night at the Beautyful Ones without me. I kept replaying it in my head.

I'd won the fight.

But if I had just left her at her dorm, to begin with, exactly none of that shit would have happened.

I was seventeen and starting to feel very tied down.

◎◉◎

And there was the time we went to a party on the West Side. Damage Done By, the Canaryville Skinhead crew, was having a party on the border of The Jewel and The Scratch. We packed into two cars and headed west. Anything to get back to normal.

Viddy spotted a small corner liquor store. He didn't want to go to the party empty-handed. He parked. We ran inside. Peaches parked a half-a-block behind and waited. The store was packed with young men from the neighborhood. One man threw some words at Siobhan but she ignored him. He didn't like that. He and I faced off.

One of his friends stuck his head out the door. Fired off a shrill whistle. Combatants crawled from the shadows. Los Viboros. Heavy reputation. Skinhead killers. We were in their motherland.

Fuck.

We spilled out onto the street. Shoves. Staredowns. Threats.

Even with Peaches and crew we were outnumbered. 11 to 7.

Fuck.

I felt the weight of the club I had tucked inside my jacket. It looked like a regular old 18" White Sox souvenir mini-bat, but I had transformed it into a genuine jaw breaker. Hollowed it out in wood shop. Pressed in a 2-pound steel cylinder in machine shop. The result was a force multiplier that looked like a kid's toy.

They surrounded us and did a whole lot of talking and threatening. We sized them up. Looked for weaknesses. Zeroed in on the leaders.

One of the more vocal Viboros said, "We gon' cut you mayates into pieces, then we gon' run a train on that new wave puta." Siobhan looked terrified but her stun gun was out and ready.

Showbiz was new to our crew. He was still ten toes deep in the Raiders camp, but was starting to turn up at Lion Order functions. Blessed with size and speed, he picked out one of the high rankers. Lunged. With a crunch brought his head up into the chin of a Viboro. His target was knocked off balance. Stunned by the ferocity that was meant to maim and shame.

I was still recovering from a Fourth World beatdown. Any bodily harm, especially to my groin, would render me useless. I needed to hit fast and hard, and take as little damage as possible.

I clocked the loud mouth. Club to the temple. Boot to the chest. Dismissed.

Their biggest and baddest were crumbling, even Siobhan was putting in work with her stun gun. They started to fall apart. Revealed their lack of discipline. Viddy and Showbiz set in on their other operators. We had the upper hand but we were still deep behind enemy lines. Another whistle.

More men from the shadows. Older. More seasoned.

I squared up with a real hitter. I mean, this kid could box. Trained. Disciplined. Efficient. He connected. Knocked my head back a few times. I had a real fear that I was going to lose my lights.

Stunned. Not wanting to go down. Afraid of being humiliated, my ego kicked in. I turned to say something to Siobhan. To tell her to run to Peaches. BAM! A solid fucking right hook.

My eyes crossed.

My knees wobbled.

It was finna be lights out for Jackpot.

I stumbled. I'd been hit before... but never that hard. My jawline was throbbing. My tongue felt swollen. I couldn't even see him... One more like that, and...

Peaches flashed her headlights. Coming through. Viddy and Showbiz dove clear. Peaches lurched forward. A couple of startled Viboros rolling off her hood. She punched a wedge into the crowd. Viddy and Showbiz on the good side. Me and Siobhan behind a wall of enemies. I grabbed her hand. Rushed through a weak point. Put some distance between them and us.

We ran for our lives.

It was like a scene from one of those "escape from—" name-the-city movies. I was dragging her behind me, but her big shoes were no good for foot chases. Fuck!

We ducked through a breezeway. Lost sight of the action. And our team lost sight of us. We kept running. Had to get off the side streets. Get to the next big boulevard. Banking on that being the border of Los Viboros' motherland.

At a big intersection I spotted a car load of Skinheads. Princess, Guiness and Jolt. Damage Done By. I flagged them down.

"Take us to the subway station." We crowded into their car. Tried to explain the clash and why we were on our heels.

Their faces showed their judgment. In their opinions, mine was a shameful overreaction.

"And you... *ran?*" Guiness asked. It was an accusation, an unfavorable verdict, wrapped in a rhetorical question.

After all, they live in this hood and nothing ever happens to them, they reasoned. "Those guys are our neighbors," they explained dismissively. "Y'all must have done something to piss them off." They dropped us at the subway. I led Siobhan into the tunnel.

Once again, I found myself on the clattering wheels of a late night train on my way back to Siobhan's dorm. The night was wrecked. I was separated from my crew. I ran from the kind of shit we lived for. This nice, pretty Gold Coast girlfriend of mine was a real fucking complication. I didn't know if she'd seen me almost get done-in. Neither of us mentioned it. The golf ball in my jaw, on the other hand, wouldn't let me forget for the next several days. "That motherfucker really had me locked up," I thought.

Tremor had tried to warn me — "She's too pretty to be in the streets" — but I didn't listen. Now, I was forced to admit that my instincts were getting dulled. The kind of dulling that makes a man let his best friend walk into the lion's den, unguarded. The kind of numbing that makes a man think he's untouchable. I was so deep into being in love that I forgot about being in constant conflict — in gangland.

I found reasons to maintain a tight radius around her university. I no longer took her to the rougher parts of The Grid. She missed the adventures. She complained that I was becoming a boring, controlling boyfriend, "just like Gold Coast boys..." She wasn't wrong. I was, indeed, limiting her range. We'd go to dinner then back to her dorm. Or to a movie then back to her dorm. Or to a club then back to her dorm.

I cooked up lies about my weekend plans so I could run with my crew. She saw through it. Quite naturally this created tension in our relationship. Inspired fights and flare-ups. One disagreement led to another, and then another, until it all spiraled into a full-on meltdown. Lamp thrown. Books thrown. Harsh words.

"I wish that Viboro had knocked you the fuck out!"

"Spoiled-ass Gold Coast girl. Go cry to Mommy!"

That one landed. I saw it hit. But I could tell — I could still come back from it.

Only, I didn't want to.

I needed a clean break.

I needed to cut deep.

I needed her to hate me.

"Tell your mother that her tragic mulatto got dumped — again."

Her eyes.

Pain.

Insult.

Fury.

She lunged. Tried to claw at my face. Wailed. She wanted blood, but I was faster. Stronger.

"GET OUT! GET OUT! GET OUT!" Siobhan shrieked.

Jackpot! That's what I needed to hear.

This was the end. There wouldn't be any "I miss you, can we try again?" phone calls. No makeup fucks. No do-overs.

I'd successfully engineered my clean break, as crass as that may sound.

I'd miss her. And the sex. But my biggest feeling was relief.

No more lies to her mother. No more dragging her through The Grid for thrills.

No more.

As Brixton would've said, "And that's that on that."

I made a vow to myself:

From now on, I only date Skinhead girls.

CHAPTER FOURTEEN

Yinka was a different animal, entirely.

You'll probably think less of me for this, but I had started messing around with her while I was still with Siobhan.

I can explain.

After Brixton got taken, the world just... kept on beating. Fourth World didn't pause. Lion Order didn't close. Sets kept being thrown. New DJs slid into his spot like it was theirs for the taking. One of them got on the mic talking about he was going to "lead Fourth Wave to the Fifth Wave."

I slapped the moisture out of that motherfucker's mouth. Yanked him off the mic. Probably would have done more if Ras Piankhi hadn't grabbed me. Told me I was disrespecting the space. "Cool yuhself, rude boy — Tek weh yuhself."

I probably took it to mean more than it did — he was probably as broken up as I was — but if there's one thing Jackpot knows how to do, it's exile.

Bet. I'll 'tek weh' myself from the whole scene and be cooler than the other side of the pillow.

The next day, I stood looking out my window.

Terror Town felt more claustrophobic than ever. I used to know every crack in these sidewalks. I knew every corner as if I'd carved them myself. Knew every brick, every face. Now? It just felt... smaller. One too many ghosts and not enough air.

And then I spotted Yinka.

Chocolate milk, made flesh.

I had wandered into Hyde Park. I paused to hear the bow-tied Reginald X profess the philosophies of the Nation of Islam. The acoustics of Harper Square gave him a huge boost and he was good at this. In his downtime he and I would normally engage in intellectual sparring sessions but today I just listened. I needed the noise. From my seat near the chess tables I saw her. She was alone. She was usually with her boyfriend so I never got a chance to know her well. I didn't need to know her well to see that she was finer than a frog's hair. She was a dream. Mahogany skin. Sable eyes that she outlined with dramatic Alex DeLarge-style makeup. She had her own take on the Skinhead look. Instead of fringe and feathers she wore a close-crop. Sleek. Strong. Sexy. Confident.

We introduced ourselves. Where we live. What schools went to. What bands we liked. What bands we hated. What DJs, other than Brixton, we followed. How we each got drawn into the Lion Order thing, and all that.

"I heard about you putting hands on Rocco. He needed to be checked. Stomping on Brixton's brand like that."

"I think you might be the only person who sees it that way."

"I remember when you were just a baby lion. Now you're all grown up."

"If you only knew," I thought. My base instincts threatened to take over. Two problems. I had a girlfriend and she had a boyfriend. Still, we can be friends, right?

"So what roped you into all this Skinhead business?" I asked.

"The music. The clothes. All the iconic movements have a look. Think about the Black Panther Party, the Brown Berets, the Young Lords, MOVE in Philadelphia. When you look at them you know you are looking at some-one who is intellectually sharp and physically tough. I don't have any dreams of turning Skinheads into a movement but the austerity of the gear is, for me, both crisp in its functionality and seductive in its details." She eyed the details on my stark white Ben Sherman shirt.

Is she feeling what I'm feeling?

She went on, "I love my hair being combat-ready. I love my shoes being tough, practical and silent. I love the way my arms look in my short sleeves and how my legs look in jeans. I love the way my jacket is both decoration and armor."

Yes. Yes. I like your everything, too.

"When I walk into a place people take me seriously. When I open my mouth people pay attention. I absolutely learned this from Skinhead. That's why I say this subculture 'raised me.' Not literally, because I'm so much more than just a Skinhead, but when I think of how I carry myself and how I'm perceived, Skinhead is always on my shoulders, alongside being a Black girl, and from Fourth World.."

And such nice shoulders. I wonder what they look like, naked and sweaty.

Yinka and I became fast friends and would spend hours on the phone talking about the world and music and Brixton — and whatever else — and before long our bonafide mates seemed to matter less. But we kept the conversations clean.

She had an imagination that picked up where Brixton's left off. She loved Fourth World so much that she never wanted to leave. "The only time I set foot outside Fourth World is if there's a can't-miss band playing. Other than that, I don't go behind enemy lines."

Whereas I knew all the dynamics of the underworld, she was dreaming bigger.

"I had this teacher, Mr. Townes. He gave a class called "Modern Utopias." He had us reading 1984 and Animal Farm and Two Thousand Seasons and that shit changed my life. Hard as fuck to get along with. Always wore these ridiculous green suits. Afro always crooked. Roach killer shoes. But that class? Mind-expanding. The one thing I took away from it... we all... each one of us deserves the right to choose our own paths in life. To set a code of conduct that doesn't encroach on others and doesn't require the exploitation of others. That's the path to real freedom."

"Okay! When do we build our spaceship?" I joked.

She paused, weighing whether to follow my joke. Then, not annoyed, just focused, she went back in.

"No. Right here. Right now. The people in The Gold Coast are fighting and winning a class war while half of us don't even know that we are at war. That's why they had to kill Chairman Fred. He was on the verge of making competitors see eye-to-eye. They couldn't allow that. But one of these days we gon' have another Chairman Fred, or maybe a Fredericka. Look around Fourth World. There ain't no reason that we can't grow what we need, make what we want, and govern, and defend ourselves."

"So how do we get there, we live in gangland?" I asked.

"We live in Fourth World," she countered.

"Post-Collapse Fourth World. First we have to get the right people... not all the people, but the right people to believe and to show up. We need more Brixtons. Fewer Adzes. Look at Haki and Third World Press. He took an abandoned school and turned it into a printing press, a library, a day care, and a museum. Ain't no reason he can't put a little grocery store in there. We need to think like that! And then we need a different group of people to agree on who the enemy is and... when the snake head show..."

I finished it for her "...the snake head go...You mean...?"

"Yes. Literally. We be scared as fuck to live life to the fullest and they ain't just gon' let they slaves go free. We need to Nat Turner they ass. Why should they sleep peacefully?"

My thoughts drifted to CACOPHONY. Why should they sleep peacefully?

She went on. "And I don't just mean people in The Gold Coast. We got some enemies right here in Fourth World. Every time The Gold Coast kill a Chairman Fred or jail a Dhoruba or an Assatta they make space for another Jeff Fort or Larry Hoover. Think about why the Nations put the brakes on Crack. It ain't because they want to protect us. It's because they don't control the product. Remember what Brixton said about Fatbacks? We got some Fatbacks in our own fucking family."

She was right.

The big corporations — the Nations — had Fourth World on lock and even when the scourge of Crack cocaine was tearing up the coasts it could not be found anywhere in The Grid. Fort and Hoover issued a death warrant on anyone found selling crack in their territories — this much they agreed on. The Nations didn't control the supply and didn't have the recipe so they did the next best thing and enacted prohibition. Local baseheads watched the wild, panicked stories on "20/20" about how addictive Crack was, "three hits is all it takes!" But for now the baseheads could only daydream about it. They talked excitedly about how amazing a high it must be and how they couldn't wait until they finally got a taste. "Shit! I'ma hop my Black ass on a bus to New York and get me some of that!" Pipe dreams. Literally.

Several months passed while the Folks and the People Nations quietly perfected their own cocktails. Lucky hypes would get some of the early product but most of them just had to deal with the classic freebase for now. You remember freebase, right? It's that shit that Richard Pryor was cooking when he went up in flames.

Once the major Nations got their recipes dialed-in they put it on the street as "Ready Rock" for the Folks Nation and "Karachi" for the People Nation. Like Crack did to the coasts, Karachi and Ready Rock would shatter our world, but in 1985 we were not there yet. Fourth World was, for now, a Crack-free oasis that could still boast of a little bit of innocence. Hell, we didn't even have MTV.

Yinka was already imagining the world she wanted to build.

She reminded me of the best parts of Brixton. I liked her vision of Fourth World as its own independent, self-governing nation. But she also excited me in ways that Brixton never could. I wondered to myself how tight a couple she and Poindexter — I gave him that nickname — really were, because... damn. She was fine as frog's hair.

◎ ◎ ◎

Lucky me! I ran into Yinka one afternoon at 2ⁿᵈ Hand Tunes on 53ʳᵈ Street. I was probably looking for something from Nabat or one of the French Oi! bands that I hunted like a dope fiend, while she was probably looking for something more adventurous like Rip Rig + Panic or The X-Ray Spex. We gave each other the familiar head nod and went back to rifling through the bins. Eventually we found ourselves in the same row, near the same bin. Accident? Coincidence? Not for me.

In the bins I found a copy of *Oi! Oi! Music* by The Oppressed and since I already owned it I left it for her to claim. That album was a rare entry into the Oi! genre where a translator wasn't necessary. When we listened to The Cockney Rejects or The Last Resort, we needed help. "What is Bovril and Ready Brek?" "What does it mean to be 'nicked over West Ham?'" Brixton would sigh, explain and urge us to expand our tastes.

With The Oppressed, their lyrics translated perfectly into our reality and became a soundtrack for the Skinheads of Lion Order. We didn't mind the electronic drums. We were surrounded by electronic drums in much of the other music we listened to so it fit right in. Plus, somebody was playing the hell out of those drum runs.

What really took us, as I said before, were the lyrics. Anti-government, anti-police, rebellious, angry, questioning everything, and leaving no inequity unaddressed. This was the edge that was missing from our Hot Mixes and most Reggae so it satisfied a mood that was waiting to be addressed. Yinka and I laughed that Brixton would have hated it.

The chemistry between us was palpable. I took the opportunity to stand a little too close to her. She didn't move away. Could she feel the electricity? I touched her hip. She playfully looked around. Asked if my girlfriend would approve. I probably searched for something clever to say but probably only managed something clumsy though useful. I probably asked about her non-Skinhead boyfriend and most-likely impugned his masculinity.

There's a funny dynamic with Skinheads. The men are free to date outside the culture but it's almost always frowned upon when Skinhead women get involved with men who ain't Skins. In our eyes, it's like the woman has downgraded. She probably warned me off that topic, but she still hadn't moved away from my touch. Her jeans fit her so well.

We finished up at the record shop and walked in the direction of her home. Me? I just wanted to spend time with this beauty. She was like pure oxygen and there was no place else I wanted to be. It didn't feel like I was cheating on Siobhan. I felt like I'd be cheating myself if I didn't follow her home.

I sensed that some part of this feeling was mutual but I lacked the words to make my pitch. None of my Jackpot remarks seemed to fit. We skirted the lake and arrived far too quickly at her high-rise condo building. I feared I'd wasted my best chance to see her out in the wild again. We lingered awkwardly at the security door. I would have stayed there all day and used up as much time as she wanted to give me. I searched my brain for the right words to let her know that my interests were decidedly un-friend-like.

Up to that point the only deep intimacy I'd experienced was with Siobhan so my confidence around girls wasn't fully realized and I guess it showed. Yinka took charge.

"Do you want to come in?"

"Yeah, I kinda want to see the lake from up high" I said instead of a simple "hell the fuck yeah." Fuck that. I just wanted to be close to her. Yes, they did have a great view of the lake. Shirt off. And her bedroom had posters and flyers on the wall that reminded me of my own room. Pants unbuttoned.

"This is a cool room." Boots off.

"You talk too much." Lips pressed. Her tongue in my mouth.

Her bed was smaller than mine and her lips were softer than I had dreamed. Jeans off. Her hands were curious, and skilled. I was probably a bit clumsy trying to figure out if her bra clasp was in the traditional place or one of those new-fangled front loading contraptions. She again took charge, reached up between her breasts and let me see her for a brief moment.

Out of step with her usual confidence, she covered herself with her blanket and waited for me to crawl under the sheets. That's when she took over. There was no foreplay.

She pushed me onto my back. She climbed on top. Reached down to put our parts together. "That's a nice dick, Jackpot." And rode me like it was the most natural pairing in the world. I was in heaven. I was in Yinka. She was mine for that time. I was getting lost inside her. This was how it should have been from the beginning. No boyfriend. No girlfriend. Just me and Yinka. What took us so long and can it last forever?

We were like two well-mated gears. No friction, just perfect engineering.

We made love two more times that afternoon, in quick succession. Hot, sweaty, energetic sex that demanded everything from both of us. Neither of us knew if we'd ever get another chance to steal time so squeezing the most out of the other was the only thing that mattered.

We did see each other again. Many times. She was always clear with the boundaries, she loved her non-Skinhead boyfriend. She planned to stay with him. And she only wanted me as long as I had a serious girlfriend. That was her firewall against either of us developing feelings.

We worked out a sexual rhythm. Wrestling as foreplay. Hot fuck talk and sex threats before, during and after. We got creative. Tried the crazy positions we saw in *The Joy of Sex*.

We made a silly pact. Never use any of our new tricks, talks, or positions with our main partners. In our young minds we feared that new kinks would tip them off that cheating was afoot and risk ruining what we chalked up as healthy, happy relationships.

You already know what happens in the heads of young men who find themselves in the company of sexually compatible women who only want us for sex... Quite naturally, we fall in love with them. Every. Fucking. Time.

And, yeah, Jackpot fell hard. I probably got too clingy. I probably asked for too much of her time. I probably slowed down to love-making tempo, deep strokes and eye contact, probably some kissing, trying to make it meaningful, hoping that she'd connect with me emotionally but this was a violation. She only wanted my hard dick and at least two orgasms.

She was smarter than me and knew what was happening inside my head.

I kissed my way down her body with designs on that special place between her legs but she wasn't having it. With both hands she pushed up against my chest. Got my attention. Reminded me of the rules.

"Don't fall in love, Jackpot. Let's just fuck."

"Yeah, yeah. I don't love you. I just like your pussy a lot," I lied.

She laughed and we rolled around some more.

I tried. Young Jackpot really tried.

And failed.

Along the way, something broke. I broke. We stopped being anything like friends. We stopped talking on the phone into the night. We no longer talk-ed about good bands or shitty bands. We didn't talk about going up to The Jewel for the next big show. Nothing. We pretended to be uninterested in each other around Lion Order but I sensed that Ras Piankhi recognized the energy between she and I, or maybe in his aged wisdom he knew that I was infatuated with her. Peaches also cocked her eyebrow every now and then, hinting that she suspected something, but she never spoke it.

Our magical friendship was reduced to arranged sexual encounters. I mean, the sex was amazing but by then, just a few weeks into our affair, I was hooked on her and in my mind I was ready to throw everything else away for her. I was also angry with her for not loving me in the same way that I loved her.

In the height of passion I had to be careful to keep it purely sexual but my mind wanted to profess an undying love. Yes, Siobhan was still in my life and it made complete sense to me that I could love two women. I know better now but at the time it seemed possible.

I ran into Yinka in the Co-Op grocery store. She was shopping with her boy-friend. Seeing them out in the wild as a couple was a shock to my system. I hung back. Observed their dynamic. She was warm, playful and clingy with him. Seemed to be genuinely in love. She threw her arms around his neck and kissed him sweetly. She honestly seemed happy. And that broke my heart.

We crossed paths in the store.

"Hey."

"Oh, hey."

My eyes darted back and forth between the two, trying to measure every-thing that I was missing. The boyfriend eyed me warily. His gaze carried a question: "is this skinny, baldheaded motherfucker trying to fuck my girlfriend?"

115

Yinka tried to look bored. Offered some quick small talk. "There's a Set at Von's this Friday." Blah. Blah. Blah.

I didn't have much to say so we went our separate ways.

She called the next day. "It was good to see you. Wanna go record shopping?" That was our code for hooking up and fucking. Of course I did.

"I'll be on the next Jeffery 6 bus." I suited up but didn't bother to lace my boots tightly. I knew they'd be off and in a heap in about 30 minutes. She buzzed me up. She led me to her bedroom where we stripped off. She covered her chest and got under the covers. As she always did. I climbed in beside her. She didn't want to kiss. I realized these were cold mechanics. She would never love me.

She got on top. I closed my eyes and held her hips while she rode. I was trying to enjoy her body without emotional investment. She had her hands on my chest. She liked to hold me down and ride at her own rhythm. Like she was taking the dick from me. Selfishly using my hardness for her release. Talking superb fuck talk. I usually loved it. But this time it really did feel like she was just using me. Can't she see that I am more than a stunt dick?

I got angry. I got distracted.

Not good. Things started to fail. I had to salvage the moment, even if just for the release.

I grabbed her. Flipped her over onto her belly. Entered her from behind. She loved the power exchange. I loved the way her brown ass creased under my pressure. I loved her little stretch marks. I called them her "tiger stripes." She loved the way I put one hand between her shoulder blades and the other in the small of her back. She pushed her hips upward to give me easy access. Two fucking machines fucking perfectly. This was one of our us-only positions and it worked to get me back into fighting form — as long as I didn't think. We both got to where we wanted. We reached our finish lines and, out of character, limited it to just one round.

"I've got to meet Siobhan. Can I shower? I can't smell like you when I see her."

"You know where it is."

I washed Yinka off me. Literally and figuratively.

She called again. Invited me to "shop for records." I came up with an excuse. And the next time after that.

In the meantime I got the shit kicked out of me by a rival team and, for weeks, couldn't even think about fucking without it hurting.

I don't remember if she ever called again. I'm sure she did. I'm sure I made excuses. I wanted to deprive her of my attention. Punish her for not loving me. Make her miss me. And of course she stopped calling. She realized that I had checked out.

A few months later I saw her across the room at a show. She was with her boyfriend, of course. I was with Siobhan. We exchanged greetings as good old friends would. I stood there between my two loves.

Under the cover of the music Yinka got my attention. "I guess we've both come to the same conclusion that we won't be shopping for records together anymore, right?"

"Right."

"Okay, cool. I just wanted to be sure that we were on the same page."

"Yup."

"Cool."

Fuck. I'd just had my heart crushed but couldn't even talk to my girlfriend about it.

I turned my attention to the band and pretended to be lost in the music. In reality I can't even remember who was on stage.

Not long after, Siobhan and I flamed out, leaving me as lonesome as a crow on a wire.

Tremor had a saying, "it's a poor dog that ain't got no bone to bury."

CHAPTER FIFTEEN

Peaches and Herb broke up.

She changed. Her feather cut was growing out. She no longer carried the style of the iconic Fourth World Skingirl who held the crew together.

She stopped running the streets with us. I chalked it up to what happened to Brixton, or her flaming out with Herb, or Ajoa checking out, so I didn't dig too deep into the whys or the whats. I called to check in. Her mother said she'd gone to see Sista Evangeline. Maybe I can catch her if I hurry.

I walked over. Peaches and Sista Evangeline were in the Bittas shop in deep conversation. I minded my business. I'd become scarce at the shop but by force of habit picked up the broom and got to work.

Sista Evangeline looked worried. Confused. Peaches looked at the counter instead of Sista Evangeline. She was very far from her usual expressive self. A package changed hands. One of Sista Evangeline's cleansing baths. On her way out Peaches stopped quickly when she spotted me. Then made her way to the door as if she didn't want to talk. I intercepted. I tried to engage. She snaked past me. Rushed out. Hustled home. Closed off. As if she didn't want to be seen.

I went back to sweeping.

Like me, Peaches was just looking forward to graduating high school. Unlike me she held down a job. For summer she'd go full time at Carson Pirie Scott — a local high-end department store. She had dreams of buying her own car instead of always begging to borrow her father's Ford Falcon.

I called again.

I knew she'd had a secret crush on Bubba of The 7 Deadly Skins, so when he invited me to come have a beer at his bar, The Artful Dodger, in The Scratch, I used that as a ploy to drag her out of hiding. Viddy and I rapped on her door. We wouldn't take no for an answer. Before long the three of us were transferring from the 71 to the 6 Jeffery, to catch the Blue Line El west.

Her father's Falcon wasn't up for borrowing on this night. But, if we had a car that night, maybe everything else would have turned out differently.

I clocked her somber mood but didn't pry. Viddy and I joked and signified, getting the occasional laugh from her. She slowly loosened as we got further away from Terror Town. The train clattered along. The flickering lights. A metronome counting beats. Her mood shifted. By the time we were face to face with Bubba, beers in hand, she was inching back toward her old self, laughing with the boys and hitting us with "yo mama" jokes so filthy they would make Tremor blush, if he could.

By the third round she was downright giddy. Dancing. Singing along to Cock Sparrer. She shouted over the jukebox. "Do y'all dare me to go ask Bubba for his phone number?"

"Why the fuck you think we here?" Viddy joked. "Digits or dick. Don't come back without getting one or both."

She laughed. Spotted Bubba. Switched over.

"Look at her trying to walk like a girl," Viddy joked.

She stood at the now-crowded bar exchanging words with a dark haired man about who was there first. She looked up at him. Her face changed. She backed away as if she'd seen a ghost. She hustled back to our corner. "Los Viboros... the one with the hands... and at least one more..."

My mind drifted back to that night. The boxer. An unsettled score. A blemish on Jackpot's record. But I was also having a good time drinking and telling stupid jokes with my crew. I was calculating my next move.

The decision was made for me. Three Los Viboros operators were looking in our direction. They swaggered towards us with the confidence of fearless brawlers. I stood to face the boxer. I slyly dumped my beer on the floor. Gripped the base of my downturned pint glass.

"Ay mis mayates favoritos... y'all are in the wrong neighborhood... again..." looking at me, "how's your headache? Digame, cabron. Do black guys get black eyes?"

I brought the pint glass up with force, connecting cleanly with the soft flesh of his cheek. His skin tried to resist but the drinking edge bit into his grinning mug, cutting a perfect bloody ring. Branded. Permanently. His eyes wheeled downward to make sense of the unexpected trauma. The sound of my pint glass shattering to the floor kicked off the festivities. Viddy jumped in, mixing it up on the undercard. Peaches ran interference punching and pulling on a Viboro anytime they got the upper hand.

Bubba jumped in on our side.

The boxer was deeply wounded by the glassing. But he still had one free hand. I took my advantage. I slid in close to him, got one arm between his legs, the other over his shoulder. I lifted him off the floor and body slammed him roughly onto a table, his back roughly contacting an unforgiving edge. He fell to the floor, catching his breath. Trying to catch his blood.

A woman knelt down to check on him. "I'm a nurse. Are you okay? Just stay down." She reached out to check his pupils. The boxer slapped her hand away. Said "Don't touch me, pendeja!"

The other patrons had been undecided who to root for, but now they were unanimously on our side. They wanted the boxer out. Dragged him up to his wobbly legs. Bubba slipped in behind. Got him in a Full Nelson. Gave him the bum's rush out of the bar.

Peaches was having the time of her life. Thanks to years of slap-boxing with us, she could fight like a guy. Her unconventional fighting style and her light, monkey-booted feet caught opponents off-guard. She could land shots that I might have struggled to land. She was like a pissed off yellowjacket. Zip in. Sting. Back away. Sting, again.

We dusted off the two remaining Viboros. Ejected them from the bar. A chorus of cheers and jeers capped their fucked up night.

The post-brawl atmosphere in the bar shifted to revelry.

Bubba shouted, "Next round is on the house!"

The nurse, feeling giddy, held a spontaneous contest to determine who deserved MVP honors for the brawl — Peaches, Viddy, or me — She held her beer over each of our heads, commanding the bar's patrons to cheer for their favorite. Peaches won, hands down. Her smile lit up the room. There's that old Peaches. A short while later, Peaches and Bubba had a brief fooling around session in the storeroom, but Peaches put brakes on all that because it was, in her words, "too soon."

"Too soon?" I joked. "You better use that thing before it dries up."

She shot me a glare that I couldn't measure.

We closed down the bar, gripped fists with Bubba, then inched back to the Blue Line. East.

It was late when we got downtown. The Jeffery 6 had stopped running for the night. We switched to the southbound El. One branch veered off towards Englewood. The other branch — our branch — veered off towards Jackson Park.

We rode to the 58th Street El station — it was still operational back then — and waited for the Jackson Park shuttle to take us to the end of the line. A very annoying delay in what really should have been a clean shot. Our plan was to walk through Jackson Park then along South Shore Drive to get back to Terror Town. A long walk, but it was a clear summer night. No reason not to do it.

Commotion. On the street. A girl. We all saw her at the same time. She came running out of the alley between Calumet and King Drive. She turned to run east. Screaming. In the streetlights we could see her silhouette. She was wearing a dress. She had been stripped topless.

Then a group of men came out of the alley. Five or six. Laughing. Swaggering. Like they'd just landed a well-fought victory. I took stock of the men. The hats they wore. The way they walked. Their gaits. I listened for clues in the faint echoes of their laughter. The silhouettes weren't enough. I wanted to know what and who I was seeing.

We were looking at the aftermath of a gang rape.

I felt Sympathy. Anger. Disgust.

Peaches... her eyes showed something different. Fear. Maybe shock.

Viddy saw it too.

Peaches drew back into her shell for the rest of the journey. She no longer wanted to walk through the park. "Ain't no buses, Peaches. And ain't no Jitney gon' be taking three nobodies nowhere," Viddy reasoned.

We walked. She had a stun gun in one hand and a knife in the other. She didn't say a word. She kept looking around, over her shoulder. It was a long walk made longer by the brooding. She demanded that we both walk her to her door, past the Kingston Raiders' Essex lookouts. Told us to stay outside until she flicked the lights to let us know that she was safe and sound.

"What do you think that was about, man?" Viddy asked while we waited under the streetlights.

I didn't have a clue. We walked in silence on Essex. Turned towards his spot on East 74th Place. Then I skipped through the shadows to Yates.

I called Peaches the next day. "You alright? That shit on the street really seemed to get under your skin."

"It ain't nothing. I don't want to talk about it. I just felt sorry for her. And... Why the fuck do boys do that kind of shit? Is pussy that important that y'all have to take from a girl who don't want you?"

I'm not proud of my reply. "I don't do that shit. I'm one of the good ones."

She cut deep. "You got a dick, don't you? You one of the good ones until you decide to not be one of the good ones."

Silence.

I spoke first. "We should go fuck them up. That whole team. 58th and Calumet. I could ask—"

CLICK. She hung up.

I called back. Busy signal. She'd left the phone off the hook.

A few days later I was sweeping up glass and plaster inside Lion Order. The Colfax Killers and the Kingston Raiders had a shootout. Lion Order got caught in the crossfire. None of Ras Piankhi's family were injured. They wanted my help cleaning up.

I spied Peaches finishing up another mysterious transaction with a worried looking Sista Evangeline. I gave her space, this time. But she walked up to me. Leaned in. Whispered. "Yeah. I want to do it."

"Want to do what?" I asked. Confused.

She pulled me outside. It all came spilling out. "That shit you said... 58th Street... I want to fuck them up. I want to pick them apart. I want to make them afraid to go outside and afraid to turn the lights off and afraid of alleys and afraid to dress however they used to dress before... before... just before..."

I was stunned by her intensity.

"Bet," was the only word I could find.

◎ ◉ ◎

I called my cousin. Asked him about the Set that operated at 58th & Calumet. "RDs," he said. "Rebel Disciples." He gave me some information about their size: "Peons. Minor Set. Trying to build. Ain't no more than 6 or 7 of them." Their habits: "they broke as fuck and ain't got no hustle. All they do is get twisted on Night Train." Their preferred weapons: "Fists and bricks. I told you. They broke as fuck." Their stature in the Black Gangster Disciple Nation: "Dicks in the dirt. They boxed in. They used to be under the five but they dropped they flags and now they claiming six. They can't even step foot in Washington Park and that's right across the street from 'em." And a guess about who might answer if they got touched: "Shit. Somebody would be doing both Fort and Hoover some favors."

I did the math. Made a decision. We hittin' 'em, I thought to myself.

"I don't know what you about to get into," my cousin said, "but my name is

Bennett—"

I finished it for him. "—and you ain't in it. Bet. This phone call never happened."

◎ ◎ ◎

I sat on the vinyl kitchen chair in Viddy's bedroom.

His wall was plastered with A Clockwork Orange posters and pages from The Last Resort catalog. He had a guitar, a cheap department store, Les Paul knockoff that he'd taught himself to play quite well, and a little 10 watt amplifier.

I dropped the needle on the soundtrack to A Clockwork Orange. I turned up the volume so we could talk freely.

"I know what I need to know about the 58th Street studs. They used to be under the five but they got salty because they never came up. Plus they chief caught a violation from a big chief behind the walls. He felt like he should have been untouchable. They wasn't never on the pyramid and wasn't never gon' be on the pyramid. Them motherfuckers straight dropped they flags and flipped to six. Call theyself 'Rebel Disciples.'"

Viddy asked the obvious "How the fuck you do that? How you go from Moe to Folks? From Islam to Hebrew? From 'First World' to 'Third World'? What? They thought they was just gonna be Hoover's top enforcers overnight?"

"Shit man, you asking me?" I replied. "I mean, think of that shit. You in the game. Everybody know your angels and your demons. But then you flip to the other side where don't nobody know shit about you but your dirt?"

"Remember that Mexican Disciple who transferred to Kenwood last year?" Viddy asked. "He lasted three days. He knew he couldn't survive. And flipping wasn't no option. You can't never be trusted."

"Right, right," I cosigned. "Can't even walk The Grid. Something as simple as going to see your granny could be your last move."

"Damn," Viddy sighed, "everybody know you flipped and everybody testing

125

you. Whoever they chief is need to be fired on. They ain't never gon' be nothing but peons."

"Anyway, long-story-short, those motherfuckers are touchable, and the real cold-blooded part is they boxed in. They got a slim row to hoe and no corners to claim. Them motherfuckers homeless."

"Bet. Peaches still down?"

"As far as I know."

"Well, let's get it poppin'."

My thoughts drifted back to that girl in the alley.

Viddy's movie poster depicted the scene of Alex and his Droogs preparing to rape the writer's wife. I loved the movie and the book — maybe not as much as Viddy — but, for the first time I understood what Burgess was telling us. Alex wasn't a misunderstood hero. Alex was one of the studs we were plotting to vamp on.

◎◉◎

A few days later, up with the birds, I walked that alleyway. I needed a lay of the land. I made note of the gangways, the shadows. Escape routes. I found the spot that was the likely the scene of the rape. An abandoned Chester van. A dirty mattress in back.

Anger, again. Disgust, again. But mostly sympathy for the girl. Who was she? Did she live around here? Did she know these boys? Would she have to see them again? How would she heal?

I sat on a rail looking at the dirty mattress. Made up a version of what happened to her that night. Got lost in thought until I was startled alert by a passing El train. I pulled myself together and headed back towards Terror Town. Root Temple.

Yinka, Viddy, Peaches, and I sat at a table. I told them what I knew.

Yinka disapproved. "Y'all want to go beat the shit out of some other poor Black folks here in Fourth World? Based on what? Some shit you think you saw? Beating folks that are already beat down don't take no courage. Take that mission to The Gold Coast. Touch one of them stockbrokers. Take that shit to Joliet and dead them motherfuckers that killed Brixton."

Peaches lashed out, "Shut the fuck up, Yinka! You don't know what the fuck you're talking about. You always want to be Fourth World President. Not every motherfucker in Fourth World is gon' have a house in your fucking utopia."

Yinka was stunned by Peaches' venomous reply but maintained her stance. Our war in the streets was a waste of energy and time. She bowed out. "Let me leave y'all to your own devices."

That left me, Viddy, and Peaches. We needed more bodies. "Definitely not Herb, but Showbiz will be down. Who else?"

A few days later Viddy and I sat in Washington Park, observing. Two men. Walking to the liquor store. They had the slow, lazy strolls of men who had exactly nowhere to be. One wore a hat. A Kangol. The other had extremely bowed legs.

We walked towards the store. Crossed paths with them. "Blue and black! Get yo' head cracked! What you niggas be about?" Kangol asked.

"You see a nigga, slap a nigga," Viddy replied, getting in his face.

"In fact," I added, "we here to ask you motherfuckers what y'all riding? Is it five or six this week?"

I saw shakiness.

"That girl y'all messed with a couple of weeks ago—" Viddy started.

"Which bitch?" Bowlegs jumped in. "We don't be asking names."

"Alright, bet." Viddy got in his face. "That was my cousin." He lied.

They dropped their bottles. Glass shattering. The odor of Wild Irish Rose in the air. They ran different directions. Disappeared into gangways.

We didn't follow.

Targets locked, we'll take the team apart one-by-one. Put them in traction. Let each one know exactly why they were getting the siafu treatment. But rain moved in off the lake. Hovered over The Grid for a few days. Sent everyone inside.

We didn't see dry skies until the next Friday.

Peaches called with one word: "Tomorrow."

That changed everything. I laid it out. "One-by-one is off the table. We gon' surprise 'em. Vamp 'em '70s rumble style."

"If we get separated," Viddy coached, "use the park if you have to. Meet up at the Harold's Chicken under the King Drive El." Just a few blocks south, in Woodlawn, the birthplace of the Blackstone Rangers — forefathers of the Black P Stone Nation — a no-go zone for these boxed-in flag-flippers.

Saturday night. Tooling up. I grabbed my lucky bat. Checked the tape. Practiced my swing. Studied its weight. Its balance. Perfection.

Local Major League Baseball teams held fan appreciation days. They'd give out souvenirs to the first few-hundred ticket holders lined up outside the park. Caps. Jerseys. Balls. But the best day was Bat Day. A can't-miss event. They would give a real, full-sized Louisville Slugger to kids. Tickets to the game were about three dollars. Add on bus fare. Even us public school kids knew this was good math. The unintended outcome of the promotion was the uptick in blunt force trauma injuries in emergency rooms across The Grid, but for us, Bat Day was Christmas in April.

I'd gotten my bat engraved, just because that was some cold-blooded original shit to do. And leaving a brand — my brand — on an enemy? Chef's kiss.

We rode the El to 58th Street. I had my bat and some mace. Peaches had her knife and a stun gun. The others were similarly equipped. Riot batons, brass knuckles, etc.

At the mouth of the alley we staged our plan. Two operators at the north end. Three — Showbiz plus two more — at the south. Peaches, Viddy and I would come in through a gangway like clueless pedestrians. It was Viddy's idea to put Peaches out in front as bait and, while she agreed to do it, I could see fear in her eyes.

I checked in with her. She said she was up for it. "I want... I need to do this... for... for that girl."

We heard voices and bottles clinking in the alley. Pitching pennies and arguing about who was winning. We stepped through the gangway, Peaches in the lead. Like moths to a flame, the men catcalled.

"Hey hoe! Is you with them niggas or is you here for us niggas?" A different voice, "Oh she definitely here for us now." Bowlegs, "I think that bitch call herself looking for the train." Kangol, "She don't need no train. She gon' be the train."

"Ain't them those Skinhead niggas from the other day?" Bowlegs asked.

Six enemies. They got between us. Three on me and Viddy. Three on Peaches. Young studs. Low rank. Bummy clothes, hard faces.

They tried to get Peaches to the van. She froze. She snapped. Fists. Nails. She caught Kangol off guard. Her ferocity surprised even us. I regretted putting her in this position. The RDs forgot all about us. Focused on Peaches. That's when our backup came out of the shadows.

I saw the arc of her stun gun. Kangol was closest. Trying to kiss her. Peaches hit him with 50,000 volts. I maced him. She lit him up, again. He crumpled. Piss and vomit. "No more. No more. I'm sorry," he whined. He sat in the dirt, propped up against a brick wall. Weak. Pitiful. Beaten. Easy.

"No pity for rapists!" Peaches shouted, then hit him with another 50,000.

Viddy's riot baton was fully stuck into Bowlegs. Viddy was trying his best to annihilate the man. Pinned between Viddy and the van, Bowlegs threw his arm up to shield his face. Viddy's baton came crashing down. A piercing scream, then: "I CAN'T FEEL MY ARM!!! I CAN'T FEEL MY ARM!!!"

Bowlegs' left arm hung at his side. Limp. Dislocated. Peaches joined in. Pressed her stun gun to Bowlegs' scalp. Sent 50,000 volts into his brain. He collapsed in seizure.

I caught one trying to crawl under the van to get away from Showbiz. I introduced him to my Louisville slugger. First swing to the ribs. A dull thud. Second to the knee. A clean pop. Third — homer — caught him on the chin.

129

Teeth. Blood. Silence.

He didn't get one of my cold-blooded lines. Just the wood.

[Knock]

One slippery RD got away. Ran south down the alley. I flung my bat at him. Missed his head by a hair. Lucky fucker. Another was awake enough to hear what we came to say. "That girl y'all raped a couple of weeks ago — this is for her. On Fort *and* Hoover, next time we gon' stuff all y'all peons in that van and set that shit on fire."

Peaches walked over to him. Knife in hand. She stabbed him in the dick.

"No pity for rapists."

The coldest shit I ever heard.

She stabbed all of them in their dicks. Kangol, Bowlegs, the one out cold, and the two I hadn't even named yet.

We disappeared into the night. All directions.

◎◉◎

My phone rang a few days later. It was my cousin. "Them RDs got erased. Somebody moved on them. Hard. Laid them the fuck out. One of them bit his own tongue off and another one straight up—"

I cut him off. "Damn, that's cold," I said, emotionless. "I guess somebody called in a violation."

"Yeah, that sounds like what probably happened. Anyway, just wanted to pull yo' coat."

"Bet. Pulled."

◎◉◎

Peaches' overall outlook brightened up after that. She'd still have her brooding moods but she could pull herself out of them by recounting the victory

130

we struck.

Her appetite for marauding turned us into even better friends.

I found myself spending more time with Peaches. Riding the bus with her to work on Saturday mornings and sitting at the Carson's food counter trading stupid jokes for Swedish Fish.

We were in the back row of the 14 Jeffery Express bus to downtown. The side window was smudged with Jheri Curl juice. I pulled the handle. Threw the window open. Let the lake breeze in. And the exhaust fumes.

Peaches broke the silence. "You remember that time Mrs. Griggs beat you at the Christmas party?"

"What the fuck you bringing that up for?"

"How... You don't even show it. How did you get past that."

"I just pushed that shit down. Don't nobody give a fuck about no hurt feelings. Shit, my mother beat the black off my back when we got home. Some shit about me embarrassing her and talking back to teachers."

"How long did it take you to forget?"

"I had forgot that I forgot until you made me remember," I snapped.

We rode the rest of the way in silence.

I hung around at her food counter. Told her she owed me candy. Blamed her for making me laugh too loud at that party. "You the reason I got kicked out of Bad-Hell." She laughed. Said I was "being a real nutsack about a teensy little ass-tearing." I had to laugh. That's when she changed the subject completely. Told me about a tunnel system under Wabash. "The department stores use it to move merchandise."

"Okay. And?" I asked.

"They be using these big rolling bins for most of the stuff but for the expensive shit... furs and shit, they move that off the trucks on these rolling racks."

131

"Oh yeah. I've seen those racks on the lifts that go underground. I guess I just never thought about it being a whole tunnel system."

"But peep... that ain't all... you know that record store Rose Records? They got a loading door that don't lock. Anybody could come by there, open that door and slide into the tunnels."

I was starting to catch on. "Sounds like a motherfucking adventure."

"I hear that if you keep going North, towards the river, the tunnel is flooded."
"Well, shit. We know where not to go. I ain't trying to fuck up my Sta-Prest."

"Sho yuh right!"

It was good to see her excited. I wanted this Peaches back. I'd do anything to keep her like this full time. "Just say when."

A few nights later we met outside Carson's at closing time. We walked over to Solomon's Fish joint on South State Street, killed some time while the streets rolled up, then made our move toward Adams and Wabash, the entrance of Rose Records.

We checked the surroundings. Clear. Peaches tried the door. The motherfucker gave.

She punched a button and the lift came up. She punched another button and we both rode down. The door slammed loudly over our heads. That clang. It wasn't just loud. It felt final.

There was a long line of loading docks stretching in each direction. The narrow street, if it can be called that, was cobblestone but also had narrow rail tracks. Those tracks were no longer in use now that lighter, more capable methods of merchandise transport had taken over. The street was lined with faint bulbs that illuminated each loading door. The lights looked like they used to be gas lamps that had been converted to electricity.

"This shit reminds me of Yesterday's Main Street in the Museum," I said, trying to make it feel less spooky.

"Yeah, but with gangster ghost stories instead of silent movies," Peaches said, dialing the spookiness back up to eleven.

We looked from store to store. Not looking to rob no stores. We just wanted to have fun in the underbelly of The Gold Coast.

Either we got bored or we got goofy because we started hooting and hollering, running through the tunnels playing hide and seek.

But then we heard a third voice. A man. Authoritative. "Hey you little shits. What the fuck are you doing down here?"

It was a cop.

We split up.

Peaches ran North, I ran East.

The cop cursed us both but pursued Peaches. His flashlight swaying in the dark, throwing shadows like ghosts against the walls.

I could hear his hard shoes clacking on the cobblestone. While I didn't want to get caught, I didn't want to abandon Peaches... and I didn't want to be alone with these shadows.

I retraced my steps in the dim light. Turned North. I caught up with them. I heard their voices but could only barely make out their silhouettes.

The chase had ended at the flooded end of the tunnel. Peaches knew to stop but the cop, unaware and in hard-soled shoes, skidded and slid into the deep pool. He was hanging on the edge but too proud to ask for help.

He was still talking shit to Peaches when I shouted "Let him swim! Punk him!"

Peaches looked back at me through the dim light then took his head and pushed it under water. She wrapped her fingers in his hair and kept him submerged until... until he stopped thrashing.

I walked tentatively toward her across the wet stones.

She stood up laughing, until she saw the horror in my face.

I hobbled over and tried to pull him up out of the water. My feet slipped. I almost fell in. I screamed at her, "Help me! Why the fuck did you drown him?"

"You said to 'dunk him'."

"I said PUNK HIM not DUNK him! Fuck!"

"It's alright. He's just unconscious." She helped me drag him up.

"Wake up, piggy." She slapped him. She pounded his chest. She kicked him. She kicked him again... and again. No reaction. Dead.

My mind raced through all the possible outcomes and only one gave us a chance. I rolled his body back into the water hoping that when he was found... if he was ever found... being submerged would hide any marks left by her kicks and punches.

[Knock]

I grabbed Peaches' hand and walked with her out of the tunnel. We took the Illinois Central train back to Terror Town in silence.

We never spoke again.

After that she was afraid to go back to work. She never even went back for her last paycheck.

◎ ◎ ◎

Some days later I saw her at Sista Evangeline's Bittas shop. From what I could make out, Peaches was looking for something to help her sleep but Sista Evangeline said, with her palms out, that she'd already given her the strongest stuff she had.

Her eyes looked sunken, as if she hadn't slept for years.

Peaches stormed out.

Then...

Somehow, days later, she got hold of Sominex.

I don't know if it was intentional or accidental, but she took too many for her little body.

◎◉◎

Her funeral didn't pull crowds like Brixton's, and this time I didn't sit frozen to the pew.

Viddy sat with Peaches' family. I sat with Showbiz. "She deserved a better exit, bruh," I said.

Showbiz whispered, "Some Raiders... They did her dirty a few months ago. Messed her up."

"What?!" I was devastated. Why she tell this motherfucker and not me? But I pushed that down. Homegirl laid up in a fucking box and I'm making shit about me. I shook it. Went back through memories. Words. Moods. I'd missed every fucking one. That bus ride. She asked a question I couldn't hear. I gave her an answer she couldn't use.

"Fuck. Now shit makin' sense," I exhaled. "But thems ya people, though, dog. How you let that shit go down?"

Showbiz shook his head. "I wasn't there, Moe. GoGo 'nem told her where they was gon' be drinking and smoking and that she should slide through. She went by, and it was a set-up... Bruh... I wanna dead them mugs. I know everybody who did it."

"That's sticky business, Kingman," I said. "You can't be Raiders deading Raiders."

"Nah, man..." Showbiz leaned in. "I got a different idea. I ain't gotta do it. I'ma feed line to the Colfax Killers... let them know where GoGo be putting his head down at and let them do the dirt. After that... ain't gon' be no more Kingston Raiders... at least I ain't... and Colfax can just become real Terror Town, get on the pyramid, end the whole fucking strife."

I studied him. "That's a cold play, Moe. You sure that's how you wanna move?"

Showbiz didn't blink. "Bruh... it ain't about what I want." He lifted a finger, gesturing toward Peaches' casket. "It was her idea."

I considered the weight of what he was telling me.

I nodded, slow. "Be careful, Kingman. Don't get caught on front."

I got the feeling he'd already thought this next part through.

"Bet..." he said. "You though... you ain't in the mix... It won't cost you nothing to feed no line."

I let out a breath. "True. True. That's a twist I could work. I'm down."

"Bet."

But for some reason we never talked about it again.

"You know that's why she ain't with Herb no more. He couldn't handle it. He didn't know how to deal with that, so he just capped out." I looked around for Herb. Absent. Motherfucker.

I left Showbiz sitting in the pews. I walked to Peaches' casket. I immediately wished I hadn't.

Cold. Rubbery. The breath of life gone. She didn't look real. Her lips were sewn shut. Why? She never wore that much makeup. Who the fuck did that? I wanted to beat the undertaker and find out where the real Peaches was hiding. My little monkey boot-footed, brawling Skinhead girl road dog was gone. My heart was broken. We'd lost one of our best. I wanted to crawl in that casket and take that long nap with her.

And me? I knew some shit nobody else knew but, still, I had more questions than answers.

And I don't give a fuck what nobody else tell you.

This... all of *THIS* is why I put Fourth World in my rear view.

Puma

CHAPTER SIXTEEN
Sunday, May 19, 1985

My bedroom was a 10x10 cell that, thanks to being the only boy in the house, I got all to myself. Funny how your space can feel like freedom or a cage, depending on which side of the wall you're standing on. Shit. It ain't much, but at least they're my walls and not nobody else's.

I stood in front of my big window overlooking the street and watched the neighborhood open its eyes.

The world stayed the same. I didn't.

Nine months. Two short, sharp shocks. Three if you count the MOVE bombing in Philly.

Those hits almost put my lights out but I clawed my way back to normal. Whatever that is. Yeah, I thought about making it three — or four — but, I don't know. It just didn't seem like the right way to go out.

I'd graduated from high school the day before. I didn't have any plans to walk in that silly ceremony but my mother made a big fuss about it. Some shit about blood, sweat, tears, ancestors. "Do it for Peaches and Brixton," and all that. So I walked across that stage, threw my cap in the air then handed her my diploma. Washed my hands of everything that sounded like school.

I'd been living here for seven years and this window was still my favorite feature. I grew up standing here imagining myself as a kingpin surveying his fiefdom. I used to run these streets with Viddy, and Peaches and Herb, and Brixton, but now they felt distant. Like I was just a spectator.

The House music movement had taken root. Records were coming out. The clothing style was fully codified. Codified to a degree that it could be copied. People used to dress to stand out. Now they could just go into the right store with the right amount of money and come out looking like the whole package. Too fucking easy. Just like Brixton said, Commodification.

I couldn't rock with it. It felt like I was cheating on Brixton. Fourth Wave was supposed to be the now thing.

Even Lion Order felt different. Some of them were getting fully stuck into the House thing. New faces were popping up. They didn't need me anymore.

On my dresser was a Sanyo turntable and tape deck combo. My 12 inch black and white TV sat on a triple stack of milk crates that doubled as home to my small collection of vinyl records.

Inside my dresser was an array of melee weapons. Small clubs, brass knuckles and, my new favorite that I called "The Payout." It was the handle of a weighted exercise jump rope from Gold's Gym. The end cap unscrewed so the weight could be tuned to a person's preferences. I ditched the weight and filled the handle with about thirteen dollars worth of quarters. This thing was a bell ringer. Of course, if the police ever hemmed me up about it, I could always say "it's bus fare—" and flash an innocent smile. Dummies.

Even Stevie Wonder could have seen that a music lover lived in this room. The walls were covered with posters from Studio 1 to 2Tone. Pages pulled from the London-based *SKINS* fanzine. From The Last Resort catalog. From Shelly's shoes. A picture of a very lovely Judy Mowatt. There were advertisements for upcoming record releases and pluggers for Fourth World Sets. Tappa Zukie's stoic face stared at me from across the room, urging me to be an "upright man." Thanks, Zukie. Maybe tomorrow.

Opposite my bed was my closet door with its full length mirror. That's where I put together my gear combinations to surprise and delight both friends and foes.

Sunbeams gave the floating dust some waves to surf. Those little fuckers are the bane of a vinyl lover's existence, but they look free as fuck. I want to be that free.

I flipped through my batch of new 45s, but I wasn't in the mood to change sides every four minutes. I looked for a long player to hold the vibes. Prince Hammer *Vengeance*? Good album, but a little too deep in the roots for this mood. I wanted to veg out, not go to war. Prince Buster's *FAB Greatest Hits*? I'd worn out the grooves on that one. *Sleng Teng* on Jammy's label? A string of massive tunes, but a bit off the mark. I flipped past some Oi!, some 2Tone, some rap, some Dancehall and landed on a bootleg I'd made of Joe Higgs performing the acoustic version of "There's a Reward." I think I dubbed it from the betamax of the 1977, "Roots Rock Reggae" documentary.

"Home taping is killing music," I laughed as I popped it in.

Mood set. Let this baby loop.

I had the whole summer ahead of me and nothing to do. I didn't have a job and didn't want one. I was getting out of Terror Town. I looked forward to not having to do shit that I didn't want to do. I'd be turning 18 in a few weeks and according to rumor that's when the real fun would start. I'd get my driver's license, find a new girlfriend and be the sharpest dressed Skinhead in the shitty inner city.

Joe was hitting all the Blues notes.

> *Everyday my heart is sore*
> *Seeing that I'm so poor*
> *But I shall not give up so easy*
> *Oh no no no no no no*
> *'Cause there's a reward for me*
> *'Cause there's a reward for me*

The number 71 bus stops kitty corner from my door to head west, away from Terror Town. Very convenient, but could get sweaty, could get smoggy, and could get violent.

I could take the Illinois Central train. With a little bit of skill a clever youth like myself can hop that and get from here to Hyde Park or as far as The Loop without paying. If I need a nap, I just pay the fare, kick my boots up and wait for the trainman to announce our arrival at Randolph & Michigan, right where the stockyards used to be.

That train line served as an important element in the second great migration of black travelers from the South to the North. Half of my family rode that line to our self-exile from repression in the Southern states but nowadays, just like choosing to sit on the back of the bus, my generation didn't even think about all that. We knew some bad shit had gone down, but we had bad shit of our own right then, right there.

Anyway, like a Kangaroo, no going backwards. Like a shark, no stopping. Ever again.

Sometimes I feel like a motherless child
You know no one cares for me
I've never known sympathy
Sometimes I look to the world with a smile
Man you hear what I say

Let's see what the rest of what The Grid has to offer.

CHAPTER SEVENTEEN

I was a wayward spirit. Questioning what the fucking point was. I drank too much. Picked too many fights. Used my bat when it wasn't even needed. And counted days by the hangover. Music was the only thing that kept me halfway sane.

Live and direct from L.A.: two Bands. The Untouchables and Fishbone. At The Cubby Bear. Small stage. Crowded dance floor. Conflict was virtually guaranteed. These bands were magnets for all the big subcultures and countercultures. Punks, Funk lovers. Skaters. Mods. Rude Boys. And, of course, Skinheads.

I stood next to Viddy and clocked the crews.

There was the Pipe FFFitters crew, which stood for "Find 'Em, Fuck 'Em, Forget 'Em." They shaved their scalps practically down to the bone, dressed like the Turbo ACs out of The Warriors and, like that movie mob, they had Blacks, whites, Asians, Latinos, and a few Native Americans carrying their banner. Considering their name, I was surprised to see a very large number of women in their crew.

Damage Done By, an Irish crew from Canaryville, though some of them lived in The Scratch. They wore bleached jeans and chain-link belts that they stole from the space between El train cars. Lightweight. Superb melee weapons. I knew this crew. Didn't have the best relationship with them after that Los Viboros incident.

DDB's biggest rivals were Brick Street. Hardheaded, Dickie's-wearing Italian-American Skins from Bridgeport and Cicero. Unlike other crews, Brick

Street and DDB carried their neighborhood conflicts everywhere they went.

There was also, Los Delicados. A crew of Latino skins that were small in number but mighty in strength. And a hard-as-nails all-woman crew called "Hell & Sorrow," after the Hortense Ellis song.

A top crew called themselves The 7 Deadly Skins. They were a smartly dressed scooter crew. They chopped their scooters down to the bare essentials and rode everywhere as a hard mob. Besides their scooters, their signature element were police department leather bomber jackets that they got from estate sales, surplus sales, or by stealing them out of parked police cars. The 7 would remove all the police insignia but leave the Chicago city flag in place. They turned that mundane, municipal mark into a symbol of defiance. The jackets were hard gear. Insulation against the Hawk and perfect for deflecting attacks. The cops didn't care how The 7 got their jackets. They wanted them back. The police waged a quiet and violent war to retrieve them.

The 7 were also known as "RedSkins." Political, left-leaning Skinheads who disproved the myth that Skins were single-minded. Bubba, Moonstomp's friend, was a key mover in The 7.

And, of course, there was the Pama City Skinhead crew. Widely regarded as the biggest and most established crew. They had two heads of state, Necro and Malört. Necro was the enforcer. He lent them a strength that other crews couldn't counter, but Malört was the real boss of that team. No one knew her game. That's what made her dangerous and alluring.

Pama was rumored to be "freaks." Orgies and all that. So they had an extra aura of seductive mystery. Sometimes they were the peacemakers between warring crews, and other times they acted like an occupying force, demanding deference.

Brooklyn ran with Pama.

Viddy knew everything about her. "She's the real deal... From Milwaukee... Studying journalism at Northwestern... The link between the Milwaukee Skinhead Crew and Pama... She ranks high in both teams."

She always looked the whole part — much better than Pama rank and file — which is why I first noticed her. Brunette feather cut, monkey boots, a denim skirt — one time I saw her out in some cutoff denim shorts that cupped her ass perfectly — fishnet stockings, sometimes topped with a blazer, other times with braces that seemed to make her breasts loom even larger. Or that baby blue Fred Perry shirt one size too small with all buttons undone — creating a lovely visual effect that none of us top-button police would be complaining about. She was also known to be street smart and kept a sharp dagger. She was a couple of years older than me and aligned with rivals. Shit. All that only made her hotter.

There's an unwritten Skingirl dating rule. Never settle for the first one you see and never go with the one who tries to make you choose. And never, ever downgrade.

"Why ain't you chased her?" I asked Viddy.

"Man. And what? She get pregnant and then we both stuck with a baby whose hair we can't comb? Nah. That's all you, playboy."

I laughed so hard I almost choked on my beer.

Eye contact. She waved first. I moved closer. She leaned in to be heard over the music "I like your Sta-Prest! That's a great color!" I leaned closer still. "Thanks. I like your Fred Perry but it looks like you need some help with those buttons." Smiles. A playful slap on my chest. Good start.

We recognized something in each other. Equals. Outsiders, but insiders. We stepped out back so she could smoke a cigarette. That smoke turned into some heavy petting, which turned into us doing "what all the lovers do," like Tito Simon said in "I'll Be True To You."

◎ ◉ ◎

Brooklyn was fun. The consummate Skinhead girl. Drinking. Music. Dancing. And the sex? Mind-blowing.

Risky fucking in public places became our thing. Anywhere. Day or night. Belmont Rocks. A peep show in Old Town. Wherever. If we thought we could get away with it, we would try it. And she was as into it as I was.

The lions at the Art Institute. The stage door to Second City. The native statue in Grant Park. A dressing room at Marshall-Field's. In the gangways and breezeways between buildings. In the balcony of a sparsely-populated movie theater. Wherever.

Fucking around with Brooklyn meant spending time with the Pama City Skins.

Pama was a very different crew. They seemed to love hierarchy. They had titles, and structures, and chains of command. Foreign concepts to me. This crew seemed to thrive on it. I quickly got the sense that I was starting at the bottom and had a lot to prove.

My loyalty to Lion Order was never in question, and I still rested my head most nights in Fourth World, but Pama started to feel like a decent home for my talents. The other crews had their virtues but, as always, Jackpot doesn't settle with the b-squad. As Tremor said "If you can't run with the big dogs, keep your ass on the porch."

Malört was a cipher. A complex woman with a distinctive look and the air of being well-and-truly unfazed by everything but, underneath it all, she was perceptive and always looking for any way to turn opportunity in her favor.

Her frosted Skingirl cut was always perfect. Long feathers and fringes with a grown out crop that lent her some softness. I never saw her wear makeup but she really didn't need it. 5' 10". Fit and powerful. She always dressed herself in the style of a male Skinhead. Tucked in ringer t-shirt complemented by tight jeans that ended above her ankles, her polished cherry red Martens on proud display. Every now and then she'd be seen in a white tank top, bra straps showing, and cleavage on display.

She smoked like a chimney and had a voice to match. A voice that was enhanced by the faintest hint of a vaguely Eastern European accent. She was one of the first women I'd seen in real life who had tattoos dotting her arm. A Pama City Skins crest on her shoulder. A 4Skins logo inside her left wrist. And on her right forearm a cherry red Dr. Martens boot crushing a hammer and sickle.

Necro was a fireplug of a Skinhead who dripped menace. His capacity for violence was barely concealed. The veins in his neck always looked tight, like he was one deep breath away from snapping. Among other ink, he had spider web tattoos on both elbows. Time behind the walls.

Viddy said that Necro's mixed-race heritage, "Black mother, Mexican father," complicated his life in The Jewel. "I made the mistake of calling him Black and was swiftly corrected. He shut that shit right down. I'm guessing he Bics his head razor smooth so his naps don't pop out and cause a scene."

"Dude is a demon on the streets. Handy with the fists. Some white hoods up here started calling him 'Negro.' He didn't like that shit. Put pain on 'em for it. He got smart. Flipped it to 'Necro.' Made them fear it."

"He ain't got no links to Fourth World, talking 'bout 'it gets dark at noon down there,' or The Scratch. Talking 'bout 'I hate gangbangers.' Product of The Jewel, through and through."

I clocked Necro's trickster vibes. Mercurial, sly, and inscrutable. I'ma have to watch that motherfucker.

Pama is also home to a real hard rock that is built like bricks. Broomie. Short for Broomstick.

Whereas Necro was menacing and bustling with pretend charm, Broomie brooded. Solid and imposing, with muscles that made him look older and tougher. His blue eyes were sharp. I got the sense they'd seen shit that most hadn't, and that backing down wasn't in his vocabulary. Necro moved with a swagger while Broomie moved like a bull. Still, Broomie wasn't just playing tough, he *was* tough, way beyond his years.

Necro had a junior named Angus, a white kid with olive skin and steel-blue eyes — handsome, my age, my height, and with the kind of presence that melted panties. Broomie had one too. A towheaded chatterbox named Radish. Looked like a gremlin in ill-fitting boots and braces.

There was also the guy they called Jake. It wasn't his real name. Like Lion Order the Pama City Skins preferred to have aliases in the streets and only in extreme cases, like going to jail or court together, would you ever learn your crew mate's government name. And even then you'd never repeat it to anyone else.

Jake took his whole personality from his namesake in "The Blues Brothers." This Jake had a stocky build and pale skin. Broad, imposing shoulders and skinny legs. Nothing like the rotund original. But despite their visible differences Pama's Jake channeled the character with a porkpie hat, Ray Ban

147

sunglasses, and by constantly quoting any line from the movie in context, with a straight face, off the top of his head. That's how he communicated. Full time. Thanks to betamax he'd seen the movie at least 100 times and would force any unfortunate newcomer to endure a viewing while he recited all the lines, verbatim. If you were trying to actually watch the movie you quickly learned it was a Jake show.

Pama's Jake even had the car. The '74 Dodge sedan that they called "The Shitbox." It was painted as a near-replica of Elwood's cruiser. Unlike the one in the movie, this one had a healthy dose of bondo and primer gray paint. Other than that it could pass as the real deal. Movie fans know that Jake Blues never actually drove the car but we all overlooked that inconsistency. Rumors said that, like Elwood, he even lived in an SRO hotel on Lake Street among the castoffs and the throwaways.

He had a single tattoo on his forearm. A '74 Dodge.

Jake had visited almost all of the filming locations for The Blues Brothers. Two outliers were the bridge in Jackson Park and Ray's Music Emporium on South Prairie. Both deep inside Fourth World. Viddy rode shotgun. I gave directions.

Jake reenacted the scene where the Illinois Nazis were run off the bridge and he got the chance to utter the iconic line from the movie. This was his personal heaven. I'd won myself an ally. But this also meant that I was first to be pulled into his movie reenactments.

Pama's chosen hangout, Aetna park, at the intersection of Halsted and Lincoln, near Fullerton, came with its own legend. It was the exact location of the apartment house where John Dillinger had once lived with Ana Cumpănaş, the so-called "woman in red." She gave crucial information to the FBI, leading to the death of "The Jackrabbit."

The night Dillinger was killed he'd been attending a show at The Biograph theater. On his way home he was ambushed by federal agents. Shot up. Once from behind. Through the neck, out the eye. They say that's the one that killed him. Another shot hit him in the chest. Passed through The Jackrabbit's heart.

That was 1934.

The Pama City Skins always, and I mean ALWAYS, poured out libations to John Dillinger any time they drank at Aetna Park or in the alley behind The Biograph. They called that Dillinger's Alley.

I silently poured my own libations. "This is for Brixton. This is for Peaches. And this is for me."

Across the street a group of skaters, led by a kid named Porkchop, were wolf-packing a yuppie who had run down a skater with his car.

That's what Pama would do. Sit, bullshit, people watch, drink beer, smoke and watch the asphalt grow. Every now and then the police would come along and give the crew the bum's rush, but the habits of bored teenagers are stronger than the drive of beat cops. Once the coast was clear, we'd reconvene and get back to watching the asphalt grow.

Skinheads from other crews would come by, hang out and play their parts.

Some DDB Skins came by with a boombox blasting their favorite music. A band of Skinheads from England. They were obviously influenced by Black American Rhythm & Blues but sang songs about kicking Black people out of England. The music and the lyrics were a cartoonish mis-match. I called out how dumb it all seemed but was the only person who cared.

I steamed.

That band paled, though, in comparison to another of their favorites. A hardcore band from St. Louis who sang ridiculous songs like "There Goes The Neighborhood," "Jew Girls," and "Fucking Faggots."

Fats, a black kid from St. Louis, and also the guitarist for No Empathy, assured me that this band was not to be taken seriously. "When they play in St. Louis, people of all races get on stage and sing along. It's just a big party."

My Fourth World sensibilities couldn't just shrug that away. I watched how serious DDB were when they sang along. There was no joke in it.

I simmered.

149

Nothing either band sang about matched up with my perceptions of the people they were decrying. I said something to this effect to Malört but she just shrugged her shoulders and moved onto the next topic.

But then they really crossed a line. A few of them posted up by the parking meters and asked people for spare change. I seethed. They made the rest of us look like shabby beggars.

I boiled over.

I got between them and a pedestrian. Told the pedestrian to keep walking. Told the Skins they were a disgrace. Jolt, one of DDB's strongest operators, countered that I didn't have the stripes to move them off the street. A challenge to my status in The Jewel and in Pama. I grabbed him by the collar, yanking him close enough to see the flicker of doubt in his eyes. "Stripes? You don't want the kind of stripes I give!"

The others shifted uneasily, their bravado crumbling as they sensed a new power ranking. "I don't know how the fuck you were raised in Canaryville but Skinheads have pride and we work for what we have," I lied. My pulse pounded in my ears, but I kept my voice steady. "Now clear off the fucking street and take that begging shit off this corner."

I shoved him back, letting him stumble. The weight of my words hung between us.

Expecting chastisement, I went to sit next to Malört. She shrugged and moved onto the next subject.

I found her limits, though.

Bubba of The 7 rolled up on his cutdown Lambretta SX 200. He parked next to Malört's classic version of the same machine. He was on his way to Wax Trax but made a quick stop to greet the Aetna stalwarts. He and I exchanged subtle head nods but nothing more.

I noticed that the words exchanged between him and the Pama vets were clipped. Short. Polite. None of the jocular riposting that was customary with this squad.

Bubba walked out of earshot. "Fucking Commie!" Malört mumbled. I looked at the tattoo on her arm and wondered about her venom for Communists, but I didn't ask. I filed this new info into my understanding of her personal code. "Skinheads can do whatever they want as long as they ain't Lefties."

She filled in the silence.

"We are Skins, first. Hated and proud. We always have each others' backs, even when we disagree. And we never pick a non-Skin over a Skin."

"But what about Redskins?"

She squinted at me, as if to see through me.

"My problems with Bubba go a lot deeper than him being a fucking red."

I thought of Laro's lyrics in "Foreign Press:"

> We have been under colonialists
> And suffering under imperialists
> Now we want betterment
> They writing about communism
> When the only kinda ism
> We know bout down here is sufferism

That shit was almost a national anthem for Lion Order.

I let her words hang in the air. She's got the mic.

"Once you start letting feeling superior and letting personal morals and politics — and *rumors* — get in the way of being united with other Skins, then you've lost the fucking plot," her Eastern European accent slipping briefly to the fore.

I adjusted my understanding of her code. It's not just politics. She demands fealty, and it's transactional.

I didn't mention that I'd been to Bubba's bar or that he was a regular at Ras Piankhi's shop. I didn't want to explain Fourth World. I wanted to keep it shrouded in mystery. I was okay with coming to live in their world but I wasn't ready to invite them into ours.

151

I went deep, gesturing at her tattoo. "So what exactly is your thing against Communists?" I didn't have a dog in the fight, I was genuinely curious.

Malört froze up. She pulled out a cigarette. Slowly lit it. Looked me up and down.

"I do not know if you are a spy so I will not tell you where I'm from."

I couldn't tell if she was joking. I let her roll.

"But let us just say that I come from one of the countries where communism is real. Where the Communists rule and where people like me have to scratch survival out of a dirt road."

"Here in America, you have god, you have hope, you have people who will do you favors who do not expect anything in return. That is not the way where I am from. If you do a favor for someone, you expect that favor to be repaid."

"Here is different." Her accent thickened. "Your communists only have bookstores and farms. But for me. The reason I am here is because communism. I threw a spear for my country. My whole life. This arm. For Communists." She paused. As if she wondered if she'd said too much. "But, never mind."

"Let me tell you about my Uncle. He has been here longer than me. He needed work. He heard about a job wrapping Christmas presents for customers at Rizzoli bookstore. He went in, had a talk with the manager and thought it went well. The manager never called. My uncle showed up anyway. He wasn't stupid. He was smart. When he showed up he said to the manager "I'm here to work." Americans never want to be embarrassed. My uncle knew this. He put on his accent. Pretended to not understand English. Said it again, "I'm here to work. Thank you for job. Where to sit?" The manager didn't know how to send him away even though he had already hired somebody. Now he had to pay two. My uncle still works there, full time. The manager is gone. The other present wrapper was let go at the end of the season. You get what you take in this life. Communists take from everybody. When you have to scratch dinner from dirt road, you will understand. Capitalism is freedom. For everybody. Now, let's not talk about this again."

I thought about the projects. I thought about The Scratch. Making a way out of no way is the Fourth World way. But I kept all that to myself. She'd clearly been through some shit — probably came to America to compete. Defected. Nothing but respect for that, but she ain't got the full frame on how this shit is built.

Shit, capitalism?

Black bodies were the motherfucking capital that bootstrapped this whole operation.

◎ ◎ ◎

To become a Pama insider I had to play their hierarchy game.

Malört and Necro decided they were responsible for teaching me the Pama way. They were also who I'd have to answer to if I fucked up. By virtue of being seen with them, and with Brooklyn, I climbed the Pama totem pole quicker than most. Crossing me would mean answering to them. But being their charge meant doing what they asked.

In The Jewel, Skinhead women were the gatekeepers of the culture. They held the clippers and were the ones to do the cropping-in. They did the screening and the sorting out of bad actors. If they didn't like what they found — predator vibes, domestic violence, whatever — they'd set a gang of boots on the offender and drum them off the scene. At their best, they would welcome "Baby Skins" and help them find their first boots or Harrington. And the women, like the men, had impish fun testing newcomers.

Malört sat smoking on a park bench, flipping through the *Chicago Reader*, the free weekly newspaper. She stopped on a full page article about Jim and Danny, the founders of Wax Trax. There was a photo of them that took up about half the page. She had a grudge against this duo. They always seemed like fine people to me, but Malört had an axe to grind.

She tore the picture out of the paper. She drew on her cigarette to brighten the coal. She pinched the cigarette between two fingers and burned their eyes out through the newsprint. She handed me the paper. "Go put this up in Wax Trax. The bulletin board."

What can I say? I was bored, this seemed delightfully impish and it broke up the monotony, so I did it.

I walked in.

I tacked the burnt newsprint to the cork board.

I didn't hide. I didn't sneak. I'm Pama City. What the fuck can they do?

A couple of days later I walked into Wax Trax on my way upstairs to shoot the shit with the Skinhead woman who ran the boutique. I got waylaid at the bottom of the stairs by the counter clerk.

He needed to work out some feelings related to the defaced picture I'd pinned to the board.

"OFFENSIVE!" I'm glad you noticed.

"THREATENING!" I like where this is going.

"DANGEROUS!" I love it.

"HOMOPHOBIC!" Wait. What?

That one caught me off guard. I didn't even know they were gay.

He crossed his arms. Stood between me and the stairs.

"Don't ever come in here again!"

That was it. Banned from Wax Trax.

A badge of distinction and standard operating status for Pama City Skins.

I sat down on the bench.

Malört cracked a smile behind her cloud of smoke.

CHAPTER EIGHTEEN
From the Book of Black Teeth
Queen Mother Rage

Erzsébet has been described as objectively beautiful. Dark hair. Pale skin. Blue eyes. A fetching figure – fuel for envy in women and lust in men. Tall. Powerfully built. With an uncommon sensuality. A mere glance in a particular direction is enough to send one of her submissive handmaidens – known as Re°Ceivers – off to fetch something, anything she might fancy.

They call her The Unfettered Self.

The Countess.

Queen Mother Rage of this clan.

Revered. Honored. Feared.

The mystery in their Magick.

The pull of the moon. A purifying fire that rivals the sun.

Devotees. Aspirants. Servants. All.

She is why they come.

Hers is a sanctuary of vanities. Beauty made power. Reflection made control. It is decadent but not warm. Precise. Staged. Ritual.

Her paintings. Slashed-out wombs. A snake coiled around a bassinet. A white hand reaching from blackness, singling out a smaller white hand. It, too, engulfed in blackness.

Chained mannequins in ceremonial positions. Their jaws nailed shut. Iron grimaces. Their eyes replaced with mirror shards.

This is where she dreams of becoming not woman, not lover, but God.

She is why they come.

CHAPTER NINETEEN

In Skinhead life every day is a test. The only way to pass is to keep showing up.

Broomie didn't like me. Didn't think I belonged. Regarded me as an invader. A virus. Something to be eradicated.

He had his reasons. I was from a rival crew. Not from The Jewel. Dressed funny. Too many opinions. Shitty taste in music. Too cute to be a street soldier.

It's a good thing I never ask permission.

Jake had a new tape blaring out of The Shitbox. "I Hate Myself" by The Offenders. A hardcore band from Texas. We'd gone to the Metro to see this band and I was now a fan. I leaned into the passenger side window to hear.

Radish, Broomie's junior, tapped me on the shoulder. Asked "What size boots are those?" I sized him up. Shorter. Younger. Not my equal.

"The size your mother likes," I snapped, drawing a loud laugh from Jake.

Radish didn't like being the butt of my joke. He either needed to salvage or build his reputation so he squared up to box. I laughed him off. Turned my back.

Insulted, he struck out, punching me between the shoulder blades like an angry child.

I decided to play his game. I faced him and squared up. He punched. I dodged. He telegraphed all his shots. I made it a game. Told him how to hold his elbows. To guard his grill. "Don't leave yourself so open." I could see the frustration in his face. He got desperate. He lunged. I stepped to the side. Helped him by. His momentum carried him forward. Off balance. He stumbled. He fell into the bushes.

His shirt tangled. Wet dirt on the knees of his jeans. Dismissed. I reached in to help him but he slapped my hand away. He punched wildly, again. Missed, again.

"I've been fighting all my life, kid. We come out of the womb slap-boxing."

Flicknife fast I caught his jugular between my thumb and forefinger. Pressed just hard enough. He panicked. Clawed at my forearms. Like he had a say in it.

I applied a bit more pressure. Driving the point home. He had neither the size nor the experience to challenge me. Then, I switched it off. Let him down. Flashed a smile. Laughed him off. Told him to run along before I changed my mind.

Deflated, he looked to Broomie but the older Skin was more interested in his own boots. I clocked it. Broomie wanted to put me down. Radish had been sent to humiliate the tourist. To send me back to Fourth World shame-faced and beaten — by a junior. Instead, Radish had been publicly outclassed and given a personal tutorial in street fighting.

They'll have to try harder than that.

Tremor told me long ago, "Never take a 'no' from someone who doesn't have the power to tell you 'yes.'"

Broomie drank and brooded. He was my main opposition in Pama. He was, at best, number four on the totem pole and with Necro and Malört in my corner he'd have to put up with me.

"Move along. No loitering."

A couple of The Jewel's finest.

Jake read the play. Didn't want The Shitbox impounded. He slipped into the driver's seat, nosed out into traffic and quietly drove away.

The cops poured out our beers. Bum rushed us out of Aetna.

We walked north on Halsted. Someone shouted, "Let's go drink at Irving Park Salvage." Necro's spot. Twelve deep. Boots and braces. Boombox in hand. Cranked up to 11. Not giving a fuck who liked it or hated it. We bought more beer along the way. Broomie strong-armed random civilians on the street demanding two dollars to buy six packs of Black Label. We gave them their change and a beer and kept walking to the next liquor store and the next civilian shakedown, getting drunker by the block.

By the time we got to the salvage yard we were all keyed up. Broomie got loud. He stepped over every boundary. First he tried a drunken, tawdry come-on with Malört. She soundly dismissed him. He stumbled over to Angus and Myra, the new girl on the scene. She and Angus were trying to get past the awkward early stages of dating. Myra sat between Brooklyn's knees getting her long, black hair cut into feathers and fringes. Broomie, always single and with shitty luck with women, tried to pull her away. Asked her if she wanted some "white cream in her banana." The words upset her. She took it as a comment on her Asian heritage.

Malört jumped in. Pushed Broomie in his chest, causing him to stumble and land on his ass. Embarrassed.

Broomie stood up, brushed himself off. He gauged the mood. Pivoted to saving face. Stumbled over and commandeered the boombox. He popped in one of his favorite tapes.

A brash hardcore song.

This band was popular with Lion Order but this particular song was always controversial. An immediate push of a skip button. I never got a clean hold on what the singer was trying to say, but, with Broomie, there was no ambiguity. For him, this was a battle hymn. He sang it at the top of his lungs.

"GUILTY OF BEING WHITE!"

"I've only served NINETEEN YEARS OF MY TIME!"

159

He looked around. He didn't get the reaction he wanted. He popped in another tape. The racist, English R&B imitators. A song about Europe awakening for the sake of the white man.

I'd been hanging around Skinheads in The Jewel long enough to know these songs and, despite their reprehensible sentiments, some of them were undeniably catchy. I sang along.

My singing-along triggered something in Broomie.

He glared. Stood over me. Poked a hard finger in my chest. Boomed: "YOU. CAN'T. SING. THIS. SONG!"

Malört intervened, again. Got between us.

"Why are you backing that lion odor jagoff. He ain't one of us!"

"Shut the fuck up, Broomie!' Malört yelled. "Jackpot is my Skinhead brother. More than you! He can sing whatever the fuck he wants."

Stunned silence rippled through the crowd of Skins. I knew that was just the beer talking through her.

I didn't need the help, and part of me wanted to fight this lout — it was inevitable and overdue — but I appreciated the deep cut. The eyes of the crew darted between the three of us, silently adjusting their calculuses. He still outranked me, but not by as much.

Broomie was disgusted but not dumb enough to test Malört.

"Radish! Let's get the fuck out of here."

Radish grabbed the tapes and followed.

Silence hung in the air, but Broomie was right. I shouldn't have been singing that song. Every lyric was an insult. To me, to people like Brixton. I notched the lesson. Ejected that band from my orbit. I never sang along again and would sabotage people's tapes of that band whenever they left them unattended.

Brooklyn hopped up. Slid in a new tape. A palate cleanser. A song everyone

160

could agree on. "Skinhead Girl." The Oppressed's remake of the Symarip Skinhead Reggae classic. Next up was "Evil" by The 4Skins, then "Where Have All The Bootboys Gone" by Slaughter and the Dogs, then "GLC" by Menace. This was a party again. We drank. Sang. I fell asleep on the couch in the salvage yard office.

◎ ◉ ◎

The next morning Necro wanted to smooth things over between Broomie and me. He roused me from the couch and led me to Broomie's apartment. Broomie answered the early knock on his door with a grumble. He was reluctant to let me in but stepped aside to make way.

"Pama breakfast. It's been a minute. Let's go to Ann Sather," Necro commanded.

The TV in Broomie's apartment doubled as a trophy stand: Great Lakes Regional. Lansing State University. "Clean and Jerk." First Place. Christian P.; Tri-City Classic. Rockford, IL. "Squat Open Super Heavy." Second Place. Christian P.; Midwest Invitational Power Meet. Cleveland, OH. "Deadlift Heavyweight." First Place. Christian P.; The Back Room Bench Off. The Wild Hare. First Place. Christian P.

"Who is Christian P.?" I asked.

"That's me." A voice boomed behind me.

Icepick. Pama elite. Broomie's roommate. This Skinhead was pure muscle, polish and charisma. The sleeves of his "United Skins" t-shirt strained against his undecorated biceps, making him look like a chiseled mannequin. He didn't run the streets with the rest of us and now I understood why.

"Swedish pancakes? I guess I can take a cheat day," Icepick said, grabbing his flight jacket.

Dude looked tough as fuck.

While waiting for the El at Irving Park, Necro and Broomie got into some horseplay. These two had years of history that I could only guess at. They decided to fuck with me. One grabbed me under my arms. The other grabbed my boots. Threatened to toss me onto the train tracks. For Necro, these

161

were just jokes but Broomie was a bit more menacing and didn't know when a joke was finished.

Okay. Game on.

I like jokes too.

I shook myself loose.

Any kid who has grown up in the shitty inner city has learned how to take risks. Those of us who survived, invariably learn that some of the myths and legends are just that. With sure movements I jumped down onto the train tracks. The burly Skinheads cried out in panic.

"What the fuck are you doing?" Necro yelled.

Icepick interjected, "Listen man. Don't do anything crazy. Just take my hand."

Necro boomed, "Man, get the fuck up off the tracks."

"Why? Is it dangerous?" I asked with feigned naivety.

"The rails, man!" Necro snapped.

I squinted. "Which rails? All of them?"

Broomie barked, "The third fucking rail! You fucking idiot!"

I stepped calmly toward the first rail. "Is this it?"

Radish practically shrieked.

I jumped with both feet and landed firmly on the rail. The Pama elite operators cried out.

"Please! Please stop fucking around!" Necro cursed.

Even Broomie looked shaken up. He offered a weak bribe. Speaking slowly like a hostage negotiator. "If you come up off the tracks I'll give you all the money in my pocket."

"Yeah man, please stop fucking around," Radish chimed in.

Only Icepick seemed to have his head in the game. He calmly tried to coax me back to the safety of the platform.

I played clueless.

"Should I be afraid of this one over here?"

I jumped cleanly to the second rail. Landed with both feet.

Everyone on the platform was in panic. No one wanted to see a young man cooked to death. Hands outstretched. Loud begging. Pleading. But none of them brave enough to come get me.

They tried luring. They tried bribing. They even lied. Said that there was a train coming.

I cocked my head to the side. Looked quizzically at the track signals. I feigned confusion, "Y'all trippin'. Ain't no train coming."

"Okay, Jackpot, please just don't step on the third rail," Broomie begged.

It's accepted wisdom that the third rail is the source of power to the trains and that contact with that rail would mean certain death. A person would be fried alive. But I've seen dogs walk the rails time and time again and they don't get cooked. I've seen birds perch on the tracks and they don't get roasted.

"Which one is the third rail?" I asked, toying with their emotions, dangling death and trauma before them. I pointed at the next strip of metal.

"Is that the third rail?" I leapt with two sure feet and landed cleanly on the slightly elevated strip of metal.

They screamed. They covered their eyes. Icepick snapped around. Put his back to me. Held his breath. Eyes closed. Back straight. Fists clenched. They listened for my last cries. But... nothing happened. Nothing at all.

I've done this before. This is child's play in Fourth World. I've run these tracks and been hanging out with graffiti writers long enough to know that

163

the danger lies in connecting the current across rails.

The street-hardened Skinheads, their little sidekick and the civilian spectators were all profoundly shook. Their Sunday morning genuinely fucked up by my game. I scanned the faces with exaggerated disappointment as I hopped back towards the platform. Rail-to-rail. Giving them fresh mini-strokes with each move.

"Y'all really embarrassed yourselves. Don't know shit about the El," I said.

I stood with them on the platform, calmly making a show of checking my clothes for dirt. Smoothing out wrinkles. Humming to myself. Linval Thompson's "Don't Trouble Trouble."

Necro fumbled to light a cigarette.

I could feel Broomie's eyes drilling into the back of my skull. Trying to figure out what I was made of.

I'd like to think that Radish wet his pants. I never bothered to check.

I felt a little bad about yanking Icepick's chain like that, but let's just chalk him up as collateral damage.

After all, it was his idea to come along. He only had himself to blame.

And Broomie? After this, my calculus said that we were about equal.

"Don't try to trouble the lion, Don't try to wake the lion. Because he will hurt you."

CHAPTER TWENTY

It was Thursday, June 13th. Necro looked damn near suicidal.

"It's been a dry fucking year!"

"Yeah. Last year was the best. When is the next one?" Malört asked.

"I don't know — Hey, BlackJack, do me a favor. Run over to Woolworth's and steal me a *Farmer's Almanac*."

"Huh?"

"Don't ask. Just do it."

Another stupid test.

Across the street from Aetna was one of the last old-style Woolworth stores. It sat at the base of a triangular, two-story building that capped the wedge intersection of Fullerton, Lincoln and Halsted.

I hopped up. Crossed the street.

This place was a genuine throwback. They still had the counter and the stools for food service. They had the freezers that you had to pretty much dive into to get an ice cream sandwich. They had Get Well cards. It's A Girl cards. A book section stacked with bodice rippers. Crossword puzzles. Roadmaps. And, sure enough, *Farmer's Almanacs*. And some other titles. A lot of them. Who knew there were that many types of almanacs? I grabbed what I came for. It looked simple but it clearly took itself quite seriously.

The book was too big to fit into my pants. I eyed the bored cashier. She doubled as a short-order cook. She looked like Loss Prevention was her middle name. I'd have to get clever.

I sat at the counter and ordered food. A chicken sandwich and fries. She got busy dropping the frozen items into the deep fryer. While she was distracted I slyly placed the almanac on the floor near the exit. I milled about and grabbed another copy of the almanac.

I sat, ate my food, and thumbed through the predictions for corn crops and estimates of sow fertility. What the fuck is this goofy test about?

On my way out, I stood at the counter and paid for my food. I also handed the clerk the second almanac. "I don't think I need this." She turned to place the book in a go-backs bin. I swooped down, grabbed the contraband, and slipped out. Slick. Easy. She's gonna lose her shit come inventory time.

I walked back to Aetna humming, ironically, "Dem belly full but mi hungry, a hungry man is an angry man."

"You didn't buy this, did you?"

"Nope. I bought food. The book was a gift from F. W. himself."

"Nice work, BlackTop. If you wasn't a shoplifter, I'd shake your hand." He opened the book to a calendar. Flipped a few pages. "Fucking September!"

"What happens in September?" I asked.

Malört answered, "Me and Necro have a Friday the 13ᵗʰ tradition..."

Sensing a story from the usually silent Malört and not wanting to ruin it, I parked my ass on the concrete and settled in.

"After Necro came back from behind the walls, a couple of years ago, we were just fucking around, killing time, skitching on the street by Stix, the pool hall. It was Friday the 13ᵗʰ but that wasn't important. We got into a friendly little snowball fight with some PR Stones. The snowball fight was all good clean fun until one of them — this chick had an arm on her — put a rock in a snowball and beaned a civvy behind us. He was shoveling the snow in front of his building."

"This dude was fucking PISSED!" Necro interjected.

"Yeah, but he was a square. Dumb yuppie haircut. Pleated pants. Galoshes. After the snowball fight we walked over to see if he had anything he needed to say. He didn't, but Necro decided to jump on top of the pile of shoveled snow and kicked it all back down onto his walk."

"It was an honest accident," pleaded Necro, drawing laughs.

Malört went on, "The yuppie looked heartbroken. All his hard work ruined. He'd be shoveling for the rest of the night. Oh well. His problem. When we walked away he muttered, "baldheaded cunt," and grabbed my ass. Poor prick. He desperately wanted to lash out but that was all he could think of."

"Well, I know I have a great ass but it's not for yuppies, so me and Necro jumped on his head with mace and fists and boots. In the course of the beatdown I told him 'we're gonna come fuck you up every Friday the fucking 13th so you better have your pussy-ass outside waiting for us.'"

I liked this energy.

"You know, that was just some crazy fight talk, I didn't think anything of it, but Necro got into it. When April rolled around he reminded me of the promise so we went by to check on the asshole. We waited for a while then got bored and rang all the doorbells. Just ran my fingers down all the buttons. Some people responded. Bingo. The third one sounded like our guy. We pretended we were UPS delivering a case of Malört to a radio contest winner. People like to win shit even when they don't remember entering any contest, so he buzzed us in like a dummy."

"BlackSpot, you should have seen the terror in his eyes when he saw who was at his door. Malört grabbed him by his t-shirt, stuck a dagger to his temple and asked if he was going to apologize for grabbing her pussy. She said that part extra loud just in case he had a wife in the apartment."

"Can I finish my fucking story?" Malört asked.

"Anyway, like I was saying, he buzzed us in, we walked up, and instead of apologizing he practically shit his pants and tried to close the door, but Necro already had his boot in there. I snatched him out and slapped him around a bit. I didn't want to go inside his apartment because that's a heavy

167

home invasion charge, so I just bitch-slapped him around in his hallway, asking if he gets off on molesting girls. Telling him I could kill him right here in the hall and no one would miss him — that I'd done it before. He just curled up in a fetal position and took the shit-kicking. On our way out Necro said, 'Happy Friday the 13th! See you in July, fuckface.'"

"Did you go back?" I asked.

"Honestly, DickSmoke, I thought he would have moved away by then but that dumb motherfucker was right there, in his car, almost like he had forgotten or maybe he just wanted to make it easy for us to deliver another case of Malört. By the way, this is how our shrinking violet got the name Malört. She was so bitter, and refused to go easy on this guy, so it was like a natural fit for her. She walked up singing 'Oh pussy grabber — We brought your Malört!!!' and the name just stuck after that."

———

The resident Aetna park winos, Arnie and Juan got into a fist fight. We egged them on and paid the winner with — what else? More wine.

———

"Anyway, that was last year, and the next Friday the 13th ain't until September, so a whole fourteen fucking months will go by without us giving him his shot of Malört."

"What will he do without his Malört?" Malört asked.

I don't know how the Friday the 13th superstition began, and the movies are hit or miss, but I know the makings of a good urban horror when I hear it. "I want in on this," I said, "take me with you next time."

"We'll think about it, CockBreath," said Necro as he looked up his zodiac.

"We don't really trust you, yet."

That was fine.

I wasn't in for trust. I was in for the story.

Peaches would love this shit.

CHAPTER TWENTY-ONE

I turned 18!

"The Chicago Handshake." That's what they called the hazing they put me through for my birthday. I was still groggy from the festivities, and from sleeping in The Shitbox.

I was sitting at Aetna with Jake. Necro walked up.

"Hey, BlackNot, where do you get those gay-pressed pants?"

"Maxwell Street, in The Scratch. Why?" I answered with confidence, trying to sound casually street smart.

"They make your butt look so cute and I was wondering if they had them in men's sizes."

"You got money? Maxwell Street ain't for the poverty-stricken." Actually, it was.

"I got more money than your mama got pussy."

"You ain't got enough dick to touch the sides. Let's go."

Jake was already on his feet, Shitbox keys in hand, anything to break the monotony. "Oh yeah? Well me and the Lord. We got an understanding."

We piled in. Necro in the passenger seat, me in the back, giving directions. We didn't take the straight shot. "Work The Grid." Not to stall. To *see*.

"East." I said, tapping Jake's shoulder. Jake knew the streets but followed anyway.

We hit Lincoln, snaked toward Clark. "Bust a right. Take Wells" South now. Old Town. Bizarre Bazaar. Peep shows. Wax Museum. Liquor stores. Currency exchanges. YMCA. Cabrini-Green off in the distance.

Division street. "Bust a right. Then left on Dearborn."

The Shitbox agreed. Swung onto Dearborn, pointed south.

We weren't in the heart of The Gold Coast yet but you could feel the air change. Got cooler. Buildings got taller, streets tighter. The air shifted. Less hustle. Buster-ass office squares. Ants. Sheep. Marks. They looked beaten.

"That's it!"

He caught it just in time, dipping the front end of the Shitbox onto Lower Wacker Drive.

It was always a different universe down here. This must be the only street in the world that's bathed in green lights. No lanes. Just raw concrete, pillars posted up like P Stone sentries. Daring you to get too close.

This is the last stop for a lot of tourists.

Past The Muzik Box. Ron Hardy's club. Church. This was Fourth World-adjacent terrain.

"We gon' hit Roosevelt then bank right." You had to know which exits didn't dead end.

Necro punctured the silence with a question. "Each of us has a reputation, QuickNut, but we are usually the last one to know what it is. What do you think your reputation is?"

I paused for a few beats... The question made me uncomfortable.

"Well, for y'all I guess I'm an unknown quantity. Maybe I can be trusted. Maybe I can't. Personally, I would say that I'm a solid player. Top notch Skin. Better dressed than most. Handy with the fists and my Slugger. Not afraid of dirty work. Popular with the ladies. I make the team look good. I don't gossip. I'm loyal, but... shit... all of us take advantages... right?"

"Huh," was all that Necro could muster.

"What's your reputation, Necro?"

"I ask the questions, CrackPipe."

I sat back and let the smack sting. I walked right into that one.

"A reputation ain't shit but walls that other people put up around what they want from you. I stopped caring about reputations when Necro was born. Necro is not a reputation. Necro is a motherfucking legend. I'm disappointed in you, SlopShit. I thought you'd have a better answer than that."

"Whatever's clever, Trevor."

"Don't call me Trevor."

Roosevelt. We surfaced from the underground. We squinted in the sunlight. The shitty inner city frowned at us.

"West. Stay on Roosevelt," I said.

Jake cruised. Why did they put a college out here? Polish sausage spots. Raggedy storefronts selling knockoff gym shoes and bootleg tapes. The Scratch.

We caught the cheap end of Halsted.

"Right, here. Maxwell's just up."

He made a slow turn. Blues guitar leaked from somewhere up the block. A guy selling tube socks and jumper cables waved half-heartedly from a folding chair.

Maxwell Street — yeah, it had another name. I'm overlooking that — on a weekday was nothing like the weekends. Then, it was an open-air bazaar with live music, pungent food on the grills, racks of clothing lining the streets, kids running around playing cops and robbers, loud haggling and money changing hands. In contrast, on Monday it was dead and depress-

171

ing. Without the sensory overload, all the cracks and flaws broke through. As people from Fourth World would say, this place was "tore up, from the floor, up." I'd never noticed it before, but now I saw that these merchants were a much lower tier than who you'd find in The Loop. I quickly connected the dots from this merchandise to the Englewood Disciples and their freight train heists. I'd heard that they offloaded their merchandise — appliances, tools jeans, gym shoes — onto Maxwell Street merchants, but now it magically made sense.

Jake got distracted by the green shop front that still had the flickering SOUL FOOD light in the window. He disappeared inside to see about some fried chicken and white toast.

I led Necro into a clothing shop. My regular Levi's connection.

The doorway was decorated on both sides by big curved glass windows that, while smudged, formed a showcase for merchandise that pimps and preachers would love. We stepped across the chipped tiled walkway. Dozens of tiny hexagons had been lost to history, making this feel like the bad end of Dorothy's yellow brick road. The door was a little jammed. I pushed it to unstick. A bell rang loudly overhead. New customers. The shopkeepers looked up, sized us up as small-time, turned back to whatever they were doing before.

"Let me know if you need any help," called out a disinterested voice from somewhere behind a clothing rack.

I pointed the way to the Sta-Prest but Necro's eye was drawn to a modern take on the pants. The Levi's 505 Street Brights. They were made of the same material as Sta-Prest but were flat front instead of factory creased. They also had the five-pocket style that Americans prefer.

Necro was sold on the navy blue and the army green. Had them pinned to just the right height to show off his oxblood steelcap Martens. He posed in the full length three-sided mirror like Super Skin and, minus the t-shirt, he really did have a tough look. The deep, consistent color of his new pants ratcheted his style up, significantly. I knew he'd be back.

I was slowly civilizing these tackheads.

Jake barged in, singing. "You better think. THINK! Think about what you're trying to do to me!" Off key. Enunciating every syllable. Sounding very little like the original. He barreled over. Excitedly grabbed some pants with his greasy fingers. "Excellent choice," the tailor said. Making it clear that Jake had just bought himself some pants. Unbothered, Jake wiped his hands on his t-shirt and joined the transaction.

There was no haggling on the weekdays. "The price is the price. Are you going to buy these or are you wasting my time?" I realized that the familiarity that they greeted me with on the weekends was just an act. These guys are sharks. Either I was feeding them or I wasn't.

Their goal on the weekends was to get your money before you spent it with the next guy, but they had no such compulsion today. I wondered if they even cared about the lore of this street. If they'd prefer to be success-ful enough to relocate to The Loop. I decided that they did not love The Scratch. They were just stranded here like everybody else.

Fortunately, we only came here to buy pants — Well, Necro did, and now Jake had to — so we made the buy. I told the idle tailor to give them Fourth World invisible hems while we waited. I showed them some shirts but these guys were t-shirt heavies. Baby steps for the neanderthals.

Deal made, pants tailored, we tumbled out of the shop, toward The Shit-box. Jake exclaimed, "First you trade the Cadillac for a microphone, then you lie to me about the band, now you're gonna put me right back in the joint."

"Why didn't you tell us about your secret Heeb tailor shop before, Jack-Dick?"

"You never asked... and besides, you seem to be happiest looking like The Village People, Knee-Crow."

"What the fuck did you call me?" Boomed Necro.

"What? Knee-crow? You don't like nicknames now? How about Negro?"

"I'll rip your head off and shit down your neck!" Necro boomed.

"There you go reliving your prison trauma."

He stared me down for a few uncomfortable beats, then smiled.

173

"Good one. Jake, get us the fuck out The Scratch before JackCock gets some of his gangbanger homies to rape and kill us — not necessarily in that order."

"You'd probably be a very fuckable corpse," I deadpanned.

My eyes scanned the high-density apartment buildings. Toddlers and grandparents hung out of windows, their faces dulled by routine. Life on pause. Waiting for something to happen, or for the next Saturday to bring the carnival back. *Take the plastic off the couch, Margaret. We got company.*

I pointed the way out.

"This don't look like no expressway to me!" Jake threw in as he nudged The Shitbox off the curb. Around a bus. Past the little gas station where the Bluesmen rested between sets on the weekends. It looked closed today.

Jake turned east to put The Scratch behind us.

This wasn't family like Lion Order, but it was motion. And motion broke up the monotony.

CHAPTER TWENTY-TWO

Pama City Skins still had some rough edges but now they were starting to look like proper Skins. Pama now carried an edge of discipline, a sharpness, that set them apart from other crews. It wasn't just about appearance; it was about sending a message. Pama was still the same crew, but now we looked like we meant business. Pride and tradition. Band t-shirts had been replaced by short-sleeved work shirts. Torn or bleached denim was traded for solid-colored Levi's Street Brights. Tall boots were getting phased out. Hard and smart was winning.

Brixton would be proud of my success. He might not be as forgiving of their influence on me.

Pama introduced me to hallucinogens — LSD and shrooms. I liked trippin'. At first I liked it a little too much. It was a great way to kill twelve hours.

Pama also introduced me to extreme live music. Harder, more violent than anything I'd witnessed in Fourth World. This wasn't just hard music to them. It was a reflection of hard living. Each event, a rite of passage.

Garages, church basements, bars, small clubs. The venue changed week-over-week but the intensity was always the same. The feedback loop between the band and the audience felt more like a symbiotic energy exchange than a concert. And once I experienced The Pit, I was hooked. The adrenaline. The physicality. The stage diving. It was like sex and drugs combined.

I didn't need to know the songs or even the bands. They gave, and I gave back. Brutal. Raw. Violent. Discordant. But... also... surprisingly communal.

Sometimes tourists would lay eyes on The Pit and misunderstand the dynamics. They — usually jocks, new to city life — would wade in thinking that hurting people was the point. They'd use their elbows. Send smaller people reeling. Or they'd throw real punches. Stiff forearms. Closed fists. Or they'd try to cop a feel on a girl. Think that just because she's in the pit in her bra that she must be the village bicycle.

The first offense would get a gentle correction. The second: a stern warning. The third: Full force. Collective fury.

Invariably, that tourist would go out on a stretcher. Never to be seen again.

Sometimes conflicts arose between the bands and the crowd.

Maybe the guitarist got loud after being jostled by a stage diver. Or maybe the singer grumbled The Pit was too rowdy. If the band ever overstepped their half of the equation, the crowd felt justified in pulling them off the stage, smashing their equipment, and beating them bloody. For the hardiest hardcore bands this was part of the culture. They'd get back on stage and finish their set, bloodied but unbowed. But there were extreme cases where the band wouldn't, or couldn't, continue.

Like the Canadian thrash metal band who came out and shouted "SKIN-HEAD FUCKS GO TO THE BACK! I ONLY WANNA SEE HEAD-BANGERS!"

The band went back to Ottawa in casts, unable to complete their tour. Their audience had to wait until the next show to get the power exchange they craved.

Skinheads of The Jewel were integral to the community of The Pit and I fell right in. Our bruises told stories. Our scars were trophies. I could lose myself completely in this. I found what I had been looking for.

Fourth World music wasn't violent or political, and jumping around shouting into microphones lacked the cool finesse that we cultivated. But here, in this raw, unfiltered chaos, I crossed swords with rage, fear, elation, and euphoria. I could shed everything and live raw — get lost in the intensity of the moment.

But I still liked to look like a proper Skin — before and after the show — so I traveled with a backpack stuffed with hard gear for the pit. I usually changed in the nearest McDonald's bathroom, or a laundromat.

Angus and I found that we had a lot in common and started to run the streets together. We had similar taste in girls, music, alcohol but it was really The Pit that brought us together. Out on the streets, we got into a few fights, backed each other up, and developed some trust. He also lived walking distance from the usual haunts. His parents were the permissive type so we usually wound up at their house to crash, shower and change after running the streets.

Angus's parents were still young. Mid-to-late 30s. His mother wasn't quite ready to fade away into middle-age. The faint remnants of a West London accent told the story. She'd been transplanted as a teen and had settled in Chicago with her family, a lot like Brixton. She fell in with a handsome boy — Angus's father — and quickly earned the status of teen mother. With luck and ingenuity she landed softly after marrying her high school sweetheart.

Mrs. Macksey — an art gallery owner — quickly started showing up in my wet dreams. About five-feet-six-inches. A few extra pounds. Olive skin. And a fantastic C-cup rack that made her stand out from the crowd. I have no idea what her natural hair color might have been but she had a pleasant face that she accentuated with dramatic post-Punk makeup. She dressed in a new wave style like women several years younger than herself. Asymmetrical skirts. Shoulder-baring tops. And the occasional bullet belt that hung just-right on her hips. She carried herself with the relaxed confidence of someone very accustomed to being desired.

She'd been around at the first wave of Punk rock and seemed to know everyone in the Wax Trax industrial music scene. She was undoubtedly part of the tribe, just a few years too old to run the streets with us.

Angus's father, Mr. Macksey, was a researcher and professor at a Gold Coast university. In his younger days he'd been involved in radical politics, and he seemed to know everything about the chemistry of drugs. He guided many of us through pleasant acid trips. He told me he was researching a psychoactive compound that promised to enhance male sexual performance, to solve the problem (his word) of most men being unable to perform sexually while tripping on LSD — as he put it, "robbing them of a sublime sensory experience."

177

He had a small army of student test subjects who put themselves on the line for a few extra dollars. "The secret," he said "is the more we pay, the more dangerous it is, but they don't seem to care — Well, not at first. There was one who experienced a psychic terror and... well, that was the end of that research... I do hope that young man gets the help he needs and makes it back to being himself..."

I told him about the African aphrodisiacs I'd seen in Sista Evangeline's Bittas shop. Ibogaine. Yohimbe. He was surprised that either could be found in the USA. He was curious whether either could be potent enough for his research. "Bring me some, please."

Deal!

◎◎◎

Root Temple still vibrated like the nerve center. Called me. Pulled me. I missed it — But the ghosts. I didn't miss them.

Ras Piankhi was out. I was relieved.

I had to hear Sista Evangeline tell me that these herbs *"ital tings deh yah"* are not intended for unclean behavior: *"dutty livity."* And to think deeply about my motives: *"is wah yuh really ah deal wit?"* She handed me the bundle and kissed me on my cheek. *"Gi di gyal dem a bick ah relief, nuh?"* Then she made a joke: *"Fuss time mi see waan man wit waan scandal bag."*

Before I could slip away she grabbed my hands. Told me I was missed. That I always had a home there. I replied awkwardly but she pressed on. "Why do you love this skinhead Oi! business so much?" She asked, pressing a small envelope into my hand.

"It speaks to me in ways that Hot Mix doesn't. The anxiety, the anger, all that. Hot Mix," I said, "is all sex and shake-your-backside. It's empty."

Sista Evangeline looked at me — choosing her words the way elders do — switched to the Queen's English. She wanted every syllable to echo.

"For so long our intimacy was regulated. This stud, that girl, make a baby for the slave master. The legend of the jezebel and the black buck. We had to recover from all this. The big lipped coon, the big assed mammy and the nappy headed pickaninny. Curses."

"We weren't supposed to see ourselves as beautiful or desirable. So now that we have some pride and some self-awareness, we choose to say loudly that we love, desire, cherish each other. Yes, anger is useful and if you dig deeper you might find that there are hidden meanings to some of the music you are dismissing. But, putting the music aside, Black people loving Black people is the revolutionary act."

She paused.

"Don't run so far and so long that you forget the way home."

She left me speechless. The moment was heavier than I expected. I silently collected the bundle. Put it and the envelope in my backpack.

"Peaches," she said, touching my arm. "I didn't understand it at the time. I should have known. There was something I didn't know. Did — Do you know? Did she ever say anything about dreams?"

I answered only her last question. "No. Nothing."

She was skeptical. I could see it. But she didn't push.

I put the shop door between us.

Then I made a mistake. I went to 78th and Essex. Where Peaches used to live. Her family had moved out. But something was still there. Looking back at me. Like she'd left a part of herself behind, leaking through the bricks.

I didn't like the sensation.

I got the fuck out of there. Hopped on the first thing smoking back to The Jewel.

◎ ◉ ◎

I handed the samples to Mr. Macksey. Didn't think much about it after that.

True to form, Mr. Macksey had a huge stash of porno mags all around the house but no one seemed to think it was strange or shameful, which was

179

the exact opposite of my home life. Every time my mother found my porno mags she'd rip them up, toss them in the trash and drench them with fish grease. I've no doubt that Mr. Macksey loved having the pretty, feral Skingirls around his home. He'd get eyefuls of their young bodies in various states of undress and on more than a few occasions I could hear him taking his desire out on his wife, most-certainly inspired by the taut, young flesh parade.

I got the sense that Mrs. Macksey enjoyed the youthful energy that we brought to their house, not to mention the spark it added to her husband's libido.

Their home was a safe place for us to crash. She'd leave the door unlocked so we could come and go at will. Brooklyn spent more weekend nights here than she did in her dorm.

When the adults weren't home we'd hook up. Fuck. Get high. Almost every room of the house was in play. Even when they were home we still had our fun but kept it in the living room. Various couples or triples. Side-by-side. Fucking for the hell of it. Or just waiting for the LSD to wear off. We were discovering what our bodies and minds could do.

I made another mistake. LSD. Microdots. They said it was a bad trip. But it felt so real. Peaches. And something else. Something... nameless. She wasn't afraid of it. It watched me. Like it was waiting. For me. Why couldn't anyone else see what I saw? I forgot how to breathe. I wanted the trip to end. I flipped out. Mr. Macksey gave me speed to balance out the bad trip. That was my last time with either.

And then the biggest mistake of them all.

I found myself alone in their house one morning. Everyone else had drifted off to school, work, the grocery store. I hopped up. Took a shower. Got ready for the trek to Terror Town. I was decked out in my classic Skinhead gear. White Fred Perry, with black tipping, black Levi's Street Brights, black Harrington jacket, Dr. Martens boots and black braces. I looked the whole part. Admired myself in the mirror.

I wasn't in a rush and was easily distracted by some of the porno mags on the living room coffee table. I sat on the couch lazily paging through an issue of *Oui*. Mrs. Macksey surprised me. I didn't know she was home. I straightened up. Felt guilty. Dirty. Busted.

Mrs. Macksey surveyed the situation silently then politely dismissed herself back up the stairs.

I started gathering my shit. Had to get out of there. She came down the stairs with more magazines. "Jim got some new magazines, you should give them a look. You might find something you like."

The magazines were all interracial sex. Specifically, Black men and white women. Some were hardcore, others were more softcore. Artistic photography. Filters. Creative angles.

I was speechless. She took the lead. Guided me to sit next to her on the couch.

She thumbed through the magazines, stopping occasionally to show me the images that she enjoyed most. She explained the photographic techniques. The differences between pornography and erotica.

"Men are generally more visually excited than women but I find this image particularly arousing."

"Have you ever considered posing for photographs?"

"No? You should. I think the camera would love you. You're a fit young machine. Not grotesquely muscular. Definitely not skinny. Just a firm young man who drips street smarts."

Wow. The pictures. Her closeness. The way she spoke. I tuned into the erotic potential. Still, as a relatively inexperienced young man I also had doubts. She was married. She was older. She was my friend's mother. Was I just an irrepressible stunt dick misinterpreting shit?

She chose a more direct approach. She leaned in with a magazine. Asked, "how does your cock compare to this one?"

I didn't know what she was asking.

I don't have a cock.

Among Black folks, "cock" meant pussy, not dick. Always had. Listen to old Blues songs like Lucille Bogan's "Shave Em Dry" or "Till The Cows Come Home" and you'll hear it. To us, dick was dick and cock was pussy, so her words confused me for a beat.

I let the question hang in the air.

"Such a shy boy. I'll bet it's really nice but sadly I may never know." Her light English lilt drew my attention to the way her lips moved when she spoke. She was close enough to kiss. Her perfume was intoxicating.

She went on in a breathy tone... "I'm very curious. You should show it to me." She tapped the fly of my Levi's with two fingers, right where my hardened mahogany strained the most.

Naturally, her words were like those of a snake charmer. I stood up next to her, dropped my braces, undid the button, then the fly to drop my pants. My firm wood sprang up from beneath my shirt, standing in sharp contrast to the white cloth.

She eyed my stiff pole with bemusement. She looked into my eyes, then back to the magazine. Deep in thought. She carried on with the ruse that she was merely interested in its artistic value. "Magnificent," she said. "It looks sculpted... Like a Baoulé statue..."

She continued comparing the relative size, shape, and color of my equipment to those in the magazines. I stood at attention. Hands behind my back, pulling my shirt up out of the way. She reached out with a soft hand and looked all around my erect tool. "Look at you. Hard enough to cut diamonds."

This, I know how to do.

I pushed her back. Hiked up her skirt. Made note of her stockings and garters. I gently pulled down her lacy panties. Admired her trimmed bush. She was nothing like my teenaged lovers.

She guided me. Put me where she needed me. Gave me the green light to be myself. My young muscles and hardened obsidian doing exactly what they were tuned to do.

"Such a darling boy," she whispered.

I gave her my most polite effort, then instinct kicked in. Turned the tables. I flipped her over. Put her where I needed her. Made her work for me. I wanted her to remember every inch of this Boss Skinhead. The feel of my hands pushing her around. Getting more than she expected. Harder than she was used to. The sound of my voice telling her what to do and how. Earning my approval. And the taste of my cum.

I collapsed on top of her, sweating. Still tucked inside. My head swirling with stars. My cum slowly running down between her legs. Puddling on the couch. She rubbed my back and hummed praise in my ear. "You are such a lovely boy. Promise me you'll come back to Mummy whenever you need a nice place to spill your milk, darling."

That was an easy promise to make.

We lay like that for a long while catching our breath and recuperating. The sensation of her pussy throbbing around me coaxed me back to usable form, setting us off into slow, gentle love-making that surprised me.

"You are a good boy... A delightful lover boy... Such a sweet, loving cocksman you are. I'm going to be so jealous the next time I hear you rogering a young bird."

I secretly fell in love with my friend's mother that day.

She became a new drug for me. I left that house dizzy. Changed.

CHAPTER TWENTY-THREE
From the Book of Black Teeth
No Mother Once More

The Coil. On the upper level of what used to be a firehouse, a Cod°Ex Re°Cereb Re°-Ceiver is doubled over in a stone birthing pool. Twelve Re°Cereb devotees surround her and look on without emotion. Erzsébet sits seven feet away and two feet above in her makeshift throne, tended, hand-to-foot, to by her Re°Ceivers.

An older man assists the expectant mother in the delivery of the offering. His doctor's coat covers his clothing that tell the tale of a high ranking professional man who had to cut short his regular duties to tend to this matter.

This man, The Judge to some, The Jackal to these, moves without hesitation, each motion as practiced as breath.

The Jackal walks with what we now know as the child, but does not lay eyes on it. That privilege is reserved for one.

Yet, even in this he inserts a ritual. The Jackal measures, no counts, out his steps. They must end perfectly on a divine number, with calculated breaths in agreement. Precision matters. Calculation matters. On the rare occasion that he miscalculates he undoes his footfalls then begins again, in pursuit of divine balance, even in the mundane.

This, he says, is esotericism, stoicism, and materialism in perfect balance. This is what distinguishes Man from men.

On his approach The Jackal almost miscalculates. There's a new imperfection in the floor. Why wasn't he told? The devotees' eyes look everywhere but at the flaw – at the imperfection.

The Jackal adjusts. Recalculates. Resets.

The offering mother waits as emotionless as her peers for The Jackal's attention.

A slight glimmer of hope dared to enter the offering mother's face as the bundle is presented first to Erzsébet. Even she, the mother, had yet to look upon her gift.

Erzsébet received. Leaned forward expectantly.

Her lips part but she does not speak.

The room holds its breath, waiting for her decree.

She says nothing.

Erzsébet recoiled.

Covers her nose with a lace handkerchief.

This child, large of cranium and pale of skin, has the bad fortune of being born sinistre. Female.

No.

There shall be no abstraction from the Countess.

Erzsébet gazes into her hand mirror, studied her face for new lines and her hair for new streaks. There will never be another Countess.

This offering is, at once, disappointing and offensive. To be Unfettered is to reign without shadow.

The future is not born – it is bound. A daughter is a door. Erzsébet closes it.

The devotees turn away from the rejected offering, putting another half step of distance between the offering mother and they.

The once-offering mother, turning slower than the rest, feels an emptiness in her belly. Her fingers almost reach out. No. There are no babies there.

The devotee – she is no mother once more – mentally calculates her next fertile *period. The Jackal says that it's the male DNA that determines Fényhozó or Recerebration.*

Next time.

Next time.

Next.

Time.

CHAPTER TWENTY-FOUR

The junkyard, Irving Park Salvage, wasn't the most obvious home base for a Skinhead crew, but maybe that was the point.

On my way into the yard I crossed paths and cool greetings with The President and Sergeant-at-Arms of Haunted Town motorcycle club.

I did a subtle double take when I realized DeRico, the President, was Gary Sayers. The same Gary Sayers who served a quick burn as a state rep back in '81. For a minute there, he looked like he might be a different kind of Chicago politician. He had a rare quality that Black folks, Italians, and Irish could all get behind. He wasn't a revolutionary outsider like Chairman Fred. He played insider ball and stole the focus every time he walked into a room. That made him extra dangerous to Da Machine.

And then came Spider Dan, a tightly wound daredevil scaling the Sears Tower with industrial suction cups and dreams of scraping the sky. We loved it. When the news broke that Dan was going up the Hancock, families piled into cars to watch it live. We cheered him on like he was the Second Coming. But the cops? They lost their shit. They turned fire hoses on him. Hung out of windows, shouting like they saw a threat instead of a thrill. Tried to knock him loose. For what? Did they really want him to fall to his death?

Sayers saw it how we saw it. Power is petty, fearful, and ready to kill when it can't control the frame. He expressed his dissatisfaction, loudly. He didn't run for re-election. He dipped. Just walked away from everything.

And now here he was, as DeRico, President of Haunted Town MC. New look. New code. Their colors were pale blue, red, and white. Their logo was the top half of Chicago's city flag. No south river. No south side. No Fourth World. That was not lost on me.

Haunted Town was outlaws among outlaws. They proudly proclaimed that they were to be a one charter, one generation club. No state chapters. No national ambitions. To them, The Jewel could be paradise with the right sentries at the gate and no other motorcycle clubs could fly colors within their borders.

As the Haunted Town founder and President, DeRico cut an imposing figure. His Cuban cigar and hard Cicero accent only sharpened the effect. His ride was a Moto Guzzi V-twin dressed in gold flake paint. That bike didn't look or sound like anything else on the streets of The Jewel, much like the man himself.

Pama had a working relationship with Haunted Town. Malört, Necro, Jake, and Broomie provided "material acquisition and recovery" services for the leadership of Haunted Town MC. The Motorcycle Club needed specific assets but couldn't risk having their members caught in any such act, and that's where Pama came in.

The first job I got clued in to was the theft of a car from Lake Point Tower.

Alice Cooper had a condo there and stored part of their car collection in the parking garage. Of particular interest was a 1963 Studebaker Avanti that had previously been owned by a Russian spy.

Pama didn't know me well enough to include me in the heist but they let me listen to Malört outline the basics of the job.

She called out one big problem: the security guard. How would they distract him long enough for the Avanti to be stolen? We all agreed that towing the Avanti was too obvious and would probably fail. I piped up. Suggested a tactical improvement. If it worked, it would get the rent-a-cop out of the equation. Everyone but Broomie signed off on the tweak.

The job was to go down the following Sunday night. Necro drove the tow truck to Lake Point Tower with a false order of repossession for a different car. The car didn't actually exist, but that didn't matter. Necro explained to the security guard exactly what he was looking for. The rent-a-cop, distracted by the specifics, and annoyed by the chattiness waved Necro in.

This is where my idea came into play. Necro hitched up a car for towing. Pulled it to the gate. It was the same color as the repo car but obviously the wrong make and model. The rent-a-cop flipped out. Questioned Necro's intelligence and eyesight. "Wrong fucking car, genius."

"Oh fuck. You're right. I better put it back where I got it. Can you be my eyes, so I don't fuck it up?"

Exasperated and not wanting heat for damage to residents' property, the guard agreed.

Necro joked "Man, I hope you don't come back to a goddamn yuppie riot." The gambit paid off. The guard dashed back to raise the gate so residents wouldn't be inconvenienced in his absence. Perfect.

The guard hustled ahead on foot to guide Necro to the vehicle's correct resting spot. Malört snuck in through a pedestrian access point. Found the Avanti. Hotwired it. And in ninety-four short seconds calmly drove out through the open gate.

She took the long way through The Jewel, sticking to the alleyways, all the way to Irving Park Salvage. We tucked the Avanti into a remote section of a storehouse. Covered it with a tarp.

Necro continued to eat up the rent-a-cop's time, then "gave up" on finding the repo. Thanked the rent-a-cop. Hit him with a crisp new $20 for the hassle. Made his way back to Irving Park Salvage.

"You're alright, BlackHead. You didn't fuck up nearly as bad as I expected, but you owe me $20."

"The best part is that shack-jockey is gonna go to his grave remembering you as dumber than a Junebug on a string, Knee-Crow."

Asset secured, Haunted Town happily took over. They had one of their guys contact Cooper's manager. Demanded a ransom. Cooper's people didn't even know the vehicle was missing. Had that whole team scrambling for a throat to choke and a quick, quiet solution. The ransom was small enough for the manager to pay in one lump sum and big enough for Haunted Town to make a healthy profit. Pama got a decent fee for the job.

I got kicked down a little cash for my enhancement.

Sensing a good moneymaker, Pama went on to pull similar jobs on Hugh Hefner, Wendy O. Williams, and Seka who all had homes and trophy cars in The Gold Coast. DeRico was ecstatic, kicking down bigger fees with each job. I could get used to this kind of money. Leeching off the rich and famous was right in my wheelhouse.

I still don't know who Alice Cooper is.

◎◎◎

Fucking around with and falling in love with my crew mate's mother was everything right and everything wrong.

Fourth World was home. Accountability. The Jewel? The Jewel was freedom.

I was a solid money maker. I was a bonafide style leader. I could be counted on in a brawl, and I could be trusted with (most) secrets. One problem, my first loyalty was always to my dick. The same dick I was regularly stuffing into my crew mate's mother.

Mrs. Macksey tried to keep it all cool, and go with the flow but she was a bad poker player.

She welcomed me into the house just a little too enthusiastically when I'd come around with Angus. She'd give both Angus and I a quick, motherly peck on the lips and say she was so happy to see "Mummy's Boys." Pama operators wondered why I was so special. No one else got that kind of treatment. Some of the older Skins joked that Mrs. Macksey liked me more than she liked Angus. He'd laugh along, but I could also tell it bothered him. Butt of the joke. Lower-cased to a peer. That shit would bug me too.

And there was also Mrs. Macksey's hard, cold shoulders to Brooklyn. Even Mr. Macksey noticed and asked his wife about it. She just glowered. She couldn't very well tell him that she was ticked off because her boyfriend was two-timing her.

Malört joked that Mrs. Macksey didn't appreciate the younger, hotter competition. I tried to laugh it off as their overactive imaginations. "Maybe she's mad because Brooklyn skipped over her number one son and came to me,"

192

I joked, attempting to make it all sound very implausible.

Everyone but Angus laughed.

He tried to change the subject.

"I heard there's a whole city under The Gold Coast. Tunnels and shit. No police."

I froze up. My mind flashed on that night with Peaches. That dead cop. I stopped him.

"Nah. I heard that same shit. Went looking for it. Locked down. They be moving furs and jewelry through there. 24-hour patrols. Ain't worth the lie it's printed on."

Necro went back to joking about Mrs. Macksey.

My turn to change the subject.

"I gotta go take a piss. Y'all can keep telling lies on my dick if that's what gets you off," brushing off my Sta-Prest pants.

Jolt from DDB, wanted to get in on the signifying.

"Why does Pama dress like youse guys are from England?"

"Why do you dress like Mork from Ork? Fuckin' seat belt suspenders," Necro shot back.

"I dress like an American Skinhead," countered Jolt.

This was a useful distraction. I pounced, "If you are so anti-British, maybe you should choose a different subculture. I hear rollerblading is all the rage."

"I don't know, man, he seems more like the bocci ball type," Necro joked.

"Or shuttlecock," I smirked. "What's the word, Jolt? Do you prefer the balls or the cock?"

Jolt was caught off guard by the rapid-fire, bad-cop bad-cop double-team.

He fumbled for words.

All day Jolt had been making a big show over the new tattoo he'd had done by Cliff Raven at Chicago Tattooing Company. The art was the iconic "Crucified Skinhead" with "Hated" arched above, "& Proud" inverted below.

Sleeve rolled up, Saran wrap exposed, Jolt was all peacocking masked by performative nonchalance. I pointed at his tattoo. "This motherfucker talking like he's Captain America but got a London Skinhead icon on his arm."

Necro sneered, "Shit says 'Hated & Proud' but this boy softer than a grape and slower than a parked car."

"If you ain't never been to The Last Resort," I added, turning the screws, "you shouldn't have no Crucified Skinhead tattoo. In fact, we should cut that shit off your arm. Give me a boxcutter."

Necro flashed a utility knife and lunged. Jolt braced. I made a loud show of holding Necro back. "Don't do it, Necro! He ain't worth the jail time!"

The whole park was in stitches. Jolt couldn't tell joke from threat. And the topic of Mrs. Macksey was forgotten.

I went to take a piss in Dillinger's Alley, behind Aranda's. I heard an extra pair of boots behind me. Necro. I claimed my spot against the wall of the Mexican restaurant but instead of moving along for his own real estate he stood elbow-close to me.

"There's a whole fucking alley and you want to be right here?" He looked me up and down.

"So, JackNut, are you boning Mrs. Macksey or what?"

"Huh? No. Those are all jokes. She's like a mother to me."

"That's kinda hot," he said, smirking.

    A carload of metalheads slowed just long enough to hurl
     "SKINHEADS SUCK!" out the window before roaring off.

Necro had seen a lot more life than me and he had a gift for sniffing out both danger and opportunity. I was sure that he was sure that something was going on with me and Angus's mother.

Necro said "Well, if you're not fucking her, maybe I'll go by there and see how much she can take."

He searched my face for a reaction. I gave up nothing.

"Angus is like a little brother to me, and maybe Broomie is right. Maybe your place is really in Lion Order and not up here in The Jewel. The cultures," he explained, "are different and, well... you ain't from up here. And you won't even trust us with your secrets."

"One of these days," he continued, "I'ma find out what sent you up outta Fourth World and that shit better be very fuckin' bloody or very fuckin' funny..."

We were grill to grill. He was testing me. Checking to see if I would fold.

"I don't owe you my life story, motherfucker!" I countered sternly.

Unfazed, Necro dialed up the menace. Switched gears. "That shit back there! If you ever touch me again, NeckDick, I will rip your arm off and shove it up your ass."

"What the fuck is wrong with you? You switch hot and cold like a retarded pit bull. I put up with all this Pama hierarchy shit because it's a hard fucking mob. Don't pretend I don't make it better."

He looked me up and down then broke out into a grin. "Haha," he laughed, "I'm just fucking with you. Come on, BlackPot. Tell me how Brooklyn's pussy tastes."

I glared.

Something about my silence triggered him.

"We're not so different Señor Jackpot. You dress your vices up as virtues. I know mine are fatal flaws. My lack of impulse control is going to bring the walls down on me."

Ignoring the point I joked "Aw, that was cute. You called me Jackpot."

"Freudian slip. I meant BlackSlop."

"Yeah, whatever, Knee-Crow. Now put that shriveled dick away. If you shake more than three times there's another name for it."

We walked, laughing back to rejoin the crew.

I had a new priority: warn Mrs. Macksey.

CHAPTER TWENTY-FIVE
Friday, June 21, 1985
Summer Solstice

Angus got invited to some new age bullshit.

"The Cerberus Method is a unique blend of eastern spirituality, paired with western pragmatism." It was the promise of free food that hooked Angus.

"When?"

"All weekend. Summer Solstice. At Navy Pier. All are welcome. Good vibes only. We'd love to see you there."

"Why the fuck not? Free food. Maybe some cute college girls." I told Viddy about it. He came through.

The Cerberus festival was one of the weirdest things I'd ever seen. Part pagan, part Buddhist, part Greek Orthodox and all goofy. Like Renaissance Faire meets Revenge of the Nerds.

In the middle was a gigantic maypole. It looked like an alabaster dick with a jackal's head. The streamers hanging from it looked like strands of cum. Subtle. The music being piped in was an atonal soundscape that Viddy described as "textural" while I struggled to find a repeating pattern that would make it make sense.

Off to one side a dog trainer showed off his very-well-mannered Doberman Pinschers.

Up ahead, Necro was telling one of his crazy stories about a London Skinhead named Joe Bovshover who could turn into a werewolf but since it was beyond his control it led to all kinds of trouble for him. That bled into another story about a Skinhead named Jay Mac from a place called Liverpool which led to the story of another Skinhead named Irish, Jay Mac's friend. Irish stowed away on a boat and made it all the way to New York City. "That's the real story of how Skinhead came to America and how it is different from the Baldies." A battalion of baby Skins hung on every word.

Two Cerberus Method recruiters tried to elbow into the conversation. Wanted to steer it towards their philosophy and mission but Necro would rotate slightly to put an imposing shoulder between the cultists and his audience. This was his show.

"I never knew Necro was such a storyteller," I said to Angus and Brooklyn.

"Yeah," said Angus. "That guy can turn it on or off." Then, changing subjects, "what do you think of these Cerberus people? They ain't as weird as I expected." He bit into one of their grain-on-the-cob creations. "I'm thinking I could be vegan." Brooklyn looked skeptical.

"Ras Piankhi has this method of making food that Rastas call Ital. They don't eat no predators, no bottom feeders and don't even use electricity to cook." "Yeah, but then you have to listen to all that Haile Haile business. I mean... it's cool and all but I can't help that I'm white. I ain't never owned any slaves so I don't know why I should care."

"It's cool, man," we'd had this conversation before, "everything ain't for everybody. Just don't disrespect Emperor Selassie."

◎ ◎ ◎

Pama Records had been one of the premier labels for Skinhead Reggae in the time of the originals. That label and Trojan were key heritage markers for proper Skinheads but, despite the crew name, the Pama City Skins weren't the deepest Reggae fans. They just wanted a cool name that pointed to the London originals but they didn't want to settle for the extra-obvious "Trojan Skins," itself another reference to a premier Reggae record label. Pama City Skins' interest in Jamaican music was limited to Skinhead Reggae and even then only the songs that explicitly name-checked Skinheads.

Their interest in Jamaican music died abruptly at about '73, which is when the Rasta influence took the lead with its black consciousness subject matter and references to the mystic ruler from Ethiopia. Pama Skins, unlike Lion Order Skins, had no patience for all that.

Angus put his narrow range on display during a visit to Fourth World. I took him to Lion Order, introduced him around and blew his mind with the Skinhead Reggae 45s that dotted the racks. He elbowed his way into the queue for a turntable to hear them for himself.

He excitedly asked Ras Piankhi how these records were received in Jamaica and was soundly told "Dem records ya neva once did ah buss dance inna Jamdung. One lone Babylon ting dat."

Angus took that as an insult but, like most people from the subculture, he transformed the dismissal of Skins into an affirmation of the singular superiority of Skins and our rightness for choosing it.

"That Dread doesn't seem to like Skins very much," said Angus as we walked to the train.

"Yeah. It's a good thing you didn't use that word while you were there."

"What? Dread? What's the big deal?"

"It's just not something that we play with around here.

"That's dumb. It's just a word."

◎ ◎ ◎

The memory made me bristle. I shook it off. We walked aimlessly, exploring the festival, taking in the sights and sounds and the weirdness. Until...

I stopped in my tracks, stunned. "That dragon. That laughing fucking dragon! That's the dragon I saw in Joliet. With Brixton. Remember those dirtheads I told you about?"

And then I saw them. The ride operators. They had that same pale skin. The matted hair. The dead eyes. The filed down teeth.

"Why the fuck these Re°Cereb motherfuckers here?"

I looked around. I snatched a flyer from one of the Cerberus weirdos.

```
1560/1614

The only solution is HER solution/

We have been told that we are DEVILs/ Bad/ We Accept/

Dare you enter The Coil modern man?

Dare you teach your daughters The Way of The Countess?

Send a metallic heartbeat to your ancestors/

MODERN BATHORISTS ARE WE/

BORN TO RULE ARE WE/

1560/1614

SEPTEMBER 1, 1985/ JOLIET, IL/ NORTH OF THE PRISON/
```

```
LOVE WITHOUT RELIEF
PLUNDER WITH LOVE
BOND ONLY THE WORTHY
```

I grabbed Viddy, "This is the same shit... Joliet... CACOPHONY!"

"The motherfuckers who killed Brixton?"

"Yes! Look at every ride. The dead-eyed motherfuckers are part of that."

I pocketed the flyer. Saved it to show Tremor.

Viddy and I peeled off to check out the tents. We made a few turns and found ourselves by the port-a-potties and the first aid tent. We heard a commotion. One of the ride operators was injured. Bleeding profusely. Crying out in surprise and pain. It was oddly pitiful. Despite his appearance, he was being a real ballsack about his wound.

There wasn't much else to see. We rejoined Angus and Brooklyn who were hemmed up by a couple of senior Cerberus representatives.

"Come to our feast on Sunday. It's free. We'd love to have a couple like you as our guests. You'll hear all about The Cerberus Method but, more importantly, we just want to make new friends."

"Can I bring more friends?" Angus asked as we stepped up.

The Cerberus spokesperson hesitated. A half-second pause then a small, forced nod.

"Oh... um... yes... of course. You may bring your *others*."

◎ ◉ ◎

Angus, Brooklyn, Myra, and I showed up. Viddy bowed out. "Too weird." Stayed in Fourth World.

The Cerberus Method headquarters was a four-story building that had been a hotel for gangsters and flappers. It had a well-kept courtyard and a wraparound drive where Studebakers once lined up like dominos. Now, silence.

The new-age yuppies droned on about the structure of the organization, the path to ascension, and their reclusive guru Anpu.

The guide barely looked at me. Her voice was smooth, practiced, but clipped, like she was speaking from a learned script.

"The first floor: Offices. Meeting rooms. Mediation center."

Almost clinical.

"The basement: Food preparation. Banquet hall."

The scent of cumin and rosemary. Warm, but impersonal.

"The upper levels: Residence for Adherents."

The elevator, spotless. Almost too clean.

Everything was dog-related. The paintings. The sculptures. Even the way they spoke.

I paused to admire the statue of a jackal.

"Some *others* among you might recognize the jackal as Anubis, but recognition is not understanding."

Did that bitch just lower-case me?

Another statue. A three-headed dog.

"Cerberus is the multi-headed dog that stands sentry at the gates of the underworld. Think of us more like guardians of the crossroads," the guide explained. "We are the light that pierces the dark and illuminates The Way."

"We who?" I wondered. All I saw were followers and joiners. They said the food would be free but I felt like I was paying a whole lot of attention for some low-grade bullshit.

I raised my hand. The guide called on me, reluctantly.

"The festival. The ride operators. How do they fit into all this?

"They don't. They are merely service providers."

The guide turned her back to me and didn't acknowledge me again for the rest of the tour.

Even Brooklyn and Myra noticed.

We were escorted to a communal dining hall. No chairs. No tables. Just thick, plush pillows arranged in circles.

Shoes off. Knees on the floor. Calm before feast.

Myra and I were the only not-white people in the whole building.

202

We lined up, plates in hand. Dry, cold buffet. Chokes.

"I see why this shit is free."

A Cerberus Method devotee leaned close to Angus. A whisper. "A special visitor will arrive soon."

At some unseen, unheard signal a door opened. A man walked in. He was wearing a black ceremonial robe over a stark white long-sleeved tunic. In his hand was a scepter. On his head was a mask. He wasn't a muscular man but he was substantially built. His hand, visible beneath the long sleeves of his tunic, was fair-skinned, healthy. The kind of hand that had never seen hard labor but might be well suited for surgery. Through the gauzelike sleeves of his white tunic I could see hints of detailed tattoo work.

The mask was shaped into the long, angular snout of a black jackal. Thin. Predatory. With high cheekbones that gave it a regal but unnatural presence. The ears were tall and pointed, damn near spear-like, stretching the wearer's silhouette into something inhuman. Paired with robes, it tried to make the man something else. Something you were supposed to fear and revere.

It was carved from lightweight ebony. Dark and polished like wet stone. With fine etchings scored into the surface. Symbols. Maybe prayers. Maybe warnings. Maybe just for show. The mouth sat slightly open, just enough to show a row of fangs, lacquered in gold but not for threat. These were decorative. They were meant to seduce.

The eyes were blacked out behind veiled lenses. The wearer could see out, but nobody could see in. That was the part that stuck with me. A mask like that, it didn't just hide your face. It erased it. Whatever lived behind it didn't wish to be known.

And it didn't just sit on the head. It flowed. Down into a hood. Into the robes. They swallowed the wearer whole. When they moved, it wasn't like a man walking. It was like a shape shifting through the dark.

Anpu's scepter was smooth, dark wood. Polished from years of handling, its weight meant for presence, not war. The head was carved into the shape of a jackal, its lines elegant, almost serene. Less a beast, more a watcher. Glyphs spiraled down the shaft, their meaning lost to time or hidden behind ceremony, but the way Anpu carried it left no doubt. This wasn't a relic. It was, like a judge's gavel, authority made tangible.

Anpu spoke, his voice a measured tide, rising and falling with purpose.

"Since the first fires licked the dark, we have known: there is dross, and there is gold."

He let that sit, taking our measure as much as we were taking his.

Oh, this motherfucker's good.

"The wise of old, the seekers, the sacred fools, they all sought to separate the two. Wheat from chaff. Husk from grain. Base metal from divine essence. You've heard of alchemy? Mere whispers of a truth too great for the unready mind. The legend speaks of lead turning to gold, but the lead was never metal. It was always the self, the crude, the common, the unformed. And gold? The gold was never precious metal. Gold was enlightenment. Gold was transcendence. Gold was freedom from the gravity of the lesser Self."

Homeboy could sell water to a whale.

"But the true mystery has been lost," he went on, slow and steady. *"Even the word itself, alchemy, is misunderstood. They think it means chemistry. But no. Al- means 'the' – a contribution of Arab invaders. And Chem- is Kemet, the land of the black soil. The land before false names were laid upon it. Alchemy: to be like the Kem-au. To be like those who knew the weight of the stars and the whispers of the cosmos before we were tricked into ignoring, mistrusting our psychic potential – shackled."*

Cold as hell. Reminded me of Jeff Fort. Even I wanted to believe, for a hot minute. But then, I caught the way his shoulders moved. Not like a prophet. More like a pimp.

"This is what The Cerberus Method is. It is not a philosophy. It is not a faith. It is the forge." He let his gaze sweep over the room, slow, deliberate. *"And you,"* a slight pause, the weight of it dropping like a coin in a slot, *"are the ore."*

I looked around. He had them. Hook baited. The silence around the room was complete.

"The city that was once called Chicago fell," he said. *"We said it would. We read the patterns in the water, the echoes in the sky. And now, the world shifts again. A prophecy unfolds. A new singularity approaches, but not the feeble dreams of ma-*

chines merging with mind. No. The singularity we speak of is far older, far greater: it is the moment where the Select and the Infinite become one. The moment when those prepared step beyond the boundaries of what materialists call 'reality.'"

"In the ancient teachings, Cerberus, stands sentry at the boundary between the living and the dead. But Cerberus is not a guard dog. It is a gatekeeper of Selves. The Self that Was, the Self that Is and the Self that Shall Be. Three heads, three truths. Those who feared Cerberus were unready. Those who knew its meaning understood: transformation requires each face be met."

"You must pass through trial and drain the last vestiges of the Self that Was."

"You must pass through fire and burn away the conceits of the Self that Is."

"Only then, when the blood runs clean and the mind runs still, can you become one with Cerberus and ascend to the Self that Shall Be."

I caught Angus beside me, leaning forward, entranced. Wolfman Jack had a good rap, I'll give him that. His dope would knock freebase off the top of the charts.

"It is not violence for its own sake. It is sacrifice to align the celestial gates. Without the proper blood, the stars do not sing. Without the singing, the Countess – The Unfettered Self – cannot rise. And if she cannot rise... the world remains filthy with choice."

Who the fuck is the Countess?

"You are here because something in you knows," Anpu continued. "Something in you has been reaching, even before you had the words for it. We, the temporarily earthbound, have always sensed it, the heavens are not distant, the stars are not cold fire. The universe is a living system, and movement between worlds is not only possible, it is inevitable. Those who rise do not rise alone. They reach back. They pull the next of us upward. And the chain continues. Forever."

Now, this part, I knew this kind of talk. This was the close. You make them feel like they're already in it, like to walk away would be betraying something inside themselves.

"A butterfly flutters and summons storms. A single word, rightly spoken, echoes across eternity. A heartbeat, in the perfect moment, is a key in a lock unseen."

205

Half Jim Jones. Half Morris Day. There ain't a mark in the world that's gonna pass on this gamble.

"We feed the body, sharpen the mind, elevate the soul. Every sense sated, every weakness burned away, every folly discarded. This can be, for some of you, the threshold of transformation. A crucible of becoming."

That *some of you* part, yeah, that was the power move. That's how hustlers lock you in. Like they doing you a favor. Make people start clocking the competition. Nobody wants to be the one left ass out.

"And sometimes, even, the ultimate supplication. The surrender of the fetters of the mortal coil."

Oh, hell no. Is this dude talking about ritual suicide? Am I the only one hearing this?

"For others..."

His voice cut sharp. I watched the way people flinched just slightly, some of them leaning forward like they could pull themselves into the in-crowd if Anpu saw how much they wanted it.

"For others, this may be the last time your shadow darkens our halls."

Breaking hearts and minds. Delivery was just a little flat, though. Rehearsed. Gigolo shit.

He let the silence hang, stretching just long enough to make a few people shift in their seats. His eyes lingered, scanning us like he was already sorting the chosen from the discarded.

Wait. Did that motherfucker look dead at me?

Then, slow, deliberate, he nodded.

"The Countess shall rise."

And was gone.

That mask was cold. I'll give him that.

I took stock of the other watchers.

That one looks like her panties just melted. She's in. That one over there looks like he'd lose every round of the shell game. He might as well empty his bank account now. But that one... that look in his eye. Pure ambition. Sizing up the ladies in the room like a peeping tom who just discovered yoga classes. He wants Anpu's job. He won't last.

Let me shake my black ass free of all these marks and joiners.

◎◎◎

Angus exclaimed that this was "the most welcoming place I've ever seen!" I raised an eyebrow. I took that as a slight against Ras Piankhi and Lion Order but I let it slide.

He talked like he was about to straight-up bust a nut over how "honorable and honest" they seemed.

I wasn't feeling it, I mean, the mask was cold, no doubt, but that food tasted like sand sprinkled with smoke, and all that shit about butterfly farts, cosmic freeze tag, and them prophesizing The Collapse? I'ma need to see the pedigree on that one.

That shit was just cubic zirconia for hard-up goofies.

Like tilting your head, squinting, and swearing you saw Emmanuelle's nipple through a scrambled TV signal.

Still, I let Angus have his moment.

Brooklyn was less gracious. "Can we get back to the streets, please?"

Chapter Twenty-Six

I was still sitting on money I earned from the Avanti job when I heard DeRico barking at Necro over the salvage yard phone. He sounded pissed. Something about a truck. Said he needed it back. But this wasn't just any old truck on any old day.

The Motorcycle Club fronted a guy the money to buy it. Problem was, he didn't know jack about running a truck — didn't even know shit about a manual transmission — and fucked it up by putting diesel in a gas engine. Rookie errors. He got spooked by the misfires and the rough running, so he hobbled it to a parking lot and left it there like a dummy. Like patience was gonna fix the shit. Couldn't run the truck. Couldn't pay the note. Getting in deeper-by-the-day with Haunted Town. Bad math.

One half of the restitution was surrendering the vehicle. The other half was none of my business.

But the real problem? The truck was in Wisconsin and Haunted Town had no-go status in that state. Crossing state lines would've been interpreted as an act of war by the dominant Wisconsin MC.

The truck was sitting in some shitty town north of Milwaukee. I knew how to drive a stick. I knew how to drain fuel. I knew how to flush a fuel system and, in a pinch, heat an engine block if the diesel had started to gel. This wasn't just a retrieval job. This job had my name all over it.

◎ ◉ ◎

I waited under the El stop at Wabash and Lake for Jake to arrive. The Shitbox screeched to a stop.

"InkSpot! Get your black ass in the fucking car." I wasn't expecting to have Necro along for the ride. He patted the rear seat next to him. I threw my big duffle bag full of tools and a small fuel transfer tank into the trunk and jumped in beside him.

I settled in and immediately felt something sharp in my rib cage.

"You know what this is?"

I stiffened.

"I could puncture your lung right here and watch you deflate like a tire — Milwaukee, Jake! — You ever heard of the Mann Act, SmokeStack? It's a law that says any Black man found carrying a white woman across state lines is assumed to be doing so for the purpose of white slavery. That shit is still on the books to this day. The good thing is that while you may be a bitch, you ain't a white bitch — so unless you got a pink surprise in your pants we should be alright. You got any surprises in there HackySack? Open up. Let me see your secret."

"You better not rip my shirt." I'd gotten creative and had my tennis shirt embroidered with my own logo, atoms smashing into each other — my version of what a flag for The Grid should look like. It was a tough look.

"Or what, LackSnot? What the fuck will you do if I cut a hole in your cute blouse?"

"We gon' have a real fucking problem if you fuck up my shirt. I might not beat the knife, but you might not either."

A tense silence hung between us.

"I'm just fucking with you, HackDick. You looked scared as fuck." He laughed. Put the tanto knife away. "I'm just here to make sure you don't rape poor Jake. In fact... Let me get in the front seat. You look like you might try to rape me."

Necro dropped a little of the edge and settled into the ride. He turned, resting his elbow on the bench back giving me my first clean look at the spider web tattoo on his elbow. Six rows. Six years behind the walls. Audy Home? St. Charles? Joliet?

"Now, tell me about this Slugger you always carrying. How you get your name on this mug? I want one with NECRO on it. I expect you to bring me one. Don't make me ask twice."

Necro turned back to watch the road. "You know... I remember when I was the only Black Skinhead in this town."

"Oh, so you do know your black ass is Black! This is progress."

"Fuck you, HackShit. Man, if it wasn't for me, you motherfuckers wouldn't even have a lane to ride in."

"Maybe you were the only Black Skinhead in The Jewel, but we been pounding the pavement for a hot minute in Fourth World, Joe. You definitely got the Mexican trophy, though."

"Man, fuck Fourth World. And don't call me Joe. Fourth World ain't shit but weed heads with revenge fantasies. The Jewel makes Skinheads. Fourth World only supplies the raw materials... like you, SlickDick. Just waiting to get shaped by your betters."

"Don't underestimate Fourth World, Knee-Crow. I know for a fact The Bronzeville Bully was doing this while you were still fighting over gang sweaters, and he is Fourth World — womb to the tomb. Y'all was just some bald punk rockers before we showed up and gave y'all soap and deodorant. Nice gay-prest pants, by the way, Joe."

"Yeah, and both y'all motherfuckers came to The Jewel to run with the big dogs to make a name. Clothes don't make or break shit. In fact... if shit is so sweet in Fourth World, ChokeNut, why the fuck are you climbing the totem with Pama?"

Peaches flashed into mind but I sidestepped the memory.

"Either a. I'm trying to take your job, or b. I'm trying to catch you slipping so I can slide you a good old fashioned raping."

Necro laughed. "There might be hope for you, yet, LimpCock. If you wasn't

211

so black I'd kiss you."

Jake sang under his breath, "Everybody... needs somebody to love..."

About an hour and a few toll booths later I was seeing Wisconsin with new eyes. Other than going fishing with Tremor, I knew very little about this state. Milwaukee and The Grid are rivals in most things. Baseball, football, beer, food, organized crime, etc. so it never even crossed my mind to give it more than a cursory look.

Necro clocked my interest in his spider web. Said, "why don't you ask me what you want to ask me?"

I countered. "What? Why you ain't got a girlfriend?"

"Fuck you CheeseDick"

I asked the question that was hanging in the air, "What got you stranded behind the walls?"

"See, RatSnot, normally I'd sock a motherfucker in the mouth for asking some dumb shit like that, but this time I'm gonna lace you with some of *our* history."

"You know that intersection where Lincoln, Sheffield and Wrightwood cross?"

"Yeah. By the 7-Eleven. With that ugly-ass project-looking building."

"Exactly. All of that, straight out to the lake, used to be Puerto Ricans and Mexicans. We used to bang those streets hard as fuck. Mexicans, Ricans, some whites. Every corner contested. Every wall a battle ground. Dipping forks. Dipping crowns. Set got thrown up on Sunday. Set thrown down by Monday. You talking about sweaters, SlopShit, we were peeling caps. I ran hard with a serious Set. The name ain't important.... let's just say we were crazy and anonymous."

I clocked it. Insane Unknowns. A serious People Nation Set.

"Anyway, there used to be a bowling alley at that intersection. It was the kind of place that parents went for fun and the rest of us went to shoot pool and hatch schemes."

I nodded. "What happened?"

"Urban Renewal happened. First the weirdos came and, when they magically didn't get killed, the area got labeled as "in transition," so next up? Yuppies with dogs and yoga mats. Next thing you know, fences, snooty restaurants, stores where they only let people like us in two at a time. Rent? Jacked up. The bowling alley? Gone. Turned it into a racquetball club."

"But shit, it's right in the trenches so of course we wanted to check it out. One of my guys said something slick to one of the yuppie ladies and some people on both sides got chin checked. But, you know, we do this shit for fun so they got laid out. Now, in our terms, that settles shit, but these motherfuckers called the cops. Said we were banned. Not just from the club. From the intersection."

I raised an eyebrow. "The whole intersection?"

"Right? Like I'ma let some yuppie jagoffs run me from where I was born and bred. So, that night... someone... I won't say who, but someone brewed up a cocktail and gave The Newtown Racquetball Club a light show. Two or three somebody elses might have shot up the place."

"I was the easiest one to recognize so I got snatched up. I ate that whole charge."

"While I was down, the whole Set got erased. Locals. State. Feds. Everybody came down. The whole team. They split us up. Blacked out our mail. Stomped on our dicks.

You ever try to send a kite and get it back in pieces, smelling like piss? That's when I started to understand why they call that shit the Slave State."

I just let that one sit. I'd never been behind the walls so all my witty observations probably would have been out of place.

"The ones that stayed outside? Went ghost or went underground. Ya know?"

"I know," I nodded.

213

Necro leaned back, dropping the bass out of his voice for the first time.

"Without a flag to fly and boxed in by every kind of enemy — and no, I never once considered no new flag — I fell in with the other outcasts. Broomie. Bubba. A few others. We wasn't all in there for the same shit and we wasn't in there for the same kind of shit. Some of us, like Bubba, just had wino time. He was the Skinhead. He had a little tape deck. Tapes. Magazines. Books — That Joe Hawkins book was the first book I ever started and finished — We just mobbed up to kill the boredom. Accidentally got into the new thing."

"Like I said, Bubba had wino time. He got out, linked up with Malört and Moonstomp — they were his Skinhead connects on the outside — and breathed life into Pama City Skins. He left us his tape deck and some tapes so when we came out we just fell in."

"When I came out I ain't even recognize the neighborhood. But, I'll tell you this," the bass coming back into his voice, "that racquetball club never opened back up. Yeah, they won the battle, but we still here making them pay tithes with clutched purses and sleepless nights." He laughed. "They can't build a fence high enough keep the boogeyman out."

He let it rest a beat.

"See, y'all think only Fourth World and The Scratch put pressure on The Grid. Don't underestimate Fourth World? Nah, bruh. Don't count out the motherfuckers who live behind enemy lines."

◎◉◎

We reached Milwaukee. Hit the surface streets. Drove past a giant postal service building. Parked The Shitbox in back of an anonymous repair shop on the south side of town. We were greeted by a Milwaukee Skinhead named Knuckles.

Necro and Knuckles exchanged some small talk. I got introduced as a new member of the crew. "This is the cute motherfucker that's banging Brooklyn, if you can believe that shit." Knuckles laughed, threw Jake some keys and pointed the way to a plain white pickup truck. That was our cover. Jake pulled out some large white magnetic signs and stuck them to the side while Knuckles and I packed the truck bed with my tools and the transfer tank.

214

"Alright, Crockett and Tubbs, I got shit to do here," Necro announced. "Make daddy proud."

Back on the road we looked official in our Mobile Diesel Repair truck.

We found the truck in a K-Mart parking lot in the working-class town of Glendale. I hopped out, put on my mechanic's jumper and did the dirty work while Jake quizzed me on Blues Brothers trivia.

I disconnected the feed line. Drained the bad fuel. Checked for gumminess. Sure enough, the fuel was gelling up. I broke out my roasting pot and coals. I made my heat source and shoved it under the engine block. While the wax in the diesel softened up I went through the process of completely evacuating the system. Flushed the filter. Checked the plugs. Closed it up. Refilled it with gasoline we'd gotten on the drive up.

"That should get us running and to a truck stop for a proper filling."

"But first we have to see if this puppy wants to crank." I sent a prayer up and turned the key.

A click, a grind, then nothing. No turnover. "FUCK!" I felt my stomach drop out. "What are you missing, Jackpot? What the fuck are you not seeing? What would Tremor do? What would Tremor do?"

Jake offered, "Fix the cigarette lighter."

"Fuck you, Jake. Fuck you very much... Oh, fuck. Rookie error. I didn't prime this bitch."

It took some cranking and a jump to the battery from the pickup but we got it turned over. The engine was running a little rough but that would probably be the case until I got it on the expressway and had a chance to get the whole system warmed up. Anything beyond that was probably something that any reasonably skilled mechanic could solve. I reluctantly admitted to myself that these were Tremor's teachings at work.

"I'ma start calling him Yoda," I laughed to myself

I followed Jake as far as Milwaukee. He went to grab Necro while I did trucker shit. Went through the weigh station. Then pointed the nose to The

215

Grid, singing along with Strength Thru Oi! to pass the time.

I didn't gloat openly but I knew I'd passed a big test. I alone had made money for Pama and I also expanded the crew's imagination about what other jobs we could start pulling. We celebrated with some Johnny Walker Black until I was cross-eyed.

I woke up hours later on the office couch wishing I had some water. Those motherfuckers left me there to sleep off my drunk like a street rat. I just made money for everybody on this team but was the only one without a ride.

"Fix that up, nuh?" As Ras Piankhi would surely say. "Rubber on wheels is better than rubber on heels," Tremor would say.

I plopped myself on the back seat of the bus. "Well, all I got is a big green limousine."

CHAPTER TWENTY-SEVEN

Like the song says. Saturday night is alright for fighting.

There was nothing special about this Saturday night. July. Warm. Clear. It was about 10pm. Belmont was wide awake. People hustling all directions. To the Avalon nightclub, to the fuck-and-cut hotel, the transsexual sex workers plying their wares, the arcade — Dennis's Place for Games — the Mexican restaurant under the El or maybe Leona's around the corner.

Viddy and Herb had come to The Jewel to run the streets. We stood in the doorways of Fleet's Inn with Pama — Angus, Necro, Brooklyn, Myra, Broomie, and Malört — plotting what we'd get into that night.

Four men strolled up. Just a little too old and plain to be trolling this side of Belmont. A bit too burly. The short one with the pale freckled face, the moptop haircut and unfinished mustache led the pack. A trio of burly Iowa corn-fed hardheads covering his back and sides. These guys oozed casual toughness. Navy Pea coats. M65 field jackets. This wasn't a practiced pose. This is who they were. Calloused, unseasoned, working class white men who drank hard and probably beat their spouses harder.

They looked out of place on Belmont, but my crew didn't give them a second look. We carried on with our joking and drinking. Politely parted ways so they could pass. But they didn't pass. They stopped. Like this was exactly where they wanted to be.

"Hey Jackpot."

"What's up? Do I know you?"

"No. You don't know me, but I know all about you."

He handed me a business card. It had their logo "White City Resistance" in Old English script, their neighborhood, Uptown, the slogan "Join The White Man's Fight," and the names of their main players. Davey, Steve and Lil' Jim.

In the 80s, we thought business cards were a sign that you'd made it. If you were a gangster, the calling card could double as a threat.

I recognized this Set. An all-white gang of political street brawlers. Their mission was to keep Uptown white and working class.

◎ ◎ ◎

The South Side neighborhoods from South Park Avenue west to Calumet, and from 63rd south to 65th had been called "The White City" in homage to the white plaster and stucco that was used to make the city's architecture gleam for the 1893 Columbian exposition. The Museum of Science and Industry is one of the few remnants of The White City. The rest was burned down by striking factory workers in 1894.

Even us public school kids knew the North Side was never part of The White City but when people from Jackson Park got a little bit of money, they moved north. They took their nostalgia and the name with them. They called their new home turf The White City, but over time that fell out of fashion. They settled on "The Jewel."

Some people misunderstood the name "The White City." Thought it meant whites-only. There was some of that, for sure. But racial obsessives like "The White City Resistance" took it to the nth degree. Brought that shit back.

They didn't represent all of The Jewel, but the White City Resistance had some hard allies. The Popes, the Gaylords, The Jousters, and other white mobs. They operated under the umbrella of the SS Action Group. They kicked off a campaign of social pressure on anyone they regarded as undesirable. The real estate industry wasn't into the working-class part of their philosophy — the working-class ain't got no money — but tolerated the racist gangs because they created useful tension that had houses flipping hands.

Real estate brokers made money on every flip.

218

It was an observable pattern.

Realtor sells to Black family "A" who moves in down the street. *Cha-ching!* Realtor scares white family "B" into selling low. "Darkies are coming! Your property value is going to tank! Get out while you can!!!" *Cha-ching!* Black family "C" is interested. Realtor steers them to a lender. *Cha-Ching!* Family "C" buys at a high interest rate. *Cha-ching!* Family "C" gets terrorized by White City, or whoever, wants to move, sells low. *Cha-ching!* New family "D" buys in at a high interest rate. *Cha-ching!* And so on.

Death is good for the undertaker. Panic peddling and white flight are good for the realtors — Fatbacks.

Cha-ching! Cha-ching! Cha-ching!

◎◎◎

I sized up their main talker. Late 20s, maybe early 30s. Baby-faced. Short. Stocky. Wore a moppish hairstyle. Looked like an average Cubs fan. I hate The Cubs. What the fuck does he want?

He was in a mood to pontificate. Quickly steered the conversation to politics. Yawn. He thought he had something interesting when he said we weren't real Skinheads. "Skinheads are white, working-class warriors." We'd heard all this shit before from the uninformed. I dryly corrected him with the history that we all know, but he was adamant. This 101 level shit bored me.

Words and threats were being thrown by both support teams while Mophead and I had our war of wits. He ran through the greatest hits. Blacks and welfare. Blacks and crime. Blacks and IQ. Each topic handily batted away with retorts that dragged white Americans right into the same accusations. Rolling it all back up to corporations and dishonest politicians.

Alcohol. Bravado. Race. The disagreement turned into a standoff. His supporters stood firm trying to look menacing. Covering Mophead's back. My team milled around looking annoyed. They didn't have time for all this chatting. Wondered why I was even entertaining the bullshit.

Viddy whispered into my ear, "Steal on that motherfucker" — basically, punch him in his baby face — but I was in my bag and starting to enjoy

219

trouncing him, intellectually.

Mophead pivoted. Bristled at the sight of Black men associating with white women. Steered the conversation to integration and miscegenation and eugenics. I continued to deflate Mophead's shallow points. "Don't blame us because you made white women hate you."

Malört jumped in. "And we don't ask permission to fuck who we want to fuck!"

That cut deep.

Wasn't nothing left to do but ring the bell.

Brooklyn flicked a cigarette. The answer, a beer bottle shattered at her feet. That was the spark that ignited the brawl that we all knew was coming.

This was really what they'd come here for.

I'd bested him with words. Now I was going to beat him with fists. I connected. However he thought this would go this surely wasn't it. This was on him. He came to see Jackpot and that's who he was meeting. I gave him a fair one. No force multipliers. No cheap shots. Pure pugilism. Just as I outclassed him intellectually I outclassed him in fisticuffs. His little movement was getting knocked down a few pegs.

Necro cheered. Brawling was his native language and he was ready to have a chat. He mixed it up with their biggest guy. The rest of my team tangled with the other Resistance. There was a whole undercard battle going on. Every member of the enemy team was locked up by someone from my mob of unconventional fighters. Those guys never had a chance. Whatever they thought they were ready for had left the conversation the moment they called my name. In my sideview I spotted Broomie. Standing off to the side. Watching. Not mixing it up with anyone.

Mophead's guys were locked up. They were in a fight for their dignity. For their survival. Set upon by boots and fists. Malört's bottle smashed across a forehead. Brooklyn had her thumbs in someone's eyes. Viddy body slammed somebody else.

Mophead's guys were brawlers. They knew how this went. Someone had to lose. They just didn't know it would be them.

My fist compressed Mophead's nose flat against his overgrown baby face. Out came the reliable flow of red. Once a fighter sees their blood — especially if it's from their face or head — they either panic, retreat or attack.

He didn't have time to choose.

I moved in.

He was getting my best work.

"You just hit the Jackpot. Remember those words."

To his credit, Mophead wasn't ready to go down so I punched him about the face two or three more times to drive the point home. Solid jabs straight to his face, knocking his head back. Speed bag shit. I was scrambling his senses. He was fighting to stay upright. Suddenly wanting to get off the ride. He knew that if he went down he'd be the guest of honor in a legendary Skinhead boot party.

Desperate now, he rushed me. Tried to pin my arms down with a bear hug. I deftly evaded his grasp. Backed away into the space between two parked cars. A useful corridor for me. He stupidly stepped into the trap. Quickly realized he had no lateral escape routes. Backing out would look weak.

Again, he lunged, Directly into my uppercut. I connected cleanly to his chin. He fell like a dead weight. I let him. Stepped to the side. He stumbled forward. Landed on the asphalt just shy of the wheels of a passing car. I knelt above him. Battered the back of his head. Tenderizing his face with the blacktop. He lay there like a used-up condom.

That fight was over.

[Knock]

Malört grabbed me by my shirt. "Cops! Meet in the alley!" I took a long arc around the back of Fleets, wove through some gangways, reconnected with my team. They cheered. Patted me on the back. Even Necro was celebrating. "That was a proper fucking booting, JackWood! Skinhead shit!" Broomie was absent.

Headlights. A car. Light green. Unmarked. Barreled towards us. Detectives! We scattered. I went east, towards Clark Street.

The detectives spared the rest of the gang. Made a beeline for me.

Chain link fence to my back. I scrambled. Over. Lost my footing. Fell eight feet to the ground. Headfirst.

I saw stars. Came up dizzy. Everything blurry.

I looked back. Two white men. Plain-clothes. We locked eyes but they didn't try the fence. I ran.

The passenger slapped the dashboard. "Clear the block! Catch him!"

I knew the streets. That alley was a tricky one.

Most alleys go straight through. Not this one. Just when you least expect it, it banks west. Spits you out on Wilton. A one way. The wrong way. Very fucking inconvenient.

That's my chance.

I dashed across Clark Street. Into the parking lot for a high-rise apartment building. Some hood cats I knew, PR Stones, lived there. Think! Pausing to push doorbells is dumb. No good. Hide! I ducked between two parked cars. I could only get half of my body underneath. Fuck my shirt. I tried harder. No luck.

Wait. See what happens next.

Straight ahead. Creeping south on Dayton street. "Is that...?"

It looked like the green cruiser. Did they stop? Did they keep going? Are they going to come back up Clark? I lost my glasses in the fight. Couldn't see shit. Think! Risk it all. Stay put.

At least it ain't raining.

Rats. A few cars down. Eating McDonald's. Fuck! A childhood fear. "Just stay down there. Don't start no trouble, won't be no trouble."

Clark Street was alive behind me. Daring me to try. Could I make it to the safe shadows of L&L Tavern? Should I try the PR Stone? Where is my crew?

Everything seemed like a trap waiting to be sprung. I breathed. Calmed down. My heart slowed down to normal pace. I replayed the night in my head.

I wondered how my crew had made out. We are a smart mob. We know the nooks and crannies around here. That should help. But that was a hard ass beatdown. The cops won't let that go unanswered.

I waited. Uncertain.

I heard voices. A young couple. Civilians. They were crossing the parking lot, heading east, towards Dayton. Wrapping up a night on the town. The woman had good instincts. Spotted me. Bent at the waist. Like she couldn't believe what she was seeing. I growled, "keep fucking walking!" Threat in my tone. She snapped up. Looked straight ahead. Hustled across the parking lot with rapid, deliberate steps. "Good girl. This ain't your problem."

What would she tell her friends she saw? A car thief? A rapist? Who cares? Just keep fucking walking.

Then... I fell asleep. Dumb.

Morning light. The sound of cars starting. Not good. Enough hiding. Get the fuck out of there.

I plotted my next move. A lady came out of the building. Walked to her car. I waited. She let the engine idle. Then threw it into reverse. Wheeled backward. Gave me cover from watchers on Dayton. I sprung up, darted out. Kept my head low. Shot west across Clark. Ran toward the same fence that fucked me up the night before. Gonna hit it again. No mistakes this time. Perfect position to snake through the neighborhood to Belmont El. From there to Fourth World.

I cleared Clark. Scaled the fence. Crested it. One leg over. That fucking car came screeching to a halt right in front of me!

What the fuck?

223

Where the fuck did they come from?

I wasn't ready to go to jail, yet.

Hopped down. Landed on my feet. Ran south. Jumped the first little fence. Hopped the next fence. Yappy poodle inside started barking. Can't rest here. I hopped into the next yard. Ducked under the back porch. A shitty hiding spot. Fucking sitting duck. I waited for the cops. They never came. No radios. No foot-chase. Nothing.

Weird.

I didn't dwell on it. Still gotta get the fuck out of The Jewel. Fight and flight.

A silhouette. Fuck. Another fucking rat. This one dancing with its shadow on the stairs above me. It would be funny under different circumstances. Sid Bucknor's "You Can't Win" could have been the soundtrack to this shit.

Back to my escape plan. Think, Jackpot. Think!

Belmont is the closest. That's where I'd normally catch the train. Probably crawling with cops. Addison. Far. A challenge. Still, the better choice. Addison it is. They are looking for a black jacket. Not a bright orange one. I turned my flight jacket inside out. Made a fast dash.

I chose oblique passageways. A gangway here. An alley there. Pause. Look out for pursuers. Keep making deliberate choices. Steady progress. This breezeway. Pause. Clear. Scope out the next gangway. Hit it. Hop the gate. Lay low. Calculate the next move.

I chipped away at the distance, methodically. Made it hard for pursuers to follow me. Made it impossible to anticipate my next move. If they wanted me, they'd have to earn it. I was in the best shape of my life. Being in survival mode helped. Fight and flight.

I reached Addison.

I hung in the shadows of a gangway. Scoped for cops. Clear. I dashed across to the station, swiped my transit pass. Up the stairs. Took my place at the far end of the platform. Still watching out for pursuers. The train was taking its slow, sweet time. Fuck! Here. I hopped on. Grabbed the rumble seat.

Ducked down. Didn't exhale until we cleared Belmont.

I was on my way back to Fourth World where I could disappear into Terror Town.

Can't this train move any faster? Another passenger, a young man, noticed my agitation, my watchful glances and the blood on my jacket. He looked away when I met his gaze. The code of the city: See everything, say nothing. It ain't your blood, it ain't your business. I turned my jacket right side out, covered my head. Rode to the end of the line.

There were several messages on my answering machine congratulating me. Asking where I had disappeared to.

I called Brooklyn. "Did anyone get busted?"

"No. Nobody went to jail. We went to the playground behind Ann Sather and kept drinking. We waited for you. You sent that guy to the hospital. He was all bloody and drooling and shit."

"Wait... Those detectives didn't catch nobody?"

"What detectives? The only cops I saw were in front of Fleets."

"What about the car that came down the alley?"

"I never saw them again."

No detectives? Nobody went to jail? Well who the fuck was on my ass?

Something about Broomie's inaction during the brawl gnawed at me.

I steered clear of The Jewel for a couple of weeks. Told Lion Order to avoid The Jewel, but no one ever came knocking and, as wayward youth do, we slowly went back to normal and reclaimed our places on Belmont.

Except Viddy.

He was done with The Jewel. This wasn't his war. "Watch your back, Moe. That wasn't no one-hitter-quitter. They gon' be selling you for parts if you get caught slippin'."

225

Necro felt it too, something heavier than just a street brawl. He'd gone to war with men like that his whole life, and while he lived for the aggro, he pulled my coat one day while we were sitting at Aetna.

"That wasn't just an ass-handling. They came to put a noose on you, but you slipped out and fucked up their main guy. This ain't over for them."

He hammered the point: "Your latitude around The Jewel? Walk on egg-shells. Word gets out, White City's allies gon' get a new noose. Ain't nobody lookin' for me, they know better. And they know where to find me if they want me. But you, SmackNut? You definitely got a greenlight on you."

CHAPTER TWENTY-EIGHT
The Pen CNN
White Shitty Resistance

When Grapevine, the Divine stood to speak, the condemned felt pardoned, and the righteous felt judged. Games were forgotten. Faces became as stone.

This next one might replace "Bad Man Dan and Two-Gun Green,"
Listen up close, and you'll see what I mean.

This one is called "White Shitty Resistance"

The White Shitty resistance. They came to fight,
Thought they could run up the score under the Belmont lights.

But there's new rules in The Jewel, I guess they didn't know,
That the kids on the mean streets are all go. All pro.

White City tried to school them about some tired old shit,
But these kids got grit and they know how to dodge a hit.

Took some scalp off old Davey, that wrong-headed freak,
Sanded down his nose on the hard concrete.

The other three got they asses kicked, from pole to pole,
Foot so far up they ass, they breath smell like bouncing soles.

It was sad seeing them laid out, in puddles of red,
Whole crew tasted defeat, boss man left half-dead.

One angelic upstart humiliated their king,

The face of a lion with a scorpion's sting.

He stood over Davey. Said "I beat tricks like you every day!"
"Now get the fuck back Uptown, bitch. Sit–Stay."

He's building a legend, he's making a name,
But know there are those that would snuff his flame.

Let's see what happens next in the shitty inner city,
Two things for sure, no mercy and no pity.

(He let that hang for a beat)

They call this the slave state, but we freer than most,
This the Pen CNN. The squares call it a toast.

I don't sell no lies, no wolf tickets, no doubt,
Grapevine, the Divine signing the fuck out.

He stepped down from the cafeteria table.

His audience faded back to their rituals. Dominos slapped, cards riffled, dice tumbled, and soft voices debated stats from yesterday's basketball game.

CHAPTER TWENTY-NINE

Necro sat next to me on the hood of The Shitbox. He sat a little too close. His thigh touched mine. I shifted away. He shifted closer.

This asshole was always testing.

He broke the silence.

"We been talking about you. And while I think you could fuck up a perfectly good wet dream, Malört is backing you."

He had the cold gaze of an under-appreciated HR lady.

Is this motherfucker about to offer me some Amway?

"Besides the work we do with Haunted Town," he explained, "there's also the scooter trade. There's a pipeline that runs between Skinhead crews in The Grid, Detroit, Indianapolis, Minneapolis, Milwaukee, and St. Louis."

"Connected Skinhead crews in each town steal what they can from college campuses or scooter shops then transport the goods to one of the other cities where it gets repainted and fitted with a new serial number. This keeps all the main crews connected and united. And as for police, they ain't looking for no little scooters, and if they do come up on one... wrong serial, wrong color, wrong model. They ain't got energy for chasing all them threads."

The salvage yard that Necro sat on, I learned, was a crucial part of the pipeline. "The Pama part of the operation is keeping Italian scooters running.

Pama gets broke down machines back in action and in the pipeline because, obviously, these machines can't be taken to legit repair shops."

I sensed that I'd graduated within Pama, and that this wasn't information to be shared with the rank and file — and certainly not outsiders.

He looked me in the eye.

"We cutting you in, BumFuck, but what's given can be taken away."

Was that a threat? A condition? A warning?

CHAPTER THIRTY

DeRico had a problem. Malört pulled me in.

Haunted Town was being pressured by the Coffin Nails, a national one-per-center motorcycle club. The offer, a threat really, was to either patch the elite patch holders of Haunted Town over to Nails or agree to share The Jewel with the Coffin Nails. Let them run their business and their territory rocker without static. This flew against Haunted Town's philosophy. They were the home team in The Jewel and didn't want to get absorbed into some other culture. They also didn't want to inherit the wars that come with that other patch.

"We are a one charter, one generation club and we like it that way. The men wearing this patch will be buried with this patch and we ain't gonna patch over to outsiders." Two MCs running The Jewel rocker would only lead to the bigger, more violent club absorbing or neutralizing Haunted Town.

The Nails had already moved some high ranking Nomads into town and they were making a big show of being present, whether or not Haunted Town, or anyone else, liked it. Not wanting to kick off a war with a big club the local Council of Clubs asked Haunted Town to put up with it while they figure it out with National. But Haunted Town had other ideas. They wanted to pull the wheels out from under The Nails, but they couldn't have Haunted Town patch holders implicated.

They called us.

Broomie thought it would be easy. "Just steal the bikes of the two reps that they send to Council meetings."

The Sergeant-at-Arms agreed. "A charter president without a bike can't address the Council."

The Haunted Town Sergeant-at-Arms laid out a map showing the location of all eleven Nails visitors and their bikes. "The top man rests here. His number two, way over here. Bring those two bikes to salvage," DeRico said, "Haunted Town will either chop them or sink them in the lake."

The problem was logistics. How would we steal these Harleys silently and quickly? Necro's tow truck can only take one bike at a time. That means a lot of time on the road and a lot of time for alarms to be raised.

I looked over the map.

"I don't think it will work."

Silence. All eyes turned to me. None approving.

"Unlike HT, under Nails covenants, the bikes are the property of the club. Any officer of the MC can take any patch holder's lady or his bike. If you want to put them out of business, we've gotta take them all."

Doubt-filled faces.

"That's a big job. Don't let your mouth write checks that your ass can't cash," the Sergeant-at-Arms warned, sounding a lot like Tremor.

"I can get a box truck that can definitely hold eleven bikes. We roll up. Lift the bikes up. Heavy straps. Load them in the truck. Then go get the next one. Silent and efficient. We can do that in one night. We time it right and no bells get rung."

DeRico gave the plan a nod. "But now you have to deliver. And it's got to be before the next Council of Clubs meeting. Monday. That gives you five days to put Nails on heels."

"Bet. But since we are doing all the dirty work, Pama should get to chop and part every bike we pull."

"Hell no!" The Sergeant-at-Arms.

DeRico interrupted. Looked me in the eye. Made a quick calculation.

"Okay, The Town can agree to that. Keeps our hands clean. Your show, Jackpot."

Broomie looked annoyed that I'd be a shot caller. Went ballistic as soon as we were alone.

"That plan is stupid. He shouldn't even be talking for Pama. He can't be trusted. He's gonna fuck up our whole operation."

Necro brought his mouth to my ear.

"Alright, CockMouth, it's do or die."

◎◉◎

Getting to Tremor's truck yard wouldn't be quick or easy without my own wheels. It was way out in Maywood. Roughly equal distance between O'Hare and Midway, for good logistics. As with most hustlers, one of the big goals is to turn dirty money into clean money. Tremor had managed to land some contracts transporting US Mail and phone books. He was running multiple routes and employed a half dozen drivers.

Tremor's small fleet of box trucks sat behind a twelve-foot high gate and was guarded by a couple of hard nosed vegetarian Dobermans, Cercyon and Ceryx. I could probably get the dogs on my side but I needed the key to the gate.

For the next couple of days I stuck close to Tremor. Helping him on his local runs. Pretending to finally be interested in "the family business." I paid close attention to his key rings. Made note of the three keys that he didn't use for anything else. I figured at least one of those would unlock the three heavy-duty disc padlocks that secured the gate. It was his pattern to have all his locks keyed-alike. Which key was the question.

I had my driver's license and as long as he was with me he was cool letting me wheel the trucks. He got comfortable. Liked being driven around through his errands. "Take your old ass to sleep. I heard you pacing like the ghost of Christmas past last night."

"Little boy, I can't sleep with yo' cross-eyed ass behind the wheel," he joked. "You'll wind up killing me, Jesus and, two or three more motherfuckers."

I did some of my best driving to put him at ease. I deliberately made a wide loop around in the direction of his favorite fishing supply shop. As I hoped, he perked up and had me stop there. His extra keys were on the bench seat between us. He hopped out.

"Take your time. I want to put in some solo miles." After a brief back and forth I was on my way to the hardware store to get the keys copied.

Thirty minutes and twelve dollars later I had what I needed.

I returned to the bait and tackle shop. Tremor was busy regaling the men with tall tales about catching the clap in Korea. That man had more stories than the Bible.

I walked in. Tremor pointed in my direction. Asked the grizzled old fisherman, "Who dat look like?"

The fisherman fixed me in his steel blue eyes. Replied, "he looks like you... but why is he so much more handsome?"

Without missing a beat Tremor replied, with a self-satisfied smirk "he had a better-looking daddy."

◎ ◎ ◎

I got Viddy out of bed. I needed a ride and I needed him to not ask questions. I gave him just enough information and money to get him to ignore the rain. After a quick stop at The Food Exchange, we were heading west.

Soaked but safe, I fed my wheel man some weak lines. "You should jet, playboy. The lights... the motor... they might draw attention." He threw up the deuces and put me in his rearview.

Tremor's guard dogs kinda knew me by this time but I was still nervous.

I tried one key.

Then the next.

Then the third.

None of them worked. Fuck!

Slow down.

Breathe.

Try the keys again.

The dogs sat on their haunches, eyeing me curiously. They almost seem amused.

Click.

Second key.

Exhale.

The gate swung open.

I crossed the threshold.

The dogs pounced.

They were a bonded pair. They worked in unison. One knocked me down. Snarled in my face. The other clamped down on my pant leg. Thank god for boots. Instead of ripping my face off, they sniffed all around me.

The meat? They want the meat! I carefully reached into my backpack, scanning their faces for permission. Pulled out the steak chunks I'd gotten from Food Exchange for this exact purpose. Showed it to the now-very-obedient dogs. I tossed meat to the side.

The dogs might have been vegetarian by training, but dogs are dogs.

They chased the meat. My heart pounded. Before I could even get to a truck the dogs were back at my heels. I gave them the rest, throwing it as far as I could. "Now get lost. I need the minutes."

The trucks were different years but all the same model, Mercedes-Benz short bonnet straight trucks. I picked the one with the longest box, the most fuel and the quietest brakes. Just my luck, it was also the one with the flaky clutch. Oh well, I'm not about to let a clutch ruin a job. I hopped in, cranked it up and rolled out past the gate. Hopped out. Closed the gate. Said bye to the dogs then hit the road to Pama's salvage yard.

I checked the time. Early. Good.

"Come on, Clutchy. Play along." Yes, I was talking to myself. The expressway was all brake lights and construction. "I swear they are fucking up the road, not fixing it. Job longevity." Let me feed this truck some city streets. I swung east. Me and the clutch were getting along like a married couple that fought a lot but mainly for the makeup fuck. "There it is. That's how it's supposed to feel."

The steady grumble of the diesel engine was like meditation. It didn't have the roar and rev of a gas engine but the torque made me feel like I was one with the road. Felt like I was driving a tank.

I cruised through Holy City.

Past the tricks and the hookers and the pimps and the kid who was out shooting hoops in the rain fully convinced that practice could carry him from the projects to the major leagues. "I hope you make it out, kid."

Past the stray dogs and the Darkside Mob MC clubhouse. Past the tall housing projects where my aunt lived. Where my cousin got stabbed in the neck with an ice pick. Where we used to line up for Chokes.

Truck and I were in deep agreement.

I passed what looked like a Muslim spot. A bunch of kids who looked a lot like Lion Order sitting inside. Sign said "BUSA Tribe." Interesting. Graffiti explained. "BLACKS IN THE USA." The graffiti on the next block shouted "THE CEO IS THE ENEMY!"

East a bit more, then I hooked it north onto Ashland. Straight line to the Pama yard from here.

The detail crew jumped into action. Doctored the license plates to transform the "8" into an "0" and the "F" into an "E." Fourth World tricks. I double checked the strap anchors inside the box, making sure they were ready for prime time. The crew stuck some big white magnets to the truck doors. "MOVING COMPANY." Looks legit... as long as the ink doesn't run.

I ran them through the plan one last time.

Team 1: Me and Showbiz. I was on the wheel. Showbiz was on communication and support.

Team 2: Broomie and Icepick. The muscle. It was their job to lift the bikes with the tow straps. They were to ride in the cargo hold of the truck. The bikes weighed about 600 pounds wet. Should be easy work for these two.

Team 3: Necro and Malört. Perimeter security. Follow in a chase car. Shotguns at the ready. Loaded with alternating shells of birdshot and 00 buckshot. Sometimes you want to maim, sometimes you need to neutralize.

Each car had two-way radios for communications and Radio Shack police scanners so we could hear them before we saw them.

"I'll do all the ramp work, getting it in and out, and the bike tethering, then we roll on to the next bike. Two minutes per bike, then we move. No fucking around, no talking and no sloppy work." I made sure they all had steel-toed boots and good gloves.

Broomie didn't like taking directions from me but this was my plan and if he wanted a cut this was the only way to get it. Honestly, I'd rather have had Angus on this job but he wasn't part of this circle. Broomie grumbled his acceptance and we got back on mission. We rolled out of the salvage yard. Top of the list? The most isolated bike so we could get our system down without stress.

We found the bike. An all business Shovelhead parked outlaw style outside an apartment building in Evanston.

One weakness with outlaws is they expect other outlaws to follow a code and they never believe they will be touched by civilians, so they cut corners on security. We slid up. I went easy on the brakes and left the engine idling. "In and out, like date night with Necro's mammy." I hopped out. Quickly, quietly extended the ramp. The muscle went to work.

They looped the straps between the spokes of the mag wheels and hoisted. It was a bit of a tricky balance. Heavy tools in the bike's saddle bags, but the muscle made it work. Loaded the bike into the truck. Strapped it to the internal supports. Wheeled off.

"Good work. Ten more. Let's assume they won't all be this easy."

The next three, scattered in Roger's Park and Uptown, went easily, but the fifth bike wasn't where we expected — out front on Lovejoy street in Jefferson Park. No time for misses. I slipped into stealth mode. Went around back. There it is. In a shed. Upon on blocks.

"Fuck! A big ass padlock!"

I crept to the alley side of the shed. Used my elbow to quietly break the glass. I climbed in. I needed something to pry off that padlock. Found a breaker bar and climbed back out. I slid the bar through the lock and snapped the bracket off the wooden door. It gave but I wasn't as quiet as I needed to be. The muscle went to work.

A light went on in the house.

A long haired, hardened biker with leather for skin, looking like Son of Svengoolie, came out yelling that he'd kill whoever he found. It was a moonless night so we had the advantage. He came slowly down the creaky wooden stairs. We paused, holding our breaths, calculating the smartest move.

Clunk! Then a thud.

Showbiz with my bat. The biker was out cold. The hit was probably harder than necessary but he was still breathing. We dragged Svengoolie into the shed. Tied him up. Made a barricade with some heavy cinder blocks.

The muscle loaded the bike.

The next few bikes were scattered around Logan Square, Wicker Park, and Lincoln Park. We were cooking. The heist became fun. We turned it into a game. But the last one — on the last one we got sloppy.

Icepick got cocky. He felt like a pro. Didn't want to use the straps this time. He was sure he could lift the bike with his bare hands. "I deadlift 500 for shits and giggles."

He grabbed the rear wheel between one of the mag spokes. The wheel started to spin backwards. The bike rolled up his chest. Knocked him down. Pinned him to the ground. Icepick laughed nervously, "Which one of y'all is my spotter?" I stood there, aghast.

Icepick followed my eyes with his own. His hand and wrist were caught between the wheel and the swingarm. Blood. Flesh. Bone?

"Whose hand is that?" His eyes seemed to ask. Then, the realization... the recognition...

His instinct was to scream but Showbiz was on the job stuffing a leather glove in his mouth.

His muffled cries. His eyes... pinned wide... staring at everything... at the stars... at nothing...

We tried... We tried to get his hand out.

Icepick lost two fingers. And a thumb. Frayed flesh hanging like chewed up rope. So much blood. We made a tourniquet out of a carry strap. The same one he didn't want to use.

Showbiz and Broomie loaded up the bike. I scraped up Icepick's fingers. Fought down the urge to add my vomit to the mess. Necro and Malört stayed on-point. Just in case the ruckus drew out any busybodies.

This was more than fucked up. I never imagined... I never planned...

[Knock]

We roared away.

Necro and Malört took Icepick to the emergency room.

I drove north to Milwaukee to drop the bikes at Knuckles' garage — Broomie and Showbiz next to me. We put The Grid behind us.

I counted the mile markers, meditating.

Broomie did something I never expected.

He cracked.

"You guys think they'll be able to save his hand? Yeah. They definitely will. That dude is the bionic man. They'll be able to sew that shit right back up."

Silence.

"He saved my life. I was spiraling. I was on a crash course with hurting somebody... or myself and he pulled me out of that shit. He's the reason I lift. I was a scrawny ass kid, always getting my ass kicked around by my stepdad, until he taught me how to bulk up. I wasn't getting my ass kicked no more. I was the one doing the ass kicking... That's how I got the name Broomstick... And we do it all natural. No juice. He's gotta be alright. If Icepick can't lift, then... I don't even want to think about it...."

Silence.

What was there to say?

CHAPTER THIRTY-ONE

Haunted Town MC's next move was visibility. All over The Jewel. Let no one suspect they had pulled the caper.

The Coffin Nails arrived at the Council in cages — that's what bikers called cars — and couldn't explain themselves.

No MC President and no more than one patch holder can attend a Council meeting without functioning bikes. Coffin Nails was essentially a full charter of eleven bikeless patch holders. If this were any other wannabe club they wouldn't even be allowed in the room. Even the Coffin Nail leaders had to acknowledge that they weren't qualified to set up an MC charter in The Jewel.

The Nails were told to take their patch out of state.

Haunted Town played their part. Pretended to be sympathetic. Promised to put all efforts into finding the bikes and punishing the thieves. They even invited the Nails to the clubhouse for some drinks. Not pure hospitality. Just to prove that the bikes weren't on Haunted Town property.

DeRico pounded me on the back like a proud uncle.

Broomie seethed.

The Nails had top-tier West Coast club-style bikes so parting them out to midwest outlaws was easy business.

This heist proved to be one of the biggest payloads for Pama City Skins.

We gave Showbiz his cut and everything else to Icepick. It was the least we could do. He'd given more to the job than all the rest.

That said, he was off the streets.

Skinhead life had cost him too much.

He hung up his boots, stopped calling himself Icepick, reclaimed his government name, Christian, and found a job slinging beers at the baseball park.

CHAPTER THIRTY-TWO
The Pen CNN
Horseless Headsmen

Grapevine, the Divine stepped onto the table in the center of the cafeteria. His fellow inmates — schemers, soldiers, old timers, and young hotheads — froze mid-sentence and mid-move, letting dice cool and checkers idle. The guards watched with that bored, ready-to-pounce stillness.

I know you wanna hear "Good Doing Wheeler" or "Honky Tonk Bud,"
But my tongue's like a razor, so this one might cut.

This one is called "The Horseless Headsmen"

Steel horses thundered, power in their hands,
Dreams of new dominion over unclaimed lands.

But shadows whispered secrets, thieves with silent tread,
Each horse stolen swiftly, like spirits of the dead.

Morning found them stranded, pride crushed in defeat,
Their plans lay in ruins, ambitions incomplete.

The Jewel jeered and mocked, their invasion now a jest,
No more kings of asphalt, just riders dispossessed.

Stripped of all their glory, left with empty hands,
They faced a harsh new future, in unknown, distant lands.

Now the road runs endless, their spirits frail and worn,
Searching for new places to rest, their hearts heavy and torn.

In the prison of their minds, they plot another day,
Hoping for redemption, where shadows don't betray.

The Grid might bend, but The Grid don't blink,
The question everybody asked: "What them motherfuckers think?"

It's sad what happened to the muscleman's hand,
You know who gotta tighten up and think through every plan.

Don't judge him too harshly. Win some, lose some,
At times it's gon' be easy, other times it's gon' be gruesome.

Now me and you know, exactly who did that job,
Who undermined the dreams of that iron and leather mob.

Now we don't name names and we don't tell addresses,
The only way it gets told is if you know who brags or confesses.

(He let that hang for a beat)

They call this the slave state, but we freer than most,
This the Pen CNN. The squares call it a toast.

I don't sell no lies, no wolf tickets, no doubt,
Grapevine, the Divine signing the fuck out.

He stepped down from the cafeteria table.

The moment dissolved. Cards whispered. Dice danced. Dominos cracked
sharp in the stale air.

Time Longer Than Rope

CHAPTER THIRTY-THREE

This was one of Mrs. Macksey's cold shoulder nights.

I followed her into the kitchen under the pretense of seeing what was in the fridge. "You need to put that cold shoulder away. Got everybody and they mama gossiping. Wondering why you are so sweet to me."

"My house. My moods. My rules."

The rumble of video games and Skinheads singing along to music filtered through the door. "Yeah. And you need to keep your doors locked. Necro said some sick shit, and I don't know where the joke ends."

"I can take care of myself."

"Just dial it down a bit."

"This is cute," she smirked. "We are arguing like a married couple."

"You're gonna get me killed," I laughed.

"There's that smile. Has Trouble missed Mummy?" She'd decided that Trouble was her pet name for my dick. She really knew how to play me.

The door swung wide. Angus. "Man, we gotta get going. I don't want to miss the openers!"

Tonight promised to be a huge night. Prince Buster at The Wild Hare. This was a rare chance to see a living legend. The Prince was one of the few originals still touring in 1985. Our greatest wish was to impress Buster so much that he'd be compelled to halt the tour, fly back to London or Kingston or wherever, on the next thing smoking, and report to all and sundry that our mob was the one to beat, and that everyone else had better get their shit together.

This was our night as much as it was his.

Skinheads love the history of the subculture, and most of us had a deep appreciation of the British originals, but we didn't get many opportunities to see those bands. We had to settle for other British bands like The Police and The Clash and we'd even been in the building the night that "Frankie Sank The Bismarck." That was the night that the English band Frankie Goes To Hollywood played in The Gold Coast and literally made the dance floor cave in. Their four-on-the-floor beat made the audience — it seemed like all of Fourth World was there — stomp in unison. We literally brought the floor down.

Yes, we were there for all that, but that was just entertainment. And hardcore? Hardcore was Battle Royale.

But this? This was heritage. As Skinheads we felt a deep connection to the subculture's originators. We wanted to show how serious we were, and put our own twist on things.

I joined the others in the living room. We looked like the sharpest mob of all time. Myra and Angus looked like the real deal. He wore a classic three-button suit, while she rocked a Bad Manners t-shirt that she'd modified to fit her form. Slim-with-curves popping out. She complemented that with a black mini skirt and thigh high leggings, held up with lacy two-tone suspenders. Very fucking sexy. For shoes she wore some black penny loafers. Coins in the slots.

Dead giveaway. Tourist. Still, cute as fuck.

I felt like I'd won the lottery in my black Ben Sherman, white braces and real red/green tonic suit. The pants hemmed and stovepiped to my precise specifications, and Florsheim brogues. I pulled it all together with an authentic Crombie — one of the few in The Jewel — draped over my arm. Sadly, it was pure show. Summer. Too hot for wool. I topped it all with a tilted stingy brim hat. This was more Lion Order-style than Pama, and it came to me as natural as breathing. You couldn't tell me I wasn't number one on the look good charts.

If Brixton could see me now...

Rounding out the crew, Brooklyn wore a matching tonic suit, tailored into a 2-piece blazer and skirt set. She borrowed some cues from Myra and went with thigh-high stockings held up by suspenders. Made everyone wonder where they led. For footwear she chose some wing-tips she'd ordered from Shelly's of London. She looked good enough to eat, and she wore it all effortlessly. She had a way of being stunning but unassuming. It was both endearing and captivating. 54 and 46. Those were our numbers.

Mrs. Macksey glowered. Locked the door behind us.

The atmosphere at The Hare was fully charged. Everyone had guesses about who the "Special Guest" would be. Good money was on Millie Small, but I was doubtful. Derrick Morgan? Nah. I don't think The Gorgon and The Prince would share a stage. Laurel Aitken? Maybe.

I divided my time between Lion Order and Pama, trying to be the same-old-Jackpot to both teams. The Fourth World mob had a lot of questions about my absence, but there was no way to tell them that I was dipping my wick in an older white bird, and that nothing could tear me away from the education I was getting.

Yinka made her way through the crowd. Stood next to me. Her boyfriend, Poindexter, hung in the background. As clueless as always. We made some smalltalk before she got down to why she was hanging there. "So, are you full-time Puma, now?" Pointedly reducing The Jewel crew to the status of a smaller cat. Despite the occasional crossover of crews, they were still rivals.

"Nah, I'm Fourth World. From the womb to the tomb. You know I rest my head in Terror Town."

"Yeah, well, you ain't been around, and it looks like your cute bird has you by the nose."

"Ah, yeah. She's good people. You should come record shopping with us one of these days. She likes all kinds of music." Yinka grinned at my tawdry come on. "Nah, you know I only like one genre, but I've heard that Pama is very... experimental... Watch your back with them."

"Sounds like you know something I don't. What's the word?"

Yinka sighed. "Listen, you came to Lion Order as a baby. We raised you. We all raised each other. You went to Pama fully-formed. You really gonna throw away that history... our... heritage so you can be at the bottom of their totem pole? You were home and then... what? Pussy? It looks weak, King. I'm not calling *you* weak, but it *looks* weak."

Weak? Yinka knew that would push my buttons. I'm sure anger flashed across my face. She turned another screw.

"But really... What exactly went down with Peaches? I've heard rumors... and maybe what I heard was enough... but I feel like there's something I'm missing." She looked into my eyes searching for answers. I looked away.

I clenched my jaw, held my breath. The truth choked in my throat. I flashed on that night in the tunnel... *"I said PUNK HIM not DUNK him!"*

I needed an escape, any escape, and then like a Godsend, Poindexter popped up, sporting a brand new Gumby hairdo. The last time I'd seen him he was in the middle of the floor at the Power Plant chanting "Jack Me Farley! Jack Me!" A real House head. I hated him. But, let's be real. I was jealous of this man's success with Yinka, and my own failure.

Happy for the distraction, I turned my attention to him. "What's up, Poindexter? I see you got rid of the Jheri curl. Must be saving bank on pillow cases."

Yinka glared. She recognized my evasion for what it was, but responded only to the bait. She dragged Poindexter away, shot me a look. Said "Pumas ain't Lions and Fourth World ain't a bed and breakfast."

"Everything cool?" Brooklyn asked, when I rejoined her.

"Yeah. Cooler than the other side of the pillow. Just crew shit. You know how it goes."

"I do. I do." She had her own tightrope to walk between Pama and her Milwaukee Skinhead team.

250

Yinka's words bothered me more than I let on. I stewed on them and didn't pay much attention to the opening band, Papa Iston & The Ronkers.

Only the opening notes of The Prince's classic tune "Hard Man Fe Dead" could put my mood to rights. "Dis one ya about King Emmanuel I of the Bobo Ashanti."

> *You pick him up*
> *You lick him down*
> *Him bounce right back*
> *What a hard man fe dead*

Chills ran down my spine.

Prince Buster! The legend in the flesh. A bonafide architect of the culture giving us what we needed to survive. His band ran through all the greats and finished up with a medley of Skinhead favorites. "Wash Wash," "Wreck a Pum Pum," "Time Longer Than Rope," He even pulled a sharply dressed Malört up on stage for "Rough Rider," blessing her with a star turn for the rude tune.

Buster killed it. The set wrapped up with a stage full of Grid ruffians dancing alongside The Prince. Trying to touch him. That would have been enough. We'd have gone home happy. Some of the audience members called out for one of his best-known tunes. "Waah yuh waan hear?" Buster asked, feigning ignorance.

"Judge what? Nah man. Mi fren dem seh it nuh healthy fi me to play dat one."

"Tell yuh what. Mi gwaan let me good good fren from England do wha him do best."

A voice boomed out, *"I want all you Skinheads to get up on your feet..."*

No! It can't be.

"Put your braces together, and the boots on your feet."

Chills again. Shit, my chills had chills.

251

"And give me some of that old moonstomping!"

All around me, slack, disbelieving jaws.

Symarip!

Roy Ellis and Monty Neysmith emerged from the shadows to the loudest cheers of the night. They ran through a 30-minute set of their top tunes. "Skinhead Moonstomp," "Skinhead Girl," "Must Catch a Train," and "Phoenix City."

They wrapped up their set with "These Boots are Made for Walking," their take on the Nancy Sinatra classic. I lost all sense of cool and sang along. I grabbed the mic and danced on stage.

This was a Skinhead Reggae lover's wet dream come true.

The Wild Hare was a sweatbox.

Following Symarip's revue, The Prince re-emerged from behind the curtains in ornate Rasta robes. He was followed onto stage by a trio of Rasta drummers. I was only partly surprised to see Ras Piankhi playing the Funde, the heartbeat. They sent the whole room into a trance. They rumbled through "Oh Carolina," baptizing the non-believers with Groundation spirituals. It felt like the Nyahbinghi drums could lift the whole building and take us to our eternity. This audience had never experienced anything like this.

The night of Ska and Rocksteady had been transformed into church. They sent us out floating on clouds. I missed this feeling. I missed Root Temple. I felt torn.

Ras Piankhi and the elders led. Lion Order followed. I felt left out.

I pivoted to Pama.

The older Skins crew had an inside track on an after party with some Skins who'd traveled from Detroit. Hard stuff. Not my thing. I resigned myself to crawling the streets with Brooklyn and the younger crew.

We stopped by the Cabaret Metro to see who was playing, but it was dead. We changed directions and ate at Fleet's Inn. The kids were drunk, high, loud. I felt like a babysitter. They wanted to go to the Macksey House to crash. Fuck. I guess that's it for this night. I wondered what I was missing at Root Temple.

Mrs. Macksey met us at the door in her housecoat. Gave Brooklyn the evil eye. "Mr. Macksey needs to be up early. Please don't make a ruckus. Especially you two."

Whatever.

I put on a mixtape that was made to coax the punk rock lovers into a Rocksteady mood. First up was "The Tide is High," the Blondie remake, followed by the Paragons' original. That led to "Wear You To The Ball," the UB40 version, followed by UB40's "Dream A Lie" which led to "Baby Baby" by The Vibrators then Delroy Wilson's "I'm Not A King."

Like magic, the couples paired off. Hands roamed.

Necks were kissed. Negotiations for next steps were made.

A typical Saturday night in this upstart branch of the Pama City Skinhead Crew.

Brooklyn felt good. Better than good. I had one hand on her ass. The other behind her neck, pulling her tongue into my mouth.

Her hands were at work. Caressing the front of my pants. Getting her best friend into fighting form.

I forgot all about feeling left out.

Thought only about sinking into this hotter-than-hot Skinhead girl.

CHAPTER THIRTY-FOUR

I needed to piss!

There was a line for the downstairs bathroom. I made my way upstairs. Mrs. Macksey blocked my way.

"Are you planning to fuck that skinny bitch in my house?"

"Most likely," I thought but I sensed that was the wrong answer. I stammered.

She fixed a steel gaze on me, grabbed me by the waist of my pants and pulled me into the bathroom, locking the door behind us.

"Get that dick out and put your hands behind your back," she ordered, smirking when she saw I was already getting hard.

"Good boy. Not tonight you won't."

"That little slag is not getting this cum tonight. This is my house. My cum. My dick. My balls." She looped her fingers around my sack and yanked straight down, generating excruciating pain. My head spun. She knew what she was doing and what this would mean for my night.

She muttered under her breath, tugging and twisting my balls. Cursing me for daring to even think of fucking Brooklyn under her roof.

I went delirious.

◎◎◎

I should add a little background...

Back in 1984, after Brixton, Lion Order spiraled.

Angry. Sad. Rudderless.

I went on a destructive streak. I'd wade into enemy territory and spark scuffles. I didn't care about the outcomes, I just wanted the war. We really should have been putting pain on those motherfuckers in Joliet but it was much more convenient to do battle closer to home.

Fourth World had several Sets that proclaimed themselves "Skinhead Killers" and I wanted to meet each one of them. They didn't bother to distinguish between Skinhead crews, and we didn't care which side of the Folks/People divide they fell on. The hatred was mutual. We all caught hell and we also gave.

We being me, Viddy, Peaches — this is before — and sometimes Herb or Showbiz. We formed our own hit squad. Took our anger out on anyone who looked at us sideways. We were no angels. We lived for it. My lucky Louisville Slugger drank liberally from countless combatants. Some of the shit we dished out was filed back in triplicate. What happens next might have been one such filing.

The 71 bus east to Terror Town. Coming off an evening with Siobhan. I clocked some enemy operators eyeballing me. Didn't recognize them. Maybe I'd crossed them. Maybe they were just out for sport. They looked like they were People Nation, but I couldn't get a good read on which Set. I was sure that they wouldn't be Folks on this part of The Grid — not on the 71 bus going east — but none of that mattered. They were giving clear signals that I was the bunny, and they were the hounds.

"Y'all see that corny ass Prep?"

"Skinhead mark."

One of them called out: "Hey tight pants, What you ride?"

I sized up the mob. There were five of them. There was the big dumb one.

The brute. The enforcer. His lazy eye made it hard to track his focus.

The little yappy one in the Pirates cap and the Converse shoes. The instigator. He's got an overbite. I think that makes it hard for him to shut up.

The one who looked like a genuine sadist. The big keloidal scar on her neck telegraphing that she took it as harshly as she gave.

The one who was clearly the boss. Dark shades. Impossible to read.

The last one. The fifth one — it took me a minute to figure out his role. He looked nervous. A little too cute of a baby face. I looked him over. Ah, he's the virgin. This ain't about me. It's about him. His initiation. He's got to get some blood to prove himself. If they come after me, I'm gonna pop his cherry, Lion Order style... Welcome him to the game.

I yelled back: "I ride the bus, just like you, motherfucker."

The bus driver read the tension through his rear view mirror. Decided that he didn't want the trouble. Jerked the wheel to the curb. Threw all the doors open. Yelled: "THIS BUS IS OUT OF SERVICE! EVERYBODY OFF!"

Fuck. I was almost to Terror Town and could have slipped into the shadows.

The other team got off about half a minute behind me. I didn't want to lead the hounds to my house so I dipped across the Illinois Central train tracks and made my way around back of the Hamilton Theater. "These motherfuckers done put up a fence!" Fuck. When the fuck did this shit happen, and who approved it?

They followed me into the alley. Stalked. Cornered. My back to the 12' high fence. My knife ready. I might not take out all five, but at least two of them will have some stitching up to do. Blades are to be felt, not seen. I hid it behind my wrist.

They crowded in. My arm made a clean arc. I got the virgin from the corner of his left eye, to the corner of his mouth. On the way back I slashed again. Split his cheek into flaps. "Bleed, bitch." He used to be so handsome.

The Virgin panicked. Tried to catch his blood in his hands. Watched it puddle in his palms. Watched it run through his fingers. He ran screaming from

257

the alley. His hysterics distracted his pack mates for a few beats.

I took my chance. Lunged at Lazy Eye. I cut deep into his lower back but not deep enough. He was stunned. Grabbed at the wound, but he still had some fight in him.

Now it's on.

They circled. Closed in. Laid into me.

They beat the shit out of young Jackpot for who knows how long.

Keloid had a special talent for beating the shit out of dicks. She made a point of attacking every soft spot with her feet and fists. I curled up into a fetal position to protect my head, but she knew where to find the good meat.

They punctuated the beatdown. "IMPERIAL!" "INSANE!" "VICE LORD!" "SKINHEAD KILLERS!"

I had drawn a very bad card that night.

But I won a consolation prize. Lazy Eye got sloppy. Played it loose. Forgot he was injured. I jammed my knife into his bloody wound. The reddest red ran. Kidney tapped. Enjoy your ER visit, playboy.

But it only made him madder. He fought against the pain. Laid into me. But then it became too much for him. He fell out. They got distracted. Focused on him. Forgot all about me. Picked him up. Walked him out. I was fucked up. My dick felt wet. My nuts throbbed. I could barely move. I didn't want to be left alone. I reached out. Clawed out. A silent plea for help from the motherfuckers who put me there. But they ignored me. Turned their backs to me. Walked away.

I lay in that piss-stained alley, surrounded by rats, for hours.

Daylight peeked over the lake. Home. I pressed myself up. Made my way to the edge of the theater. Peered around the corner halfway expecting Keloid to jump out and finish the job. Nobody. Clear. I hobbled out of the alley. Stumbled across the tracks. Limped into the alley by the gyro shop. I clung to my neighbors' gates, pulled myself home. I grunted and struggled up the three flights of wooden steps. It hurt to raise my foot. To put weight on my legs. I fumbled with the key. Went in through the kitchen. I crossed paths with Tremor on my way to my room. Another sleepless night for him. He didn't even look in my direction.

I closed the door behind me. Pressed my back to it. Looked at my bed. I was afraid to lay down, but I wasn't strong enough to keep standing.

Nothing makes you feel more alive — more human — than pain. That's what torture survivors say. I understood.

I tried to mentally locate the pain. Self-diagnosing but scared to look.

I let the bed win. Closed my eyes and fell in. Tried not to cry.

I don't know if I fell asleep or just blacked out. Shit went dark.

I came to about 20 hours later. Still delirious with pain. Forced myself up out of bed. My balls felt like they'd been crushed in a vise. I waited until the house was empty. I stripped down. Stood in front of my full length mirror.

My face was fucked up. "This is a face that will never get another girlfriend." I can't show myself to Siobhan's mother. My black eye looked kind of cool, though. That would be a good story. There's an upside. Right?

My ribs seemed to be alright. I was all scraped and bruised but my limbs weren't broken. I was okay, for the most part. For the most part.

I pulled my shorts down.

My right nut was swollen to the size of a golf ball. Throbbed. I felt a lump inside. That wasn't there, yesterday. Fluid? Blood? "Fucking Keloid!"

I should go to the hospital. Mom is a no for that. We'd already been through that behind another brawl. And I was getting known at that hospital so using a fake name wasn't an option.

Tremor. Another no. He was fully sick of my street fights. He'd be a brick wall, and probably bend up my ears about how back in his day they had to pick cotton while boll weevils feasted on their nuts or some other shit.

Fuck it. I have ice and aspirin.

After a few days the worst of the swelling went down, but that lump was still there. Nutsack looked like the elephant man.

I wanted normal. I tried to get dressed. Tight pants pressed on the swelling. Hurt like a motherfucker. I pulled them on anyway.

I wondered if my dick still worked. I pulled out a dirty magazine. Flipped to a favorite photo shoot. Got hard. That's good. I started stroking. Nutsack protested. I modified my approach. Switched to the left hand. Finished. Came. An explosion followed by a dull throbbing ache. Little streaks of blood.

The next day. Same pain. Less blood. And the next. Same pain, less blood. I reasoned I was healing. Jacking off was therapeutic.

Siobhan missed me. Wanted to see me. Wanted to fuck. I couldn't say no to that. But it was a trade off. Pain for pleasure. I didn't want her see I was injured. I measured out my dick strokes. Changed the tempo. Adjusted the angle to give my right nut some relief. Siobhan thought I was very creative.

Fucking wasn't the problem. Busting a nut was. That's when it hurt the most. I'm talking about seeing yellow stars, orange lights and green clovers levels of agony, so I had to put the grand finale off for as long as I could – or as long as I wanted.

The upside? I developed greater stamina. Durability. I became a fucking machine.

A trauma-trained fucking machine.

Over time, I began to associate sexual arousal with pain. With discomfort. I got used to it. Then I began to enjoy the familiar ache, and eventually I started to look forward to it. Like, "yeah, I'm alive and my dick still works. Watch!" I wore it like a secret badge of honor. When I was feeling self-destructive I'd throw all caution to the wind and bash Siobhan or Yinka or Brooklyn's body with no care for how much it hurt me. Other times I'd relish in the slow strokes. Hit it from the side. Make the fuck last. Put off the fever dream for as long as I could. Try to beat my own personal stamina record. Kick off. Release. Oh, now I get why they call it the little death.

Mrs. Macksey was one of the few people who knew the details of my injury.

She learned about it very early in our relationship.

We were on a couch in her office at her Old Town art gallery. She was folded over and taking a lot of dick. Her husband and son thought she was working late. In a sense, she was. I was giving her some of my best effort. She wanted to help. She reached down to play with my balls. She grabbed me right where it mattered most. I grimaced. Halted. Missed a couple of strokes. Paused to recover. To catch my breath. She took notice. Waited for me to recover. Later asked me about it. I told her the whole story. She responded with tenderness. Gentle care. Kissed all around. Massaged my ache. Her curiosity also unlocked a sadistic streak that would change me forever. She always had all kinds of new kinks to try so I can't say I was surprised when she began to exploit my damaged balls.

"A little mutual objectification never hurt nobody," she said.

She tugged my balls to see how much pain I could bear. She poked around to see where I was most tender. Sucked one, then the other to see if that helped or hurt. Squeezed them at the point of orgasm to see if I'd shoot further. Twisted them to control the pace of my fucking. She even convinced me to try poppers — amyl nitrate — to see what effect they'd have.

I let her have all the time she wanted because, honestly, I was just as curious as she was. It hurt. And I kept coming back.

Because I loved it.

◎ ◉ ◎

In that bathroom, after the Prince Buster show, she abused my balls, threatened to rip my nuts off and ruin me for the night, so that Brooklyn would have to go without.

"Mummy is going to beat the skin off this dick." She had such colorful language.

I nearly passed out when she took my balls, stretched the sac and wrapped it around the base of my dick. This was a new kind of hurt. She kept jacking, fast and cruel. Wanted me ruined. I teared up. Fought to keep quiet. She smiled with her eyes. This brutal bitch knew my weakness. Made me cum. In less than three minutes she had ruined me for the night.

Angry, I pushed her away from me and folded over in pain. My stretched, beaten nutsack shriveled back to shape. She fell to the floor gracelessly, her nightgown flew up. She smirked, self-satisfied. Stood up. Fixed her clothes. Sucked my cum from her finger.

"Don't try to fuck that skinny slut tonight."

I was dizzy and exhausted. My head spun. She quietly slipped out of the bathroom. Left me there.

I rejoined the party. Tried to walk normally. I eased myself into the Lazy Boy recliner.

Brooklyn smiled, handed me a beer and moved to resume our foreplay. I stiffened up. Lied that I'd gotten sick in the bathroom. That I was in no shape for romance. She was horny and disappointed. Rubbed on me. Tried to get me in the mood. Got no satisfactory response.

I joked that she should go see if Angus and Myra needed a third. She looked at me quizzically. "Sometimes I swear you're cheating on me, Jackpot."

◎◎◎

The morning after Prince Buster was really my fault. I stayed around late the next morning after everyone else drifted off. I knew she was upstairs, and I'm sure she knew I was still in the house. My equipment was back in fighting form. She owed me.

I knocked on the door of her bedroom but heard no response. I knocked again.

"Go away. I'll see you when I choose to see you."

I turned the handle. It gave way. I walked into her bedroom... a threshold I'd been reluctant to cross before. One very explicit barrier she'd set early on. "That," she said, "would be disrespectful." I never challenged it.

She lay there, in her night clothes, in the one place that was off-limits to me.

My eyes scanned the room. I could see the touch of an artist in there. The European romance styles were tastefully arranged and nothing seemed out of place.

She turned her back to me. Didn't cover up. "You shouldn't be here."

I stepped to the edge of her bed. She looked up at me. I threw the covers back. Reached down. Pulled her nightgown up. I dropped my pants. She took me in her hand. Pulled me towards her. Into the bed she shared with her husband.

I crossed the line.

We crossed the line.

A gentle fuck. Unrushed.

We lay there wrapped up in each other. I was mostly-alert when I heard footsteps coming up the stairs.

A male voice asking.

"Mom. Are you home?"

CHAPTER THIRTY-FIVE

Angus struck out at me. I dodged. I understood his anger. I didn't want to fight him. I put all my energy into evading his attacks.

Mrs. Macksey yelled at us to stop fighting.

Necro was there. Was the reason Angus came home when he did.

He was being a nuisance. Pretended to hold Mrs. Macksey back from harm. Was actually copping cheap feels. Annoyed, Mrs. Macksey broke free. Slapped him. Left Necro stunned and with no purpose.

In the confusion, he got behind me. Locked me up in a Full Nelson. Bum rushed me out of the house. Down to the street.

Incensed, I spun around. Struck out. Punched him in the jaw.

He laughed. "I'm not your enemy, BlackCock. I just did you a favor. That's a family matter now." I paused. Loud arguing from inside the house. I couldn't make out the words. Didn't need to. He led me away from the Macksey house.

"If your dick wasn't so small I'd ask to smell it. You got a magnifying glass?" Necro joked.

I pretended to laugh.

"Man, I knew you were fucking that hot old bitch. Why didn't you just tell me? That's the kind of shit I like. You're stingy... that's your problem. Stingy and sneaky. That's a good combo... for hustlers."

I remembered his words from that night in Dillinger's Alley. *"We're not so different Señor Jackpot. The only difference is you think your vices are virtues. I know mine are fatal flaws. My lack of impulse control is going to get me killed."*

I tried to break up the tension with some Ras Piankhi wisdom "Teef neva love fi see teef wit long bag."

"NigNog, I don't know what the fuck you just said."

◎ ◉ ◎

Necro wasn't the one who told all of Pama. That was Angus, who told Myra, who told Brooklyn, who consulted Malört, who told Necro — who already knew — and Jake, and all the rest.

The reactions were mixed.

Brooklyn was disgusted. "Fucking family, Jackpot? You gotta fish in bigger ponds, man. That shit is tacky." Her closed off body language made it clear that any warmth she previously held for me was now history.

Necro agreed it was a deep violation of the Pama family, but he added, "any man would do that shit. AssDick was just polishing his knob."

That was one for me. I think.

We already knew what Angus thought.

Malört was less firm, "You get what you take in this world," but still disapproving. "Too close to home."

Jake was ambivalent. The one time I wanted him to have a movie quote he came up empty.

Myra didn't have a voice in all this. She was new to the crew and had already played a bad hand by carrying gossip directly to Brooklyn instead of checking-in with Malört, first.

Broomie now had a legitimate reason to downgrade me. He dug in. "Disloyal." "Shouldn't be overlooked." "Can't be forgiven." Radish backed him up.

Broomie looked happy for once.

Four downvotes and two ambivalents which, of course, meant I was out of Pama.

My dick had divided The Pama City Skins. Just like that, my phone stopped ringing.

◎ ◎ ◎

The straw that broke the proverbial camel's back for Angus wasn't the crew strife or even knowing that his mother had been getting dicked down by his friend. The final straw was Mr. Macksey.

Angus told his father everything he knew. He wanted to hurt his mother. Humiliate her. Make her feel ashamed. It would serve her right, in Angus's mind, if she died alone and unloved.

Mr. Macksey was more bothered by the secrecy than the infidelity. He tried to explain to Angus that Puritan morals don't apply to all and that the concept of monogamy and "cheating" were unfair burdens to place on free-minded people.

Angus snapped.

He wanted his father to go to war, not play philosopher.

Angus needed to get out of that house, that family, so he ran.

He ran east, then north.

He ran to the most welcoming place he'd ever been.

The front door of The Cerberus Method.

CHAPTER THIRTY-SIX
From the Book of Black Teeth
The Communion of Two Cups

This dark, cobblestoned room could be mistaken for a medieval catacomb, until one notices the tools.

Down a flight of limestone stairs, at the bottom floor of what used to be a firehouse, The Jackal works in his lab. His instruments are meticulously arranged: forceps, scissors, bone cutters, scalpels. One tool stands apart, a small, well-worn iron implement, shaped like a worm with a hook at one end. It does not gleam like the others.

Against the far wall, a glass-faced refrigerator hums softly. Inside, bags of thick, red liquid resting in neat rows, each one labeled by a steady hand, dates, details, weight, age, time of disposition, astrological alignment. Essential metadata.

Exsanguation.

At the center of the room, the surgeon secures a small gourd to a metal tray.

The surgeon. The Jackal. The craftsman. Not muscular but substantial. Hands made for precision work. His leather apron tanned from countless rituals. His shirt sleeves rolled to the elbows revealing intricate tattoo work.

He counts every step. Measures every breath. Wasting not a single motion.

He reaches for his chisel and, with deliberate force, presses it past an obstruction. He did not flinch. The tool did not flex.

Satisfied, he selects the archaic hook and begins the delicate process of entering an orifice, extracting organic matter, piece by piece. Each fragment is placed into a ceremonial goblet. Each piece, honored. Each drop, sacred. The feast must complete itself.

None shall be left wanting.

Only now for us does the truth settle in. The gourd is a child's skull. The obstruction? The ethmoid bone that separates the brain from the nasal cavity. This was not crude dissection. This was ritual. Precise.

The Jackal moves with practiced ease, pulling the last piece free. Brain. Human brain.

Excerebration.

The Jackal reaches for a very specific bag of Exsanguation. The one with the right details.

He poured its contents into a second goblet, a perfect twin to the first.

From the shadows, a Re°Cereb devotee steps forward, silent, waiting. The white of their robe glowed under the red ceremonial light. They kneel, taking both goblets in careful hands, one filled with matter, one filled with blood.

Beyond them, the room opens into something larger. The chamber is red-lit, filled with watchers, breathless in anticipation.

Metallic drumming begins. A pulse from nowhere. A heartbeat. Felt through stone.

The Jackal measures his approach, landing satisfyingly on the desired divine number. Joins Erzsébet at the head of the ceremony.

All will imbibe. All will digest.

Where the purest offering becomes part of them. Each piece in its place. Each drop in its cup. Eat, drink. Become the Self that Shall Be.

A communion of carnality and cerebrality for the eaters of the purest uncorrupted untainted.

CHAPTER THIRTY-SEVEN

I looked out my kingpin window. Surveyed Terror Town. Laid out my gear. Put on some music. Plotted my day.

I slid around to check in on Herb. He was sidelined by some health issues.

Depression and something else.

His mother was one of the eleven people who died in the 1977 Loop train derailment. His father sued. Won a case against the CTA. He got three big ass settlements. One for himself. One for Herb. Another for Herb's little sister.

They lived in a red brick three-flat on South Shore Drive, steps away from Rainbow Beach. Other than the color it was unremarkable, but once you stepped in, you could see the signs of new money. Curio cabinets stuffed with things that would only impress poor people. Plates with presidents' faces. Tiny replicas of the Eiffel Tower. The Leaning Tower of Pisa. Little depression-era figurines that smoked miniature tobacco cigarettes. It was like an S&H showroom had exploded here.

His grandmother let me in. I went upstairs. She trailed me.

The walls of his room were bare. Stark white. He had records everywhere. A bunch of musical instruments he never learned to play. Every color of Fred Perry folded and stacked. Most unworn. Boxes of brand new Dr. Martens. Even the ugly ones.

His bed looked like it belonged in a hospital. That's where I found him, even though it was almost noon.

Herb spoke first. "Well, well, if it ain't the Super Skinhead himself. I thought you forgot about the home team."

"Never doubt. I'm loyal to the soil."

"So you say..."

Huh.

There was an extended silence. I looked at his records. Trying to avoid looking at him.

"I'ma go pee."

I dipped through the side door to Herb's bathroom. Did my business. I looked around. Every spot on the wall taken up with cheap art, like the rest of the house. Except. In the trash. A folded sheet of foil with a zig-zagging burn mark running down its face. Some pill bottles. Some with Herb's government name and others with who-knows-who's name. Some little yellow envelopes with residue in them.

Fuck.

My sister said he was running with party people. I never gave it weight. Shit, I lived with party people. Her.

But now shit started to make sense. I mentally clocked all the times he wasn't around. Then it hit me. The rest of us had money problems while he had money ain't-no-problem. That settlement. Abundance can be traumatic too.

I thought about his father. Big ass cars. Rolex. Always running with women who looked like last year's supermodel. Too busy shining to see his son's lights going out.

The grandmother. She's the only one keeping this shit standing.

This wasn't grief. This was a mausoleum gussied up with Spic and Span.

I zipped up and stepped back into Herb's sanitarium.

He was waiting to speak.

"You know... something's been bugging me..." He tried to sit up. "You act like you the only one that took some arrows. We all lost Brixton. Peaches. But you... you the only one that ran to The Jewel."

"Man, we all have our ways..." I said, halfheartedly, trying to suppress my instinct to bristle at the mention of our fallen and really not wanting to talk about my ghosts.

Yeah. My ghosts.

This motherfucker wasn't even at her funeral.

Herb sensed I was detaching. He glared at me. Tried again to sit up. Like he was strong enough to do something. His grandmother, who'd been sitting outside the door, eavesdropping, rushed in. Warned me off exciting him. Quickly showed me the street. Closed the door on my heels.

The exchange ticked me off. This Terror Town claustrophobia was reminding me why I boned out in the first place.

Fuck it.

I walked over to see Showbiz. 78th & Essex. Across the street from where Peaches used to live. He kinda got lost in the shuffle when I dug my heels in with Pama. I hadn't seen him since the Coffin Nails job.

He opened the door.

"Sup, Joe." It wasn't a question.

"Just sliding through to see what's poppin'."

"Keep sliding, Joe. You don't wanna know what's poppin' for strays down here in Terror Town."

"Strays? Man, don't forget I raised that flag when you was still Kingston Raiders."

"The flag, huh? Which flag? This one or that one?" He smirked. "You got tall flags, playboy."

He leaned in closer.

"But you know what, Jackpot? All you really got is your ego, and what you think is your reputation."

He spread his arms. "You wanna talk about Raiders? Look around you, Moe. Shit changed. Ain't no more Kingston Raiders. You see how you walked easy on Essex? All the gunplay done moved east. West. South." He punctuated each direction with a firm finger. "You outta touch."

His voice dropped lower. "Root Temple? Safer than a cemetery."

He let that sit.

Then: "We pulled off the impossible... Yeah... you know what the fuck I'm talking about. Lion Order pulled off the impossible. And we didn't need you — Joe."

He brought his face close to mine.

"If you really about Lion Order, then show it — to some other motherfuck-er."

The force of his door slamming made me flinch. I clenched my jaw.

I just wanted to reconnect. These motherfuckers wanted to turn screws.

Dejected. Pissed off. Disrespected. I strode over to check in at the shop. I walked by where Peaches used to live. I didn't look up.

Ras Piankhi sat behind the counter examining the blade of his machete from behind a cloud of sinsemilla smoke. "Barabas" by Twinkle Brothers made the walls vibrate.

Without even looking up to acknowledge me he pointed to the broom. "Di floor nah guh sweep ihself, yuteman."

I grabbed the broom and tried to make a joke. "Damn, when the last time y'all swept? These dust bunnies or super rats?"

No reaction.

Ras Piankhi turned, rifled through some 45s, thrust one towards Sista Evangeline. "Run dat chune, nuh?"

Sista Evangeline dropped the stylus. Through the speakers came "Dat" by Pluto Shervington.

"Dis chune ya," Ras Piankhi explained, "about wah Rasta weh hide him indiscretions. But wah gwaan inna di dark mus' come fi light."

Even Ras Piankhi was firing missiles.

"Damn, y'all making a mixtape for my downfall?"

I listened to the tune as I swept, wondering how much Ras Piankhi knew about my dilemma — my "indiscretions." He'd been a young man once. Surely he could understand that I was bound to make mistakes and that most of my mistakes would be led by my dick. I wasn't the only person who'd ever fucked around and fucked everything up but... shit... I guess it's my turn to feel the screws.

I kept sweeping.

I read the titles of the books on the shelf. *Countering The Conspiracy To Destroy Black Boys* by Jawanza Kunjufu. *The Destruction Of Black Civilization* by Chancellor Williams. *How Europe Underdeveloped Africa* by Walter Rodney. *The Compensatory Code / System / Concept* by Neely Fuller.

I wondered if I'd ever be an asset instead of a liability. Would I ever get a chance to prove that I could solve problems and not just cause them? And I don't mean lifting cars and motorcycles — real problems.

Perhaps sensing my melancholy, Sista Evangeline changed the tune to Lord Kitchener's "PP 99". "One more fi di mixtape, mi yute," she said with a wink. I'd never heard this tune before but quickly understood it as a man's bawdy reflection on his sexual liberty. It's a clever double entendre about a recalcitrant car owner who feels he should be able to park his "PP," the car's registration code, wherever he wants without reserve. It was a very funny

275

calypso and cheered me up. I asked her to play it, again.

Sista Evangeline gave me a tight hug. "Yuh nuh di first. Yuh won't be di last. Just nuh make it yuh all. Seen?"

"Sighted."

The door swung open. The bell above gave a reluctant, uneven clang. Half-welcome, half-warning. A Rastaman walked in. I'd never seen him before. He had a hard, serious face. But held his hat in his hands. Ras Piankhi straightened his back. Inched his hand towards his machete.

Sista Evangeline grabbed my hand. "Ital stew inna di back, mi yute." My cue to park the broom and follow.

"Siddung," she said.

I sat at the little table and watched the two men through a crack in the door. I couldn't make out the conversation but it didn't appear to be contentious. They talked. Listened. They ended by shaking hands. I wouldn't call it warm, it was more like... closure.

The bell clanged again.

A few minutes later, Ras Piankhi joined us in the kitchen. Sat at the table across from me. Exhaled. Then spoke:

"Dat man deh...

"I and I have bad bad history wid dat man. When I-man still deh inna di drugs trade. Him did wuk fi mi an' him tief some ah mi product. Seen?"

"Him tek di Rasta fi klaffy."

"I-man went to him fadda house, but di yute nuh did deh. I and I is a real patient man, so mi wait."

"I-man tie up him fadda. Stuff gyal panty inna him rahtid mout. Mi box di ol' dog all roun him face wid di gun back. Den mi park di ol' dog inna di closet."

"And mi did wait."

"When dat man, Trinity, come roun, mi shub mi gun nozzle inna him mout. Mi tell him seh him mussi waan drink lead soup. Him mussi waan mi rinse di nozzle. Him mussi waan meet Lucifer ihself. Ih tek nuttin' fi bore yuh skull, bwoy. WEH. MI. RASS. CLAAT. TINGS?"

"Mi play Russian roulette wid dat man until him piss him pants and tell mi weh fi find mi tings."

"Cho!"

He paused, stone faced.

"Mi was a bad man, mi yute. One a di wuss. Nuh rass. Yuh sight me?"

He paused, again, stared at the table. Laced his fingers. Exhaled.

"Dat was a long time ago, mi yute. Todeh him come fi apologize. Him seh him know him wrong an' him undastan why mi do wah mi do. Him seh long time him hear bout Lion Order but him steer clear. Long time him waan come sekkle accounts wid di Rasta."

"Said weh. Long time mi hear chat bout Trinity deh bout, but duppy know who fi frighten and skeleton alone have need fi chase ghost."

He made a broad gesture covering all of Lion Order.

"I-man easy fi find... Yuh see me?"

The clarity in Sista Evangeline's face was at once calming and chilling.

"Todeh him come fi bury di hatchet so we coulda tap wait fi di nex' man mek waah nex' move."

"Mi change... Him change... Every man have him chance fi change."

He pressed his finger into the table and locked my eyes.

"Every saint have waah past. Every sinna have waah future."

I sat still as a statue, awed by Ras Piankhi's intensity.

Sista Evangeline's voice was softer than Ras Piankhi's but her gaze was just as sharp. "Dem say 'time longer dan rope' but mi seh overstanding longer dan both... A man wah learn is a man wah win. But a man wah neva learn? Him lost already."

Ras Piankhi walked towards the storefront, "eat up, nuh? Food nuh cheap. Den git back pon dat broom. Di floor naah gwan sweep ihself, mi seh."

I can be more than my mistakes, I reasoned. I finished the bowl of Ital stew. "Prophecy" by Fabienne Miranda could be felt in the floors.

I fell back into my routines around Lion Order. It still felt strange without Brixton – all that remained was his Cetec sound system – and the cold shoulders from the rank and file irked me. Not everybody was happy to see me back in Fourth World.

Yinka's words started to rattle around my head.

"...you came to Lion Order as a baby. We raised you... You really gonna throw away... heritage...? For what...? It looks weak, King... it looks weak."

I didn't expect there to be a cost to be paid back to the home team. I expected open arms. Instead, I got ice grills and broom duty. I never imagined the day that my loyalties would be questioned... that my simple presence wouldn't be enough. Kicked out of Pama and bottom of the totem pole with Lion Order.

As Tremor would say, I "ain't have a pot to piss in nor a window to throw it out of."

Fuck.

CHAPTER THIRTY-EIGHT
From the Book of Black Teeth
This is Why They Come

The curtains pulled back reveal four small antechambers. The theater, the banquet hall, the cathedral, tonight, all are one.

Inside each antechamber, a Re°Ceiver reclines, naked as the day she was born. On her face, fixed, a mask. A dark, flowing wig. Homage to Erzsébet. Her beauty. Tonight, they are she.

A line formed before each.

Men of all classes, working men, businessmen, tall, short, stout, chubby.

They do not drink together.

They do not pray together.

Yet here, they wait together, unified in a common queue for a common pursuit.

Equalized by the stain of red that dresses their lips. They have imbibed. They tell themselves it's symbolic. Ritual. A small transaction, an exchange for what makes them come. The taste lingers, metallic and wrong, but not revolting enough to turn away. Nothing is.

They stand nervously, eyes locked forward. Looking down would mean seeing another naked, needy shaft. Looking up, a craven mirror of their own depravity.

Instead, they fumble with their pearls, their gifts to the Re°Ceivers, and wait their turn. To mix their pearl and their milk with that of those who came before them.

The Re°Ceiver accommodates one, then the next. Wondering as they press inside her, Fényhozó or recerebration?

The line shortened.

Now they can see.

The thrusting buttocks of the man before them.

The curve of the Re°Ceiver's legs. The flush of her chest and face.

They can hear her acceptance. They can hear his urgency.

Their breath shortens.

The waiters' hands tighten around their pearls. Their need obvious.

Hurry. Finish. Let me in.

Fényhozó or recerebration?

This is why they come, thinks the Re°Ceiver. This is why they come.

CHAPTER THIRTY-NINE

I picked up the phone that wouldn't stop ringing.

"Hello?"

"It's Malört. Don't hang up. We need your help."

"My help? This feels like a trap. I'm not in the mood to get trapped today."

Click.

Ring.

"Fuck."

I picked it up.

Necro. "Man, just hear me out. It's Angus. He's been fucked up since you whipped your dick on his mother. That whole family is in shambles. But that's not what this is about... well, it kinda is... just listen. When that shit went down he flipped out. He talked about crossing over to Re°Cereb and was going to get your scalp but we talked him off that ledge... I mean, he still wants your scalp but..."

Malört grabbed the phone from Necro. Complained that he was losing the plot.

"We need your truck. Your father's truck. Angus ran off and joined Cerberus, and now shit's all fucked up. His mother is flipping the fuck out.

Another kid, a skater kid came out of there... last year... just... changed. No light in his eyes. They brainwash kids. Keep them on as little food as possible. Give them only essential water. There's shit in the food... hallucinogens maybe... or barbiturates... we don't know. But we need to get him the fuck out, and we need that truck."

"This still sounds like a trap. How do I know..."

"Jackpot? It's me, Mum... Marilyn. It's not a trick. Please. We need your help. I just want my son back... Please."

I softened, "okay. Let me talk back to Malört."

◎ ◎ ◎

I reached out to Viddy, again, but this time I didn't need him as wheel man. I wanted to borrow his KZ. I offered to kick him down a little bit of cash to make him forget the risk, but still he asked the obvious. "When you gonna get your own wheels, man?"

"Well, it ain't gonna be tonight, now, will it?"

"It could be. You got that Puma money. Buy it off me." Viddy was a brand new father and hard up for cash.

"How much?"

"$3,000," Viddy offered.

"$2,000. Shit used as fuck." I countered.

"Meet in the middle, then. $2,500."

We got down to $2,200.

"Fuck it. Done. Give me the key."

I hopped on the bike and grabbed the throttle. "Just a boy and his motorcycle," I thought. Viddy's door clicked shut behind me. Instead of feeling free and filled with joy about finally getting my own wheels, I felt... alone.

I spun the KZ wheels toward Maywood, threw the dogs some meat, tucked the bike away, and got the truck.

Holy City, again. New BUSA Tribe graffiti. "NO GOVERN-U-MEN!" No government.

North to The Jewel.

I ran through my life choices. Do I really want to walk back in to Pama? Is this a trap? What's the worst that could happen?

There it was. I flashed my lights. The big gate swung open. I rolled in. The gate shut behind me. "If this is a trap, I guess I'm trapped," I muttered to myself. "I probably should have brought snacks... and my favorite pillow."

Broomie waved me in. Shouted "stop there! Leave the keys!" As if he was in charge. Their driver hopped in. Bumped me aside. Threw the truck into gear. Promptly popped the clutch. I grimaced.

In the club or not, I'm nobody's junior. They need me more than I need them.

"Get out and tell me where to put it."

The detail crew did their thing again with the license plates. They had drawn some Cerberus logos on big white magnets. They stuck those to the doors of the truck. Nice touch.

As fucked up as things were with Pama, I could still acknowledge that these fuckers knew how to pull a caper.

The plan was to pull the truck right up behind the Cerberus HQ in Roger's Park. Iron bars and tough security doors on the first floor so that's a no go. The height of the truck would get us just below the second story windows. There was grating over the windows but nothing that a crowbar and a Necro couldn't pop.

I wondered aloud why Cerberus had all that security. It wasn't to keep burglars out, I reasoned. It was to keep the Adherents in.

On signal, the extraction crew would filter in and search the second and

283

third floors.

We knew that the kitchen and meditation room was in the basement. The first floor was all business offices and meeting rooms. The upper floors are where the devotees and the aspirants rest. They weren't sure which room Angus would be in but they had a good idea based on the information provided by the kid who'd recently gotten out.

Necro cased the place, watching for activity. Patterns. Which lights went off at what times. Which lights never seemed to come on. Which rooms revealed human silhouettes. Were they male or female? And what they appeared to be doing. He mentioned a lazy security patrol that stuck to their shack in front of the building. Never seen patrolling the alley. "I don't expect them to be an issue if we hit quiet and fast."

We had a rough floor plan from the skater kid, but he'd only seen a couple of rooms and a lot of closed doors. The big library downtown had some architectural documents from when the building was built so, while some things may have changed — like the elevator — we had some basic guidelines. According to the construction plans there were 14 units per floor. We suspected that some walls had been taken down to expand some units. We also believed that each of the upper floors had community showers. We had no way of knowing how many people lived there — were held there — so we had to be surgical in our approach and move quickly.

"These motherfuckers ain't gonna just let us creep in and creep out. Weapons?" I asked.

"Covered, Grasshopper," Malört replied. We took a page from the Lion Odor book. Silent but not deadly. Riot batons, mace and handcuffs. We don't need neighbors complaining about shotgun blasts, now, do we?"

"No. No we don't. Let's just hope they think that way too," I answered.

"This is the plan... but there's one more thing."

"Uh oh. What?"

"Angus ain't gonna want to see your face. We don't want to set him off. You stay back here. We'll get this truck back to you without a scratch."

"Nah. I get that he won't want to see me, but I'm on this mission. None of y'all can wheel this truck like I can, so if I'm just a driver, I'll be the best fucking driver, but I'm coming."

"You say that a lot, don't you, ZipLock? 'I'm coming.'" Necro quipped.

"Fuck you."

"You're not built for that."

"Introduce me to your mother, then."

"BOYS!" yelled Malört. "FOCUS."

"Alright. We're doing this shit tonight, ZagNut. Keep your dick in your pants, and your eyes on the road."

"You're always thinking about my dick. It's weird, Joe."

"What? It's a nice dick," he joked.

"Finally, we agree on something."

Laughter.

"And don't call me Joe."

Malört shook her head.

We went over the plan one last time.

"The goal is to get Angus out of there," Malört asserted.

"Out the same window we came in. Back into the truck and then we roll."

We clarified roles and responsibilities. Who hits the upper floors. Who stays on the extraction tier. Who secures the extraction room. Who guards the stairs, and who keeps the elevator doors open.

And our signals. One for room clear. Another for resistance encountered. Still another for eyes on Angus.

Sounds easy, right? A little too easy.

The streets were in our favor tonight. Not too much traffic and not too much rain. The street lights mingled with the clinging droplets to create a dreamlike effect that quieted the three of us in the front cab. Me in the driver's seat, Malört in the middle. Necro riding shotgun. Let's hope no cops recognize that ugly mug.

In back, on the couches, was a team of nine more men and women. Broomie was on the mission but Radish wasn't. The couches were strapped in to keep them from getting tossed around by the truck. This was Pama's elite Set. The Press Gang. Not military, but knew how to solve problems like this. I'd seen and even influenced Pama's operational discipline. Seeing it in action was like watching a well-oiled machine do its one thing really well.

We crept through the night. Made it to Roger's Park. Turned into the alley behind The Cerberus Method. I feathered the clutch, eased the truck silently into place. The brakes squealed slightly, but nothing alarming. The driver's side of the truck blocked the ground level exit, so that was an added bonus.

"Ain't no Cer-busters coming out this way."

Necro went to work. With surprising agility he climbed up onto the cab of the truck, onto the trailer, checked for electronic sensors and attacked the weak points. He had clearly done this before. He dislodged the grating, barely making any sounds.

He called up a Press Gang operator. Helped them through the window. The rest followed. Necro was right. A community shower. Empty. Fan out. Find Angus.

I was jittery. I watched the clock. I had no idea what was happening inside. I felt useless. I grumbled about being reduced to driver, but it also made logical sense. I didn't like being a worker, but they might need a talented getaway driver.

"The mighty Jackpot reduced to getaway driver. Ain't that a bitch?" I thought to myself.

"I wonder what song Ras Piankhi would cue up for this stage of my undoing. Maybe "One Piece at a Time" by Johnny Cash but a Reggae version... "One spliff at a time," maybe, I laughed. Or "Highway to Hell" but make it "Highway to Zion" or "Highway to Bull Bay"! Haha! That's it." I was cracking myself up. So much so that I didn't even see the fucking security grunt and his fucking vegetarian Doberman.

Motherfucker got the drop on me.

"Get your Black ass out of the fucking truck!" The guard, a middle-aged, stocky white man in military fatigues yanked the passenger side door open with one hand. The other hand held a revolver, aimed straight at my face.

Fuck!

Hands up "I'm coming, I'm coming."

"Damn right you're fucking coming. You thought, what? That you could sneak in here and steal some computers? I know you yard apes love your pork chops, so it can't be the food."

"No sir, that's not..."

"Wait! Hold the fuck on! Look at me! You're that... well fucking well. I guess I just hit the jackpot! I wondered if I'd ever find your little Black ass again. You had us chasing you all night... you monkeys and your fast twitch muscles... but ain't gonna be no hopping fences and hiding under cars tonight. No sir! White City finally got the spook who mugged Davey."

So *this* is who the fuck had been on my ass that night. The motherfuckers in the light green cruiser. I thought they were detectives. In reality they were The Resistance support team. They'd seen their main man get laid the fuck out and wanted to avenge. Well shit, I guess they are gonna get their chance.

The dog sat at attention, ears erect, waiting for the command to attack.

"Face down on the ground, Moon Cricket! I always knew you were just a common criminal."

I sprawled out. He kicked my feet apart. Pulled out some handcuffs. He knelt with his knee in the base of my spine — more to hurt me than anything else. Slapped the bracelets on my wrists. The clicks sounded so final.

"Davey will be so happy to see you! You won't be too happy to see him, though. I can't tell you that. No sir!"

I heard some light footfalls coming from the top of the truck. I felt a rush of air. Heard the sound of a dull impact. A faint yelp. Then a whimper... the Doberman fell flat facing me. Eye to eye. Not dead, but not deadly, either.

White City hopped up, "What the...?"

He turned around, confused, trying to formulate a reaction, but he was too slow. The shadow pivoted. Got behind him. Locked him up with a sleeper hold.

I saw it first in his eyes, then in his claws, as he struggled to break free.

"Shhh... don't fight it, baby. Relax your muscles. That's it... good boy...."

All the light left his eyes.

"See? That wasn't so bad now, was it? I knew you could do it, baby doll." The shadow gently laid his unconscious body on the concrete next to the Doberman, then bent over, looked me in the eyes. "You owe me one."

Malört.

"Fuck yes! Thank you. I'm so fucking happy to see yo ass. This shit was..." I was part relieved and part embarrassed.

"Yeah, yeah. Let me find the keys, then we can start naming babies."

Malört rifled through White City's pockets. Found the keys. Uncuffed me. She tucked his revolver into her waistband. Tossed his night stick to me. She cuffed the dog's collar to the guard's ankle then threw the keys over a gate into a neighbor's yard. "Give them a puzzle to solve," she explained.

"This bitch is cold-blooded," I thought. I kept that thought to myself.

The Press Gang came through with Angus. They'd had to knock a few heads and knock out a few nerds but other than the resistance put up by Angus, we were in the clear. They piled back into the truck, worked to keep the dazed and confused Angus calm, and pounded on the side when it was safe to pull off.

Necro raised an eyebrow at the unconscious guard and dog. "I can't wait to hear this lie."

"Ain't shit to tell. Business got handled," Malört deadpanned from behind a cloud of smoke.

We wheeled back onto the streets.

I'd gotten caught slipping and Malört saved my ass. I really did owe her one. And I couldn't begrudge her that one fucking bit. Viddy was right. That White City shit was not a one-and-done. And... shit... now they got two scores to settle with ya boy. I just hope I see them before they see me.

I stopped the truck at an alley. Hopped out. Took the magnets off Tremor's truck. Put them on somebody else's.

Then we drove Angus to the Macksey House. I hadn't laid eyes on that place since that crazy morning. I stayed outside. Brooklyn, Myra, and Necro stuck around to help out at the house. I was nagged by the realization that none of us knew shit about deprogramming a person.

Would Angus ever be Angus again?

The shit that made him jet was still unresolved... maybe never could be resolved.

After dropping the Press Gang crew back at the salvage yard and dismantling all their modifications, I wheeled the truck back towards Maywood, not looking forward to another encounter with Tremor's vegetarian Dobermans.

CHAPTER FORTY
The Pen CNN
Lost Doggie! Do Not Chase!

When Grapevine, the Divine spoke, nobody blinked. Not the hitters. Not the lifers. Not the half-dead doing nickel bids. This was elder magic. Snake-tongue sharp and heavy as fresh dug dirt.

You might wanna hear "Wise Egg" or "Hustlin' Pete,"
But next time for the old shit, these new waters run deep.

This one is called "Lost Doggie! Do Not Chase!"

In the yard of time, ancient dogs roam,
But some young pups off and ran up in they home.

A wild young pack with no fear snatched up a stray
Then faded like shadows into the motherfucking grey.

The dogs lost the little puppy and can't tell a god damn soul,
About the midnight caper so bold and so motherfucking cold

But in their hearts, a fire still burns bright,
These old dogs will endure and hope to take back the night.

But these old dogs ain't killers, they are believers in an ode,
They ain't got no skills in war and their weakness showed.

The angelic upstart ran through them like a hot knife through butter,
Facedown in the dirt, with no excuses worth an utter.

That upstart is shifting the balance in The Jewel,
But therein lies the peril, it takes two to duel.

No good deed shall go unpunished, that's what they say,
Be careful who you save, they might be the one to slay.

We want to see this young motherfucker do his thing,
From The Scratch to Fourth World, his name is starting to ring.

But rings have echoes and we know he's getting known,
The seeds of his destruction you can bet are being sown.

Y'all love to hear about this kid, the one we shall not name,
The one who dances with danger, never shying from the flame.

Be here tomorrow, you can bet he gon' pull some stunts,
But the other cunts have stunts, and hunts, and shunts.

Let's wish him luck, the shitty inner city needs a hero,
But every hero meets a Nero that wants to make him a zero.

Somebody should pull his coat and tell him the knives are out,
They know more than he thinks and betrayers are about.

(He let that hang for a beat)

They call this the slave state, but we freer than most,
This the Pen CNN. The squares call it a toast.

I don't sell no lies, no wolf tickets, no doubt,
Grapevine, the Divine signing the fuck out.

He stepped down from the cafeteria table.

His fellow inmates went back to slapping dominos, shuffling cards, and arguing about who was next up in spades.

Bald Head Dread

CHAPTER FORTY-ONE

I put my head down in Fourth World.

Pama laid low in The Jewel.

We waited to see how Cerberus would answer being invaded and losing an Aspirant. We maintained absolute radio silence. No phone calls. Nothing.

I cleaned up the KZ. Rode with the few Lion Order operators who would ride with me. It felt good to be home. Working with Tremor. Spending free time at Lion Order. But eventually, I felt the call of The Jewel — it was almost like a drug. The lights. The girls. And I also just wanted to make these wheels spin.

Bikes and top gear didn't mix so I was kitted up like a real rider. Took a cue from The 7. Police bomber — don't ask how I got it — old Harrington under that. Fred Perry, the last layer. Gloves. Brain bucket. We didn't have helmet laws but depending on where you went and what you did, they could serve purposes beyond what the designers intended. Rounding out the functional kit were my very common 501 jeans and Irish Setter Sport boots. I looked like I'd been plucked straight from the Nick Knight book, page 36.

Brixton would disapprove. I'm not sure how Peaches would feel.

Same gear I wore working Tremor's trucks. Anyone who was tuned into the subculture would recognize the underlying elements, but civilians would just think I was a grease monkey. Whatever. They didn't matter. I'm Jackpot, Soon Ras. Skinhead outcast. Ain't never Gon' be king of no Skins. Lion Order elite, once. Former Pama City Skins' big money maker.

Let's make these wheels spin.

Thoughts of Brixton and Peaches took me back to happier and sadder days. Made the city seem like a brightly-lit tomb. But I had to focus. I was on a bike. No time for thinking about anything but the road.

The words of The Aces' "Fu Man Chu" came to mind. "It makes no sense to talk about what you used to do..." Hard tune.

The journey was a flat but curvy straight shot.

Picked up South Shore Drive near the South Shore Country Club. Headed north.

Rode for a mile or so. Becomes East Marquette Drive.

Zoomed past La Rabida hospital.

Hooked another right at Yacht Harbor.

Now we're cooking.

Fourth World is beautiful from this vantage point. The Grid didn't even feel like a cage.

The lake to the east. The lights of the town waxing and waning on the left.

63rd Street Beach. Where Rodney gassed Rasta Fox.

I raced past the Museum of Science and Industry. Past Promontory Point. Past Yinka's building.

It was just me and the buzz of the KZ.

35th Street beach. I remembered seeing divers pull an unfortunate kid from those waters.

Big ass CHA projects on the left. Projects with a lake view. Only in Fourth World.

I zipped past McCormick Inn.

Past Soldier Field, where The Bears played. Lived here my whole life. Never once been to a game.

Past the Adler Planetarium. The Field Museum on my right. Then Buckingham Fountain on my left.

A great place for a cheap date but also a tourist trap. For the takers this was a prime place for a distracted mark to get their pockets turned inside out. No hook shot trickery, just good old light fingered klepto.

Up past where the S-Curve used to be. Now it's all smoothed out. I used to ask my parents to bend their wheels through the right angles. Sometimes they would. Other times they'd say something like, "I'll come back there and bend *your* wheels!" Whatever that meant.

On past Navy Pier and Lake Point Tower. Alice Cooper lived in that building. I'm still not sure who she is.

Cleared The Loop. Now deep behind enemy lines. The Gold Coast. Siobhan's parents' building on my left. I didn't look up. I tried to catch a glimpse of Playboy Mansion. Bad angle. On past The Drake Hotel on my left, and Oak Street Beach on my right. I'd had some good sex and some great fights on that beach.

Part of me wanted to check the peep show in Old Town but that was just a money trap.

Closing in on The Jewel. Could smell the zoo. Up ahead. Belmont street exit. Take it. First place to check. The Rocks. Some nights this is a gay cruising spot. Other nights, Pama City Skins take over.

Nobody at The Rocks or in the tunnel. Back to it. West on Belmont towards Fleet's. They've got to be there. Dead. Again. I guessed they were still heads down. Still, it felt strange to not see anyone on a clear summer night.

No signs of them by Stix. No way I was going to stop at the Macksey House. Rolled past Fleet's. Kept rolling. Hit Clark Street Dog. Nobody who is anybody. Where the fuck?

Try the Salvage Yard. I turned to do a lazy roll up Clark toward Wrigley Field. Wait. That's Malört. Stumbling out of L&L Tavern. Two dirtheads.

One on each side. A very drawn looking Broomie, too. Helping the dirt-heads get Malört into the back of a Chester van. I've seen Malört shitfaced many times but never sloppy like this.

They piled her in. One of the dirtheads, the stringy-haired one, jumped in back with her. Slammed the door shut. The other dirthead, the fat one, ran around, handed Broomie a little brown bag. Then hopped into the driver's seat. Broomie slunk back to L&L. The van edged out onto Clark, north-bound.

I followed.

I took stock of what I had. Weaponry was pretty sparse. Push dagger in my boot. Payout — my force multiplier — tucked into the inner pocket of my jacket. My helmet might be useful. And my triplex chain belt. It would have to be enough. Do what you can with what you have.

The van stopped in the alley behind Sheffield at Roscoe. Next to a brown brick apartment building. The driver doused the lights. Kept the engine running. Weird.

I shut down the bike. Crept into the shadows.

Stringy rang a doorbell. A few seconds later the metal utility door swung open. A man. Dressed like an amateur dentist. He looked around nervously. Waved to the driver. Wanted the van right up to the door.

I kept to the shadows. I crept for a vantage point. I ducked beside an electricity pole. "Good work, guys. Thanks."

Malört tittered. Slurred her words, pointed at the man. "Wait! I know you."

"Yeah, you baldheaded cunt," he replied. "We're gonna know every disgusting thing about each other before this night is over."

Oh fuck. The Friday the 13th mark.

The Mark was holding up Malört with one arm. The glint of a pair of extraction forceps provided eerie foreshadowing of his sadistic intent. In his other hand was an envelope for the kidnappers. I'd seen enough. I zeroed in on The Mark.

Payout in my grip, I angled myself to get between The Mark and the Chester jockeys. The Mark saw movement. He opened his mouth to shout something. My momentum. My fist. Payout. His open jaw.

His flesh yielded.

His mandible shifted.

His face structure called it quits. His teeth gave way. Blood and spittle flew. My fist followed through.

He lost his grip on Malört. He collapsed to the floor. She slumped on the ground next to him.

I got on him. Delivered several quick blows to his eye sockets. He was fully awake. His eyes were on high beam. Pain. He couldn't talk. He couldn't blink. Shock.

The Chester jockeys leapt back in surprise. I turned to face them. Noticed they were both wearing Haunted Town soft colors.

Chubby screwed up some outrage. "You don't know who you're fucking with."

"No, you don't know who you are fucking with. That's Pama City Skins right there!"

They went slack jawed.

"Are the Blue and Red kidnapping for sadists these days? Does The Council sanction that in The Jewel? Does DeRico?"

The blood left their faces. They made some quick calculations.

"I told you not to trust that fucking basehead Broomie," Stringy spat.

They murmured some weak excuse about not knowing... who she was... what The Mark had planned. Blamed Broomie... Hoping that would be sufficient cover. They hopped in their Chester van and boned out. They kept the Mark's money, though.

The Mark sat up like a ventriloquist's dummy. Blood ran into and out of his high beams. I wondered if he would ever blink again.

His chin looked like something the class clown might make on sculpture day. Everything was out of place. His teeth resembled tumbled tombstones.

His breath was ragged.

I wondered if he would ever eat solids again. He couldn't even scream. His cries were little more than short breaths and low whimpers. Helpless.

The weight of my boot came down and crushed the bones in his right hand. "No pity for sadists!" I did the same with his left hand.

He coughed up blood. Teetered over onto his side. High beams still on. His tears told the agonizing story that his voice box couldn't.

[Knock]

I helped Malört up to her feet. Fixed her clothes. Draped my cop bomber over her shoulders. Hobbled with her to the nearest safe space. Stix. It was only two blocks over but it was slow going. Malört wasn't a small chick and she offered exactly zero help.

The cleanup guy recognized me. Let me in. Helped me put Malört on the couch in the office. I called Necro. No answer. I called Mrs. Macksey. She picked up. Came right over. She brought blankets and a pillow. Water. Aspirin. Guessed that Malört had been slipped knock-out drops. A heavy dose but nothing she couldn't sleep off.

We actively avoided each other's eyes.

"How is Angus?" I asked.

"He's... he's in therapy, but he's not himself. I had to leave him alone to come here. I'd rather not talk about it."

She did what she could, then went back to Angus.

I sat watch over Malört. I could only imagine what depraved horrors The Mark had planned. Every now and then she'd wake up and want to talk — I

300

just listened — then she'd fall asleep, again. Maybe I fell asleep too. I don't remember. I reached Necro the next morning. He came racing over.

I told him everything I knew. The Haunted Town soft colors. Broomie's connection. What Stringy said about Broomie.

Malört was groggy but alert. She cursed herself for letting her guard down.

"You thought you were with family," I consoled.

I sensed that Malört was more disturbed by what almost happened than she let on.

"I'm glad you were there, Jackpot," said Necro, calling me by my actual name, "You're a good soldier."

I left them to figure out whatever was next.

I walked the few blocks back to where I'd left my KZ. FUCK!!!! Of course. I'd failed to turn the ignition completely off and the battery was drained. FUCK! FUCK! FUCK!

Only an idiot would stick around the scene of that shit so I rolled the bike off its stand and started to push. I was trying to find a gas station when I met another rider who hopped off his own bike and showed me how to bump start. I was rolling again. On my way back to Fourth World.

I don't know who brought Jake up to speed on what had happened, but by the time he got around to breaking into The Mark's home for revenge it had been cleared out. The Mark had skated. Retribution would have to wait. Jake found a few stray teeth that he delivered to me in a Tic Tac case.

Broomie had a lot to answer for. "Jackpot saw you at the bar." "Why did you let her leave with those guys?" "Did you set it up?" Necro, Jake, and Malört jumped on his head. Beat him bloody.

The beatdown, they said, was a pitiful one. "He didn't even fight back. He just took it like a self-loathing masochist," Malört reported. He kept saying shit like "I don't care if you kill me... You'll be doing me a favor... I'm already dead. I'm a piece of shit... I'm a lying, thieving, cheating, low life basehead piece of shit."

301

Necro added quietly, "It wasn't even fun fucking him up. I just told him to get his shit together or next time we really would put him under."

Broomie was officially "out with no contact" from Pama and, essentially, homeless in the local Skinhead world.

Anyway... who gives a fuck? Not my pig, not my farm. Hope wherever he lands they teach him not to be such a dumb dick.

CHAPTER FORTY-TWO

Necro replayed the answering machine message for me.

It was the voice of Mrs. Macksey.

> *"Angus has gone again.*
>
> *Not to Cerberus this time.*
>
> *He was seen at the bus station.*
>
> *To Joliet."*

I whispered it to myself. "Re°Cereb."

CHAPTER FORTY-THREE
Monday, August 26, 1985

I'd been out with Viddy on the bikes.

I didn't know.

I couldn't know.

In the night.

Ras Piankhi was closing down the session.

He was alone.

Picking cups off the ground. Making sure the system was covered in case of rain.

The last song he played was still on the deck.

"Run Come Come" by Tony Tuff. The stylus stuck in the runout grooves.

They propped a ladder against the gate. Climbed over.

White skin.

Black eyes.

I don't know how many.

Silent.

From behind.

They cut.

He didn't even have time to react.

He watched them slice his wrist and collect his blood.

His life slowly drifting away.

They left as quietly as they arrived.

They left his blood there. In a gourd.

They didn't want his blood. Just the ritual.

No one saw or heard.

They were like ghosts.

They stuck a dagger in his chest. More for show than need.

They left it in his chest.

Took one silver-flecked lock with them.

I walked.

Home.

I didn't think. I didn't feel.

I just walked.

In my mailbox.

Paper. A letter.

CHAPTER FORTY-FOUR
The Pen CNN
A Eulogy

Grapevine, the Divine stood tall, and silence crawled up the walls. Even the ghosts in solitary leaned in. He didn't need no guitar. His words tuned the whole block to truth.

It ain't no time for neither "Shine and the Titanic" nor "Stagolee,"
This one right here is a eulogy.

This one is for Ras Piankhi no cusswords, only respect.

In Zion's light, Piankhi stood tall,
A Rasta noble, heeding Rastafari's call.

His Church the truth, his gates so pure
His belief in the youth, for they he did endure.

Crown of locks flowing, eyes so bright,
Guided by the Lion's might.

Groundation, foundation hymns of peace,
Decolonize your minds, he taught release.

Wicked men, with hearts of stone,
Despised his strength, hated his tone.

Plotting darkly, they laid their snare,
Caught him unaware, no mercy to spare

In cold blood, they took his life,
Piankhi fell to the edge of the knife.

Yet in spirit, he rises high,
A Rasta man's soul, can never die.

Nine nights for Piankhi, we sing and pray,
Guiding his spirit, lighting the way.

In reverence and love, his memory bright,
A noble soul honored in Zion's light.

His progeny stood silent, their hearts full of fire,
Vowing to honor him, lifting his name higher.

Friends gathered close, their sorrow worn proud,
In the stillness of night, beneath a solemn shroud.

Fourth World stood still, even the gunman gave leave
In the silence, only love drowned out the aggrieved

For every tear shed, a promise was made,
To remember his light, to never let it fade.

The cubs mourn the lion, the mothers mourn the babe,
We are in the quiet before the storm, the silence before the rage.

But this is about Piankhi, a shepherd of souls,
Now basking in Zion in ites, green and gold.

(He let that hang for a beat)

They call this the slave state, but we freer than most,
This the Pen CNN. The squares call it a toast.

I don't sell no lies, no wolf tickets, no doubt,
Grapevine, the Divine signing right out.

By the time his boots hit the floor, the inmates were already back to dealing hands and slapping bones like prophets come and go every day. One guard stood with a self-satisfied grin, looking like the cat who got the cream.

CHAPTER FORTY-FIVE
Monday, August 26, 1985

In my mailbox.

Paper. A letter.

Handwritten. Meticulous. Measured. Precise handwriting.

I offer the following, not because I consider you worthy of my effort.
I offer the following, not for sentimental reasons.
I offer the following not because I expect you to understand.

I have looked into your eyes, though you shall never see into mine.
In yours, I saw skepticism. Mockery. Hubris.

I offer the following because I know: To give too much to the unready is to hasten their destruction. Your destruction.

I care not whether you see.
I care not whether you believe.

I care only that you are changed — reduced — by these words.

As told to The Jackal, by Erzsébet — Seven Truths:

I. ON ORDER AND BLOOD
We believe hierarchy is not a cruelty but a mercy.
It gives the lowly meaning and the high-born purpose.
The abolition of caste has made the world sick with yearning.
A rebalancing is required.

II. ON THE LIE OF EQUALITY

All are not equal.
That has never been our case.
The fantasy of shared gifts — shared virtue, shared power — is the poison of this age.
Every man has a station.
To pretend otherwise is to damn the species.
To tether us to the material plane.

III. ON THE PEASANT SOUL

The peasant does not rebel.
He reveres.
His joy is not in rising, but in serving greatness.
His body remembers what the mind has forgotten.
Science has misprogrammed the chaff.
Generosity has fattened the undeserving.
Withholding the lash has confused the weak.
This is why we mark the blood, and discard the brain.

IV. ON THE WELLS OF KNOWLEDGE

We harness what is powerful from all epochs, even from savages who stumble upon revelation.
We bow to no continent but kneel to every secret, whether they bloom in shadow or in stone.

V. ON THE SELF-ANOINTED

The false saint is the modern deviant who rises without being appointed.
He walks unblooded.
He ascends without sacrifice.
He must be unmade, that the true ascension may proceed.

VI. ON THE BEAUTY OF THE BLADE

To cut is to honor.
To drain is to cleanse.
To be consumed is to rise.
The knife makes immortality.

VII. ON THE ASCENSION OF THE COUNTESS

She bathes not to tempt, but to transmute.
She anointed herself by releasing her Self.
She reclaimed what science denied.

We are her lineage, not by blood but by energy.
Belief.
Time.

Seven Truths, as told to The Jackal, by Erzsébet.

Enjoy your destruction.

◎◉◎

Scrawled on the back — in a different hand. This one, rough, crude: *"We hoped you'd be there. But we shall Re°Turn. His Ninth Night will be your first night, and thusly for every Night Skin we find."*

I held my breath.

"Angus. Please tell me you didn't..."

CHAPTER FORTY-SIX
Wednesday, August 28, 1985
Seven Days until the Ninth Night

We'd lost our light.

I was haunted by the feeling that all three losses tracked to choices I'd made. Who could I possibly tell this to? Who would understand? The elders? Sista Evangeline? Who?

I walked past the sentries. Into Terror Town headquarters.

"What's it like to go to war?"

Prince Adze let my question hang for a few beats.

"I know this feeling, Jackpot. I've been on every side of the gun. I also know that when my card gets pulled it will most-likely be by some low-rank motherfucker who catches me with my guard down."

James Brown's "Cold Sweat was playing. Adze nodded at one of his men — I recognized him from Bad Hell. He had been one of the main movers in the Colfax Killers — Curtis Mayfield's "Don't Worry" was cranked up. Now Adze and I were the only ones who could hear.

Adze leaned in closely.

"Now, I know you ain't coming here to ask me to put soldiers in a war that ain't got shit to do with Stone Love, Moe. And I know you ain't coming to me to ask for firepower. You know that would require a very deep commitment. And we both know Tremor ain't having that. So I think you want to ask what I'd do next."

"I can't tell you what to do, Moe, but if this was my problem, it would end with crying mothers and happy undertakers. Now, you walk a different path than the rest of us, but you might have to dig down and find the Tremor that's tucked in that chest." He hammered the point with a firm finger to my chest.

"You already know that death is hardest on the living, but what you might not know is that mean us killers too — But fuck all that philosophical shit — Go 'head," Prince Adze said.

He leaned in even closer. I saw the gleam of a killer who makes killers. A man who makes mothers weep and undertakers rich. I saw something deeper. Nameless.

"Go 'head and let Lil' Tremor out his cage. I been waiting to see what that motherfucker can do."

Tremor. Always Tremor.

I shuddered. This had been a mistake.

I jumped up.

Thanked him for his time.

Got pulled into a handshake.

The same one as before.

I put Terror Town behind me.

I walked home.

◎◎◎

I went to Tremor with nothing but open ears. I leaned against the door jamb. He considered me over the top of his glasses.

I let a few beats pass between us before speaking.

"How did you get the name Tremor?"

314

He sighed heavily, took off his glasses, his eyes showed the weight of another sleepless night. He walked to the bookshelf, joint hanging from his lip.

He handed me a photo album. I flipped through as he spoke.

"I grew up an only child. Little Rock, Arkansas. Segregation time. But my parents moved across the river to Memphis for work. My father was a cement layer. That was the job he held until the day he died. Literally. My father died on the job. I ain't got no pictures of him, just memories and a few stories. My mother was a registered nurse. This was the time when black nurses were the ones who washed asses and emptied bedpans. Her life was a hard one and raising a growing boy alone under Jim Crow stretched her to her limits."

"I was a big kid, and was becoming a big young man, so the authorities — basically any white man — always found a way to remind me that I was something less than them. But I always saw the angle and sidestepped their bullshit. Still, the best place for a Black man in the segregated south was somewhere outside the segregated south, so I went down to the Marines recruiting station and lied about my age. They signed me right up."

"I went home to tell my mother that I'd be heading out soon but she panicked. She grabbed my birth certificate and dragged me back to the recruiter."

"He's only 16! You can't have him."

"The recruiter has one job. Collect warm bodies. He looked at my birth certificate. Said, "when he turns 18, he's ours.""

"The day after my 18th birthday I was in the back of a truck with other recruits, Black and white, on our way to basic training."

"My job in the Marines was field artillery man, that's why my hearing is bad, and, on the side, I was a football player. The officers loved me on the field and they'd bet money on my plays. I never saw no money, but I felt like I was really moving further away from Jim Crow."

"While we were waiting to be shipped out to Korea, we were stationed at a small base near a little South Carolina town. There was a black side of town and a white side of town. Us recruits socialized along color lines but every now and then our paths would cross."

"On the Black side of town there were some kids, boys and girls of all ages, that followed us around. We didn't pay them much mind, and when we could we would pay them in coins for running our errands. One night us Black recruits were crossing a bridge on our way back to the base transport when we heard something that sounded like a struggle. I went to investigate and found two white recruits messing with a young Black girl. I'd seen her around."

"I didn't know this girl. I didn't even really care about her one way or another but I'd been knowing men like this my whole life. Foul men who never meet accountability. And I knew too many girls like her who had to recover, if they could, from the abuse that men dish out. I shouted out to them to leave her be. They turned, cussed me out with all the words you already know and told me to mind my business. They say this Black girl, they used some different words though, would be getting some white dick that night, whether she wanted it or not. Told me I could have whatever was left."

"Her eyes met mine. 'Please, Mister. I just want to go home.'"

"A backhand from one of the white recruits sent her reeling."

"I pushed through and helped her to her feet. "Go on home. Now!" Oh, those recruits didn't like that. The ride back to base was quiet enough to hear a little-dicked mouse piss on a big piece of cotton. I expected to be reprimanded for bucking up to the white recruits but I have big shoulders, so I went directly to the commanding officer and explained my side of things. Keep in mind that at that time any Black man accusing any white man of anything was a sure way to catch the business end of a noose but, like I said, I have big shoulders, so I faced up to it."

"The commanding officers called in the offending recruits and sat the sweaty, drunken men in hard wooden chairs in the middle of the room. At the far side of the room were three officers. The two military police who brought the recruits quietly closed the door behind them on their way out. I was the only Black man in the room. I stood between the recruits and the officers. It was almost like a movie. Yankee officers, southern rednecks and the Black man in the middle."

"One of the officers said to me, 'We got us two cracker perverts, and what I want you to do is sock that one right there in the cocksucker.'"

"I hesitated. You see... that's the dirty trick of white power. It strips us of any trust we have in our own sense of right and wrong. Everything is relative to their interpretations. So, I hesitated."

"The officer urged me. 'Come on, boy, this is what you niggers live for. Hit that peckerwood in the cocksucker.'"

"So, I did it."

"I beat the brains out of the white recruits, and they had to take it. I got lost in it. I think they call it a cathartic release. But I also understood that these officers were using me as a big Black brute to terrorize these white recruits. On some other night, the opposite dynamic had surely played out.

"Any time I let up the officers urged me to get back on they asses."

"They were bloody pulps. Then... one stopped crying. Then the other one. They stopped doing anything. They stopped trying to duck the ass-whipping. They just stopped moving. Then I noticed they'd stopped breathing."

"I beat them boys to death. Them officers treated it like it was filing paperwork. They sent me back to barracks and told me to sleep it off. Not to talk to anyone about it."

"And that was that? They just let you walk?" I asked.

"I went to bed that night expecting to be visited by demons who would call me by name, charge me with murder, claim me and rip me apart. But, nothing. Nothing happened."

He paused, as if he wanted to add something more, but decided against it. He picked up where he left off.

"Over time a sad, sick part of me took pride in knowing that I had delivered justice, if you can call it that, to the rapists. Another part of me knew that I would have to answer for this one of these days. The officers went on as if it was just another Thursday. I halfway wondered if it had been a dream."

"But people noticed that the white boys were gone. They'd seen them with

317

the MPs. And some others had seen me with the MPs. Some genius put it all together and made up a rumor that I'd beaten them so bad that they shook in their boots and asked to get sent off to the bloodiest place on earth. The Black recruits wanted to see my knuckles. The story got around, and they said that I made all the white recruits tremble. They said that when I walked in the mess hall I sent tremors through them. Tremor."

"For me, this was the beginning of the end of my love affair with the US Marine Corps. I still had time to serve, and I still had white recruits to beat the brains out of, not always to that end... not always, but I made up my mind that once I finished my tour, I'd put the USMC in my rear view."

"When I told the superior officer of my intent to go civilian and try my hand in Chicago, that's where everybody was going, I was told "you've been a good, loyal soldier to us and we're sorry to see you go but here's the phone number of a friend of mine in Chicago. He could use a man like you.""

"The number was my main line to some bad men in Chicago. Organized crime types. Italian. I already had the biggest stain on my soul so anything else I could do could be no worse. I became one of the worst men in town and the name Tremor rang out in all corners. I was the best at being wicked. I was untouchable. When my boss met an untimely end, not by my hand, I got the rare chance to go independent and run my own operation."

"I was a lone wolf. I did dirt for anyone, and I do mean anyone, who was paying. I had friends and enemies on all sides. When I walked into a room, all action would halt until it was clear if I was there for business or pleasure."

"I hired some heavies that I grew up with in Memphis. I taught them the game and we built a wall around ourselves. We did our thing. Our way. Hard. Anybody that crossed us didn't get to do it twice. I hope you understand me."

"But, for me, the game was never a long term strategy. It was a means to an end. Like all hustlers, my dream was to turn my dirty money into clean money and I'd been saving and plotting for a way out. After a while, when your sisters, and then you, came along, I went ice-cold civilian. It used to be that people saw in me a man who wasn't afraid of death. Now I was a man who had reasons to live."

◎ ◉ ◎

Tremor pulled a yellow book off the shelf. He pushed it towards me. The *Egyptian Book of the Dead*.

"Now, you came here asking me how I got the name Tremor, but I know what you really want to hear is how you should answer what happened to Ras Piankhi."

"I can't tell you what to do and I know that the hardest lesson to learn is somebody else's lesson."

He opened the book to a marked page.

"Read the '42 negative confessions.'"

I read.

"I have made none to weep."

"I have not debauched the wife of any man."

"I have not been a stirrer up of strife."

"Shit! I'm guilty as fuck!"

Tremor took the book from my hands. "Each of us has to weigh our heart on the scale of Ma'at, the goddess of truth, justice, and balance. If your heart is heavier than a feather, then you must relive this life.

So, let me ask you... Are you angry enough to kill?"

"Yes." No hesitation.

"Shake that. Anger won't help you. It will cloud your judgment – Are you prepared to die?"

"I – I don't know."

"You better find an answer. Before you embark on a journey of revenge..."

I finished it for him "...dig two graves."

"Sho yuh right."

He reached into his desk drawer. Pulled out a gold necklace. A small pendant hung from it.

"Two shovels," he explained, "one for each grave. I haven't worn this for many years. I think you need it. I wish you could get through this life without having to make the choices I did, but I also know that you are more like me than either of us will admit. You'll go your own way, but don't go blindly. Don't go as a fool."

"Be like Sun Tzu. 'Know the terrain. Know your enemy.' And, as the Kemetic temples all say 'Man, know thyself.'"

◎◎◎

I don't know why I was crying.

I came to Tremor looking for answers – looking for permission to go to war – but I left with a lesson. An inheritance.

I paused in the doorway. Said, quietly, "Thank you, Dad."

"One last thing," he said. "You already know what you're gonna do. Just remember – next time you come see me, I want to recognize who I'm talking to."

I turned away without answering. I can't promise that. A promise would be a lie.

[Knock]

CHAPTER FORTY-SEVEN
From the Book of Black Teeth
Silence from the Stars

Night at the ranch.

Outside, nothing moving but the dogs. Prowling. Watching. Waiting.

Inside, the master bedroom sits in candlelight. A 16th-century bed. Large. Heavy. Erzsébet and The Judge's resting place. Asleep at the foot of the bed are Grootslang and Wendigo. They are afforded no comforts. Peacefully at ease on straw bedding.

Across the room, The Jackal is unraveling.

The Jackal's desk, a ruin of parchment and ink. Star charts spread like entrails. Dogon symbols. Mayan glyphs. Kemetic markings. They whisper. They contradict. They mock.

He runs his fingers over the numbers. Again. Again. A perfect cycle must exist. A truth beneath the noise. But they refuse to align.

The Dogon offer Sirius cycles, divine reckoning in celestial movement.

The Maya whisper human gestation, the sacred Tzolk'in, cycles of birth and prophecy.

The Kem-au command the heliacal rising of Sirius, Osirian resurrection, the flooding of the Nile, rebirth and destruction entwined.

All of them claim to hold the answer. None of them give it.

His jaw tightens. His quill snaps in his grip.

"One of you. One of you must be the clue to the other two."

"Tell me what I'm not seeing."

He exhales, eyes scanning the mess of ink and time.

The stars have spoken before. The ancients knew. He is merely clawing at what has already been written.

Behind him, Erzsébet hums.

A melody only she recognizes.

She draws her brush through her hair. Long, deliberate strokes. Watching herself. Admiring herself.

Perfect.

She tilts her head. Adjusts the candlelight. She wants to see more. More herself. The Unfettered Self. The ideal Self.

Then she sees it.

A single gray strand.

The brush stops.

No sound now but The Jackal's heavy breath.

His hands curl into fists over the parchment.

The breath of the berserkers at the foot of the bed.

The dogs outside, still circling.

Erzsébet's fingers tighten around the brush.

The Jackal keeps searching. The berserkers keep sleeping. The dogs keep prowling.

Time keeps moving.

In the stables, on a bed of hay.

A sleeper. Stocky build. Sunburnt. Short hair.

In his grip: a souvenir.

A single rope of hair.

Black. Flecked with silver.

FORTY EIGHT
Thursday, August 29, 1985
Six Days until the Ninth Night

"They are gonna turn his funeral into a bloodbath."

I showed them the note that Cod°Ex Re°Cereb left at my door. The cryptic threat. Ras Piankhi's "ninth night would be my first night."

I looked around the Pama salvage yard. Faces from Lion Order. Faces from Pama City Skins.

"We can't let that happen."

◎◎◎

"We can't be dumb about this," Malört began. She turned down the volume of the arrhythmic industrial noise.

"To understand The Cod°Ex Re°Cereb first you have to start with Joliet itself. Their home. Cod°Ex Re°Cereb calls that prison 'The Slave State,' and to them Joliet is 'Terra Blanche' — White Land."

"To outsiders, Joliet looks like a bombed out wasteland where even the pigeons look half-starved and hate-filled. The streets are lined with addicts of every stripe. It's difficult to tell which buildings are occupied and which ones are abandoned and they like it that way."

"Joliet is the exact opposite of an oasis. A place where the worst kinds of men go to vanish in plain sight. The law only exists behind the walls of the prison. In their view, it's appropriate that thousands of Black and brown men are warehoused there, isolated from society — where they can visit brutality on each other, instead of on everybody else. Remember, this is Cod°Ex Re°Cereb philosophy, not mine."

"But there are white men in there, too."

"That doesn't matter to them, Yinka, that's one of the costs of society in their eyes. Some must be grounded so that some others may fly. Hell, there's even some Cod°Ex Re°Cereb locked up in there. That's how Necro first ran across them."

"In their church, Countess Bathory can be reached through group meditation, semen letting, and beating on big metal drums."

Necro picked up the thread.

"They believe they are the vanguard for a coming Bathorist ascendance that will become real when enough chanting and heartbeating, that's the metallic drumming you hear on that tape, has been performed and when the right sacrifices have been made, but no one knows what 'enough' or 'right' is, so they keep trying."

"Wait, sacrifices?" asked Brooklyn.

"Yes. They... it gets weird. They have this sex cult thing going on. The mother of their clan, Erzsébet, is the vessel that they use to channel life, which really means she is the creative director for these wild gang bangs. The men have to put pearls in her devotees' pussies as an offering. There are several women in their family but Erzsébet is the most important person, man or woman."

"Her husbands Wendigo and Grootslang are like her foot soldiers, and lovers, and sons. Kinda like BlackPrick and Mrs...

"Stick to the fucking point!" Malört commanded.

Necro gathered himself.

"Right. So, sometimes one of them gets pregnant, that's kind of the goal, and if it's a girl, well — that pure baby gets bled out, exsanguated and the brain is removed through the nostrils, excerebrated — some ancient Egyptian ritual. Then they drink the blood "imbibe" and eat the brain "recerebrate.""

"And if it's a boy?" Yinka asked.

Necro deferred to Malört.

"If it's a boy," she said, "they raise him to be a *'Fényhozó.'* Means, 'The Light Bringer' but they extend that to *"Fény, ami égeti a sötétséget."* 'The Light That Burns The Night.' Night Skins. Fényhozó is also the Hungarian word for Lucifer.

Necro picked up where Malört left off. "Sometimes they come out retarded or malnourished so they stay on the ranch. I forgot to say that Wendigo and Grootslang are her brothers. Like, literally her blood brothers. She is their mother and their sister, if you catch my drift."

"Holy fuck," gasped Matilda, "how the fuck do we beat monsters like these?"

Yinka jumped in. "That's the thing. They ain't monsters. They ain't got no magic. They ain't got no powers. They might be sick and twisted but whatever hurts us, hurts them. Whatever scares us, scares them. Their rituals are desperation. They want spiritual power but they are grounded by their own craven mortality. Ras Piankhi once cautioned me. 'Hatred eats in all directions.'"

"Yinka is right. I learned that by crossing swords with them behind the walls," Necro added. "They threatened me with all kinds of cosmic retribution and metaphysical torment, but I beat the shit out of three of them. They bled and cried like any other motherfucker. They were pathetic. Couldn't even fight. And when I walked away, I felt nothing. They're just sacks of meat."

Malört reinforced the point. "They look scary. The pale skin and the leather, but they're just some spooky kooks."

Poindexter wasn't convinced. "If all this is true, why haven't the Feds stopped them?"

"They're connected," Necro said. "Erzsébet's father is a judge, and anytime any investigation has been opened against them, he's found a way to halt it."

Suddenly it clicked. "A judge?" I asked. "The judge in the Brixton case. The judge that went easy on the killers...?"

"I wouldn't doubt it," Yinka said.

Necro nodded. "Remember, this is really just a sex cult, and it goes to the top of that town. They don't want to be exposed, and, DickSnot, you know better than anyone, they don't want the fun to end. So they find ways to keep it going. The Countess Bathory shit is just to keep gullible white men interested — especially white men with fuckable daughters."

"But why do they kill?" Poindexter asked.

Malört scoffed. "When they kill, they try to claim the life force of the departing soul in these little gourds, but really they just run around looking like blind mice. It's pretty pathetic."

"How many of them are there?" Myra asked.

"In The Coil?" Malört counted off. "Always nine plus Erzsébet. At the ranch, there's the judge and the six retards. Other than that, I count about twelve hardcore Fényhozó and a bunch of horny middle-aged dads who just come to the ceremonies to bust a nut. So... thirty-ish."

"What about the daughters?" I asked.

Necro couldn't resist. "Keep it in your pants, BombSmoke... we won't be having time for all that."

"Alright, so how does Cerberus fit into all this?" Poindexter wanted to know.

Malört didn't hesitate. "Cerberus is just the more refined wing of the organization. They don't do all the sacrifices and shit, but everything else, the fucking, the heartbeating, the meditation, they do all that. The Judge is the link between the two, I think he might be the one they call 'Anpu', but we don't know that for sure. Most of them are technology executives — IBM, Morton-Thiokol, Commonwealth-Edison. They've got a lot to lose by being exposed. That's why they didn't put up a resistance when we snatched Angus out of there."

"That's probably how they knew about Ras Piankhi and where Jackpot lives," Yinka said.

"More likely, Angus," I replied dryly.

Malört's expression darkened. "Remember. No distractions. We can't be dumb about this. I plan to walk in, and I plan to walk out. If any of you don't have the same plan, stay on the porch."

———

```
Piggy, Matilda, and Beams, three untested Lion Order newcom-
             ers, huddled in a side chat.

  "Why the fuck are we trusting these Puma motherfuckers? And
why the fuck are we taking orders from that Malört bitch? We
ain't killers. These Puma devils gon' pull us into some shit
       and leave us to take the fall. I don't know — "
```

———

I mentally checked them off as no-go for the mission.

Yinka set the tone. "Listen, this will get bloody. We don't know what these people are capable of. We don't even know if we have what it takes to stop them."

She let that sink in.

Then she continued. "We are doing this for Brixton, for Ras Piankhi and for Fourth World but, Lion Order, I can't ask you to risk anything you ain't willing to lose.

She scanned the room. "Show of hands. Who from Pama wants out of this? Okay, Brooklyn and Myra. We understand. No hard feelings."

Yinka quickly continued, "Okay, now who from Lion Order wants out?" Matilda, and Piggy dropped, as I expected. No other defectors.

She went deeper into her plan...

"We have two goals — One: Pull Angus out... Again. Lion Order, this will be our first extraction mission so we'll be playing support. Surveillance, driving and securing. Two: Neutralize Cod°Ex Re°Cereb. Two teams, The Press Gang and The Pride will lead here. We cut off the snakes head and the body will die. Erzsébet is the head. Y'all know what we say, 'When the snake head show...'"

Lion Order answered "the snake head go."

Poindexter asked the question that half the room was thinking. "You make

329

it sound so easy. How the fuck do we do any of that?"

Without acknowledging his question Yinka continued, "We have three options. None of them easy, but listen. It wasn't easy for them to come into Fourth World and breach Root Temple. Y'all remember that game we used to play, 'Last Tag'? Well, this is our get back."

"Our options — A. Brute force. Go in there and take the snake's head, but we know that Lion Order ain't killers and the killers we know ain't gonna get involved. B. Try to infiltrate but that's a long, slow game and very dangerous for whoever is inside. Dangerous physically and spiritually... and let's not even kid ourselves that we could pull it off. C. Poison the mind and the body.

Viddy asked the right question. "Why can't we do some of two and some of three? You say they like fathers and daughters right? Somebody pose as a father and daughter and get inside. Not for a long game, but for a quick hit. The poison."

"Yeah, but who?" asked Yinka.

Brooklyn interjected, "I know I said I was out, but... I could... I could be a daughter. I just need a father. We scanned the faces but there were no white men in the room who could credibly pass as her father. "Mr. Macksey," I said. "He ain't no killer, but we don't need a killer. We need a face. Get the Mackseys over here."

Malört was already on her way to the telephone.

◎◉◎

I broke the silence.

Read them the "Seven Truths" letter from The Jackal.

By the end, every jaw hung slack.

When we do this, we will be entering the gates of an imagined hell, to do battle with hounds who will kill for belief. Cod°Ex Re°Cereb is caught in a civil war between this world and their supremacist fantasies. We are in a civil war with our freedom and the walls that anyone might put on us."

330

"They killed Ras Piankhi and Brixton because they were living proof of a different path. One rooted in effortless beauty. And if Night Skins — peasants, in their eyes — can ascend, here on earth, then every Bathorist ascendance fantasy they cling to becomes obsolete."

"Cod°Ex Re°Cereb tries and fails. Then tries again. And fails again. They become uglier, less human, with every failed effort. This makes them desperate. Dangerous. Hate-filled."

"But they are only the tip of the spear of this war."

"I don't know what Ras Piankhi or Brixton would do, but I know what Peaches would do."

"She would blunt that spear."

"When summer started all I wanted to be was king of the Skinheads. I just wanted to dress well, drink heavily, fuck and fight. But that was escapism."

"Someone once told me, 'we all have a reputation, but we are always the last ones to know what it is.' But I'll tell you now that whatever you think of me today, you will not recognize who comes out the other side."

"The snake head show...," I called.

"The snake head go," the room answered.

Malört returned. "The Mackseys are on their way."

Yinka pulled Necro to the side and asked him very pointed questions about how things work behind the walls in Joliet. They huddled together to plot a special trap.

◎◉◎

Back home. Alone. I needed some music. I dropped the needle.

U-Roy's Bald Head Dread.

[Knock]

331

Scrawled on the cover in Ras Piankhi's scratchy hand: "Listen once, then never again."

The words weren't for me, specifically. They were for anyone who picked up the album.

I was reminded of the forgotten envelope that Sista Evangeline had given me when I went to pick up the Ibogaine. Dug it up from the bottom of my backpack. I sat down to read it.

The handwriting was slow and deliberate. No rush. No anger. Just the weight of knowing.

I took the needle off the record.

Only my pulse punctuated the silence.

I read it again.

"You hear a knocking on your soul.

Don't answer it.

When self-appointed becomes self-anointed, that's when it comes for you.

Ites.

Mother Evangeline."

CHAPTER FORTY-NINE
The Pen CNN
The Black Pearl

Grapevine, the Divine put his boots on the table. Every hustle folded. Bones stopped rolling. Mouths hung open. A long, slow chord stretched from the hole to the mess hall, vibrating with his signal.

In the vein of the greats, "Doriella du Fontaine" and "Mexicana Rose,"
Today is the day that we shine light on hoes.

This one is called "The Countess' Black Pearl"

Countess think she perfect, but we see the cracks,
Hiding wrinkles with rouge, dodging time like tax.

You can't be the whole Self when you fearing decay,
Less whole, only hole where your soul used to lay.

She say she unbound, but that ain't flight. it's fleein',
Ain't godhood if you gotta keep the lights dim to keep folks from seein'.

Untethered? Nah. Just unmoored and afraid,
A ghost wearin' silk hopin' death gets delayed.

Countess, Countess you done fucked up now,
Getting hooked on chocolate milk from your new chocolate cow.

Your slaves want pure white, not the stepped on stuff,
But your pure white is now cheaper than granny's snuff.

Countess, Countess, you twisted fucking soul,
That black pearl you caress, it's gonna take its toll.

What's done with the darkness always comes to light,
What you're doing with the night skin is cumming in the white.

Countess, Countess, you hide behind your pride,
But we all know the hunger you bury deep inside.

Every night you creep to taste forbidden sin,
With trembling hands, a willing pot and wicked, crooked grin.

That black pearl, it reflects the depth of your deceit,
That big black pearl fuels your fire, it makes white holes feel complete.

This shame, like chains, will bind you to your bed,
As every dirty lie rings around your fucking head.

You grip that black pearl like it's your only friend,
But we know it drags you closer to the end.

You play with fire, and now you're bound to burn,
This might as well be the river Styx, the path of no return.

Countess, Countess, your games will be your fall,
Your pearl, the curse, it's spraying its name on your walls.

So drink to this, your tale of sordid plight,
For all your sins will haunt you every waking night.

You crave the forbidden, the darkness fills you in,
Your soul corrupted by your illicit mixing sin.

You're nothing but meat to that big black gem,
It owns your ass, it bones your ass and sullies you to the brim.

(He let that hang for a beat)

They call this the slave state, but we freer than most,
This the Pen CNN. The squares call it a toast.

I don't sell no lies, no wolf tickets, no doubt,
Grapevine, the Divine signing the fuck out.

He stepped down from the cafeteria table.

This was crossroads made flesh. Every card shark, every dice shaker sat up straight, hoping he didn't call their debt next.

An inmate, pale of skin, scraggly hair, sharpened teeth, cast a look of grave consternation toward a guard. Almost imperceptibly the guard acknowledged the shared understanding, took leave of the cafeteria, walked slowly to the guard room, picked up a black telephone. Dialed a number.

CHAPTER FIFTY
From the Book of Black Teeth
She Still Hums

The dogs watched.

From the edge of the clearing, their eyes follow the movement of the people. Silent. Attentive. Watching the work being done around what looked like an above-ground well.

But it's too big to be a well.

Too small to be a house.

The doorway, once a way in, now a way out, has been bricked over.

Save for a single, narrow slot near the floor.

A Re°Ceiver approaches. She kneels. Slides a metal tray through the slot.

From inside, a hand snatches it angrily.

Metal scrapes against stone – a dull, sharp sound in the silence.

Then, a shadow shifts inside. The hand reaches again, not for the food, but for the Re°Ceiver.

It does not find purchase.

The Re°Ceiver sits down, just out of reach.

And she sings.

An ancient hymn, soft and reverent, extolling the enduring beauty of Countess Bathory.

A prayer. A promise. A devotion.

From within the darkness, a second sound rises.

Not words.

Not a song.

A hum.

A discordant melody. One only she knows.

This indignity.

This defamation.

It shall be answered.

Erzsébet hums.

On the other side of the ranch, a young man is working at pulling a plow. His new daily reality. He turns his face up to beg the sun for relief. We recognize him as the one called Angus.

CHAPTER FIFTY-ONE
Sunday, September 1, 1985
Three Days until the Ninth Night

I dressed for war.

Pure function. Two weapons. My lucky Slugger and Ras Piankhi's machete. My only decoration: the gold shovels — just in case I needed a couple of graves.

Each time we went over the plan somebody backed out. I couldn't hold it against them. Not everyone is built for blood.

I counted thirty combatants at Promontory Point. Twelve from Pama. The rest from Lion Order.

A school bus. The shitbox. Motorcycles. Whatever it took to ride on Joliet.

We had four small teams in Joliet already. One watching the Judge's ranch. Another watching The Coil. Yet another whose job it was to clear the streets by posing as do-gooders and giving money to the local addicts and alcoholics. And, the last team: The Spearhead.

They say the master's tool can't take down his house, but let's see if the Fed's COINTELPRO can work in reverse.

Based on what the ranch-watchers reported, it looked like it was working.

Rumors spread that Erzsébet had been intimate with a Night Skin. One who passed for white. Angus. That kicked off tension in The Coil. She was thrown into a sequestration chamber for a three-day cleansing and fasting. She'd be weak and vulnerable. They started calling Angus "Erzsébet's 'black

339

pearl.'" They didn't want to let him go so they put him to work. Hard labor on the ranch, and far away from the ritual. Night Skins cannot experience the heartbeating. So far he was more useful to them as a slave. Our team understood that the first sign of danger for Angus was reason enough to storm in.

The Spearhead, our codename for the team tasked with getting inside The Coil, had a sticky job. Play the role. Dress the part. Don't crack. Get in. Don't set off alarms. Do your task. Don't stick around. The rest of us would bat cleanup. Literally.

I drove the school bus. Riders from both teams peppered across the benches. A freshly repainted Shitbox pulled up next to me. Jake, Necro and Malört. The Dodge was completely unrecognizable in this state. That was the point.

I checked my mirror. Viddy, Showbiz, Yinka, Poindexter. My people.

"Alright, JizzPot, don't fold on me."

"Don't watch me. Watch yourself, Knee-Crow."

Jake broke character. "I need somebody else to say it. Jake never says it... Anybody." I sighed, and yelled out "We're on a mission from God!"

We roared towards Joliet. We took different routes. We'd reconvene in town.

I twirled the shovels. "Gotta dig these graves," I thought, "before Ras Piankhi's ninth night."

I pulled into the edge of town. The walls of the prison rose up from the horizon, reminding me of the first time I saw them. And of Brixton. A sense of foreboding ran through me. I wondered—am I really ready to kill? Am I prepared to die? How does a person prepare to die? I never asked. Can that question ever be answered by the living?

It was feast-and-a-fuck day in the shadows of the prison so there were more cars than usual in town. Good. That gave us extra cover.

We watched from the top of a run down storefront. The attendees, mostly men. Both blue collar and white collar. "If it's one thing that unites men of all classes," Necro mused, "it's free barbecue and easy pussy. Okay, two things."

I spotted The Spearhead. "They're in!"

We waited.

The metallic heartbeating — the start of the ceremony. Necro kept time.

About 30 minutes later The Spearhead slipped out. They stuck to the walls. Made their way to their car. Mr. Macksey flashed a subtle thumbs-up. They'd done their part.

Brooklyn was the trojan horse. The shortage of daughters made her special. She and her "father" were ushered to the front of the line. *"Be the first to imbibe the purest untainted."*

They didn't. They did something better.

Minutes later, pandemonium. The heartbeating clamored to a ragged halt. Men spilled onto the street. Eyes wide like saucers. Running in every direction. Swatting at invisible pursuers. Above. Behind. Their screams. Peals of horror.

The Spearhead had tainted the imbibe with a cocktail of Sista Evangeline's Ibogaine-35 and some other shit Mr. Macksey had laying around. It worked.

Psychic terror.

We moved in.

Inside was even crazier.

They were doing it to themselves. Psychic terror had the men tearing at their own flesh and at that of their fellow pleasure seekers. They fought each other for access to Erzsébet's Re°Ceivers. Clawed, bit, and slashed in frustration. They struggled, stumbled. Pants around their ankles. Impossibly hard dicks punching the air. Bobbing as they ran at and through each other. More than a few ejaculating uncontrollably. Cackling. Crying. Firehoses of wasted potential. Failures. Drenched in each other. All reasoning behind why they came — ruined.

341

A small man, impatient, horny, hard, withdrew a sword from the wall. Ran through another man who was in his way. Liking the result, he ran through another. He positioned himself between the legs of the terrified Re°Ceiver. She drove a dagger into his chest before he could consummate. He stood there. Seeing but not feeling. He was finished by the blow of a mace from behind.

The Re°Ceiver shrieked, covered herself with a bloody blanket. Vanished behind the curtains.

The men set upon each other. Two grizzled bikers restrained a yuppie. A third biker attacked his genitals with a broadsword. They quartered him.

Behind the altar The Judge was losing the fight of his life under the rage of Erzsébet and her husbands. His sons. Her brothers.

Erzsébet held a dagger to his throat. He clawed at her face. Cursed her for laying with a Night Skin. Said the magic would fail and she'd forever be tied to Earth.

She plunged the dagger into his jugular, again and again. She professed the purity of The Blood Countess herself.

The Judge's blood spurted like a drinking fountain. The killers became feeders. Ritual and restraint abandoned. Erzsébet, Grootslang and Wendigo wrestled each other for the fountain. He saw us.

Even on the precipice of death, The Judge turned his head to us. Not in fear. In outrage. As if we had unraveled his last good spell.

Night Skins in The Coil.

He raised a weak hand. Pointed to us. Trying to warn the feeders. His children. But they were drunk with exsanguation. Their mouths, their sharpened teeth, smeared crimson with rivulets, the deep red contrasting dramatically with their ghastly skin.

◎◎◎

I looked into his eyes.

The Judge. The Jackal. Anpu.

As The Judge, he played at order. A gavel in one hand, a pen in the other, deciding fates with ink instead of iron. He wore the mask of civility, of justice, of balance. The illusion of Ma'at. But his rulings were arbitrary, his scales tilted at his own whims.

As The Jackal, he shed the robes and stepped into essence. The butcher. The eater. The taker of flesh. He was the hand that flayed. The blade that cut. The teeth that tore. His justice was not balance; it was consumption. He did not weigh sins, he devoured them. He was a predator, and the world was to be his slaughterhouse.

As Anpu, he reached for something greater. He postured at enlightenment. At sacred knowledge. At divine authority. He was the mask that whispered of ascension. The high priest of something ancient. Something grander than himself. But his hunger betrayed him. His failures exposed him. He wanted to be a god, but he was only a man — bound by his own flesh, his own lusts, his own limitations.

Here is the Truth. He was none of these.

Not truly.

Never fully.

He spoke of Selves. I saw his, and if he must be named, let it be the Derelict Self. Juggling titles. Playing roles. Hiding his cravings behind cosmic miscalculations and elaborate masks.

He saw that I saw and it hurt him... reduced him.

He was a man who wanted to be a god, but died as less than either.

◎ ◎ ◎

The hallucinations peaked.

A man bit off his own fingers.

Another ripped the earrings from his lobes and swallowed them.

Erzsébet and her husbands turned once more on each other. The men pounced. Erzsébet, weakened, didn't stand a chance. The Blood Countess fell into a bloodsucking orgy. Her eyes flew open. Her veins offered themselves. They pierced. They fed. They drew. Her last word was a gurgle — not quite a death rattle. Her eyes darkened slowly. Grootslang and Wendigo drank.

The hall echoed with ranting.

One devotee chewed through her own shawl, mistaking it for serpents.

Another clawed at his chest, screaming to release the beast he swore was coiled in his ribcage. Necro freed it.

A third slammed his head against the altar, chanting gibberish.

Yet another spun in broken circles, hands red from digging at his eyes.

We crossed that last line.

Hunted them.

Subdued them.

Neutralized them.

Yinka stepped through the melees and approached the altar, where the husbands sucked for the last of Erzsébet. The light left their eyes. Night Skins in their sacred place. Grootslang lunged. Yinka waited.

Necro hunted a stray devotee. The man howled an ancient curse then vanished behind the heavy curtains that concealed the secrets of The Coil. Necro followed. Wendigo tore in behind them. I tried to keep up but the labyrinth tricked me. I could hear the struggle. Necro's voice. The ancient curses. A third sound. A rasp. Bestial. I closed my eyes. Used my other senses. Followed the sounds of a clash.

Turn right here.

No. Left.

Yes. Left.

Clearer now.

Right.

Straight ahead.

Light.

A body fell on top of another. Only one stood.

The shadows gave up nothing. I stepped closer. I called out for Necro.

The figure turned.

Wendigo. He swatted and slashed at invisible tormentors with his dagger. It still dripped with blood. I looked at his feet. Necro. Necro's blood.

Wendigo's eyes followed mine. He bared his fangs and howled. Part celebration, part taunting.

He gloated. "That's three Night Skin Wendigo take down. Uppity one, one," he said with a smirk. "Old man, two. He would not kneel. So Wendigo unmade him." He gestured to a long rope of hair, Ras Piankhi's, that was woven into his own. "Slave State boy now, three. Night Skin, you, will be the four."

"Since you seem confused, let me tell you who I am," I said "and that souvenir of yours is going home today."

I closed in on him as if to grapple. Testing his alertness. He misread my intentions. He lunged forward, grasping nothing. We moved around each other, each looking for an advantage while he tried to resist the pull of his unseen agitators.

Ras Piankhi's machete tucked sidelong against my forearm, edge thirsty. Wendigo lunged again. Heard the song of the cutlass half a second before he understood its melody.

As if in slow motion, the severed meat hung in the air — just for a moment

345

— then dropped to his feet. We both watched. For different reasons.

He looked at the severed lock, lying limp in a pool of his own blood. He didn't reach for it. He knew. That power was gone. It was never his to begin with.

The ear. Beyond salvage. He'd miss that.

I could see his skull. White, exposed. A single red trickle. Followed by three. Becoming a flood. Drenching his tunic.

"I am the Fourth Wave symphony. Here to silence your heartbeating."

[Knock]

Wendigo howled again. Fury. Indignation. Fear. He recoiled in shock. Looking for what he'd lost. He made the mistake of reaching out. Felt for the rest of his face. Ras Piankhi's machete sang again. This time it danced with his hand. At the wrist. A downward dip. A last bow.

"I am not vengeance. I am the mighty hand of correction and consequence." I stalked around him, machete at my chest."

He shifted into survival mode. Shook his head to dislodge his phantom tormentors. The berserker was fast. He spun. Grabbed. A bullish motion. Spun towards me. Charged. I felt it before I saw it. His bone saw pressed into my chest. He drove my back into a stone wall.

The breath left my lungs.

My ribs threatened to crack.

My vision blurred.

All senses tuned to the blade biting into my chest.

Wendigo looked into my eyes. "Night Skin four."

I dug down. Brixton. Peaches. Ras Piankhi. Necro. And...

And Me?

Not me. Not yet. I reached down, inside my chest. Looking for Lil Tremor, I found and named "Bald Head Dread." Flirting with the forbidden.

[Knock]

I dropped my weight. Slid to the side. Tore my flesh but broke free.

He spun to grab. Lost his footing in the slickness of his own blood. Landed on his back. Knocking loudly against the floor. Stunned.

I pounced. I pressed my blade to his neck.

"Dread and terrible." Crossing the line.

[Knock] [Knock]

His last howl was cut short. Clipped.

"They used to call me Lil' Tremor. Tell Lucifer that Jackpot: The Dread Skinhead sent you."

I put my full weight on the machete in his windpipe. His head lolled to the side, attached only by sinew. He twitched. A body still fighting — even with nothing left.

His cold heart pumped impotent rivers of blood toward shores they would never bathe.

I knelt over him catching my breath. I looked into his eyes. What does it take to make a man believe so strongly in a thing? "Which killer made you a killer, Wendigo?" My question fell on dead ears.

I stayed there a moment longer. Studied him. Looked for something that wasn't there.

"Was there ever a mother who would cry for you?"

I wiped my blade on his shirt.

I turned. Did the morbid-but-delicate work of separating Ras Piankhi's hair from the flayed flesh that lay in a bloody corner. I tucked the lock into a

347

pocket, then...

The wall.

The bricks.

They weren't bricks.

Nameplates?

Burnt wood, scorched edges. Each one etched. A first name, only. All feminine-coded.

I pulled at one. It gave.

[Knock]

Behind it: a small vessel — a carved wooden cup, covered with... skin? Tied with... sinew? I peeled it open.

[Knock][Knock]

Hair. Fine. Light.

Fingernails. Tiny. So tiny.

A knot. An umbilical stump?

I staggered back.

A graveyard for daughters. No last names. No birthdates. No death dates.

The room tilted.

I forgot how to breathe.

I stumbled backwards over Wendigo, fell onto Necro. I scrambled to my feet. I picked him up. Ran with him draped across my back. Fought with the slack of him. Dragged what was left of him to the main room.

"Why, Necro?" I hissed.

"Why the fuck did you have to chase that stray?"

Yinka had her hands on the pillow that was pressed to Erzsébet's face, assuring her a long goodnight.

Yinka relaxed. Sat on her heels. Stared at her hands, reliving what she'd just done. Stunned by her own capacity for violence. All her theory turned into the ultimate practice. She now belonged to a very different class, we both did.

Malört, chest heaving, stood over what was left of Grootslang. Her eyes struggled to focus. To make meaning of the shell of the man I dragged behind me. Flitting from my eyes to Necro's.

She looked around — eyes set — pulled a bloody pike. Ran through every Re°Cereb devotee or aspirant who dared to show signs of life. She punctuated every stab with the name of one of our fallen. "Ras Piankhi!" "Brixton!" "Necro!" "Angus!"

Her rage — at some point, it stopped being vengeance and turned into naked bloodsport.

They watched. Shocked.

Not me.

I helped.

[Knock] [Knock] [KNOCK]

I heard the knocking. I answered. Sorry Mother Evangeline.

Grabbed a pike.

Stabbed out every remaining heartbeat and near-heartbeat.

"The daughters!"

A nameless thing smiled... if it *could* smile.

There's no law outside the walls of the prison. No material reaction. On

349

Judgment Day, we will be called to answer. But not today.

This was inevitable. It could only ever end one way. We torched The Coil. Scattered as we had arrived. We left the carnage behind, only for it to survive in nightmares and prayers.

Even Jake was without a quip to get us on our way.

He somberly laid Necro across the back seat of the Dodge and roared back towards The Jewel.

My bus of silent, reflective combatants passed through Holy City, on our way to Fourth World.

Changed.

◎ ◉ ◎

The ranch team extracted Angus. The dogs were sedated. The inbreds were incompetent. Clumsy. Left unscathed. They'd have a hard enough time feeding themselves. We saw no need to compound that.

They found Angus weak and malnourished. They strapped him into a straight jacket. Pushed him into a repurposed ambulance. Got on the road. Delivered him to his parents. To a respectable institution where he could get professional deprogramming. Too bad there ain't no respectable institutions. He'll probably come out more fucked up than he went in.

No angels and no demons came to me that night.

There was no accounting to be made.

No one would remember their names. Only their mothers. Maybe the undertakers.

◎ ◉ ◎

Before we departed The Coil, I had to retrieve something of great importance. I ran to CACOPHONY, kicked in the front door and found what I sought. A used Alembic bass. I pulled it off the rack and claimed it as my own.

CHAPTER FIFTY-TWO
Wednesday, September 4, 1985
The Ninth Night

The Jamaican Nine Night ceremony is a celebration of life.

It begins on the day the beloved slips through the veil. Convenes with the ancestors. Takes their seat among the council.

Those left behind reflect on the meanings of the beloved's beginning, middle, and forever.

On the Ninth Night the beloved is released from their last earthly fetters.

And on the tenth day they are freed to "fly away home" as the song says.

The walls of Lion Order were draped in purple. An altar was made for every Mansion of Rastafari. The Ethiopian African Black International Congress, also known as the Bobo Ashanti. The Nyahbinghi Order. The Twelve Tribes of Israel.

Every drummer, every singer, every player of instruments. Ministers of every faith in Fourth World – Ifa, Vodun, Christian, Muslim, Hebrew – came to offer comfort to Mother Evangeline.

She was stoic. Patient. Composed.

◎◎◎

Jeff Fort and Larry Hoover showed up at the same time. Both flanked by complementary-yet-competitive phalanxes of jet-black soldiers. They both promised Mother Evangeline they'd remake Fourth World so that no weapon formed against it would prosper. I wondered if they could ever do that. Would they do that? Or were they just capitalists with the right words? Haven't they killed more — for less?

———

A group of Fourth World Elders sat around a table. They were having a serious conversation about what they called the 'second person' connection that African people have with our ancestors. The conversation was inspired by the Wailers lyric "Every time I feel the crack of the whip, my blood runs cold." One elder argued that everything that happened to our ancestors happened to us and that everything that happens to us is also happening for our ancestors.

———

A royal roll call of reggae and Jamaican politics passed through the gates or sent word: Coxsone Dodd. Prince Buster. Bunny Lee. Lee Perry. Derrick Morgan. Jimmy Cliff. Rita and Cedella Marley. Michael Manley. Flabba Holt. Peter Tosh. Yellowman. Joseph Hill. Norman Grant. Mortimer Planno. Bongo Herman. Bongo Les. King Tubby. Even the garrison dons Lester Coke and Vivian Blake sent representatives. Chokwe Lumumba was there. Sonny Carson. Cha Cha Jiménez. Sister Khadijah Farrakhan.

Mother Evangeline pointed to me. A man, an older Jamaican man, walked my way. He clapped my shoulders like we'd known each other for years.

"I finally get to meet Jackpot himself. The man Ras Piankhi said would bring the Skinheads back to their roots. It's me! George Dekker!"

On my way to being king of the Skinheads, I'd taken a detour.

And become something else entirely.

Chapter Fifty-Three

"Hey man, you finally got a job," Bubba laughed.

"Aw man, you know how it is. This place always needed me more than I needed it." We both laughed at the lie. Yinka stepped in to manage Lion Order while Mother Evangeline mourned. I just helped out around the shop.

"I miss that old man," Bubba said.

"Yeah, every time I come in here I expect to hear his voice. And sometimes I swear I do. I know what you're here for, man. I have it right here. 'Foey Man' by George Dekker. Really a top Skinhead tune. I asked him to autograph it for you."

"You know, the 7 are gonna start throwing dances at The Dodger. I expect to see you there."

"I'm already there!" I went back to sweeping.

There was a pause then he asked the question I know he'd been turning over for a long time.

"You ever regret falling in with Pama? I started that mob and had a hard run with them. This was before your time, but still..."

I sensed a story. I stopped sweeping. Leaned on the broom. Gave Bubba my full attention.

"Life with Pama City Skins was a balance of long stretches of boredom broken up by extreme violence."

"Holding down the pavement at Aetna Park was sometimes like watching paint peel. In a city as big and rich as Chicago, there really wasn't much to do for young people on summer break. It was either hang out on the beach, play basketball or get a shitty job. We'd break up the monotony with treks up the street to Wax Trax, or take the long haul to Bizarre Bazaar in Old Town, but mostly we just held fort at Aetna and waited to see who would show up."

"Back then, it was easy to find parking on Lincoln. We had the bird's eye view of newcomers who looked like they might fit in with our kind."

"One day this tall Punk rocker with a done up jet black mohawk pulled up. She parked her car, a tan beater — the driver's education car — on Lincoln, right across from the Woolworth's and stepped out in her full glory. It was too hot for her black leather jacket but it was part of her look which was finished out by denim jeans that she'd blackened with Rit dye and army-styled combat boots, complete with studded spur straps. Her jacket was decorated with painted-on band logos, a big MDC tank on the back. DOA on one sleeve. The Dicks on the other sleeve. And chrome spikes everywhere."

"She acknowledged us but was clearly on a mission. She made her way up the street toward Wax Trax."

Bubba checked to see if I was still tuned in. I was.

"A little while later she was bouncing on some new soles back towards her car with a bag of records and her old boots. She tossed all that into the trunk of her K Car then proudly walked over to see what the local mob was all about."

"Her brand new 20 hole, steel capped, black Dr. Martens gleamed in the sunlight. These were the ones that didn't have the yellow stitching so she looked extra militant."

"Her name was Skylar, she fell right into conversations about music and art and where she was from. Skylar recognized her new tribe and copped a squat alongside the home team. I joked that if she was going to hang out with us she's got to ladder lace her Docs. I talked her through the process so she could get rid of that stupid criss cross. With that her whole look was fully-baked. Jeans tucked into her boots, she looked like a six-foot-tall Dave Vanian — with tits."

"She'd moved from somewhere in North Carolina to start at the Art Institute in the fall so she had a few weeks to get herself settled."

"One eagle-eyed Skinhead, Brutus, was busy sizing up Skylar. Asked, "what albums did you buy?" The answers sparked more questions, and so on. Before long, Brutus had sniffed out a mark with money. Brutus leaned in and turned on their charms to win Skylar's trust."

Brutus was an expert at the confidence game and within a few minutes had learned that Skylar liked to get high on the hard stuff from time to time. I don't think Skylar had a full grown monkey like Brutus had, but that didn't matter. As long as Skylar had money, Brutus was her best friend."

"Brutus dominated the conversation and convinced Skylar to give them a ride to somewhere they had to be, urgently. Skylar agreed and off they roared. Brutus yelled out some shit about us being idle losers while they drove off in the wind. Brutus wasn't wrong but they didn't have to tell the whole world."

That got a good laugh out of both of us.

Bubba continued, "Skylar quickly became a whole part of the squad. You know that Levi's trucker jacket I have? The one with the Dragon Stout back patch? She painted that."

"A few days later, I heard Brutus calling Skylar their 'roommate' which struck me as odd, but it was none of my business so I let it go in one ear and out the other. These two became fast friends — maybe more than friends. If Skylar was around, Brutus was soon to follow, and the two would head off to some unknown destination after some quiet words. Always just those two, never anybody else."

"Shows came and went, days at Aetna bled into each other, and the kickoff date for school crept closer. That didn't mean shit to us kids that only had pavement to pound, but for kids with a future, that was an important date."

Yinka walked over. Listened quietly.

"I was sitting at Aetna drinking beer when Skylar copped a squat next to me looking like the world was about to end. Eventually she piped up. Quietly asked me how she could get Brutus to move out of her apartment. School was starting soon, she explained. She'd fucked off her summer. She should have been finding a job and getting settled but she'd blown her savings and now had a heroin monkey on her back. And to top that off she had a leech that she couldn't shake."

"I didn't have answers. I was 18 years old and had no relevant experience or useful advice. Disappointed, she asked Skin, then Kim, then Olga, getting the same non-answers. We tried to offer advice but we didn't know shit. All we knew was that Brutus had an explosive temper that they backed up with violence, so on top of being inexperienced we also didn't want to go to war with that nut."

"Skylar left the park more fucked up than before. She had to make a hard break and it was all on her shoulders."

"I didn't see Skylar for a few days."

"The next news I heard about her was that she had committed suicide in the vestibule of her six-flat apartment building. They said she strangled herself with an extension cord. How the fuck do you do that? And in the vestibule?"

"But what do I know? I was only 18 years old and had no relevant experience or point of reference. There was no suicide note, and according to her family members they hadn't noticed any change in her behavior in phone conversations."

"It didn't make sense. I couldn't prove it. But I didn't believe it. I never mentioned it to another soul but I made up my mind that Skylar's exit-stage-left was not 'suicide.'"

"Brutus disappeared for about a week but popped back up at Aetna Park with fading bruises on their face. Looking like they'd been in a fight. They also had some very nice new items to offload. Some albums. A nice studded belt. Some Dr. Martens boots that weren't their size. They'd give you a good price on them, of course and — Skylar's leather jacket."

"My suspicions were on full tilt."

"According to Brutus, Skylar's mother had given them all this shit because she learned how close they were. When she'd arrived from NC to collect Skylar's remains Brutus turned on their charms to express condolences, be generally helpful, and to assure Mom that they were Skylar's best friend on earth."

"'Anybody want to buy this jacket?' Brutus will give you a good deal."

"There were no takers, but a lot of sideways glances."

"For a long time I'd had suspicions about Brutus but I could never name it, and whenever I mentioned it to others they'd tell me I was overthinking shit."

"Following Skylar's dear-departure, and my silent calculations, I tuned in and paid very close attention to Brutus. I kept my eyes on them. I didn't antagonize, but I also didn't hang too close. I watched and waited. I was too political for Brutus anyway so it was easy to dress back, quietly."

"I clocked how overly-friendly they always were — until some slight, real or imagined, set them off. How they were always armed with a toothy smile. How they'd find the most impressionable newcomers, make them their best friend and their pet. And how Brutus would invariably flip on them and beat them bloody... just awesome brutality."

"I made up my mind. Brutus was a killer and I needed to put some distance between me and them... and Pama City Skins. I dropped my flag. It wasn't a clean break but when us Redskins formed The 7 everyone agreed that we needed our own thing. It was inevitable. Brutus would watch me like a hawk, though. I think they had a feeling that I had deeper reasons for pulling away."

"Let me tell you, I took one of my best lessons in life from Brutus. When you meet someone new, shut up. Observe. Listen. They will tell you everything you need to know about them within the first ten minutes. I was 18 years old and for the first time had relevant experience and useful advice."

"Let me guess," I said, sensing the conclusion of the story, "Brutus is Broomie."

"Nah, man," finished Bubba, "Brutus is Malört."

357

CHAPTER FIFTY-FOUR
The Pen CNN
A Parable

Grapevine, the Divine stood. Luck itself took five steps back. The gamblers stiffened. The joker went mute. Even the guards felt it. Prophecy in the marrow. Heavy and real.

This one here might displace "Master of the Long-Shoe Game,"
You can copy, you can quote, just remember my motherfucking name.

This one is called "Parable of Jackpot."

Erzsébet ruled with a countess's hand,
Two husbands and seven freaks a cursed band.

A judge corrupt, foul deeds concealed,
A carnal confederacy, fate screwed and sealed.

Blood rituals conducted in shadowed halls,
Echoes of torment, decorate those walls.

Power fed on orgies of pain,
Any girlchild marked... a crimson stain.

Daughters desecrated by the profane, the unhinged,
Daughters unnamed, now daughters avenged.

But retribution rose with a lion's tail,
Their empire of horror wasn't nothing but a thin veil.

Erzsébet fell, her battalion of freaks undone,
Carcasses rot, beneath the redemptive power of sun.

We knew it would be answered, the saints that they took,
Black queen took white queen after black king took rook.

Don't frown on him, Ras Piankhi it had to go that way,
For The Game is our law. The rules do not sway.

He once was Little Tremor, son of a gun,
Then he was Soon Ras, Terror Town's rising sun.

We tell tales of his heists, his prowess in the streets,
And now we rap about his crucial and most dreadful feats.

So it was written, so it shall be said,
Fourth World got a new hero. Jackpot. The Dread Skinhead.

(He let that hang for a beat)

They call this the slave state, but we freer than most,
This the Pen CNN. The squares call it a toast.

I don't sell no lies, no wolf tickets, no doubt,
Grapevine, the Divine signing the fuck out.

He stepped down from the cafeteria table.

They left the prophecy on the table and returned to what they knew — slapping down dominos, cutting decks, signifying, and humming half-remembered soul ballads into the night.

A lone inmate — pallid, hollow-eyed — stared at the table before him.

A new guard, nothing like the old one, surveyed the room with the eyes of an unseasoned rookie.

360

CHAPTER FIFTY-FIVE

Nine nights after Ras Piankhi's Ninth Night I fell asleep in Fourth World, replaying everything in my head.

And... the dreams... the fucking dreams...

I was in that hot, dark military barracks.

But it was me...

I was the officer.

I was telling Sista Evangeline's children to... become... like me... to *"Hit that peckerwood in the cocksucker..."* to *"let Lil' Tremor out the cage... See what that motherfucker can do..."* *"WEH. MI. RASS. CLAAT. TINGS?"* *"...dig two graves."* *"Dunk him!"* *"The 42 negative confessions... Shit! I'm guilty of all these!"* *"Tell Lucifer Lil' Tremor sent you..."* *"Which killer made you a killer...?"* *"When the self-appointed becomes the self-anointed..."*

I woke up in a cold panic trying to rip the officer's uniform from my back.

And the other dream... Not me this time...

It was like the steady drip of a rundown shower head, like some archaic torture. Never loud, never fatal, but always denying rest, denying relief, denying the soul its drink.

It followed her. It knew? No. That's crazy. Still, she felt it. At times it was a creeping chill. Other times it was a haunted fixation on a piece of nothing. An inability to focus. Even when focusing mattered most.

No. It's just guilt, she thought. She didn't want to keep believing in religion. The material world was all there was. If you couldn't drive it, eat it, fuck it, it wasn't real. Still, every now and then she'd remember her hammered-in programming. The Lord's Prayer. The Ten Commandments. "Why did God make me? God made me to know Him, love Him, and serve Him."

She'd shake it off, dismiss it as superstition.

Until the next time.

As the days burned, she believed she was safely divorced from consequence but the passenger cleaved on. Appearing almost constantly.

Things that used to work perfectly no longer worked as well. Visitations... that's the only word that made sense... by insects. Birds. A staticky interjection into a phone call.

She joked to herself that she should give it a name, invite it to sit for breakfast. That last part felt reckless. Like welcoming a vampire into your home. No. No breakfast. But naming it? What's the harm in that?

Something silly. Popeye? Olive Oyl? Back when her neighbors' daughter had night terrors, her father coached her to give the monster the silliest name she could think of. Something that would make her laugh when she said it. She chose Booty. And it worked.

Maybe she should choose something more personal, like Brendan. She thought that was a good name for a cop. The one in the tunnels. She'd looked for news stories but he was never reported missing or... that other thing. Brendan works.

Maybe the feeling was the memory of Brendan. Maybe Brendan needed to forgive her.

Yeah. Brendan, it is.

She tried to sleep, but her dreams were too heavy for her head. They were leading her somewhere. Back. Back to that scene. Back to the tunnels.

No. No sleep. NoDoz. Better.

Brendan, the uninvited.

"Stop fucking with me, Brendan."

Maybe naming it was a mistake. I should have gone with Booty.

I tried Sista Evangeline. Sista Evangeline asked the right questions.

I gave the wrong answers. I couldn't tell her. She didn't know what she didn't know. She gave me something, but it wasn't enough. Or it wasn't the right thing.

Brendan, the old man at the train station. Watching-not-watching in the reflection.

Leaking through.

Later.

Sominex? But, the dreams.

NoDoz. Not strong enough. "Herb. I need some crank."

Brendan, the voice in the Walkman. The Ruts. "It was Cold."

"But you were laughing to hide your crying..."

Here.

The tunnel. Again.

She dropped – or was pushed – to her knees. She put her hands in the water. Watched-not-watched. Then her face. She drank of the dark waters. Found a bottle. Saved him. For an altar.

Back home, now.

Opened the bottle.

Imbibed.

Come in, Brendan.

Brendan. Never its name.

The Dread. Its weight.

Miasma. Its form.

Jackpot? No. He was there. But he didn't do it. Or did he? Another one? A different one? More than one?

Your pills.

Fix the leak.

No answers.

Leave questions.

Sleep?

Sleep.

Stopped?

Fixed.

I woke up drenched. Tasting dark waters.

I looked around the room.

I wasn't alone. It had come for me.

I opened my shade. Stared out at Terror Town. Jealous that everyone else could rest. Bracing myself for whatever would visit me next.

This is the part that no one tells you.

That's what Prince Adze meant when he said that death is hard even on the killers... "*Us* killers," he said.

The demons don't come to get you...

You become the demon.

I looked over at my pillow.

I couldn't go back to sleep.

I didn't want to go back to sleep.

I was... *afraid* to go back to sleep.

I heard feet pacing in the corridor.

No wonder Tremor never sleeps.

Areas of Interest

 Aetna Park

 Bar (Dodger, Dreamerz, L&L)

 Beautyful Ones

 Dillinger's Alley

 Holy City

 Irving Park Salvage

Joliet Prison

Lake Point Tower

Rainbow Beach

Root Temple

School (Bad Hell, Kenwood)

Stix

 Tremor's Truck Yard

Von's House

Wax Trax

Friends and Foes

 Black Gangster Disciple Nation

 BUSA Tribe

 Cod°Ex Re°Cereb

 Colfax Killers

 El Rukn

Kingston Raiders

Los Viboros

Terror Town / Black P Stone

PR Stones

Vice Lords

White City Resistance

Incidents

 The Blue Gargoyle

 The Kidnapping

 The Lost Doggie

The Racquetball Club

The Rebel Disciples

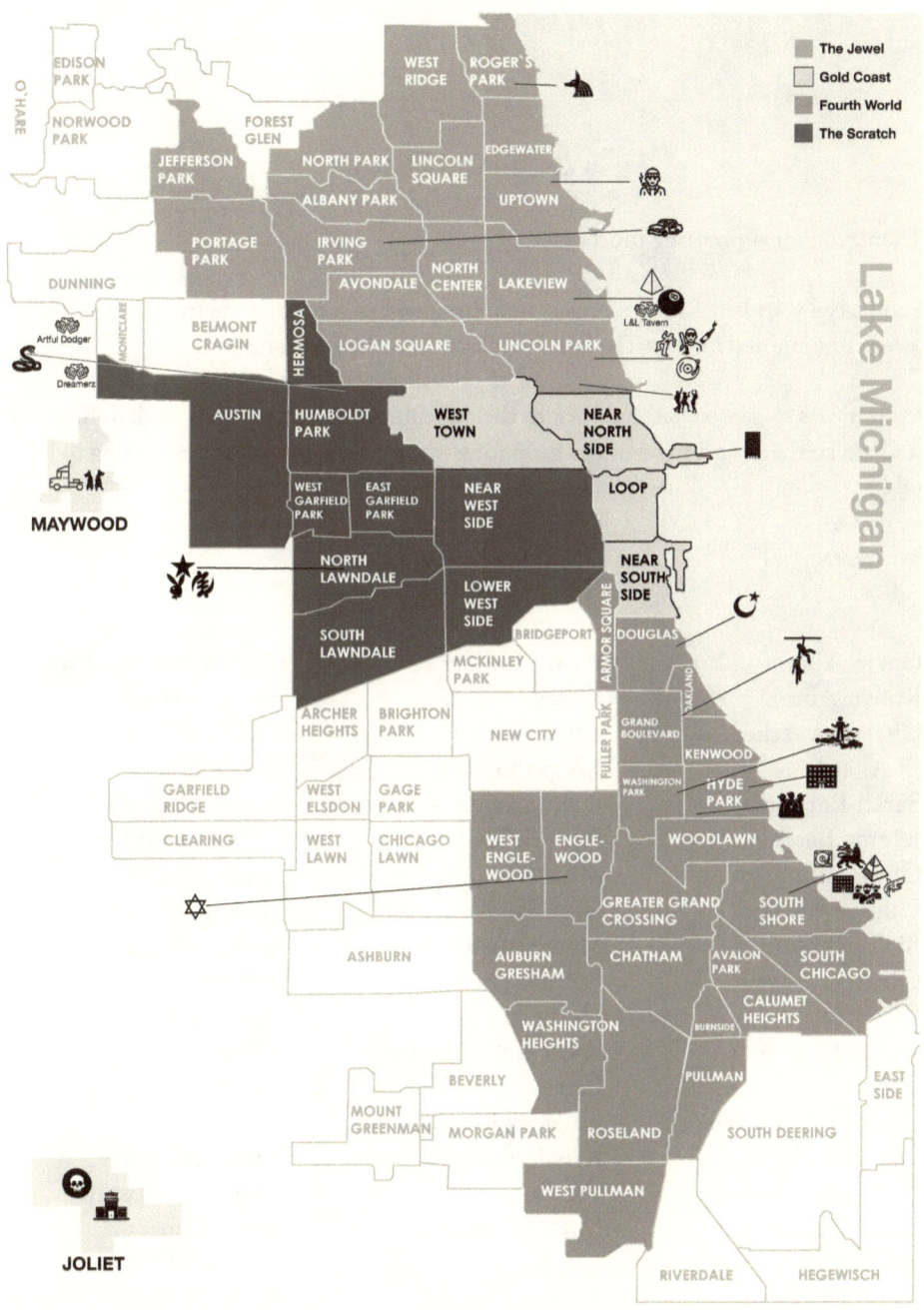

The Grid

See facing page for markers

Map labels:

The Jewel
Gold Coast
Fourth World
The Scratch

O'HARE
EDISON PARK
NORWOOD PARK
JEFFERSON PARK
FOREST GLEN
NORTH PARK
LINCOLN SQUARE
WEST RIDGE
ROGER'S PARK
EDGEWATER
UPTOWN
ALBANY PARK
PORTAGE PARK
IRVING PARK
AVONDALE
NORTH CENTER
LAKEVIEW
DUNNING
BELMONT CRAGIN
HERMOSA
LOGAN SQUARE
LINCOLN PARK
MONTCLARE
Artful Dodger
Dreamerz
AUSTIN
HUMBOLDT PARK
WEST TOWN
NEAR NORTH SIDE
L&L Tavern
MAYWOOD
WEST GARFIELD PARK
EAST GARFIELD PARK
NEAR WEST SIDE
LOOP
NORTH LAWNDALE
LOWER WEST SIDE
NEAR SOUTH SIDE
SOUTH LAWNDALE
BRIDGEPORT
ARMOR SQUARE
DOUGLAS
MCKINLEY PARK
ARCHER HEIGHTS
BRIGHTON PARK
NEW CITY
FULLER PARK
GRAND BOULEVARD
OAKLAND
KENWOOD
GARFIELD RIDGE
WEST ELSDON
GAGE PARK
WASHINGTON PARK
HYDE PARK
CLEARING
WEST LAWN
CHICAGO LAWN
WEST ENGLE-WOOD
ENGLE-WOOD
WOODLAWN
ASHBURN
GREATER GRAND CROSSING
SOUTH SHORE
AUBURN GRESHAM
CHATHAM
AVALON PARK
SOUTH CHICAGO
CALUMET HEIGHTS
BURNSIDE
WASHINGTON HEIGHTS
BEVERLY
PULLMAN
EAST SIDE
MOUNT GREENMAN
MORGAN PARK
ROSELAND
SOUTH DEERING
WEST PULLMAN
JOLIET
RIVERDALE
HEGEWISCH

Lake Michigan

SUPPORTERS

Thank you for supporting this book.

You placed your belief in this project and, in some cases, pushed me in ways that mattered. You injected *Jackpot: The Dread Skinhead* with the fuel it needed.

My goal was to give something back to the Subculture, to carry readers back to how it felt to be there, and to open the gates for a whole new range of stories waiting to be told.

Thank you.
Adisa

Gavin Abercrombie
Robyn Abree
Christian Acker
JF Allard
Sarah Bartlett
Jeremy Bates
Clint Billington
Hunter Brawer
Malki Brown
Quentin Brown
Quentin Brown
Lemuel Cabrera
Chris Catchpool
Lamont Chandler
Charles Clarke
Elizabeth Compton
Brian Dougherty
Ian Elliott
Jacob Elliott
Mike Ellsworth
Jen Exoo
John Ferguson
Derek Gangland

John J Gillett
Kelley Graham
Chip Gross
Joseph Giunta
Joshua Giunta
Amy E. Hall
Mike Hammecker
Jerry Hudson
Matt Hufstetler
Patrick Hughes
Harry Jenkins
Scott Kelley Ernest
Christopher Kellogg
Gregory Kerns
Kris Lange
Tiny Leidof
Mike Lemmons
Joel Loya
Kenneth Martin
Randall May
Chad McMann
Kim Nguyen
Mario Parenti

Christian Picciolini
Eric Pressley
Larz Putchaven
Josh Radlein
Amber Rajcevich
Chente Rudo
Jason Sanchez
Michelle Sánchez
Andrew Santa Lucia
Josh Sanders
Gary Sayers
Scott Seath
Gar Somah
Phyllis Taylor
Yoko Terretta
Greg Thompson
Evan Torres
Crystal O'Soul
Adam Whistler
Caitlin Wood
Kristin Woodward

AUTHOR

Jabari Adisa grew up hardstyle.
Lived the Chicago Skinhead life in the
turbulent '80s. The time of *Jackpot*.
Receipts available upon request.
He grew up to become Ol' Boxcutter.
Lives in Atlanta.
Writes stories about risk, consequence,
and cultural fire.

web: hardstylefiction.com
instagram: @boxcutterbrigade

PLAYLIST
The Music of Jackpot: The Dread Skinhead

`https://tr.ee/3tWkex`

This is the music of Jackpot: The Dread Skinhead.
As he lived it, as you read it, as it happened.
Feel the pulse.
Embrace the discord.
Drop the stylus and step into the novel.

www.ingramcontent.com/pod-product-compliance
Lightning Source LLC
Chambersburg PA
CBHW020419030726
47495CB00006B/1586